EAT THE RICH
A Millie Thatcher Novel

By
Steve K Peacock

Copyright © 2024 Steve K Peacock

All rights reserved.

One

'So, I was thinking. When this is all over, how would you like an evening out on my boat?'

Somehow, he hadn't picked the exact worst time to try and chat me up, but it was pretty bloody close. A tip for all of you out there trying to get in a girl's knickers: at least wait until after she's finished reciting the most menacing fucking Latin.

Oh, introductions. Hi, I'm Millie Thatcher – ghost hunter, sort of a wizard, and a runeskald. Those are all loaded terms, so I'll get into them later, after I've finished getting my hooks into you with a bit of dramatic action. All the good books start *in medias res*.

There's that Latin again.

Anyway, he was trying his luck with me, and I was soul-deep in some rather infernal incantations. About ten metres ahead of us, something was trying to claw its way out of a crypt. It was the family repose of the horny shit who was accompanying me, though I had made it my mission to refuse to learn his name. It was something pompous and double-barrelled, filling their name full of vowels to make up for the conspicuous absence of a chin.

The creature in the tomb had been scratching at the heavy stone for hours without rest, and while I was pleased to find out it didn't have the strength to lift the damn thing – ruled out most of the more dangerous critters that pop up in graves – it was only going to be a matter of time before it carved its way through. The Latin was supposed to re-sanctify the tomb, but it didn't seem to be working.

I snapped the book shut and frisbeed it across the room. 'Right. Fuck that. Hand me that bag, Pugwash.'

The little cogs in the guy's brain crunched against each other as he awkwardly tried to change gear. He froze for a moment until I snapped my fingers in front of his eyes. 'Bag. Yes. Of course. This one?'

'There's only the one,' I said, yanking a weathered leather satchel from his grip. Rooting around inside, my fingers plucked up a couple loose poker chips that were laying at the bottom. 'Family history pop quiz, Pugwash. As precise as possible, please, or we'll probably die horribly. How long has this guy been dead?'

'Uh,' he stalled. 'Three hundred years, maybe?'

'Three hundred?' I asked, counting out six poker chips. 'You sure?'

He shrugged. 'Not really.'

'I need you to be sure here, mate.'

'Uh, give me a second,' he said, whipping out his phone. He tapped at the screen a few times. 'Three hundred and twenty-nine years, according to Wikipedia.'

Of course, he had a Wikipedia page. His family probably

Eat The Rich

owned half of Hertfordshire.

Three hundred and twenty-nine. I counted out a seventh chip just to be safe, then set about arranging them atop the sarcophagus. One chip went on each of the four corners, with the remaining ones placed in a stack in line with where the dead bastard's heart should have been. Helpfully, the family had been unable to resist having some bored stonemason carve some flowery sigil onto the thing, at more or less exactly where I needed to put the chips. May as well have carved a bloody great bullseye into it.

As the last poker chip clicked into place, they each began to glow blue with sharp and angular designs – runes – letting me know everything was set. Again, I rifled through my bag until I found a pig iron nail and a broad-headed mallet. Carefully, I held the nail on top of the stack, point aimed at the centre of the glowing rune, and took a deep breath.

'Ok, Pugwash, important information coming up,' I said. 'Hold your breath, close your eyes, and try not to shit yourself if you feel something touch your face.'

He opened his mouth to protest, but I was already hoisting the mallet up and ready to strike. Seeing this, he gulped down a breath and screwed his eyes shut. I did the same, then brough the mallet down hard onto the nail.

The air turned cold. I could feel something delicate crawling over my face, that same horrible feeling you get when you walk into a spiderweb you didn't see. Fighting the urge to swipe it away or worse, open my eyes, I let it waltz up my face and into my hairline, then down my back. Then it was pulled away suddenly, the wispy threads trying in vain to find some purchase on my skin. Everything went still.

There was a loud crash as the lid of the sarcophagus slammed down hard, fusing with the sides on which it was resting. Slowly, I opened one eye to survey the scene. A huge crack ran corner to corner across the stone lid, passing directly underneath the stack of chips. All the chips had been obliterated as I had expected, blackened and scorched discs that were unrecognisable apart from the one I had driven the nail through. That one was still intact, the nail glowing red hot in its centre.

I picked it up gingerly and gave the nail a little wiggle. It was secure.

Turning around, I clapped Pugwash hard on the shoulder. 'You can breath again, mate. Job's done.'

He blinked his eyes open. 'It... It is?'

'Yep. And this is for you,' I said, handing him the pierced chip along with a folded piece of paper. 'Keep that safe. That nail comes out of that chip, whatever's trying to scratch its way out of that coffin gets back to scratching, understand?'

'I think so,' he said. 'And the paper?'

'My invoice,' I said. 'Two grand. My PayPal. One week. And no, I don't want a trip on your fucking boat.'

*

The money was already in my account by the time I reached my hotel.

Eat The Rich

The woman on reception – barely older than me but with a resting bitch face that matched my own – barely acknowledged me as she slid the key across the desk. I snatched it up with equal grumpiness and made for my room.

I was tired. I'd spent the best part of the day underground and breathing in the dust of rotting corpses – I needed a shower. The water was mercifully warm, which was a far cry from how things tended to be at home.

There was a lot of dust to wash off, so I took my time before finally climbing out of the shower and into a warm towel. It wasn't just the dust, mind – I knew what would be waiting for me when I left the bathroom.

I wrung as much water as I could out of my hair, taking some of the dye with it, and readied myself to meet a god.

Loki Laufeyjarson was sat at the room's small desk, his feet on the tabletop, leaning back. His chair was balanced on its hind legs, and he was rocking it back and forwards with impatience. 'Another fine job, Millie. I don't mind telling you, you're fast becoming my favourite.'

'Great,' I said, walking right past him and pulling another towel from a cupboard. 'Because I live for your approval.'

His expression darkened for a moment. 'You should. After all, without me, I wonder what path your life would have ended up following. Besides, you're really taking to being a proper runeskald! That little sealing ritual? Inspired!'

I shrugged. 'Yep.'

'Always so confident,' he said. 'Even when you're not. Keep up the good work. I'll pop by again next time to give you the praise you deserve.'

He didn't even have the decency to snap his fingers and disappear in a cloud of smoke. Irritating bastard just vanished the moment I blinked.

You're probably more than a little confused. I did sort of dump you in at the deep end there without much in the way of context, but now my hooks have well and truly dragged you this many pages into the excellent book, I guess I can get you up to speed.

First off, magic is real – in case you didn't work that out from using rune-inscribed poker chips to destroy an undead horror. I'm technically a wizard, but I'm very shit at that sort of magic. My training was sort of interrupted by the British Government getting all authoritarian and making my mentor's heart explode like an overstuffed sausage. If you want to hear all about that stuff, go track down Jameson Parker's longwinded rants.

Luckily, I'm not totally useless. I suck at your standard fireballs and fairy dust sort of magic, but I'm a fucking hero at rune magic. That's the runeskald bit, building spells and rituals out of runes used by ancient Norsemen, taught to them by Loki Laufeyjarson. Yeah, the same one kicking up his heels in my hotel room.

It's a whole thing. Upshot is I have a god borderline stalking me, but it's kind of ok? He doesn't do much beside point me in the direction of *stories* that will make me a stronger runeskald. Got to be good at stories to make the magic work for you, apparently.

There, you're all caught up. More or less. Anything else will become apparent in time, I think.

Anyway, Loki gets some credit for being the one to lead me to Pugwash and his haunted crypt. I'm a London girl, born and bred, but we're talking *inner* London. I didn't run in the sort of circles that would drag me out to Hereford, and yet here I was.

That's as much credit as he's getting though.

I wrapped the fresh towel around my damp hair and threw myself on the bed. For a moment, I let myself sink into the soft sheets, then shuffled over to the far side of the bed and fished around in the bedside cabinet. My journal was taped to the underside of the drawer, and I tore it free before setting about adding Pugwash's job to the tally.

Slim pickings. I was building a reputation — a good one this time, not the drunken disasterpiece I had been known as until recently — but it was slow going. There were a couple of good jobs, some freelance work for the chief partisan of the magical world, helping to hobble the government's Orwellian system of controlling mages, that sort of thing. I'd kicked more than my fair share of ghosts in the bollocks too. But jobs like this one, *paying* jobs, were not coming in as regularly as I'd like.

I fought off the sadness by wasting a chunk of my hazard pay on a disgustingly greasy pizza, then checked my emails and went to sleep.

Come the morning I'd have a train to catch early if I wanted to get back to London in time to do fuck all with a good portion of my day.

Two

Pugwash had sent me several emails overnight, all of which I dutifully ignored. By the time I was on the train, he'd sent me three or four more, tracked down my long-abandoned Twitter account and DMed me there, and even somehow found me on Facebook despite my very discrete profile name of *Real Human Woman*.

That was a little concerning, I won't lie. Nobody likes a stalker, especially one with a budget, but curiosity got the better of me and I took a look at the bilge he was so desperate to send me. I'd been expecting dick pics mostly, he was definitely that sort of guy, but I was surprised to find nothing of the sort. Instead, he was trying, very insistently, to refer one of his friends to me.

A referral. Like a proper professional business. I'd done some *networking* and I hadn't even meant to.

It was a little sobering to see that he had taken the liberty of doling out my location to this friend of his without my consent, though. Evidently, his cyberstalking skills went so far as to sleuthing out the most likely trains I would have taken, cheerfully informing me his friend would be waiting for me at the station when I arrived.

I wrote several emails for Pugwash that were full of the vilest filth ever smashed out of a digital keyboard, but I decided against sending them. Don't take that the wrong way – I would have been more than happy to shred his presumptuous little brain – but if I engaged with him now, he'd probably take that as a sign to keep in touch. That was a hassle I could do without.

Instead, I took the time to reorganise my bag. At first glance, the utter catastrophe that you'd see inside the thing might lead you to believe that there's no organisation involved, but that's where you'd be wrong. Small things at the bottom, leading up layer by layer to the heavy things at the top. You want the items suitable for twatting people to be the ones your hand finds first. This is doubly true when meeting a stranger at a train station.

When the train pulled into London, I made a point of being one of the last people to get off. Stations don't really empty in cities, but if you hang around long enough you can find a sort of *low tide* situation. I had hoped that it would have given me a momentary advantage, that I could scope out the person who would be waiting for me, but in the end, I hadn't needed it. The idiot couldn't have made himself more obvious if he had tried.

First off, he was reading a newspaper – or pretending to. He was holding the Financial Times, opened so wide that he'd fostered a little clearing around him, which was a comical scene in itself. Ever seen a teenager reading that stonking huge bastard of a paper? Yeah, didn't think so. He might as well have cut eye holes into it, that might have actually cut a more authentic image. If that wasn't enough, he was dressed like someone who had been kicked off the set of Downton Abbey for getting far too into character. In a way I had to respect the balls of him, showing up in central London wearing one of those suit jackets with the tails on and uncomfortably white gloves.

As I stepped down from the train, I saw his eyebrows rise over the surface of the paper. It was a reaction I was used to, a moment of profound disappointment and confusion at seeing that the person you were supposed to be meeting was, well, *me.* He took it better than most, I suppose, taking only a few seconds to regain his stiff upper lip.

He folded the paper under his arm and strode confidently over to me, the heels of his extremely shiny shoes click-clacking on the platform floor. 'Ms Thatcher? Bertie De'Ath, at your service.'

I looked him up and down with disdain. 'I've got, like, ten seconds of patience here before I tell you to get fucked. Don't waste them.'

He looked confused. 'I wasn't expecting hostility. You came highly recommended.'

'I tend to get a little hostile when people I don't know are lying in wait for me.'

'Ah,' he said. 'Monty didn't actually ask you, did he? That little rat.'

'Monty?'

'Montague Battenberg-Fiennes? The young gentleman you

just assisted with his... *Family issue.*'

The young man looked around sheepishly with those last words, seemingly checking if anyone was listening. They weren't, of course. Why would they? Perhaps because he had the tell-tale accent of a man whose name opened doors, where those cut-glass tones would be enough to draw attention and get the owner thinking he was the centre of the universe.

Posh, is what I'm saying.

'If you've got a similar fuck up in the family—'

He raised a gloved hand, rudely interrupting me. 'No, nothing of that kind.   There is quite a real problem though. The faculty have hired professionals to look into it, to no success. They weren't keen on contacting you, but Monty put in a good word with me, and I passed it on, and—'

'If you're trying to neg me into looking into your problem, it's not the best way to hire me. Just give me the details.'

'Well, it's not me that's hiring you, per se. I'm the head prefect of Fury College—'

'You don't say.'

'—where students and faculty are turning up dead.'

I gestured at him to continue. 'And?'

'And partially, or in some cases wholly, eaten.'

Fuck sake. I really wanted to tell him to get lost, but if he was going to dangle that right in front of my face, I had to hear him out, didn't I? Just weird enough to get my juices flowing. 'What sort of eaten? Dahmer, Donner, or Dinner?'

'Pardon?'

'Fetish, food, or feral? Don't make me do another round of alliteration, I'm struggling here.'

He looked around once again. 'The faculty suspect the latter rather than anything else, at least so far as they will tell me. Wild dogs is the current lead theory.'

'Occam's Rottweiler.'

'Impossible,' he spat. 'The last time there were wild dogs on college grounds, the faculty organised a hunt and had them all shot. They were pedigree game dogs; we do not get strays.'

'Not selling me on wanting to help you here,' I said. 'And I'm not seeing why you thought you needed me.'

'The college has internal measures that have historically proven quite adept at dealing with matters like these,' he said. 'Unfortunately, they have as yet failed to resolve the matter. In fact, they were the first to recommend that an outside expert might be required. This recommendation was met with significant pushback from the faculty, but needs must, as they say.'

The last time I was able to honestly state that my reputation had preceded me, I was being forcibly denied entry to a pub. It was weird to be able to use it positively for once. 'As an expert, I command a *considerable fee*.'

'Considerably less than what the college stands to lose if it gets out that students are getting devoured on campus, I assure you,' he said. 'The headmaster and the provost have already given their assent, and seeing as I represent the student body in these matters, I have too.'

'That was fast. I only finished up with Pugwash yesterday.'

'The notion of hiring outside help precedes the notion of that outside help being *you*,' he said. 'But this is where we are at, I suppose.'

I couldn't help but smile. 'I'm your last choice and you *hate* that. Lucky for you, I don't have a big problem with being the bottom of the list as long as the money's good.'

'Does that mean you'll return to the college with me?'

It wasn't so long ago that I would have turned him down flat, even with such an interesting scenario to explore. But this whole runeskald thing had gotten under my skin, and why spend time trying to up my game if I wasn't going to put it to use. Plus, rinsing a load of baby Tories was something that should never be avoided. Doing my part for the ethical redistribution of wealth.

I nodded in agreement. 'Sure, I'll take a look.'

'Very well, follow me.'

Without even time to take a breath, he set off down the platform at an almost military march – back straight, footsteps heavy, arms swinging in perfect time. I almost had to run to keep up with him, my overstuffed satchel bouncing uncomfortably against my hip.

He was mercifully quiet as he cut a path through the people now filing onto the platform for the next train. As I followed, I caught a few people turning their heads to watch as he pushed past, a mix of confusion and interest on their faces. Those expressions soured the moment they saw me tagging along behind him, but I tried not to dwell on that thought too much.

At the end of the platform, he shared a handshake with a man in a high-vis jacket who subsequently opened the ticket barriers for us and ushered us through. We hoofed it across the station to the furthest platform, through another set of barriers via handshake, and onto a waiting train. It was absolutely heaving, a quick glance telling me that every seat and square inch of aisle space was taken. Undeterred, De'Ath shoved through the gaggle of people in the vestibule of one carriage and pulled me through into the next one.

It was a carriage out of time, like something from one of a film from the golden age of Hollywood. It made the other carriage look like a cattle car which, I suppose, it was when you think about it. Cram as many people in as possible, maximise profits, minimise comforts. Those considerations were flipped on their head in here – lots of space, seats with cushions that weren't stuffed with old foam, and completely without the smell of piss that somehow permeates your usual train car.

'Trying to show off?' I asked him.

He gave me a curt nod and pointed at a chair. 'Sit here. The

College Car is old and the suspension can be a little stiff when moving away. I shall just inform the driver we are aboard.'

'I'm sure he'll be thrilled.'

'I expect he will,' De'Ath said. The college paid him a month's salary to hold the train for my return journey.'

Stepping out of the carriage once again, I heard the door lock behind him and felt my stomach drop a little.

Maybe I had been a little too reckless here. I had expected rich and stupid, even stupidly rich, but not this level of wealthy. A private car with a chauffeur? Sure, that was fine. First class on a normal train? Absolutely. Commandeering a public train to haul a Victorian dining room around at a whim? Nuh-uh, that was *conspiracy rich*.

That's the sort of rich where they find you all carved up and stuffed in a bread bin near Kensington Gardens. It's the obscene level of wealth that melts brains and makes people start thinking NFTs are nifty and the blood of young people can lengthen your life. Being a young person, I can tell you that my blood, if anything, will shorten lives, incidentally.

To set my mind at ease, I took a reading of my runes.

Ordinarily, I'm not one for prophecy. My education never reached that bit of rune magic, and there's enough complexity in the shit I *can* do that I'm not overly interested in adding a whole new string to my comically splintered bow. But, that said, bounce some runes across a table a few times and you'll at least get the basics down.

Eat The Rich

Weal and woe was all the stones said – the runic equivalent of a magic 8-ball telling you to ask again later. Thoroughly unhelpful and did little to put my mind at ease. I prepared a spell, just in case, and waited for De'Ath to return.

It didn't take him long to return after my failed attempt at prophecy, and he did so with a stack of papers held tightly between both hands. He slammed it down on the table in front of me and pulled a fountain pen from his pocket. 'Sign this and then we can begin.'

'What is it?'

'Standard Non-Disclosure Agreement,' he said. 'The college is very keen on protecting its reputation. This one is comparatively light compared to the one I had to sign when I got my prefect's badge.'

'You're all very serious and stuffy, aren't you?'

He allowed himself a tiny chuckle. 'You'll find I'm something of a rebel amongst my peers.'

'Is that so?'

'I've been known to crack a window on occasion,' he said. 'Let some of the stuffiness out. Here.'

He took the fountain pen back from me and swapped it with a cheap ballpoint pen. 'Excuse me?'

'I notice you're left-handed, you'll get ink everywhere.'

'I can use a fountain pen.'

'I'm sure you can.'

I narrowed my eyes and rolled the ballpoint over my fingers a few times, then turned my attention to the stack of paper and started to read. A document that many pages long is just begging you *not* to read it, and I wasn't about to let De'Ath slip something by me.

*

The NDA was long and wordy, and it took most of our travel time for me to decipher what I could of it. I couldn't find any references to relinquishing my soul, my first born, my sexual autonomy, any of the usual shady shit that shows up in these things. I was still greeted by a feeling that I had fucked up the moment I put pen to paper, though.

De'Ath stayed quiet for the journey, letting me read through the contract in silence, and giving me time to myself once I had done so. He was always watching, however, out the side of his eye. I mean, look, there's been shifty and then there was whatever he was doing. Maybe it was just upper-class indifference to a grotty peasant girl like me, but I was starting to feel like I was being tested.

The fuckers had come and sought me out, putting me at the advantage, and still they couldn't turn off the condescending, sneering, superior looks. I just needed to use what was left of the train journey as practice – surely it would get worse once I actually reached their *glorious* college.

Once we arrived at *this* station, I was ferried from the train to the sort of car I had been expecting from the beginning, and inside of twenty minutes I was deposited outside the rear gates of the college, next to the dumpsters. Hard not to take that as a message.

De'Ath had abandoned me again, but only for five minutes this time. I kicked some pebbles around for a bit until he returned with a man following behind him. He was middle aged, rocking a bushy moustache that was seemingly designed to draw attention from his balding head, and some actual fucking *tweed clothes*. I thought tweed was a joke we all shared, not a thing people could actually buy and *wear*.

I bet when they first invented dolls for boys, they went with a look like this. Aspirational boredom. The exact look of a man who would unironically call fucking *a bit of rumpy pumpy*. Dear god, he turned the air grey.

Not very impressive, to be clear. In case you missed that.

The man looked me up and down as if he was appraising some weird deep-sea fish. 'Been mingling with the natives have we, De'Ath?'

'She doesn't look much, I grant you, sir,' he replied. 'But Monty doesn't tell tall tales, and he says she's good for it.'

The man was quiet for a moment, again peering at me from down his nose. 'A change of clothes will have to be procured. A shower. If the dye can be scrubbed from that hair, a comb run through it, the length of it may just help disguise her enough to let her on campus.'

I blinked. 'You want to say that again, to my face this time?'

'I was,' the man said. 'Perhaps if you took the time to listen before you spoke, to consider what you are being told—'

Well, I had heard quite enough out of him. Closing what little ground there was between us, I got right up in his face, seething. Not exactly easy when you're barely over five feet tall, but my chunky boots added a helpful couple of inches. Without those inches, I don't think I would have even reached his chin, but as it was I had just enough height to make him recoil backwards in shock.

'Who the *fuck* are you, mate?' I asked.

'He's the vice provost,' De'Ath said. 'James Dayne.'

My eyes never left the moustache of the old man. 'He could be the pissing King himself, he doesn't get to talk to me like I'm *the help*.'

A pencil-thin smile carved its way onto the face of the vice provost. 'Yes. Quite right. Very well, I'm convinced.'

He took a few confident steps backward, putting some space between us. By the time he had come to a halt, something had changed in his demeanour; he looked a touch less austere. For my part, I suspect I looked a little confused. 'Convinced of what?'

'Your credentials,' he said. 'Sorry about the rude welcome. People have impressions about the sort of person who ends up in a college like this one.'

'Rich arseholes, you mean?'

'Indeed,' he said, not missing a beat. 'And we certainly count plenty of those amongst our number. I wanted to just give you a little test to see if you had the backbone to deal with them.'

'You couldn't have just asked? You had to be a twat about it?'

The smile grew a little wider, but it didn't reach his eyes. 'To get an effective understanding of you, precisely. Are you prepared to get to work, or do you need time to freshen up? Don't let the character I was portraying moments ago put you off – the test is over, I won't be judging you should you need to wash off the journey before we begin.'

'I'll get a lay of the land, then settle in and get to work,' I said. 'Might as well start with the good stuff. Want to give me a heads-up of what to expect?'

Dayne sniffed. 'Stares, I would expect. No audible catcalls, we do drill a surface level of decorum into them, but—'

'I meant in terms of the whole cannibalism thing.'

'Of course, you did,' he said. 'De'Ath, you can return to class now. I'll see the young lady on from here.'

De'Ath snapped a very official nod and headed off towards the main gate. Dayne waited for him to be out of sight and then led me the opposite way, through the *staff entrance* and into the college.

He hadn't been wrong about the staring. While he escorted me through the staff areas, things weren't too oppressive. A few teachers' heads turned, a few stiff upper lips writhed, but nothing altogether out of the ordinary. The staff areas of the college were tiny compared to the bulk of the buildings however, and it didn't take five minutes before we emerged out into the perfectly presented central quad.

Take away their frock coats and their plummy voices, and the experience was weirdly like walking into an old pub. At a basic level, all men react to strange women the same way – stare great big burning holes into her until she either crumbles under the weight of social pressure or last long enough to become part of the background noise in their heads. I wasn't about to crumble, but there is something unique about the sort of pressure you can get from hundreds of pairs of teenage boarders at a private school. Wasn't really prepared for that.

Like chinless children of the corn, it seemed as though the entire college ground to a halt to watch me make my way across the quad and into one of the dorm buildings. Inside, Dayne waved off a pair of upper classmen that were weakly guarding the sort of staircase that creaks like a coffin lid in a light breeze. He led me up it, down a corridor at the top, and stopped outside a hefty wooden door.

Reaching into his pocket, he pulled out an equally chunky key and unlocked the door. 'I understand you are a professional, but I'd still take a moment to compose yourself and prepare if I were you. When you're ready, I'll open the door.'

I sucked my teeth dismissively and pushed past him, throwing the door open defiantly.

It was a small dormitory, designed for four students. There

was a quarter of the room for each student, and while they all seemed to share the same unbearably boring style there were a few little touches that lent some personality to each section. One of them had a scarf in the team colours of what was probably some polo team or another, a second a bust of a dead Roman general looming right over his headboard. You know, normal teenage boy shit.

Only one bed stood out though, the one absolutely fucking *drenched* in gore.

'Fucking *CHRIST*,' I spat, slamming the door again. 'What the fuck?!'

Dayne's eyes were focused down the corridor over my head, steadfastly refusing to look me in the face. 'I believe I did warn you.'

'I was told eaten. *Eaten.* Not gnawed on like bargain bucket gristle. There's a *skeleton* in there.'

With slightly less bravado this time, I opened the door again and stepped inside for a closer look. The gore on the bedsheets looked like chunky jam, thick gobbets of flesh drying into black specks on the white fabric. It didn't take a coroner to work out the poor kid had been picked clean by teeth rather than blades – once I was close enough to get a good look at the bones, I could see the teeth marks. My bargain bucket analogy had been right on the money, he'd been gnawed on extensively, to the point that there wasn't an inch of bone that hadn't been marked.

My stomach started to settle – if you're going to deal with

ghosts and shit, your stomach's going to get used to gross corpses pretty fast – and I hunched down over the mess. 'How long ago did this happen?'

'This one, two nights ago,' Dayne said from the doorway.

'And you haven't cleaned up after him?'

'The head of the Dee Society recommended we leave the scene untouched for the benefit of our...' he stopped and cleared his throat pointedly. 'For our *outside contractor*.'

I sighed. 'Remind me to buy him a drink.'

Behind me, I heard Dayne step into the room and close the door behind him. 'For what it's worth, the others weren't nearly as brutal as this. Deadly, indeed, but the boys were found in a dignified repose.'

'Interesting change in methodology,' I said. 'Don't give me that look, I know long words.'

Dayne, again, didn't miss a beat. 'The young man was Harry de Pfeffel, a first year. Well liked, by all accounts. Should you wish to interview his roommates, they've been distributed throughout the other dormitories, but I can summon them if you wish.'

'No need right now,' I said, shaking my head. 'I doubt they'll be able to say much. Unless one of them is the killer, I suppose.'

'The Dee Society explored that possibility, but there was no—'

Eat The Rich

'That's the second time you've mentioned the Dee Society,' I interrupted. 'Who are they?'

Dayne took a moment to choose his words before he spoke again. 'They are our... in-house solutions team for matters like these.'

'Ah, yes, Bertie-boy mentioned them,' I said. 'Get a lot of weird shit then?'

'Our fair share. We are a storied establishment.'

'I'm sure.'

I crossed the room to one of the pristine areas and fished around in a desk for a pen or pencil of some kind. Underneath a discarded exercise book, I found a fountain pen – expensive metal, a family crest inlaid on the clip – and hurried back to the corpse. Trying to avoid thinking about how this must have looked, I started to poke and prod at the skeleton with the pen, pushing aside the moist lumps of flesh and muscle, scraping away the dry bits, in the hope of getting a closer look at the bite marks.

They didn't seem familiar, but it's not like I'm a shitting dentist. I snapped a photo on my phone, another addition to my camera roll of horror, and made a mental note to look into that later. Maybe I'd get lucky and find someone had spun up a wiki page devoted to the teeth of flesh-eating monsters while I wasn't looking.

Still, it did expose something more immediately curious.

'Is this exactly how the body was found?' I asked.

'Yes,' Dayne said. 'No-one has interfered with anything, at least not physically.'

'Physically?'

'The Dee Society—'

I threw up a hand. 'I'll just talk to them about whatever it was they were doing, don't strain yourself.

He looked relieved. 'Very well.'

It hadn't registered when I first entered the room, but it was *weird* how pristine the skeleton's pose had been. I'm not enough of a bad bitch goth to do much pondering over human remains, so I'm not embarrassed to say that I didn't realise at first how weird it was that the skeleton was just, you know, *there* like that. He looked like he'd just lay there happily and content while someone chewed his *literal face off*.

Scraping off some of the gore gave me some indication as to why that was. The killer had eaten the flesh, the muscle, probably even the marrow, but they'd left the ligaments. They'd slurped all the juicy bits right off the bone, and left behind a macabre Pinocchio, *sans* strings.

Well, that had to be a clue, right? Chomp through all that flesh, gnash at all those bones, and take the time and care to leave something *that* untouched? Definitely not an accident, at least.

I pulled a small pouch from my satchel, opened it, and took out the contents. Without looking, I started to roll myself a cigarette. It was finished in seconds, and I tucked it behind my ear before pulling a small penknife from my pocket and flicking it open. Holding it firmly in my left hand, I hopped up onto the bed and straddled the hollow chest of the dead boy, leaning down over him and placing the tip of the blade against the front of the skull.

'What *on Earth* are you doing?' Dayne spluttered. 'Is that really necessary?'

My eyes fixed on the forehead of the skull, I slipped the cigarette into my mouth. 'Would you tell the pope how to shit in the woods? Let me work.'

Slowly, carefully, I etched a rune into the skull's forehead. It only took a few minutes, but that can feel like an eternity with those hollow pits staring back at you. Once it was done, I snapped the knife shut and returned it to a pocket, then I lit the cigarette and took a few puffs. It tasted fucking rancid – no tobacco or weed here, just a madcap blend of wiccan wonder-herbs – but that was how I knew I'd gotten the balance right.

A couple more puffs, just to get the room nice and smoky, then I stubbed the cigarette out on the rune.

The room turned ice-cold for a moment. A shallow breeze crept up from the floor, tickling the curtains and scratching at the back of my throat. Then it was gone as quickly as it had arrived.

'Sleep well, kid,' I said, climbing down from his ribcage. 'Your torment's done.'

'Torment?' Dayne said, his composure a little cracked. 'What torment?'

'Just exorcised the poor sod,' I said, flicking a glob of dried flesh from my trousers. 'A death like that, he was bound to linger if something wasn't done about it. Now, I suppose I should have a word with this Dee Society you keep banging on about, hadn't I?'

Three

Dayne led me as far as the main building, leaving me at the entrance. He had told me that the Dee Society made their lair in the back of the library, which tracked. Books and creepy shit go hand in hand, so even if you're not a massive nerd you're going to have to visit a library once in a while. Then again, if you were the sort to join a society dedicated to seeking out creepy shit, on the balance of probabilities you *were* going to be a massive nerd.

Classes were in session now, so at least I didn't have to deal with the staring while I awkwardly made my way through the halls. Dayne's pressing business that kept him from directly guiding me to the library – whatever that had been – was not so pressing that he had been unable to give me directions. I hadn't listened though, which was on me. I had mistakenly assumed the layout of a fucking school would make sense.

By the time I found the library, the whole atmosphere of the school was starting to get to me. The bloody bricks were radiating patriarchal energy – probably *literally*, I should have tried using my *magic eyes* to check – and it was starting to make me feel unsafe. The library helped put me a little at ease, thankfully. It was equally as empty as the halls had been, but all libraries have the same energy. Every library hates every person, regardless of colour or creed – whoever you are, you're there to steal from it.

That's why you have to be quiet in a library. You're doing a heist.

The librarian, an old man with glassy eyes and grey teeth, was the first person who hadn't paused to look me up and down the moment he saw me. Before I could say anything, however, he directed me towards the far wall and went back to stamping the returned books.

A lot of leather-bound books in that room. They had to match the upholstery I suppose, all those rich red leather armchairs. If it hadn't been for the books, the layout would have been more like a lounge, I guess.

If it hadn't been for the books? Come on, Millie. A library without books isn't a library. Idiot.

True to Dayne's word, I found the Dee Society huddled up at the back wall of the library. Immediately, I knew they were *my people*. For one thing, not one of them was wearing the stupid college tie – bonus points already. Shirts untucked? More points. All that greased hair scruffed about like electrified pompoms? Ding-ding-ding, *jackpot.*

One of them noticed me and pried himself away from a stack of books he had been using as a backrest. He was the first person of colour I'd seen since arriving at that hellhole. 'You're the contractor?'

I shrugged. 'Very prim and proper way of referring to me, but sure.'

'Azizi Igbinedion. The others,' he paused to wave his hand around idly at the other members of the group, all either asleep or nose deep in a book. 'They will introduce themselves in time, I expect. As a group, we are not accustomed to being social.'

'You're not doing a bad job.'

'I'm the most senior of our group,' he said. 'Aside from the Professor.'

'The Professor?'

'Our faculty liaison sponsor. He will be in class now, but I will arrange a meeting if you like,' he said. A smile split his face like a precious geode as he sat down again. He indicated for me to join him. 'Anything you would ask the Professor, you can ask me.'

I slid down onto the floor next to him, pulling my knees up to my chest. In the distance, the rhythmic thudding of the librarian's stamp was the only sound other than our voices. 'Didn't think you'd all be students. I was led to believe you were a professional group.'

'Build's character, apparently,' he replied. 'The *official* position of the school is that we have to earn our keep somehow, and the best way to do that is to do the work they don't want to do themselves. Or don't want to pay someone else to do for them. Used to be cleaning, maintenance, that sort of thing. As the years tick by, the focus has shifted somewhat.'

'Earn your keep?'

'We're scholarship students. The token poor they let into their little club for good publicity.'

'All of you?'

'Yep,' he said. 'Anyway, enough about us. You're here to do what we can't, and I'd be very happy to help you do that.'

I crossed my legs, letting my knees fall away from my chest. 'Apart from the dead kid, what I saw says you were going about things the right way.'

'You've seen the body?'

'First place I went,' I said. 'Dayne was very keen on me getting started immediately.'

'Not surprised,' Azizi said. 'The other victims had no standing, but not Harry.'

I leant forward. 'Slow down. Standing?'

'More scholarship students. The Dee Society is all scholarship students, but not all scholarship students are Dee Society. Get me?'

'But Harry de Pfeffel doesn't fit that pattern.'

Azizi's eyes fell. 'Harry… Harry was complicated. We failed him.'

'Go on.'

'Harry was one of us,' he said. 'Or was going to be. A scholarship student, but his family are old blood. His father frittered the fortune away on the crypto boom but still had the connections to get Harry in here.'

I nodded along as he spoke. 'They could sweep the poors under the rug, but people are going to pay attention to a dead kid with connections.'

'Exactly. There's usually a death or two a year here, nothing big. Easy enough to say a kid burned out, and people will believe it. We're up to five this year, though. Harry was just the first one with enough clout for his death to be a problem.'

'Well, that's even more fucking grim than I expected of this place.'

He shrugged. 'It's not as bad as it sounds. If they can keep things under wraps, the Society has time to look into things. But now they need to be seen to be doing things, we aren't enough.'

'Christ, this PR bollocks gets on my tits.'

'And mine,' he said with a wink. 'So, tell me what you need to know.'

I thought for a moment. 'Let's start with the basics. What have you ruled out?'

He kicked out at one of the other boys, rousing him just long enough for him to pull a notebook out of a backpack and hand it to Azizi. 'Very little, to my shame. Take a look.'

He held out the book and I took it from him. I flicked through the pages, wanting to find the last entry and work backwards. There were a lot more than I expected.

'Someone's thorough.'

'Unlike some, I am in this school on merit alone,' he said. 'Preparation is a difficult skill to switch off.'

'Lycanthrope, zombie, voodoo zombie, doppelganger… Won't lie, I wouldn't have thought of some of these.'

He narrowed his eyes at me. 'Why not?'

I choked on my tongue. It was a weird sensation, realising I didn't *want* to be rude to someone, and yet I'd just painted myself into a corner where the only answer I could give would sound like I was making a dig. Instead, I stammered. 'Well… I… The thing is…'

Azizi smiled. 'Don't worry, if you're going slap my ego down a little, I will understand.'

There was a blush trying to make its way to my cheeks, I could feel it. I needed to answer before it took hold. 'They're all too conspicuous, and none of their feeding patterns fit. Lycanthropes have set hunting times, and they aren't nearly this picky. Non-voodoo zombies are pretty conspicuous, and their voodoo mates don't eat. Doppelgangers—'

'Only eat the hearts,' he interrupted. 'To consume the soul of whoever they are wanting to replace.'

'You can add your common-or-garden variety ghost to that list too,' I said. 'No teeth to chomp with.'

'Noted,' he said. 'There's a lot of different types of ghost though, right?'

I flopped my head from side to side noncommittally. 'Eh, I guess. You tend to get a feel for them after a while though.'

'We are playing catch-up,' Azizi said quietly. 'And we are catching up too slowly. You are ahead on the reading so, tell us, what horrors are still in play?'

Frowning, I rubbed at the side of my neck. 'Way too many creepy little fuckers to count, if I'm honest. Tell me about the other killings.'

Another kick, another notebook extracted from a sleepy library lad. 'There are signs of escalation. The first kills were reserved, only a couple of bites. At first, that led us to the possibility of a vampire—'

'Reasonable.'

'—But we couldn't find a genus in our research that consumes the flesh, just the vitae.'

I nodded approvingly, hoping he wouldn't press me on that issue. The more he spoke, the more it was becoming abundantly clear that I was out of my depth. True, I might know my way around the odd necromantic horror, but I was hardly an expert. I didn't know shit about vampires, and I knew even less about *how to research vampires* than Azizi and his lot did.

But I did like the way he looked at me while he thought I *did* know this shit – like someone who had their shit together, a professional, *an authority.* That was a feeling I wanted to hold onto, even if it meant playing up my expertise a little.

'When did they start getting more thorough?'

'With Harry,' he said. 'Real jump in confidence there, as far as I can tell.'

I ran a hand through my hair, thinking. It didn't fit any undead shit I had heard of, that much was true, but even living psychos can be relied upon to act a certain way. Dead ones, on the whole, tended to be even more strict when it came to their patterns. Never known one to jump to the end of the line like this.

I took the notebook from his waiting hands. 'I'll look into it. Can you get me a list of all the scholarship students? Should probably keep an eye on them, all things considered.'

He nodded. 'I'll head by the administration office and throw my weight around. You'll have it by the end of the day.'

Now, call me a miserable fucking cynic, but I don't trust people who are as helpful as Azizi was being. You fuck up bad enough that they have to bring in someone to do your job for you, you're going to be at least a little pissed off about it. I mean, Christ, I used to get grumpy enough when my ex told me I was doing the washing up wrong, and that's piddly-shit compared to failing to stop classmates getting *fucking eaten.*

On my way out of the library, I turned around long enough to give him one last look of suspicion, but Azizi had gone back to lounging confidently and was seemingly ignoring me. Rude. Probably not rude enough to count as suspicious, but still *rude*.

Eat The Rich

Honestly, I was at a loss on how to start this investigation. When it's something I know about, this part is easy – they all work the same way really, so you just run a finger down the right page in the playbook until you hit the bit they last did, then go wait for them at the next bit. It's always a lot harder when you actually have to think about shit.

First things first, I needed the lay of the land. Finding the library had been far too embarrassing an experience – if I was going to take this seriously and find whatever hungry horror was munching through the student body, I didn't want to have to worry about getting lost again. So, I picked a direction and set off walking, hoping I could put together some sort of mental map.

It took me a while. The college didn't look too big from the outside, but the corridors twisted and bent over themselves in ways that would make the hotel from the Shining jealous. Unfortunately for me, this wasn't magic at work, just confusingly old-fashioned architecture.

On the plus side, a lot of corridors meant a lot of classrooms, and *that* meant plenty of opportunities to get the real read of the atmosphere.

Take several hundred young guys and squash them into a dudes-only boarding school, it's going to take a while for someone like me to push through that outer layer of testosterone. We've covered that before. Thing is, once they've all had a chance to ogle, you get a chance to sit in the eye of the hurricane and see just how things are swirling around you. Ultimately, men are easier to read than picture books.

The kids had been defiant and, yeah, horny when I arrived. A couple of hours stalking the halls as they moved between classes, however, had seen my novelty wear off. Well, a bit. Enough, in any case, to start seeing the fear begin to creep through.

You can't hide deaths on school grounds – everyone knows the urban legend that a dead student gets everyone an A – but listening to them as I walked past started to open some interesting points to consider.

The kids were shit scared and Harry de Pfeffel had been the one that tipped them over the edge. He was the talk of the town, right down to the gruesome brutality of the whole thing. Curious that such details made it out, but then I supposed his roommates had been the ones to find him.

Flicking through Azizi's notebook, I started adding some notes of my own on a blank page:

Brazen, bold. Was shy? Escalated too fast to be truly nervous early. Wanted them scared?

I tapped my pen against the page a few times. That made sense, right? A spectacle, something that people would be talking about. That was where I needed to start – start at the side-effects and work backwards. Wasn't much of a revelation, but it gave me *something* at least.

Groaning, I stretched out my arms to pop my spine. I had done a lot of travelling today, far too much sitting, and I could feel a cramp brewing. Couple that with the fact I was starting to feel how slowly my brain was moving, it was clear that I needed to take Dayne up on that offer of a room.

Snapping the notebook shut – I'd made a start, it would keep a little longer – I went looking for the old bugger and, I'd hoped, somewhere I could relax.

*

Dayne had been easy to find. He was giving a lecture on some dead poet or another, one so uninteresting that the class didn't seem to mind my interruption. Begrudgingly, he escorted me out of the main building and off to one of the newer additions to the site. It had that horrible concrete madness of the 60s going for it, but that still put it at almost a century younger than everywhere else I had been on campus.

The room itself was nothing special, but at that point anything on a higher tier than a wet cardboard box would have been enough. I did my best to be patient as I waited for Dayne to fuck off again, then threw myself face down on the bed and fell into the limp, restless sleep you get when your important parts are thumping pain signals into your brain at regular intervals.

Sleep doesn't really work the same when you've been fucking about with runes for a few years. You know that whole lucid dreaming thing? Once you've worked a few runic spells, you kind of forget how *not* to do that. You want to know why that happens, ask someone smarter than me – all

I know is that it makes for a great way to relax.

A dream tried, ever so optimistically, to take form in my mind. As soon as those first hints of it started to take shape, I grabbed them and started to twist them into something else, something of my own design. My own little sanctuary.

While the room I was sleeping in may have been drab and uninspired, I'd turned the one in my mind into something pretty bloody awesome. Spacious, comfy, every book I had ever read, and in the centre of it all, a huge wooden table. Upon its surface was carved a web of channels and slots, perfectly shaped to fit the little stones that were resting in a box on the nearest bookshelf. Scattered around this tabletop, flashcards of various colours were laid out neatly, some joined together by a gentle blue glow from the channels in the table.

My thoughts on the matter, carefully arranged.

I wasn't ready to look at them yet. A cursory glance told me that I had subconsciously made a couple of connections already, but it was too soon to start getting caught up in all that. For now, what I needed was in a pile over by the suitably gothic fireplace – the third book from the bottom in a dusty stack of old tomes and cracked parchments.

The book was a stout old thing, clad in purple leather that was coming apart at the spine. I had never actually seen the book in person, nor known the English translation of its title, so the outside was only a rough approximation. I *had* read the insides though, or at least some cheap and nasty photocopies of it, which was enough for here.

Eat The Rich

Azizi had his sources of research, and I had mine. I started to flip through the book, hoping that something would all but leap off the pages and catch my eye. It wouldn't, but then that wasn't the real reason I had cracked the thing open.

'Whatcha reading?'

I barely turned, tilting my head just enough to glance over my shoulder at the chipper interloper. 'A book. Hello, Loki.'

Once again, the Norse god himself had decided to stop in and bother me. 'Come on, kiddo. Surely you know by now that you can't just hope to find all the answers you need in some little half-remembered book. Reading the tales of others isn't what a real Runeskald should be doing.'

'Do you bother the others like this?' I asked, closing the book carefully.

He shrugged. 'They're boring now. You're the new hotness, and you're the one most in need of my expert tutelage.'

'Lucky me,' I said, hiding a smile.

Loki sucks. He's an arrogant, pompous, *problematic*, pervy little shit. But, as I said, Azizi has his ways of research and I have mine.

'You think I show up in many dreams?' he said with a wink. 'Well, I do. I show up in fewer like this, *fully clothed*.'

'Keep it in your pants,' I said. 'This is a professional space. You're here because—'

'Because I can't keep watching you make the same amateur

mistakes over and over again,' he interrupted. 'The book learning, honestly—'

It was my turn to interrupt now. 'Cracking a book makes you show up *every goddamn time*, mate. You're getting predictable, and that's the point.'

He rolled his eyes and pushed his tongue against the inside of his cheek. 'Well played. I like this side of you.'

'I want to know what's going on at this school.'

'Then do the legwork, Columbo. Ask around. Look into things.'

'The longer I take on this the more kids are going to die,' I snapped. 'So, sure, I'm asking for a nudge in the right direction here to get started.'

'And rob you of that sense of personal growth when you work it out for yourself? What sort of handsome mentor would I be if I did that? Besides, you've already started so well.'

I scowled. 'Yeah, right.'

Walking around me, he perched on a nearby bit of furniture and lifted my chin. 'Don't pout. You were smart to try and rule out the usual suspects. And you were right to focus on the motive. Chin up, sweetheart, you'll get there.'

Again, I hid my smile. Yes, Loki sucks. He's so very much an arrogant, pompous, *problematic*, pervy little shit. But he's also the god of mischief, which means he is almost pathologically compelled to fall for bullshit. There was no doubt in my mind that he knew I was really hamming it up with my talk of doubting myself, but I also knew he'd appreciate all that shit. Game knows game, and while I had hardly excelled as a runeskald in the traditional sense, the one thing I was born to do was talk a good game.

'Thanks mate, you've been ever so helpful.'

And he had been. Granted, he hadn't told me anything new, but he had confirmed what I had already been thinking – this was something I hadn't run into before, and the whole spectacle of it was important. With that locked in, I had a base to build from. Might not sound like much, but it helps.

Loki shot me another wink, his sign of respect from one player to another. 'You're coming along nicely. Might even get your skills up enough to keep the wolf from the door.'

I woke up with a start.

Someone had been knocking on my door, but I was too groggy to pull myself together in time to answer. By the time I rolled to my feet and wiped the drool away, whoever it was had posted a sheet of paper under my door and disappeared back down the corridor.

I picked it up and read it – a list of names, signed by Azizi. A few had been struck through, lines had been drawn between them, joining them up in true conspiracy theorist fashion. Spidery handwriting in the margins tried and failed to find a compelling arcane link between the victims, beyond the obvious.

But, sometimes, you had to accept the obvious, didn't you?

Even basic patterns can reveal shit. Over-analysis is the bane of the perennially keen.

It was so simple, I had to double check myself because, despite what I just said, I still felt like a fucking idiot even giving the theory time of day. And yet, there had been enough dead now to accept that it was, somehow, fact.

Our killer was working in alphabetical order.

What a boring fuck.

Four

'Milton Gracemere?' I all but shouted, throwing open a door.

I had slept most of the day away in taking a trip to my little mental sanctuary and classes were over now. This meant that if I was going to find the next name on the list, I was going to have to go door to door through the dormitories. The lads had been less than helpful.

If I had taken the time to track down a faculty member, it was possible there was a list somewhere of which room every student was in, but I didn't think I had the time to waste. It was already starting to get dark, and if I knew anything about teenage boys left to their own devices, if I didn't find Gracemere before lights-out, then I really was leaving things to chance. What were the odds he'd still be in *his* room?

I'd worked my way through a couple of floors of bewildered boys before I finally found him, secreted away in one of the few single-occupancy dorm rooms. They were little more than closets, tucked next to the fire escape that I can only assume had been begrudgingly bolted to the back of the old building. Fitting, in a way, as he had the look of a podgy Harry Potter.

Gracemere had been sat on his bed, his nose in a book, when

I threw the door open and shouted his name right in his face. His rheumy, shocked eyes widened at me, and he struggled to respond. 'W...wha...*what?*'

'Up!' I snapped. 'Get up. Now. We need to go.'

The poor lad's brain was totally fried. Everything just ground to a halt inside his skull. 'Go where? Excuse me, who are you?'

'Bro,' I said, trying and failing to seem mysterious and intimidating between my hurried breaths. 'A weird goth bursts into your room and you want to take the time to ask questions? I appreciate the impulse, but let's do that later. For now, try this on for size: come with me if you want to live.'

All but grabbing him by the scruff of the neck, I yanked him off his bed and out into the hall. He staggered along behind me, bent double to make a smaller target. I've watched films, I've seen how the Secret Service do this shit. Luckily, the worst he got thrown his way was the amused giggling of his classmates, completely oblivious to what was going on.

In considerably less time than it had taken me to find the bloody lad, I had dragged him back to the room they had given me and shoved him down onto the grey fabric armchair. He tried to get back up, but stopped when I shot a glance at him as I started to rifle through my bag. I quickly found what I was looking for: a couple of loose tablets of gum and a tiger's eye gem about the size of a twenty pence piece. It had a patchwork of tiny runes carved into its surface – a job that had taken days and caused me to spend a lot more money on Amazon getting the tools to do it than I had wanted.

I popped the gum in my mouth and tossed him the gem. 'In your mouth, under the tongue. Hold it there until I say otherwise.'

'Is this drugs?'

'Mate, it's a rock,' I said. 'Just get it in your gob.'

The poor guy had no resistance in him at all. I'm not exactly an expert on family dynamics, but I recognised the signs of a guy who had spent his life bitched about every which way from Sunday by the women in his family, and I respect that. They don't start getting ideas that they need explanations immediately; they can read when it's the time to just fucking shut up and listen.

He placed the gem in his mouth as I turned to lock the door. Once that was done, I pulled out the gum and jammed it into the lock, gooing up the mechanism and sealing the room. Allowing myself one breath, I then pulled a chunky paint pen from deeper in my bag and scrawled even more runes across the walls. By the time I was done, the room was a metaphysical fortress, and nothing was getting in or out until I broke the seal.

Exhausted, I clicked the cap back on the pen and slumped down against the door. 'You can spit that out now, matey.'

He awkwardly flicked the gem out of his mouth and onto the floor. I drummed a boot heel against the floor and the gem obediently rolled over and into my hand – just a party trick, one of the few bits of arcane magic I can muster without giving myself a headache. The boy's face was white as a sheet.

'I... Um... Look,' he said. 'I don't really know what's going on here. Is this hazing? I've heard about hazing.'

I shrugged, still trying to get my breath back. 'What sort of hazing goes on at this shithole?'

'I don't know! I'm confused!'

My heart had finally stopped pounding in my ears. 'Ok, bullet points. I'm a wizard, basically. Someone is trying to kill you. I just used a lot of very cool-looking magic to buy you a bit of time while we work out our next move.'

'We? Wait—'

'We,' I interrupted. 'Just because you're on the list, doesn't mean you get to avoid pulling your weight. I'm a shit white knight, and I find people live longer if they take a bit of responsibility.'

Now he was up, his eyes practically bulging. 'Let me out. This is ridiculous!'

'Sit. Down.'

He sat down. There's that little bit of family programming again, telling him when to shut up and listen. 'Did you say someone is trying to kill me?'

'Probably,' I said. 'I mean, yeah, I did say that, but they're only *probably* trying to kill you at this stage. Unless you're not Milton Gracemere, in which case *I* might end up being the one trying to kill you. Christ, I need to exercise more.'

'Um, I am Milton Gracemere.'

'Excellent. We're back to *probable* target then. That's heading in the right direction.'

'I don't understand,' he said. There was a look in his eye that I recognised, one that said he'd get trapped in a loop if I let him start asking questions.

Instead, I interrupted him by shoving the list of names I had been given into his hands. 'Here. Study this, spot the connection.'

Whether he spotted the link or not didn't matter, I just needed him to shut up for a minute. I had pushed this situation into a high tempo, but now I had him secured I needed to bring things back to a more appropriate level. Like, right, I had no reason to believe he was in *immediate* danger – the big spike in confidence notwithstanding, the previous pattern didn't make it seem like he was going to strike just yet.

But he would be preparing. A bit of chaos surrounding his target might put him off his game a little.

Reaching into my pocket, I retrieved a little metal device about the size of a pocket watch. On its surface, a dozen fine cogs and sprockets interlocked and helped sell the appearance of a pocket watch even more, albeit one that had been turned inside out. I rolled my thumb over the largest cog, clicking the others into a new setting. In the centre, a panel slid open and delivered a smooth token of white marble, another rune carved into it.

Think you've got the hang of this whole runeskald magic shit? It's all rocks and squiggles, mate. Rocks and squiggles.

This rock was carved with a truesight rune. A very useful rune and well worth keeping a few in your gaudy, clockpunk magic dispenser. Slam that bugger against your third eye and you get about a minute of being able to see through the petty temporal nonsense that separates us all. Veils and spells and glamours.

And walls.

Which is what I wanted to see through right then.

The runestone splintered against my forehead and time ground to a moist crawl – that's the best description for it I can come up with. Behind me, I heard Gracemere's confused whining stretching out like miserable word spaghetti. In front of me, everything went sort of greenish, yellowish, purple and I started to become aware of the people out in the corridor.

My, let's call it *enthusiasm*, at tracking down Gracemere had made a hell of a lot of noise and drawn a lot of attention. Kids were starting to amass in the hallway outside, shuffling awkwardly, waiting for someone with an outdated moustache to come and tell them what to do. I recognised some of the faces from my crazy-bitch-dash from room to room, but it clearly hadn't taken long for the news to spread. Half a dozen of the little shits had already pressed their heads against the door, not knowing my runes would mean they wouldn't hear shit.

Kids being kids. What a surprise. Fantastic bit of sleuthing you've done there, Millie. Great story this is, barricading yourself in a bedroom with a bewildered child and using cool magic to make up for the door lacking a peephole.

Really glad I bought this book.

Well, calm your tits a moment and chill. I wasn't making a scene just for the sake of it all. I was fishing.

Like I said before, I wanted to put our culprit off his game with a bit of highly conspicuous teenage drama. My thinking was that there would be something going on out there that didn't belong — I just had to find it.

Nothing in the hallway — just the confused kids and now the miserable moustache brigade trying in vain to shove them back towards their own beds. I needed to look further, reach deeper. Truesight runes give you a bit of leeway on this, a *zoom function* of a kind. I just had to hope the weird shit was happening close by.

I know if I was working out the best way to hunt down a child and eat all his flesh off, I'd want to take a personal interest in what was going on if he got dragged into a heavily warded room. That's basic.

Floor by floor, I swept my gaze over each room in the building. A lot of things going on that an impressionable young woman wouldn't want to see, but nothing that could connect to my big-bitch-drama.

Then, at the very edge of my vision, something caught my eye.

There was a shimmering, hazy *thing* lurking around just outside the building. I couldn't get a clear view of it, and that's what made me suspicious. You deal with magic daily, you take routine precautions to make yourself harder to scry, but it's not like this posh-boy factory was fucking Hogwarts – no reason for anyone here to have warded themselves.

No, before you ask, not even the Dee Society. Like, honestly, they might be great at knowing the Dewey Decimal code for spooky shit, but they didn't know their arseholes from their elbows when it came to magic. Even this simple bit of warding – the equivalent of those shitty LED-laced caps to blind CCTV cameras – would be beyond *them*.

'There's the fucker,' I muttered to myself.

He'd be gone before I could get there, but that was fine. If I went down there now, all unprepared and unarmed, it'd probably end up with him making me his next snack. Plus, you know, there was the issue of the whole school clogging up the corridors between us all.

The sound of someone pounding on the door brought me back to myself, snapping me out of the spell. The hammering was dull and distant, muted by the wards I had set up. They hadn't even pried the gum out of the keyhole yet – we had all the time in the world.

I turned back to Gracemere. 'Finished reading yet?'

'Yes,' he said, his face suddenly ghost-white. 'I didn't... No-one said there was a pattern or anything. They said the murders were tragic and unrelated.'

'That's authority figures for you. Keeping important shit from people so they don't panic? Always leads to panic. Anyone stand out as the potential scumbag behind this? Any bullies, that sort of thing?'

'Bullies?' he nearly managed a laugh but caught himself. 'I don't think I could narrow down *that* list. We're not popular, everyone hates us. We're the mud in the water.'

'Tough break.'

'Eh, you get used to it,' he said. 'I've never met an inventive bully, and I don't think I've seen any murderous ones...'

Poor, dumb idiot. He'd never met real bullies. They don't really come into their own until you hit secondary school, and they won't have a need to get inventive if they've got money. The rich have the dubious privilege of throwing money at their first dumb idea, but the poor have to scheme and plan and plot — they have to treat every shot as their only shot.

Which did raise questions about the shady shit lurking around outside the school. If he was a particularly switched on posh boy, then we were fucked seven ways from Sunday. One of the main things you can count on when dealing with wizards is that even the best of them are marginalised these days; limited resources breeds ingenuity, true, but it comes with restrictions.

Unrestricted and smart? Big oof.

But then we had the alternative, which was possibly worse — self-hating poor kid, making a name for himself. Fuelled by desperation and *issues*, no telling where such a brain could end up.

The dull hammering on the door was growing louder, a failing on my part. The runes had been quick and dirty, but they should have held a lot longer before they started failing. Would have been a bad look if I'd needed them to hold, but they had at least lasted long enough to meet their purpose.

Besides, even without the runes, the chewing gum would keep them at bay.

I turned my attention back to Gracemere. 'Right, let's get freaky weird about all this instead. Tell me about the weird shit that you've run into at this school. The unexplained or the out of the ordinary.'

'Like what?'

'Ghosts, zombies, man-eating trees, sex-dreams about snakes with your mum's face, that sort of thing.'

'Are you serious?'

'Mate, look at the shit I've scrawled on the walls. This is a fucking elaborate prank if I'm not serious.'

He went quiet for a moment. 'I don't think it counts, but...'

'Go on.'

'I've not been dreaming lately. Like, at all.'

Hmm, curious. 'A lot of people don't dream.'

'Yeah, but, like, I lucid dream,' he said. 'I read an article online and taught myself to do it. Kind of helps. With the bullying.'

Escaping into a dream world probably isn't the healthiest way to address bullying, but it's not like I'm qualified to give a kid life advice. 'Every night?'

He nodded. 'Every night. It's really easy once you know how. If you're, like, a wizard or whatever, I'm guessing you'd know all about that.'

'Not really,' I said with a shrug. 'It's a dangerous practice for people with power; opens too many doors. How long since you last dreamed?'

'I don't know,' he replied. 'A couple of weeks? I just thought I was too stressed out to sleep properly. You know, with exams and classes and the complete lack of friends...'

'Sure, school is hell,' I said, cutting him off. There was something to this, though. 'So, you're not dreaming and you're sleeping badly?'

'Like weirdly badly, yeah.'

'Wake up tired, sleepwalk through the day, that sort of thing?'

'Yeah, exactly.'

That narrowed things down a little. Not much, but it was a start. Kind of hinted towards a psychic attack of some kind, actually.

The mind has pretty excellent natural defences, that's why mind magic is so notoriously hard to pull off properly. Even an undefended mind is more than capable to kicking spells in the bollocks. But the energy to do that has to come from somewhere and, as we all know, sleep is where you regenerate your mental faculties.

Fucked up sleep patterns definitely count as potential evidence in that regard.

But did that narrow things down? Not much. Pretty much every horrible thing likes to dole out psychic damage whenever it can — even your common ghost has the capability to fuck with the mind, it just kind of comes as part of the package when you go all malevolent.

But it was better than nothing, I supposed.

There was a noise from the door behind me and I turned in time to see it being awkwardly removed from its hinges. The protracted hammering from the hallway had overloaded the runes, protective sigils snapping impotently as the door began to move. It slid out of the frame, borne on the backs of a pair of spindly students. A third was stood to the side with a mallet in one hand and a spike in the other. The hinge pins were on the floor by his feet, glowing softly with the dissipating magic.

Outside the door, I could see other students too, but they had pushed back to form a bubble of empty space around Dayne. He was stood front and centre, waiting for his top tier students to finish extracting the door. He gave a sniff of approval as they set it down on the wall next to the frame, then stepped through into the room.

'Gracemere,' he said. 'Run along, now. You'll sleep in Perkins' room tonight.'

'I... yes sir.'

'I require a word with Miss Thatcher,' he said, his tone suspiciously restrained. 'And that goes for the rest of you too. Back to your rooms.'

The gaggle didn't want to disperse, so instead opted to dismantle. This, in practice, meant that they drifted away exactly as slowly as they could get away with and, I'm pretty sure, meant they would reform at the minimum safe distance to hear my impending bollocking while still avoiding being caught in the splash zone.

I crossed my arms and waited patiently for Dayne to work himself up into a lather. Better men than him had shouted at me before, and I figured he needed to give himself a run-up anyway.

'Students are not allowed to mingle in another's room after lights-out,' he said once the gaggle was out of sight. His voice was clipped and breathy, like he was physically struggling not to shout.

'I'm not a student.'

'You *kidnapped* one! When we agreed to bringing you onto campus, there were certain conditions that we assumed you would meet.'

I crossed my arms. 'I didn't agree to any conditions.'

'We didn't think it would be necessary to specify you *not kidnap children*, Miss Thatcher.'

'It's protective custody, dickhead.'

'No,' he snapped, jabbing a finger at me. 'What it is is unacceptable behaviour, young lady. You are here at the invitation of this school, and that invitation can be rescinded at any time. Just because we have need of your services, do not take that to mean that you have free rein to damage the reputation of this college.'

I slapped his hand away and got up in his grill. 'I wasn't aware keeping the kids safe would damage the reputation. *Do excuse me,* I need to keep that Gracemere kid safe.'

Dayne's hand locked around my wrist as I went to leave. 'He will be fine, but we are not finished here.'

'I am,' I said, prying my hand free. 'And if you want me to actually do this job, maybe open your mind a little to my methods.'

His eyes narrows and his nostrils flared. Honestly, I wouldn't have been surprised to see him go all cartoon and have steam burst out of his ears. When he spoke again, his teeth were so gritted I could hear them squeaking off each other. 'If I didn't have an open mind, Miss Thatcher, you wouldn't be here at all. The board of trustees that oversee this college is staffed by some of the most powerful people in the

Eat The Rich

country—'

'Rich twats.'

'That's as maybe,' he continued. 'But the fact remains they are the authority on this campus and it is my job to see their wishes are respected. I get very little leeway in the requests I make of them, and the fact that I have been able to negotiate some slack for you should speak volumes as to how open my mind is.'

'That sounds hard,' I said. 'But I don't care about inter-office bullshit. You hired me for a job, so get out of my way and let me do it.'

He took one very long, deep, excruciatingly slow breath. 'Gladly. If you can just restrict your more chaotic impulses just a tad.'

'I work how I work. You should have looked me up before you hired me.'

'Fine. If you want to keep acting this way, then I'll have De'Ath shadow you. He can make sure the college's interests are respected.'

Once more, I squared up to him. If he wanted a pissing contest, then he could fucking have one — and I'd win. I was the one holding all the cards here, and he knew it. 'If you assign me a babysitter, I'll walk. Fuck your job, fuck your kids, peace out.'

I could see it in his eyes; he knew I'd fucked him.

Five

Dayne had issued De'Ath a little notebook, and the prissy little shit was taking a lot of glee in writing down everything I was doing.

'Do you know shorthand or something?' I snapped, quickening my pace in the hope he would fall behind. 'How can you write so pissing fast?'

He didn't miss a step. 'Yes, actually. Took it as an elective so I'll know what my future secretaries will really think about me.'

So, yes, I folded first. But, in my defence, I couldn't just fuck off now and leave the kids to die, right? I might have made overtures to that effect, but even I'm not such a disastrous human being that I could leave actual children to horrible deaths.

I had just been hoping that Dayne thought I was that level of a disaster. Apparently not.

It could have been worse; at least De'Ath wasn't a total fucktrumpet.

He had been following me while I tried to track the mystery man's magical signature across the campus, and he had barely remarked upon how lost I must have looked. Without magical senses, it must have seemed like I was wandering the grounds randomly, flitting about in a way that gave off the impression I knew what I was doing. And yet, outside of noting it down in that stupid pad, he was content to let me just blither around.

Which was good, because my arcane senses were about as powerful as a sparrow's fart.

I'd found the scent, lost it, and found it again so many times that I was getting turned around. Frankly, it was giving me a headache.

'This isn't working,' I said, rubbing my temples.

'What isn't?'

'Short version? There's someone here somewhere that is doing a proper lurk, and I'm trying to find him.'

De'Ath shook his head and scribbled something in his notebook. 'Oh, I shouldn't think so. Someone would have noticed.'

'The point, darling brain genius, is that they wouldn't notice him. He's using magic to be invisible.'

'I managed to grasp that inference, yes,' he said. 'But everything that happens on this campus leaves a trace. You can be as careful as you like, word will get out. Sneak out for a cheeky pint in town, smuggle in a girl, toke up in one of the bathrooms, someone always knows, even if they don't do anything about it.'

'Is that so? And how, pray tell, do they do that?'

'I couldn't say.'

But then, he didn't need to say, did he?

Cameras.

I hadn't seen any cameras on my frantic tour, but that didn't mean they weren't there. They made them small these days, hide them basically anywhere. And sure, they wouldn't *tell* the kids they had all these secret cameras, but they might let a rumour form, slip out there amongst the kiddos. Maybe they'd have a few trusted pupils lead the charge, just to make sure it stuck.

If you can never be sure they're watching, you can never know when they're not.

'Well, I don't need you to say, but I do need you to show me where all those cameras record to.'

De'Ath was going to be an expert at poker when he got older. 'I don't believe I mentioned cameras.'

'You didn't need to,' I said, plastering a real shit-eater of a grin on my face. 'But you're still going to show me where they are, or I'll have to make you.'

'Are you threatening me?'

'Not really. Just a little. I'm promising the use of *violent sexual language* if you don't tell me.'

He bristled. 'In a *school?*'

'Try me.'

Eat The Rich

*

Someone other than me had been skulking around the school, yet it was clear that no-one else had noticed. Another little fact to pin to the big board of crazy theories I was going to need if I wanted to clear this up.

De'Ath had ultimately submitted to my charms – namely the ones that involved me throwing insults at him until he gave me what I wanted so that I would go away. In this case, he was happy enough to give me the best part of half an hour in the security room that *officially* did not exist, provided I stopped using *unladylike language*. I'm not a monster, so I ceased the moment he shut the door and locked me in with all those lovely screens.

Of course, they had a security room. The college might have looked like something from an Edwardian nightmare, but that was all for effect. If they were going to be responsible for the twatty future of the country, that twatty future was going to need protecting.

And the twatty past that had spawned the twatty future were the sort of people that think hiding tiny webcams about the place would be sufficient. *Watching was basically as good as doing*, the rallying cry of basically every MP.

I took a seat in front of the chunky keyboard that controlled the system and started spooling through the footage almost at random. I didn't bother watching the footage of the killings – if there had been anything useful on there, they wouldn't have needed me. Besides, I had the sneaking suspicion that one of the moustache brigade would have eradicated anything of that sort to make sure it didn't stand a chance of leaking.

Instead, I was looking for traces of my sneaky little pal. Orbs, that's what I was after, essentially.

If you've been lucky enough to avoid one of those television piss parties that claim to be ghost hunters, here's the rundown on what an orb is. It's a weird orb seen on a camera screen. Usually, a speck of dust or a cobweb, if you actually *know* what you're looking for a real weird orb can tell you a lot about what was going on.

For example, the orbs on this footage were super bloody weird. They're supposed to creep and float about, currents kicked up in the wake of some significant dead thing tromping about all moodily. They're *supposed* to be rare, perhaps showing up in a quick burst of one or two over the space of a couple of minutes, then naffing off for the rest of the night.

What they're most definitely not supposed to do is show up in such numbers, and with such coherency, that they could spell out a message.

Or, in this case, a rune.

The design wasn't one I recognised, but its shape was unmistakable – sharp, efficient, powerful. It was there, on every camera at the same time, on the day of each of the murders. The orbs would blink into being ten minutes before the murder, arrange themselves, then blink out again twenty minutes later.

Eat The Rich

How the hell did someone miss this? Might as well have been scratching his message into the pissing lens.

I spooled through more footage, desperate to find some context for all this. Nothing. If my spooky compadre had been walking the halls since the first murder, even the cameras weren't picking him up. All of this meant he had a far greater skill in warding than I had thought when I caught a glimpse of him. And *that* meant...

Shit. He had *wanted* me to see him. Was it paranoid of me to assume that these runes were meant for me? It's not like there had been any warning I was going to be called down to this shithole, so how could he have known about it before me?

I mean, unless he was one of the people that made the case for me coming here in the first place.

If that was the case, I was *fucked*.

Slowly, I got up and moved over to the door, checking the handle. De'Ath had locked it from the outside, as he had said he would, but I slid the small deadbolt across to make myself feel better. The bolt wasn't even as thick as a pencil, but I tried not to dwell on that bit of information.

My mind was on fire, and I needed to make the most of it before the paranoia finished digging its heels in. Fight first, flight later. Lots of flight. A whole long-haul flight.

I upended my bag on the floor and grabbed my little flick knife, popped it open, and started sketching out this new rune on the floor. I needed to reverse engineer it, work out what it *meant*. What spell it held was important, sure, but I was more interested in how it had gotten here – was this another runeskald?

What a hell of a way to meet a colleague if it was, right? Nothing like sitting down for a meeting of the minds over an eviscerated child. Why yes, thank you, I will have another slice of the brie – it pairs well with my *fucking Merlot.*

Runes are tricky things. There's your basic alphabet, your building blocks that you need if you're going to try and get anything done. These are pretty weak on their own, but they have a great deal of versatility. Anyone with a pen and the fingers to hold it can probably get something out of this. Baby magic for babies — you can still make sounds that kinda-sorta resemble letters even when you're a little babbler.

It's making them into words, and then sentences, where you start to grow. It's the same with runes. Downside, of course, is that no-one is ever speaking the same bloody language.

This guy liked a lot of redundancies in his runes, that was apparent immediately. He'd based it around the rune for *air*, using it as the central spoke to build off from. Not all of the lines made sense to me, blending together at weird angles that only ended up obscuring the shapes to the eye. What I could make out told me that at the core he'd woven several different variations of *air* together. A curious move.

Then there were the other runes wound into it. Carving them into the floor to fill out the shape, there were connections present that I had never thought of before. Kind of embarrassing, if I'm honest. I've never considered myself an expert in the field or anything, but this was like singing fucking Frere Jacques at a school talent show and having the Foo Fighters take your spot on the stage when you were done.

I'm going to end up all technical and boring if I keep this up — don't want this to be a textbook, no-one ever gets to the end of those. I'll dumb it down for the sake of enjoyment. With the core being *air,* that probably meant one of two things: communication or observation. If it was observation, then he was laying a trap for me to spring. If it was communication, it was probably still a trap — you don't go that fucking extra if you're on the level.

Finishing the last stroke of the knife, I blew away the dust from my etching. It almost matched the one in the recordings, though I'd made the lines a bit straighter, the corners a little sharper. This was probably a mistake, seeing as it made the rune look a damn sight more foreboding than when it had been rendered by floating ghost balls.

Fuck it.

I dripped a tiny spark of magic into the rune and let it fly. Jump starting runes with arcane magic is *poor form* according to Laufeyjarson, but what does form matter? It works, and it's nice and fast, unlike all the traditional methods. For a moment, I thought it might have worked a little too well here — the rune soaked up my power greedily and, at first, didn't seem to react. When it did, the light it vomited out filled the entire room and sent me reeling.

Falling back, I hit the rear of my head against the table that held the security monitors. Little black spots started swimming across my vision, though whether they had come from the bright light or the blow to the head I couldn't tell you. It was probably the light, because if it had been the smack to the brain then I wouldn't have had the wherewithal to realise that those featureless spots were merging together into the shape of a face.

This guy loved his weird mosaics, right?

'Young Miss Thatcher,' the face seemed to say. I say *seemed* because the face moved in a way that certainly indicated it had lips, but they were lost in the blackness. Plus, the sound didn't seem to be coming from anywhere in particular. 'It's a pleasure to finally meet you.'

I winced. 'This is *meeting*, is it?'

'It's close enough,' he said. 'I would have liked to have met you in person, but I couldn't know exactly when you would arrive and I didn't have time to wait around.'

Even when I screwed my eyes shut, the face just hung there in front of me. 'Naturally, got some more children to snack on you rotten little pissbag?'

'You English, with your capacity for vulgarity. It impresses me.'

'Come meet me in person, I'll leave you with a banger of an impression.'

So, yeah, the hope had been that I'd sound a little tough

there, but I don't know if I managed it. Judging from the smile that I think I saw spread across his face — it was empty space surrounded by darkness, but it had a smile-like shape to it — I was fairly certain I'd fucked it.

He let the smile linger for a moment. 'I think you've got the wrong idea about me. We're both hunting the same monster here.'

'Sure we are.'

'We are,' he said. 'I'm your reinforcements.'

'My reinforcements?' I spat. 'Reinforcing me before I even got here — *before I even heard about here* — and sent by who?'

'Take a guess.'

A little fire of rage sparked to life in me. 'That patronising little prick! He told me this was *my* shout.'

'It is! Master Loki merely—'

I cut him off. '*Master* Loki? Jesus fucking Christ.'

Right, I'm not an idiot. I know that Laufeyjarson's interest in me isn't as innocent and mentorial as he wanted me to think it was, but I'd always flagged it as the type where he would let me wade into shit creek by myself so he could be my white knight when I got in too deep. Didn't think it was the type where he would send a chaperone to make sure I behave.

'You're new,' the man said. 'Ma— *Loki* has every faith in you, but there's so few of us these days he wanted to be sure you had a little backup in case you needed it.'

The pain was subsiding now, and the face was fading away with it. 'And he knew all that before I even knew this job existed?'

'Maybe this would be easier in person,' he said, the outline of the face barely visible at all now. 'You're at the college, right? I can be back there tomorrow morning. We'll meet face to face and I'll do a better job of introducing myself.'

'You've done a piss poor job here. Not even told me your name.'

The face shifted in what might have been a wink, it was hard to tell. 'Wolfgang.'

Then he was gone.

*

I toyed with the idea of spending the rest of the night looming over Gracemere like a bedraggled crow, but thought better of it. If Wolfgang was the killer after all, then he wouldn't be around to be a problem tonight — assuming he was telling the truth about anything, which I admit was a bit of a naive leap on my part. If he *wasn't* our killer, then the actual villain wouldn't dare risk exposing themselves after the massive rigmarole I had stirred up.

For now, Gracemere was probably safe enough.

Leaving the security room, De'Ath was my constant companion. He didn't bother talking to me, but I could tell from how he lurked that he was disappointed in me, and that he hoped I gave even a little bit of a shit about what he thought of me. Naturally, I didn't. If they had done any research on me at all beyond the grapevine of the Old Boys Club, they would have known what to expect of me.

Things had started to die down now, at least. The faculty had ushered the nosy little snots back to their beds, leaving the halls empty once again. This gave me the opportunity to follow up on the one lead I had left — the figure I had seen whilst scrying.

Whoever he was, he had been snooping around behind the dormitories. It was hardly an out of the way place in any way that mattered, but I could recognise the sort of seclusion it offered before De'Ath bothered to chime in.

'Is there a reason you've decided to investigate this area in particular?' he asked, scribbling something down in the little notebook Dayne had given him.

I shrugged. 'Maybe I just had the urge to explore.'

'Hmm,' he said, then sniffed loudly. 'That figures.'

'Does it?'

He caught himself, a slight hint of pink flushing his cheeks at the realisation that he had actually said that last part out loud. 'I... What I mean to say is—'

'I know what you meant,' I said. 'A quiet little corner between the outer wall and the back of the dorms? I know a grotty little makeout point when I see one. An *asmooch-*

bush.'

'What?'

'Amuse-bouche, *asmooch-bush?* Forget it. There a girls school nearby, or has the student body finally started to accept the *student body*?'

The answer didn't matter. I just wanted to see him squirm. And he *did* squirm. 'Wyvern College is less than a mile away over the fields behind this college. We have visitors on occasion. And, of course, there are the... *private indiscretions* that are bound to occur among adolescents who reside in close proximity to one another.'

The lengths people would go to to avoid saying that these horny young men were wanking each other off in the bushes.

I gave De'Ath a crumb of mercy and stopped asking him questions about the *sex hedge*. A few bare branches barred the way into the little clearing, but they were easy enough to clamber over. Following in the footsteps of many a sexual adventurer, I folded myself through the gaps, my stockings catching on one and adding an extra tear to my collection. The flustered upper-classman elected not to follow me.

Immediately, I could tell that this was a place that belonged to the students — which was *awesome*. From the moment I had stepped foot on the grounds of the college, there had been a sort of sterility in the air, so thick that you could taste it. Class and tradition and *the way things have always been done* had stripped the place and its students of any

Eat The Rich

expression or individuality. That's not unique to posh schools, only much more noticeable.

Here, though, the air was very different. It wasn't just the smell — and if you know the smell I mean, *you know the smell I mean* — but there was a very clear feeling that there was to be no thought given here to propriety and *station*. That sort of stuff still managed to sneak its way in, naturally, but it wasn't something that was enforced as it was in the college proper.

The regular visitors had made the little clearing quite comfortable. A couple of pieces of old furniture — no doubt chosen for the ease of *straddling* — had been nicely arranged. Sheets of fabric in dark greens and earthy browns were tied to the hedge all around the interior circumference, blocking the view between the already dense leaves in an inconspicuous way. There was even one such sheet for covering the entrance, but that was rolled up and pinned above the opening.

Really bloody odd place for our prime suspect to linger about.

I tapped at the panels on the little device I had pinned to my belt and it spat out a sleek little token for me. Clasping it tightly in my hands, I started to walk the perimeter. It didn't take me long to find what I was looking for.

The rune in my grip started to vibrate gently when I reached a spot as close to the main wall as the bushes would let me walk. I slipped the rune back into the device and knelt down into the mud for a closer look.

Too many footprints to pick out a prime candidate — and even if I had found one, was I going to go door to door and demand to see everyone's shoes? No, the reaction from the rune told me there was something important to find here. Something *dead*.

Clawing through the mud, I carved a small trench that ran as deep as my fingers could go. The top layer of dirt was loose and pliant, but the soil underneath had been compacted by decades of visitors. That was fine, I shouldn't need to dig that deep to find what I was after.

Sweeping my hand through the muck, something sharp and barbed prodded me painfully in my palm. I yelped and fell back in shock, yanking my hand out of the mud. With it came the culprit — a spur of yellowed bone, roughly two inches long and about as thick around as a ballpoint pen. One end, the one that was embedded in my hand, had been snapped to a set of jagged and hooked points, while the other was filed down so as to be easy to hold. All across the surface, intricate designs had been scrimshawed. They were too fine to make out in what little light was present.

Plus, you know, I was too busy freaking out over the *fucking bone spear* that was jutting out of my hand.

The damned thing had only gone half a centimetre deep, but that still meant several of those nasty hooks had settled in. Pulling it out meant making the wound that much worse, but it was either that or leave it in, giving it a chance to work its way even deeper until it came out the other side. So, I grabbed the bastard and yanked it out, coming up with new and radical swear words as I did so.

With the skewer out, I could take a better look at it. Turning it over in my fingers, it felt even lighter than it looked. The tip was red with my blood now, and it had already started to channel down the thin lines of the scrimshawing, the bright red contrasting with the pale yellow.

Honestly, I had no idea what the bloody thing was. Obviously, you don't find things like that just laying around in a school on the reg, so it was clearly something left behind by the killer. Why he had left it behind though, and what he had made it for, that was a total mystery.

I didn't like that it was holding onto my blood like that either. Undead things like blood, that's pretty universal. It tastes like life, so quite a lot of them have their uses for it. Again, this wasn't narrowing down the suspect pool much, but it did start pumping shit into my anxiety engines.

No way this had been used only once. It had been too carefully crafted to be disposable. The barbs might have looked like the ragged sheer lines of a fractured bone, but they'd been purposefully honed. This was a *tool*, and that meant it had probably tasted more than just my blood.

Jesus, I was going to have to get a blood test in the morning.

Still, why leave this behind?

Looking around, I found a small battery powered lantern tucked behind a reclined deckchair. Flicking it on, an atmospheric pink light did its best to provide some better visibility. It washed out the colours and found some properly scary places to put some shadows, but it would do the job of letting me get a better look at the scrimshaw.

My blood had finished working its way through all the lines now. I could make out some tiny little figures, but that was about all. If I wanted to see more, I'd need a magnifying glass, like trying to get a look at those ludicrous little statues carved into the eyes of needles.

The wound in my palm was starting to itch. Looking at it, I could see a patchwork of black veins rising to the surface around the edges of the puncture. Poison? It would make sense — if this was some sort of dart, the barbed hooks would keep it in place long enough to deliver its payload.

I tried to turn and make my way back out towards De'Ath, but my legs wouldn't budge. They had taken root, so much so that I didn't have the strength to move them at all. After that, it only took another second or so to lose the strength to keep me upright. I sank slowly down to my knees, then feel forward onto my face.

The burning in my palm spread up my arm, across my chest to my heart, which started beating it around my whole body in a lovely rhythmic pain. I mean that sincerely, too — it fucking hurt, but it had that narcotic soothing quality that would scare the shit out of you if it wasn't mucking about with your brain at the same time.

Laying there, face pressed into the dirt and completely paralysed, I didn't care what came next. If this was how I was going to die, I'd thank them for it.

Six

I was extremely pissed off come the morning, at whoever had left that dart behind but also, mostly, at myself.

Ready to die? Fuck off.

It had been a very long night and I had been awake for the entire thing. I had breathed in so much dirt that it felt like the back of my throat was going to be caked in the shit for days — I'd be coughing up earthworms. Whatever drug had been pumped into my system had kept me from feeling the cold, or much of anything at all, but its effect on my mind had been quick to drain away. That obedient, compliant, *meek* feeling had given way to the terror of realising I was completely defenceless and trapped in my own useless body.

For hours.

Once the feeling started coming back, I didn't know if I was going to cry or scream. I think I elected to do both.

De'Ath had been useless. Not once had he checked on me during the entire night, not that he could have done anything if he had. If this was the same drug the killer had used to incapacitate his victims, no wonder he could take his time flaying de Pfeffel without resistance. How would De'Ath have even begun to snap me out of that level of paralysis? I doubt he had the arm on him to slap me awake, after all.

I pushed myself up into a sitting position and hocked up a loogie that was, at best, eighty percent soil. Very ladylike of me. At least the burning had gone, replaced with the familiar icy chill of having spent the night in a place you most definitely shouldn't have. The shivering hadn't started yet, but it would come.

The little bone dart was on the floor nearby, and this time I was careful when I picked it up. It slid quite comfortably into one of the small pockets on my shorts — I just had to hope the denim would provide enough protection to stop it stabbing me again. Either way, I couldn't leave it laying around here for anyone to find, and it would definitely break if I put it in my bag. It would *probably* be fine.

In a rude contrast to how they had been before my dirt nap, my legs were weak as piss now. I managed to walk, but it was the gangly wobble of a hungover idiot instead of the confident stride of a fucking badass. Stumbling through the privet and falling on my arse again was not the image I had wanted to convey, but *c'est la vie.*

De'Ath was still there, looking down his nose as I folded my legs underneath me and tried to get back up. 'You were in there for a while.'

'Going for your A-Level in obvious bollocks, I see,' I grumbled. 'Didn't think it was worth checking on me after the first *two pissing hours?*'

He shrugged slowly, but I saw the glimmer in his eye — smugness with a hint of pleasure, the old Rich Twat Special. 'I saw nothing to be concerned about. Besides, it would be a little unseemly of me to go scrambling around in the muck like that.'

The utter barefaced pomposity of the second sentence fooled neither of us, which was probably the point. If it wasn't for the fact that he had all the sinister presence of an imploded cupcake, that might have put him on my radar as *a little bit suss*.

As it was, he was just a rude prick.

'Does this place keep a chauffeur on staff or something?' I asked, getting back to my feet. 'Or a number for a taxi service that doesn't charge through the nose?'

'A car can certainly be arranged, if it is for business use.'

'Then arrange one.'

'Very well, and I'll let my teachers know I'll be absent from a few lessons.'

I shot him a well practised scowl. 'You bloody well won't. You're not coming with me.'

'The vice provost was very clear that —'

'That you chaperone me *on college grounds*, not off them. I don't need you staring at my arse when I'm doing serious business.'

De'Ath had referred to himself as a bit of a rebel when we had met, but any good will that had built up had been thoroughly undone by this whole chaperone bullshit. I could tell he liked the power of looking over my shoulder, second-guessing my every action. Didn't need that energy clogging up my pores.

He deflated a little, realising at last that there was a limit to this little dose of power he had been given. 'You will, um... You will come back, won't you?'

I blinked. 'You think I'm doing a runner?'

'There are many here, at least amongst those who know the reality of the situation, who wouldn't blame you.' He was continuing to deflate — was it possible I'd misread him?

'Frankly, I don't give a tinker's fig whether anyone else would blame me,' I said. 'I'd blame me.'

Gently, he nodded. 'I'll go arrange the car for you.'

*

I had enough time for a quick shower and a change of clothes before the car was ready. As I'd come from one job to another so fast, I didn't have much in the way of clothes to change into — I swapped out the short jeans and torn stockings for a baggy pair of longer jeans that had better structural integrity, but I was forced to pair it with a white button-up shirt from the wardrobe in my room. Someone had left me with a full selection of the school's uniform, but the shirt was bad enough.

Naturally, I roughed it up a little before I dared head outside in the bloody thing. Still, the ensemble knocked a year or two off my age, which was going to make my whole grumpy-authority bit a little harder to pull off.

Eat The Rich

Thankfully, the driver of the car didn't seem to give a shit. He had the stoic silence of a lifetime spent keeping his eyes forward and his ears switched off, pretending not to hear the sort of bilge routinely spouted by people who can afford both a big car and someone else to drive it. He took me into town without fuss, though he did park a little further away from my destination than I had liked.

'To spare you the looks, Young Miss,' he had said. 'People are liable to talk if they see you emerge from this car before heading inside.'

Again, I didn't much care if people were going to talk or not, but the driver had a grandfatherly quality to him that put me off having that fight. It wasn't a long walk anyway.

My destination, if you haven't worked it out yet, was the nearest clinic I could find that — according to my hurried Google-fu — would test my blood with as few questions asked as possible. They wouldn't test it for sedatives and magical trash, I'd have to do that myself later, but they'd put a rush on the *other* things. Doubly so if I told them a guy with shifty eyes and the facial hair of a repeat offender jabbed me when I wasn't looking.

It took a couple of hours to be seen, and it would take a couple of days to get the full results, but the act of putting the ball in motion did wonders for shutting up my worried brain. Just file all the *terrifying blood illnesses* away now, leave them be until you got the results back. Back to the proper worries, there's a good girl.

They gave me a chocolate biscuit on the way out. Name

brand, too. How the other half live, eh?

I was fiddling with the bandage on my palm when I felt his eyes on me. He was behind me, leaning against the wall near the door of the clinic — not so much a sixth sense as a manifestation of my paranoia. At least it was public, no danger of anything kicking off here.

He must have realised I had spotted him because I felt him shift a little, pushing himself off the brickwork. 'They tie them tight on purpose.'

'Excuse me?'

'The bandages,' he said, still behind me.

I turned. 'I'm going to go out on a limb and say you're Wolfgang.'

'A very educated guess,' he said, smiling. 'It's a pleasure to meet you.'

Look, I'm not going to say he wasn't hot as fuck because, let's face it, he was. I've got eyes, and he had stylish stubble, piercing eyes, and probably abs for days. And an accent. *And* rocked clothes that seemed to drape over him like some sort of gorgeous old painting.

But, if anything, I'm always going to be more suspicious of the hotties — life has treated them a little too well for them not to have an agenda or two bubbling beneath the surface.

'Charmed, I'm sure,' I replied, refusing to shake his hand. 'Nothing a girl loves more than being stalked to a clinic.'

Eat The Rich

'I didn't stalk you. I said I would come and meet you today, and this is me keeping that promise.'

'Didn't want to leave an extremely fucking *extra* message in floating rune orbs this time?'

He looked away bashfully. 'Not very subtle, I admit. But it did the job, let you know I was serious. Let you know I was *like you*.'

He wasn't like me — his runework was annoyingly better for one thing — but best not to push back on that point just yet. 'How did you find me?'

'I asked the young man, the one with the silly name.'

'Bertie De'Ath.'

'Yes, him,' her said, grin widening. 'He said they'd organised a car into town for you. I figured maybe you had run into one of these little things and, quite understandably, had a reaction.'

Carefully, he slid his thumb and index finger into one of his pockets and slowly pulled out a bundle of familiar bone darts. Holding them by the sharp end — the barbs covered with little rubber protectors — he handed the bundle to me. I took it, slipped off the rubber band that held them together, and studied them.

'Where did you get these?'

'Same place you got yours,' he said. 'Roughly. Found them on the grounds of the college.'

The darts were all very similar to each other, but a closer look exposed a few little differences. The colour of the bone was different in each of them, the jagged barbs presented in unique patterns and, most obviously, the etchings had nothing in common bar how fine the detailing was. The patterns ranged from images of small figures to what looked to be a broad vista, one was a tableau of some kind and another was an abstract collection of swooping lines.

I counted them off one at a time. 'One for each killing.'

'Plus the one you found,' he said. 'I would say that means you saved a life last night.'

'The stuff he loads these with would definitely put someone on their arse long enough to be flayed alive without complaint,' I said, snapping the band back around the darts. 'No-one mentioned finding them though. Come to think of it, no-one mentioned you either.'

'I blend in.'

'With that face?' I snorted. 'Going to call bullshit on that, bro.'

'Try being low-key sometime. You'll be surprised how easy it is to go unnoticed. Come on, let's have a seat.'

We found a bench and sat down, far enough way from the bustle of people that we could talk without worry of being overheard, but close enough that I had the safety of still being in sight of the general public. Wolfgang was saying a lot of the right things, but I wasn't sold.

'You'll be wanting to analyse the sedative, I'm guessing,' Wolfgang said as we sat down. 'I've already done it. I think it's Dead Man's Blood.'

'You sure?' I asked.

'Ran the runes twice to make certain. That's what they told me.'

I frowned and turned the bundle over in my hands again. 'That doesn't make sense. I remember reading about that stuff, it's only supposed to work on dead things that eat other dead things.'

'*Totenfresser.*'

'Yeah, alright, Captain Keen. We've both read books, you don't need to try and break out the scientific language.'

'I suspect your books did not have the German name for such creatures.'

'No, I guess not,' I conceded. 'But still, as I'm not one of those, Dead Man's Blood shouldn't have much of an effect on me outside of an eventual case of sepsis. Unless...'

I *had* read something about this once. What the hell had it been? It was a story, not a text book, more folklore than science — that was why it had stuck with me when so much of what I had learned with Wingard had faded. It was right there, just out of reach.

'There is no unless,' Wolfgang said. His pride was getting the better of him. 'The runes do not make mistakes, if you read them right.'

'And you read them right, did you? Are you sure?'

His nostrils flared a little. 'I am the oldest living practitioner of the art. Master Loki himself saw to my training, put his hopes in me to keep the power of the runeskald alive. I don't say that as a boast, just to state my credentials. It's why I'm the one that was sent to help you, to back you up.'

'I don't need another mentor, thanks.'

'And I don't intend to be one,' he said. 'As I said before, you're running this show. I'm a, well, a safety net.'

'One with a bloody great tear in it,' I said.

'Pardon?'

It had come back to me, the memory I had been scrabbling for. 'These little fuckers aren't laced with Dead Man's Blood. It's *Sangfroid*.'

'Go on,' he said, coldly.

'It's made from Dead Man's Blood, maybe that confused the runes,' I said charitably. 'But that's old European, Sangfroid is the product of some offshoot of Creole Voodoo. It's a poison; chills the blood, preps a person for grisly sacrifices. *I'm surprised you didn't know that, you arrogant fuck.*'

I do like smacking down people who think they're better than me. Usually, doing that doesn't end with them pulling out a wry grin and a piece of paper. 'I did. Needed to see if you did too.'

'What's this?' I said, taking the paper from him.

'The address of the only person in the area who might know enough about this branch of magic to help fill in some gaps.'

I looked at the address, confused. 'What the fuck is an expert on Voodoo doing in Middle England?'

'How does an expert in Nordic rune magic find his way from Germany to Middle England?' Wolfgang said. 'Life can take us all down paths that are unfamiliar.'

'Oh good, aphorisms. Love those.'

Wolfgang shrugged and crossed his arms. 'Fine, a more straightforward answer. I suspect they're going to be someone with too much time on their hands and a fetish for the exotic.'

'Now, that makes more sense.'

*

'How did you find this address?' I asked Wolfgang.

'I had help,' he said, sheepishly. 'Very competent help. Usually.'

'Hmm.'

The address had led us to a weird little house just off the main street. It was wedged into what had once been the last crack of space between the end of an old footbridge and some hellish development put up in the 60s. The modern day had happened around this little house, and it had categorically refused to acknowledge it, with the sort of stubbornness only the old can muster.

It was not, however, lived in by the old.

The woman who had answered the door was in her early thirties, the gentle off-white of a playing card, and had a colourful band of cloth woven into her short hair. In her hands, a large novelty mug was steaming. It smelled vaguely of tea, in the way any leaf dunked in hot water for a moment is, technically, a tea.

'Can I help you?' she asked.

'I doubt it,' I said. 'But fuck it, let's try our luck anyway. I need a refresher on the finer points of *Sanfroid*. The poison, not—'

The woman nodded sagely. 'Of course the poison. You wouldn't come to me for French lessons, right? Come in!'

It was the fastest I had ever been invited into someone's house. She might not have been old, but she did her best to walk like she was — an affectation of entropy, all hunched over and face stretched into some imperious grimace.

She led the pair of us through to a small reception room next to the even smaller entrance hall. Inside, I could see that her home was cramped but long, like someone had squeezed her house out of a toothpaste tube. Wolfgang was almost too broad to fit into the room comfortably, but I didn't have a problem.

'So, *travellers*,' the woman said as she flopped lazily into an arm chair. 'What can Mama Mistral do for you?'

She was laying it all on a bit thick. 'Sangfroid.'

Eat The Rich

'Yes, but what about it?'

I pulled the bundle of darts from my pocket and rolled them across her rather kitsch coffee table towards her. 'What do you make of these?'

Her eyes snapped open so violently that they began to bulge. 'Oh. Shit.'

'That bad?' Wolfgang asked.

'You're professionals,' she said, the act melting away and leaving quite   a plain woman behind.

I nodded. 'Get many amateurs?'

'Almost exclusively,' Mistral said. 'Look, normally, I pull this grift on idiots from the internet, but I don't play when pros come knocking.'

'How do you know we're professionals?' Wolfgang said, leaning forward in his chair. It creaked in satisfaction.

She sighed, idly running the tip of one of the darts over the end of her finger. 'Because an amateur wouldn't come here with the weapons of a Nightmare.'

Seven

'Pull the other one,' I said. 'It'll ring like a campanologist's wet dream. A Nightmare? Come the fuck on.'

Mistral held up her hands. 'Look, I don't want any part of this, all right? I'm coming clean right out the gate here and hoping that will get rid of you before things get bad.'

'Before things get bad?' I said, looking around the room. The decorations were exactly as you'd expect of a white girl very into Voodoo — shrunken heads and bone charms hanging on the walls, jars of unspeakable things, incense everywhere. It was as cliche as it comes. 'Looks to me like you're all prepared for the worst. A lot of *juju* lining these walls.'

She shook her head. 'No. All props from old films. It's all part of the con.'

Wolfgang snapped his fingers to draw her attention. 'But you know enough to be scared, unlike us.'

'I read around the subject. I couldn't help it. And these things,' she indicated the darts. 'You see these in a book, you remember them.'

'Go on,' I said.

'I really shouldn't. For all our sakes.'

'Stop fannying about, for the love of God.'

Defeated, Mistral pinched the bridge of her nose. 'Okay. Fine. Here we go. A Nightmare isn't a dream, or rather, it wasn't a dream originally. We took that word from very real, very horrible little creatures. Using those darts, they render their prey helpless before they feed. Painful but discreet, when the victim wakes up they think the whole thing was, well...'

'A Nightmare,' I finished for her. 'No-one is waking up from these Nightmares.'

Mistral frowned. 'What? The whole thing with Nightmares is that they repeat. They don't just feed on you once, they feed on you for life, stripping you away slice by slice while you're meant to be asleep.'

'Our one is flaying kids to death. In one go.'

'Impossible. They're too cruel for that.'

I didn't like being on the back foot. I had approximate knowledge of many things, was an encyclopedia with alternating pages ripped out or coloured in with magic marker. If Nightmares were as dangerous as this woman wanted me to believe, I would have stumbled across them in my studies, what I'd had of them. Wingard had made sure I knew where all the most interesting monster manuals were and had made it very clear I was never to read them, all while knowing that I most definitely would be cracking those fuckers open the moment he turned his back.

And not one of them had mentioned Nightmares.

I crossed one leg over the other and sank back in my chair. 'Too cruel to skin children alive, but not so cruel that certain groups in this society, ones that aren't playing dress-up and actually know their shit, wouldn't write about them?'

'They write about them quite often,' Wolfgang said. His eyes had turned hard and were boring a hole right through Mama Mistral. 'And then someone comes and convinces them to have *not* written about them.'

'What?'

He placed his hands over his ears and nodded at Mama Mistral, who dutifully covered her own. When he was sure she wasn't listening, he turned back to me. 'Are you familiar with the vow that binds?'

Bit of a dick question, that. If you already know about the vow, it's perfectly fine. If you don't, you've just fucked up that person's life forever.

'Jesus. Yes, luckily for you I've already had that particular bit of innocence smashed to buggery. How is it relevant?'

'Nightmares, I think, are kind of the same,' he said. 'Memetic viruses. Parasitic ideas that can pass from person to person, burrowing into a brain.'

I had always hated the vow that binds, but that at least made sense. Once you know the rules, you can't unknow them — therefore, you've got to follow them. Fair's fair, equals peaquals, it only hurt you if you were an oathbreaking piece of shit.

It didn't hurt you just to *know* about.

'How does that track?' I asked. 'I highly doubt these kids have heard about the grisly backstory of such an everyday word as *Nightmare*. And even if they had, would that be enough to draw the thing's attention?'

Wolfgang took one long, slow breath. 'Maybe. Maybe not. In either case, I'm not suggesting that having that information in your head is the only way to make you a target — would really limit the menu for them if it were — but I suspect it makes you a more tempting one.'

'So, what, self-censoring information about them out of textbooks is *mental hygiene* or something?'

'Makes sense to me,' he said with a nod. 'Just another

unspoken nudge to make a killer pick one victim over another.'

'It makes a certain sort of sense,' I conceded. 'If you believe in this memetic virus shit.'

'The kids don't *need* to know about Nightmares—'

I waved a hand, continuing the thought. 'They're already big bags of fear and insecurity, they're probably tasty enough even without knowing. Could just be bad luck the critter shacked up here.'

'Right,' he continued. 'But knowing about it would be enough to turn its head, draw a little attention.'

'Which means that, now we do know about it, we're potential targets.' I said.

'If the theory holds.'

I thought about it for a moment, then smiled. 'Perfect.'

'What?'

'Think about it,' I said, kicking my feet up on the table. 'If we're on its list now, then all we have to do is find a way to get it to bump us up. The closer we are to the top of the page, the safer those kids are.'

'I am starting to see why Master Loki likes you.'

My smile faltered a little. 'Right. You can stay here with

the Voodoo Queen of New Bore-leans and find out whatever is left to find out. I need to get back to the school and start making a nuisance of myself.'

'You think the Nightmare is at the school right now?'

I shrugged. There were a lot of theories rocking around my brain now, but I wasn't in a mood to share them. But, between you and me, I think we both know that this beastie wasn't going to stray far from its hunting grounds. It was a hunch before, but now it had graduated to a full theory.

Wolfgang didn't press me, but I do kind of wish he had. Him sitting back and following my lead was making my blood run cold — people *approving* of me usually means they are just waiting for my big stupid head to slip into the noose I hadn't realised they were holding. It was definitely possible I was misreading him, or just paranoid, but I wasn't ready to let my guard down on that front just yet.

Without another word, I left him in that little crooked house and made my way back to the college.

*

The driver had been very understanding, and I enjoyed the hip-and-cool-dad style of fist bump he gave me once he returned me to Tory Toddler Town. No-one was waiting for me, no De'Ath to chaperone my rebellious arse and keep me out of trouble. So, naturally, I did what any good disasterpiece does when left to their own devices.

I went to the library.

Azizi was alone today, the other members of the Dee Society so conspicuous by their absences that I could make out their silhouettes on the floor where they should have been. They'd *discoloured* the carpet.

'How goes the hunt, Ms Thatcher?' Azizi asked, his nose poking over the top of a glossy textbook.

'Slowly,' I said. 'Thank you for getting me that list though, it helped clear up a few things to start with.'

He snapped the book shut. 'I heard! Methodical and alphabetical, I'm not sure I would have caught that. I don't think any of us would have.'

'You would have. Eventually. Once you stopped overthinking the problem. Think less, you'll live longer. Still got a list of all the suspect critters you ruled out?'

'I think so,' he said, yanking a book from the shelf above his head. 'Here.'

I took it and flicked through it again. 'I notice you haven't ruled out Nightmares.'

'Should we have?'

I ignored his question. 'Don't suppose you noticed a handsome German guy snooping about the campus a day or so before I showed up?'

'I don't think so. What did he look like?'

The words caught in my throat as I said them, my voice cracking a little with surprise at myself. 'Blond, blue eyes, stubble, a smile that can turn heads and unmake beds. You know the type.'

Azizi chuckled. 'I think anyone like that snooping around here would draw the attention of the moustaches pretty quickly. I haven't heard of that happening, why?'

'Never mind,' I said. 'Do me a favour, yeah? Get your buddies together and find me what you can on Nightmares. I've got some things that need verifying.'

'Sounds like the hunt *is* going well then,' he said with a smile.

I held my hand out flat and rocked it a little. 'Ehh. We'll see.'

Now, saying that Azizi was trustworthy might be taking things too far, but he was certainly *easier* to trust than Wolfgang. The kid was closer to my age for one, hadn't been all mysterious and weird, and didn't keep name dropping Loki Laufeyjarson like a starstruck loser. If he came back with the same info as Wolfgang though, that would help me put a nagging doubt to sleep.

After leaving Mistral I had tucked the darts into my bag at last — made a little safe zone for them and everything so nothing would crush them — but knowing they were there was making it heavier. That and all the suspicion.

Wolfgang shows up, does all manner of suss business, and immediately leads me straight to the most likely suspect? He just *happens* to already have the address of a local Voodoo expert? *He just happens* to know all the important shit about Nightmares, but didn't tell me until his little expert set me up to hear them first?

I mean, look, it's been clear immediately that he wasn't on the level, yeah? Not suspicious enough to peg him as the villain — or even *a* villain — but definitely sufficient to not just gobble up all his easy bullshit like a good little hog.

With not much else to do, I took myself back to my room to finally, properly, get some real sleep. Laying face down in the dirt gives a certain quality of rest, true, but that quality is god awful. My eyes felt like they were grinding against my sockets with every movement, and the noise rattled around my brain painfully.

Have you ever been so tired that you just want to cry? Actually, let me rephrase that: so tired that you *want* to cry but you can't because you lack the basic energy to pump tears up from wherever they hang out before they come squirting out your eyes? The moment I realised I had nothing to do but wait for a while, that's when I noticed I'd hit that point. Couldn't even muster a sob, just a quiet melting of consciousness.

I didn't sleep. I tried, but at the last moment I'd remember the Nightmare and the stupid survival centre of my brain overrode common sense. There's that memetic quality at work, I guess. Still, I stared at the ceiling long enough that time thickened into a sort of lumpy soup and soaked up plenty of hours. That was, in a way, something *like* rest.

Tired, vulnerable, and paranoid. I wanted to call the few people I felt I could trust, talk it through with them. Jameson Parker would take my call if I tried, but even with his contact details called up on my phone I couldn't will myself to press the button. If I wanted to stand on my own feet here — which I did — I couldn't go calling up the man who'd decided he was basically my warlock foster dad. There was a chance he'd want to help, and I already had one allegedly well-meaning dude threatening to sideline me on my own case.

Kaitlyn van Ives would be a less dangerous call in that regard. She'd listen to why I was calling, not what I was talking about. If I wanted advice, she'd give it — albeit with a heavy dose of smug superiority — and if I didn't she wouldn't try to butt in.

Of course, she hadn't been taking my calls for over a month at this point, so why bother?

Everyone and their mother had been lining up to mentor me lately, and Wolfgang was just the latest addition to the list. Maybe that was why I was so determined to prove him wrong and to convince myself he was so suss. If he really had just swanned in with the answer, what did that say about me as a runeskald?

Introspection is fucking annoying. Once you get started, it's bloody hard to shift. Worse when you *can't pissing sleep.*

After a few hours — I think, like I said, time had become porridge — I rolled out of bed and back into the hallways of the college. The upside of spending a long time moping is that it lets your brain work on other problems in the background. It had come up with something pro-active for me to do, thank fuck.

First, I had to find my way to the centre of the college. This was easier said than done. The footprint of the campus had grown and shrunk so many times over the centuries the shitty place had existed, and this meant that working out its metaphysical dimensions was a bit of a crap shoot. Sounds like bollocks, and it kind of is.

I did a few calculations, got annoyed with them, ripped the paper to shreds, threw the pencil I had used into a bush, then decided to just use wherever was in the centre of the map. The school chapel, coincidentally enough. That would do.

The idea my distracted brain had come up with was a sort of tracking spell. That's a pretty simple bit of thaumaturgy if you're a skilled mage — which I'm not. Besides, for actual thaumaturgy you need something connected intimately to your target, like blood or hair or a tooth. I was hoping to use the darts, but I didn't think the bone was sourced from our killer, and the sangfroid most certainly wouldn't be.

That doesn't matter with rune magic as much, though. Rune magic was all stories, the theme was more important than the actual content. In fact, doing this all in a chapel was especially helpful — it was like calling God a wanker, which was thematically appropriate for the acts of the killer, Nightmare or not.

The chapel was small. The pews were arranged so that they faced into the central aisle rather than up at the pulpit, staggered so that each row was a little higher than the one before it. Felt more like a courtroom than a church, somehow.

I picked a point about halfway down the aisle and sat down on the cold stone floor. My trusty pen knife was out again, whittling a steady stream of dust from the end of a piece of chalk. Carving a fucking rune into the flagstones of a holy site isn't something I'm squeamish about, but it would definitely dull my lovely knife.

The way I was sitting, the chalk dust fell into the space marked out by my crossed legs, the little clearing. Once a suitable pile had been formed — pretty much the entirety of one stick of chalk — I reached in with my finger and started to draw.

So, I might be pretty crap when it comes to working arcane magic, but I can still *feel* it. It has a flow, a beat, and if you leave something in one place long enough it gathers a sort of dust. Cobwebs of magic, I guess. Your average runeskald might not think to use them, but I'm resourceful as fuck.

The chalk dust, given enough encouragement, would stick to the webs. I'd be able to trace out a sort of compass with it, though it wouldn't be overly accurate on its own. Thicker lines would indicate more magic in general, but also a stronger association with my subconscious desire, whatever that was. Hopefully, it would be our killer and not, say, a hot teacher or a slice of pepperoni pizza in the staff room fridge.

Left alone, that was the problem with magic — it loved to be vague and chaotic and to fuck with you. You had to dial it in, and I didn't have the skill to do that.

Hence the runes.

Honestly, it's a bit like ChatGPT prompting, except the

outcome isn't utter trash stolen from a million different people. Once all the chalk had settled, I just had to tweak things by telling it what I was after.

Awkwardly, I shifted my weight and started to tap at the device on my belt. I was going to need a lot of different runes here, but I could at least cut down some of the work by using some of the rune tokens. Scuttling backwards a little, I began arranging the little stones around the outside of the chalk pattern, each one clacking pleasingly against the floor. For the ones I didn't have prepared in stone, those were worth risking a bit of my knife's sharpness.

I might have gone a little overboard. Once I was done, a three metre section of the floor was covered in runestones and etchings. The place looked like the spawning ground of a serial killer.

Climbing up the pews, I got a bird's eye view of my creation. I had been very precise, overly so, working so many redundancies into the directions that the chances of a false positive were practically zero. If you'd tried to translate it into English, it would have come out like the most convoluted and incomprehensible legal document since they accidentally made Smack legal for about half an hour in the early 2000s.

But that didn't matter. The magic would understand. You get the syntax right, it always understands. It just needed me to hit the runic equivalent of the enter key.

I lit a cigarette off a half-melted prayer candle — because I'm edgy and cool — and took one long, deep drag. There were a hundred different ways to seal a rune spell, but this had always been my favourite. The nicotine hit got the neurons firing, the blood pumping, and got me ready to fucking leg it if something went wrong — always a good stance to be in when you're messing with magic, a nice fuck you to complacency.

One last puff, then I flicked the stub at the centre of the design. I missed, but that didn't really matter. As the smouldering smoke ricocheted off one of the outer rune stones, I felt a shift in the air. A tingling static ran up my arms, the back of my neck, over my scalp.

All at once, the runes lit up, a wave of colour sweeping around the circle like a neon clock, slowing until it stopped as a thin line pointing in one very definite direction. I traced it with my eyes, over the opposite pews and out the stained glass window. There was only one building in that direction.

Trotting down one side of the aisle and over towards where the runes were pointing, I felt a dull rumble from the stone beneath me. The static in the air pricked up even higher and I smelled the hair on my arms singe.

The shockwave hit almost half a second before the sound. It threw me off my feet and slammed me into the pews behind me before peppering me with dozens of little marble tokens kicked up from the floor. Then I got smacked in the tits with the godawful thunderclap and the sound of glass shattering and stone cracking.

When I opened my eyes, I would have been speechless if anyone had been around to talk to. Or, not so much speechless as stuck in an endless *fucking hell* loop.

Something had carved a jagged rent through the side of the church, like some great whip had slashed straight through the masonry, glass, pews, everything. Worse still, it traced over the line of my spell perfectly, leaving a deep gash in the floor where the illuminated runes had been.

It had obliterated the rest of the design.

Cold air rushed through the fresh gap in the wall, knocking some sense back into me. Through that same gap, I could see scorched grass point along that same line and up to the building.

So, yeah, that wasn't supposed to happen.

If you fuck up a rune spell, it's not supposed to explode. And if it somehow *does* explode, it's supposed to go big or go home, not something so violent but very contained. Not on its own. That meant an outside influence, a show of strength, a counterspell.

Counterspell.

Oh my god, you fucking idiot.

He'd been shielded when I had scryed him the night before and invisible on the cameras. Veiled or glamoured or something else, whatever, but he'd been working a constant counterspell to keep me off his scent. The bastard had been on his guard and I'd just thrown a sloppy punch his way, hadn't set my feet or anything. He'd basically Judoed my magic back at me and knocked me right on my fucking arse.

Stumbling out of the chapel, I did my best to run for the building. Through the stained glass I couldn't make it out, but from outside it was easy to see it was the main teaching building — old crushed stone construction, complete with charming wooden beams carving lines in a facade now marred by a huge stonking burn line.

The scorch mark was pointing right to a window on the first floor. It was open and from inside I could hear screaming. Children were pouring out, throwing open fire doors and bolting through the main entrance, but whatever was going on in that room was drowning them out completely.

Head down, I picked up my pace and threw myself through the main door of the building.

Eat The Rich

Eight

Inside, the building was sheer chaos. Trying to force my way against the current meant I may have smacked a couple of the younger kids upside the head just from trying to keep my balance. It didn't seem to slow them down much.

I reached a set of stairs and started to force my way up them. The screaming was growing louder now, continuing to block out the terrified yelping of the students I was elbowing aside. It was too loud, like it was bleeding out of the walls. This was only made worse by the realisation that the screaming wasn't getting louder in time with me getting closer. Just louder.

The torrent of scared students started to thin once I reached the top of the stairs, giving me the space to break into a sprint. The door to the classroom was closed, letting me use it as a brake so I didn't feel the need to try and slow down to open in. I crashed right through, rolling awkwardly across the ground and smashing into the teacher's desk.

Gracemere was in the middle of the room, just hanging in the air. His back was arched and his chest was puffed

Eat The Rich

out, arms splayed behind him so tight that I half expected his ribs to tear open. I had expected him to be the source of the screaming, but I could see now that his face was blank.

The screaming was coming from the creature crouched underneath him, working away like a gross little mechanic on a car.

It had its knees curled up around its ears, its uncomfortably long legs still almost too long to let it fit under the boy. Knobbly fingers were picking away at bare flesh, the back of Gracemere's shirt having been cleanly cut open like you would plastic wrapping. One hand was massaging the surface flesh gently while the other slid firmly into another delicate incision, this one running down the side of the spine.

You ever seen someone skin an animal? I saw it on TV once, and this was exactly like that. Except, you know, the animal wasn't floating in the air and the guy doing the skinning wasn't *disconcertingly gangly.*

The creature didn't seem to give a shit I was there — I started to creep around the room to get a better view of it and it didn't slow down, look up, nothing. It had pried free enough of Gracemere's skin now that its whole hand was in there, gently working more loose.

'Oi!' I shouted. A universal bellow, everyone knows what that means.

The creature froze for a moment and fell silent, then slowly turned its head to look at me. At first, I thought it looked like an old man — sharp cheekbones, loose skin, a general leathery look — but something was off. Looking at it made my eyes water and blur, and when I wiped away the tears I noticed that its face went beyond gaunt, through emaciated, and was halfway to fully skeletal. The lips and gums had receded enough to expose the teeth and the skin on the nose was almost translucent.

Tears of dust ran down the cheeks in loose clouds, trickling down from orbs of porcelain where the eyes should have been.

Really fucking creepy, right? He looked like the guy that would always be at the bus stop at night when you're coming home alone from the club and you're just a little too drunk or high to deal with that shit so you take a taxi instead and then wonder why your bank has blocked your card when you try to buy a breakfast roll from Greggs in the morning.

Just me?

Anyway, as long as it was staring — if that's the right word for a thing that doesn't really have eyes — at me then it wasn't unwrapping Gracemere like a ready meal. I needed to keep its attention on me.

'So, you're the one causing all the trouble, huh?' I said.

Eat The Rich

'I'm going to go out on a limb and say you're not a Nightmare. *Nightmarish,* sure, but an actual Nightmare?'

A drop of blood plopped from Gracemere's back, landing on the creature's face. Without breaking its gaze, the teeth parted and a long tongue climbed the weathered flesh. It lapped at the blood and then retreated, the creature swallowing noisily.

Again, the teeth parted and the tongue slithered out from between them. 'Begone, little bard.'

Its voice sounded strained, breathy. Ironic for something I was pretty sure wasn't breathing. I crossed my arms arms and glared. 'That's not how this works, mate. You don't tell *me* to fuck off, yeah? I tell you to fuck off. And I'm telling you now: get your hands out of that kid and fuck right off.'

'Leave me to my work,' it said, turning its attention back towards the boy.

I kicked out at a desk. It barely moved, but the legs screeched against the floor all the same. 'Don't you fucking ignore me, you grimy bitch. Eyes down here, mate.'

Once again, the face turned back to me. Pretty sure Gracemere tried too, but the poor bastard couldn't move his head.

'I am working,' the creature said, his tone a bit more abrasive this time. Impressive for a thing that sounded like it gargled sandpaper already. 'Necessary maintenance must be performed.'

'Do you get off on being cryptic or something?'

It started to withdraw the hand that was wriggling around inside the kid's back. 'Do not interfere, little bard. Thrice I warn, no more.'

The words set something whirring deep in the back of my head, but I couldn't wait for my brain to track down whatever memory it was grabbing at. I needed to keep the creature busy, to make sure its hands stayed out of Gracemere, at least until I could figure out how to get rid of it. Didn't seem to be a ghost, so that was like 80% of my expertise down the shitter. Whatever this thing was, it didn't fit neatly into the other 20% of undead bollocks either.

But if I could piss it off, the kid would be momentarily safe. Couldn't flay the poor bugger if it was trying to rip my throat out, I guessed. That's the Jameson Parker method — one of the few things he's taught me that I'll admit to being useful.

'Buddy, I've been interfering in shit since the day I was born. I am a nosy bitch. So, put the kid down and indulge me, yeah?'

Eat The Rich

Slowly, the creature began to unfold itself and step out from under Gracemere. At its full height the bastard's wispy hair was almost touching the ceiling, and as those blank eyes started peering down at me from all the way up there I started to wonder if I had just made a very big mistake.

Because, here's the thing: I'm not what you might call *combat capable*.

I've tangled with ghosts and zombies and shit, but one of the things you learn very quickly there is that you don't want to actually be fighting them. What you want to do is obliterate them or exorcise them or generally kick them into another dimension or something before they are close enough to sink their teeth into you.

This ugly bastard had serrated teeth.

It took an unnaturally fast step towards me, thing fingers probing for something to grab hold of. Luckily, I was faster. I dropped to the floor and scrambled under the nearest desk as the creature lurched forward, disappearing behind it. The thing recovered quickly, turning fast and using this newfound speed to start upending desks, hurling them so hard against the wall that they broke into pieces.

At this rate, I was going to run out of places to hide very quickly — skittering around under the tables would keep him occupied for a moment, but I needed a better plan if it was going to keep me alive.

The little contraption on my belt slapped against my hip as I changed direction, and I started to take stock of my options. As spells went, I had a couple of heavy hitters on call, but they were too heavy. Any spell I could use to fight this gangly fucker was just as likely to take me and the kid out too, considering the tight confines of the classroom. Might be worth the risk, though.

Could I banish it? Bind it? Can't really build a trap *around* the rampaging lion, got to control the space and lure it in. Right?

My attention divided, I didn't see the pool of blood until it was too late. Gracemere had been dripping steadily and a worryingly massive puddle had formed underneath him. It had spread across the floor and under the desks closest to him, and I had completely failed to notice it.

Zipping from one desk to the next, my path took me directly through the warm blood. My hands lost traction, sending me face down into the sticky stuff while my legs kept fighting for purchase. Bony fingers tightened around my ankle and hauled me back, wrenching me painfully up into the air. A second hand came down and pressed hard against my chest, the fingers seeming to push into the gaps between my ribs and lock there like hooks. Letting go of my ankle, the creature slowly turned me the right way up.

The creature pulled me close, so all I could see were the porcelain orbs grinding in the sockets. 'You are not on the work order, little bard. Do not think that absolves you of punishment.'

The first notes of a scream of terror took form in my throat. I tried to contain them, but the hooks flexed and I could feel my rib cage flex along with them. 'Let's... Look, I fucked up... Can't kill a girl for fucking up! Right?'

The dry tongue flicked across the teeth again. 'Beg for your life, little bard.'

'What?'

'Beg,' it said again. 'Debase yourself. *Humiliate* yourself. Take sandpaper to yourself and abrade that gleaming surface. Tarnish your being for my amusement and perhaps, if I deem it so, I will forgive you.'

You know what, I considered it. Don't tell me you wouldn't — fucking horrifying skeleton man has you at his mercy like that, the smart person is going to beg. Like, fuck pride, what good was having pride if you were dead? Besides, it was hard to have much confidence in myself while I was painted in the still warm blood of an exsanguinating teenager.

I could feel it dripping from my fingers, hear it *pitter-*

pattering onto the floor.

If there had been any hope that begging would have saved me, I might have done it, but it doesn't take a genius to know this fuckface was grandstanding. It wanted me to break first, and *your girl don't play that way*.

There was still one card up my — very soaked — sleeve.

'I don't understand,' I coughed. There was blood in my mouth now, hopefully mine. 'Broad daylight. No subtlety. This doesn't fit.'

'You have elected to forego humility, then?'

I snorted down a mouthful of blood. 'Thinking out loud. Helps me forget that I'm shit scared.'

'There is no need to be scared of what comes next, little bard,' it said. 'The pain will last only until you cannot bear it any longer, then a little longer after that. At the cusp of your pain blending into pleasure, that is when you'll expire.'

'Oh, I'm not scared of that third-rate attempt at a threat,' I said, marshalling what little strength I had. 'I'm more concerned with how much *this* is going to hurt.'

I brought up my hands and grabbed at the creature's head. With my thumbs, I daubed a quick and dirty sigil onto the thing's forehead. Blood makes for better runes than chalk any day of the week — there's old power in blood, the kind that at a fundamental level keeps any kind of magic ticking over, a universal constant — and the blood of a victim holds a grudge.

The sigil was nothing special really, a couple of thumb strokes to form the symbol for *release*. One of the most basic signs, the runic equivalent of double-tapping the clear key on a calculator, resetting all your magical manoeuvres so you can start fresh.

If cast properly.

If cast improperly — say, with the blood of someone who holds a pretty major grudge — you're not double tapping the clear key any more. Instead, you're smashing the ever-living fuck out of the calculator with a sledgehammer.

Either way, whatever sums you were doing are gone, yeah?

Thankfully for me, so was the man-eating skeleton bastard.

The spell went off like a bomb, throwing me back across the room and into the wall. The creature took it worse, though — everything from eyebrows to arsehole was just gone, and everything else was little more than a smouldering pile. Even as I watched, it was melting away, leaving behind a gelatinous goo that was already mixing with Gracemere's blood.

Pulling myself back to my feet, I took the poor kid in my arms and broke whatever spell was holding him in the air. He was limp and a lot heavier than he looked, though judging by his complexion he was much lighter than he should have been. He'd lost far too much blood, he needed an ambulance.

My head was pounding. Did I have a phone? I probably did. In my bag, right? Where had that gone? Fuck, lost in the utter mad chaos of the classroom, no doubt. Needed to find one, had to save him.

Stumbling out of the classroom, the noise of the world came rushing back in. More screaming, more terror, fresher and more purposeful than it had been when I fought my way in. Still children were fleeing from classrooms and down the stairs, but now they were being pursued by tall, dark shapes. Shapes with long, spindly legs. Shapes with paper-thin skin pulled tight over old bones.

Shapes with porcelain eyes.

The pain in my chest tightened, driving me down to my knees. There was blood on my shirt and by that point I couldn't remember if it was mine or not. Someone ran past me, bumping my shoulder as they did, and I flopped weakly to the floor. I heard them struggle to stop, then come running back my way.

More footsteps followed and a face slid into view. Not that I could make it out, the pain in my chest was sending white-hot sparks of pain through my entire nervous system. I could, at least, make out what they said.

'Get her up. Get her up! We must leave now!'

*

When I came to, someone was hovering over me and prying my eyes open. She didn't have a bad face to wake up to, although the dark bags and the sunken cheeks did line up a little too cleanly with the tall bastard with the porcelain eyes.

Seeing that I was awake, she snapped her hand back from my face and turned away to talk to someone off above my head. 'Yo, she's awake.'

She helped me upright and I saw that I was sitting on a foam crash mat. I didn't recognise the room but I did recognise the general ethos — brickwork coated in thick white paint; a little cold but had a distant stink of sweat; a room so cavernous that a fart would echo — it was a sports hall or something very much like it.

My guess? I was still on the college grounds.

'Give her some air,' said someone behind me, muscling the woman out the way as he stepped around. The sharp, Germanic tone of his voice tinged with what sounded like genuine concern. 'Finish the warding.'

I blinked some awareness back into my pounding head. Standing there, Wolfgang was really playing up the handsome hero bullshit. His shirt, already tight enough to leave little to the imagination, had been torn from one shoulder all the way across his chest. His hair was damp with sweat.

Bastard had the perfect jawline for the grungy look too.

The woman nodded and wandered off, leaving me with the sweaty German. He watched her for a moment, then offered me a hand. He smelled of ozone and frosty mornings — the telltale signs of someone having knocked out a few rune spells in quick succession. I took his hand and let him pull me to my feet.

'Saved my life, did you?' I asked.

He nodded. 'Probably. Not sure exactly what it did to you, but resetting your central nervous system seems to have sorted you out.'

'Thanks, I guess,' I grunted. 'Awfully convenient of you to show up then, though.'

A coldness ran across his face. When he spoke again, his voice was like ice. '*I came to help you.* The Voodoo expert came up with more ideas on how to deal with

Nightmares and I thought you might benefit from knowing what they were.'

'And?'

'I don't think they're appropriate now,' he said. 'I don't know what those things are, but they aren't Nightmares.'

A light clicked on in my brain. 'I know what they are. I think. *Outsiders*.'

Wolfgang took a long time to let that sink in. Anyone else would have probably shut me down immediately, but apparently he was going to take me at my word or something, which was weird as fuck.

He *should* have shut me down. People who deal in the magical side of the world can still fall victim to the same sort of pigheadedly stubborn brainworms that cause people to flat-out reject scary notions. Outsiders, however, were immune to even that sort of shit. Everyone knew that they were real in the same way oxygen is real — it's vaguely everywhere, but you don't really want to wake up one day and be able to *see* it.

'The campus is crawling with them,' he said eventually. 'That would mean—'

'That the biggest incursion of these fuckers in a century has, somehow, happened at a school for posh twats.'

What he had *meant* to say was that this many of them meant we were utterly fucked, but I couldn't let those words come out of his mouth. If I heard them, they were real. Keeping them unspoken, though, let me tap into that same pigheadedness I mentioned before and maintain my belief that everything wasn't completely and utterly buggered to fuckery.

Right, you need context.

Outsider is a very broad term that means anything from another plane of existence. There are loads of them, in theory, and they're all weird as shit. Walking across planes is some of the hardest magic to pull off and one of the few things basically every arcane-minded wizard agrees upon is a *dick move*. Wingard once told me of a mage down in Cornwall who tried to take up planeswalking — my old mentor and some of his actual enemies tracked the guy down and kicked his bollocks so far up his throat that he had a new pair of tonsils.

One of the many books Wingard had expressly forbidden me from reading was one he had confiscated from that dude, and naturally that meant it was one I had skimmed. Even as solid as my memory is though, this was still a book I only half remembered.

Wolfgang's brow was as furrowed in thought as I suspected my whole face was now. 'If there was someone here with the power to summon across the veil, we'd know.'

'Not necessarily,' I said, shaking my head. It was coming back to me now. 'You don't summon Outsiders. That's the trick — you can open the door, but they have to knock first.'

'Judging from the amount out there, that's a lot of knocking.'

'And a lot of dead kids if we don't do something.'

'You got some ideas?'

My mind went blank. The books had a lot to say about dealing with Outsiders — your typical fae-style contract where every loophole that could be exploited to ruin your day would, absolutely, be exploited to ruin your day — but very little about *dealing* with them. That wizard had apparently not thought that sort of information would be helpful.

Then again, it couldn't be that hard, right? I'd already splattered one of the bastards across a classroom, so they were eminently killable.

'Wards are done,' the young woman said, interrupting us. She had walked up beside Wolfgang and was standing there, her hands behind her back and her chest puffed up like an overeager copper. 'Walid is heading to the roof to get a look at what we're dealing with.'

Wolfgang gave her a curt nod. 'Good. Go over the wards once more, Su-Yin, just to be safe.'

'Of course,' she said, turning to leave.

Before, all I had seen of her was her tired face. Now, I could get a better look at her and saw that if anyone had carried me out of that dorm building, I would put money on it being her. Su-Yin was tall, broad, and had a silhouette like an ancient Greek statue. There had clearly been a lot of muscle mass on those bones, though it seemed as though she'd lost some of it recently, and quickly too — her shirt hung loose in awkward places, a bit too much space in the sleeves, and her belt had a kink in one of the notches that showed how tight she usually wore it, which was not where it was currently buckled.

There were a lot of things to notice about her, maybe you've managed to get that impression too.

Wolfgang was watching her too, his gaze lingering curiously. 'You picked up an entourage yet?'

The words took a moment to soak into my skull. 'What?'

'Ah, I see,' he said, sinking down into that pose that youth workers just fucking love when they are getting ready to drop *some high quality life advice, yo*. 'You're that early on in your career. Short version for you: every frontman needs a backing band.'

I nodded over to Su-Yin. She was dutifully going over the wards again. 'That's what she is to you, a backup singer?'

He shrugged. 'She and Walid are reliable, dependable, and very capable. You're going to need people like that, people you can rely on, if you want to make a proper go of this.'

'So I can lead them to their deaths in a school full of extra-dimensional skeletons? Yeah, no thanks.'

'Or,' he said, slapping me on the shoulder. 'You do your job and keep them alive.'

Nine

Eventually, I managed to convince Wolfgang to fuck off for a bit and leave me alone. Despite having the poor woman go over the wards another two times, he didn't seem to trust Su-Yin quite as much as he had wanted me to think. He was getting off on the whole *mentor* shit.

I, however, had more important things to deal with than one handsome guy's enormous ego.

Walid, whoever he was, might have been up on the roof and doing some recon, but seeing as I'm not the sort of person to just wait around for others to do the work for me, I wanted to be *doing something*. Be proactive, not reactive.

I took myself away to the toilets and laid out another little space to work in. Honestly, it's the first time I've been in a gents toilets and felt safe being near the floor — the amount of piss was surprisingly negligible. There was enough dry tiles on the floor to make for a solid little canvas to build my spell upon.

A little cog had been whirring in the background of my head for a while now, and I had to see to it. Now, Mama

Mistral had been decidedly useless all told — only way you could connect Outsiders to voodoo was by some *exceptional* lateral thinking — but she'd confirmed the sangfroid, and I couldn't shake that being important.

Why would Outsiders go around wielding the weapons of a Nightmare? It didn't make sense, and yet, there were definitely Outsiders beyond these walls, carving up kids like gangly butchers. But they clearly didn't need to use sangfroid to do that.

That was a detail that I just couldn't make fit, no matter how hard I hammered on that specific jigsaw piece. I had to be missing something, and it was getting right on my tits.

I needed more. More information, more data. I had the facts that both sangfroid and Outsiders were involved, and I needed to find the point that connected the two. If I didn't have that information yet, I'd need to find it. There weren't many avenues open to me with regards to researching Outsiders, but I could still look a little deeper into sangfroid.

Sangfroid means cold blood, dead blood, and that had to come from somewhere. Chances were, the source of the blood would have some useful information. So, all things considered, where was the harm in a little seance, eh?

Well, not exactly a séance. I'm not a medium, that's a

skill you're either born with or develop from a horrific brain injury. But like all gothlings with a handbag full of cheap mascara and a bookcase stuffed with legitimate magical tomes, I'd done more than my fair share of necromancy.

And if you tell anyone that, I'll stick pins in your unmentionables until you die.

Necromancy is bastard magic; a weird Frankenstein's monster of the arcane, runic, a few bits and bobs from African and Eastern magic, all stitched together and shaken about. It's the magical equivalent of a dirty pint. Thing is, if you make a living telling ghosts to piss off, you soon realise it'd be to your benefit to find a way to tell them to fucking come back on occasion too.

I lay the darts down on the floor in a pleasing arc. They hadn't come out of the scrap with the Outsider unharmed — a couple had snapped at the tip, and one had broken clean in half — but they'd still be good enough for what I needed. The runes would fill in the gaps.

Reaching down to the device on my hip, I clicked a couple of commands into the buttons and waited for the runes to be dispensed. A spring twanged deep inside the mechanism, followed by a heavy stream of little tokens. It vomited every rat-bastard little rune stone out and onto the floor, the flow trickling through my fingers. The device had fared much worse in the scrap than the darts had. No more shortcuts, I supposed.

The knife was pressed into service once again, doing its duty at making a royal mess of the floor of the toilets, and then came the hard bit — the arcane bit. Calling on that power required focus and a certainty of purpose, a calm that you may have noticed I don't possess. At least, I usually don't. When it comes to the dead, you can't help but be chill as fuck, they kind of rub off on you that way.

Feeding my pitiful amount of power into that of the runes, I felt the air turn cold and the hairs on the back of my neck suddenly shot bolt upright. That was good, setting the stage nicely. All I had to do was reach out, one by one, down the line of mortality that was woven into each dart — the lives ended as a result of each one, both in their creation and their execution — start at the end and reel myself back to the beginning.

All a bit flowery, seeing it written down like that, but that's arcane magic for you. Might be that you're starting to understand why I prefer runes.

Anyway, the tracks were easy to follow, and once I was sure I was following the right ones I wrapped them around my metaphorical arm and started to yank those fuckers out of the light like big spooky fish. Sad thing is, they didn't even struggle.

Until they started to manifest in front of me, it hadn't occurred to me that they would be kids.

'Try not to freak out,' I said in my best calming voice. 'But I need to ask you a few questions.'

All five of them stared at me for a moment, unblinking. When they spoke, the words rolled down the line of them, a Mexican wave of speech, a different word from each mouth. Ghosts are weird. 'You pulled *me us* back from *my our* rest?'

'Yeah, kind of,' I said. 'To find out who killed you, though! That's a good reason.'

'As if justice is any good to *me us* now,' they said. 'But *I we* don't really know the rules, so *I we* guess this is fine? Ask away.'

I crossed my arms. 'Who killed you?'

'A monster,' they said.

'Yeah, I figured, but what I meant was—'

'Called *me us* its work, even as it ripped out bones. Made *me us* watch as it carved the next weapon.'

The Outsider that had been skinning Gracemere had waffled on about *doing its job* or something too. I'd filed that away for a quieter moment, and it seemed that moment had arrived. 'Why was it targeting you?'

'Don't you know?'

'I figured it was a class thing,' I said. 'You were all scholarship students, here on a free ride. But then, I don't see how an Outsider could be made to give a fuck about something that petty.'

'*I we* didn't have a scholarship,' they said.

A ripple passed over the group suddenly, like a wave travelling up a pool, crashing against the edge and bouncing back again. But it didn't bounce, it held in the kid on the end. He was short and squat, wild straw-blond hair so fine that it must have been able to catch a breeze on even the stillest day.

This kid seemed more alive than the others now, as if they were fading into the background. Judging by the look on his face, this required a lot of effort to pull off. 'I lied. My father's an MP, he got a donor to pay for me.'

'De Pfeffel?'

'Yes,' the boy said. 'I think that was my name, right? Struggling to think clearly.'

'Being dead will do that to you,' I said, trying my best not to rush him. 'You don't have a connection to the world anymore, so organising your thoughts might get tricky. I need you to try though, yeah?'

He nodded. 'Who are you?'

'The unlucky cow trying to solve your murder.'

'*Name,*' De Pfeffel seethed through his teeth. '*Give your name. Your name. YOUR NAME.*'

I scooted backwards on my arse a few centimetres. 'You all right there, De Pfeffel?'

The boy's expression changed and his eyes grew wider. 'That wasn't me. Was it me? I didn't mean to!'

Now, I kept my face neutral but inside I was shitting a whole house's worth of bricks. Anything asking for your name like that is bad news, but doubly so when its a ghost.

See, this is why you shouldn't fuck with necromancy and, in case you were wondering, the main reason I didn't consider trying this earlier. You're lucky to bring back the dead shit you're actually after, and if you do there's bound to be something that tagged along for the ride.

'Chill, kiddo,' I said. I was on a timer now. 'Don't need to worry about that, just tell me what you meant to say.'

De Pfeffel licked his lips. 'I just wanted to join the Dee Society. They only take scholarship students.'

Eat The Rich

'Huh. I thought they were for the outcasts.'

'Sure, they are,' he said. 'But, like, messing around with magic and shit? That's the inside track. My dad says I'll be set for life if I make the right connections here, but how sad is that? Sucking up to people, always owing someone something.'

'You figured lying your way into the Dee Society would be good for you? What?'

'That magic stuff is real power. I just wanted to learn.'

Poor dumb bastard. From what I'd seen, the Dee Society might have had the knowledge of wizards, but they didn't have the skills. You can read every book on magic under the sun, but if you don't have the spark in your blood you're not going to be able to do shit. At least, not without runes and sigils and calculations and all that — none of which I could see the Dees knowing about, and certainly not the sort of thing De Pfeffel wanted to learn.

You could see it in his face — he was a rat, a poser, just so infatuated with the idea that he didn't take the time to think things through. I think I might have been one of those when I started, but I'd had just enough spark to make me worth someone's time. De Pfeffel, not so much, and somehow, that had gotten him killed.

The temperature had dropped another few degrees and

I could feel ice starting to form on my eyelashes. Summoning five ghosts at once had been pretty bloody stupid, but it had been manageable. If the temperature was dropping more, though, then that was just another alarm screaming in my ears.

I scooted forwards again, back to all my magical shit. 'Right, well, thanks for you help. I think you can all piss off back to the afterlife now. What do you say?'

De Pfeffel blinked slowly, confusion creeping into every spectral pore. *'Your name. Speak your name. GIVE ME YOUR NAME, BITCH. LAUFEYJARSON'S WHORE. YOU PROSTITUTE YOURSELF TO THE LAUGHING STOCK OF THE GODS—'*

Snatching up my knife, I scored a line through a couple of the runes on the tiles and broke the spell. Everything snapped back in an almost comical fashion — number one on the list of proofs for the existence of a god: you break the spell summoning a ghost and they catapult back to hell like they've got a bungee cord tied to their knackers. Really kills the whole spooky vibe they're got going.

The first time.

It wears off after that, especially when you get spat at by something wearing the spectral skin of a dead child.

The less said about that, the better. It could have been

all manner of things that live in the dark spaces between the living and the dead, and probably not worth my time going over really. Just one of the dangers of fucking about with necromancy.

Which is why you should never do it. Unless you're a bad ass bitch with ice in her veins like me, then you've got *fuck around and find out* privileges. Go nuts.

I packed up what could be packed up from the spell, let everything I had just heard sit for a moment, then rejoined the others. If my absence had been noticed, no-one seemed interested in commenting on it.

Wolfgang was over by the main entrance, Su-Yin slumped against the wall next to him. She was hugging her knees, head flopped down in a very uncomfortable power nap. In front of her, a young man that I assumed must have been Walid was whispering to the German, arms a little too animated for such a secretive volume. I considered butting in, or at least sidling close enough to eavesdrop, but I found myself not really caring enough to do either.

Instead, I milled around for a little, doing that blind wandering autopilot thing that people do when they're doing *big thinking*.

I also took the time to have a nosy gander out what windows the sports hall had. It was weirdly calm and far too quiet out there. The Outsiders should have been prowling around for fresh meat — fine, the student body and the faculty had piss all chance of fighting them off, but you'd expect them to try, or at least run. But then, did I want to look out the window and see a massacre, was that the level of cynicism I'd reached?

Not quite.

But I had reached the level that couldn't help but ask the question: What job are they here to do? Maybe that purpose was the thing keeping them in check. Hearing them talk about their work once was coincidence or, more likely, an artistic turn of phrase from a bony monstrosity. Twice and beyond, that was a clue.

I was starting to see the appeal of an entourage, especially as something to bounce your ideas off. The freedom of working alone and finding your feet is great, don't get me wrong, but watching Wolfgang and Walid discussing things made more a little jealous. All I had was my brain, and that thing never shut the fuck up long enough for me to get a word in edgways.

As if reading my mind, Su-Yin's head shot upright and she got back to her feet — nap over. On unsteady legs, she crossed the hall and stood next to me, staring out. 'Apologies for the view.'

'It's fine,' I said. 'Not like you built the school.'

'I meant the warding,' she replied, the corners of her

mouth twitching, hoping they'd be allowed to have a little fun. 'I thought I'd made them secure enough but they can be a bit twitchy at the best of times and —'

'I do know how temperamental arcane wards can be,' I snapped. I don't even know why, but something about her presence was irritating me. I pushed it back down. 'I'm not as dumb as I look. I don't need the foundation degree.'

Her face turned ashen, but the pleasant demeanour never wavered. 'I should have known. Sorry if I offended.'

I waved her words away. 'Nah, you didn't. I'm just feeling like a grumpy cow right now, I'm sure you understand.'

'I do,' she said with a nod. 'We can't stay locked in here for long. Ma— That is, *Wolfgang*, is trying to work out an attack plan.'

Interesting slip of the tongue she made there. Caught herself fast enough to decapitate it. I'd just file that away for the future. 'He wants to fight them?'

'How else do we stop them?'

It wasn't a question — this was *never* a question, at least not one that whoever asked it wants an answer to. They already had their answer, it was woven into the fabric of the phony question, they just wanted the peace of mind that came part-and-parcel with the barest shred of consent from someone else. What she wanted was for me to shrug and let her get her rocks off by cracking heads.

'You want to swim down to R'Lyeh next, punch Cthulhu in the teeth too?' I wanted her try to understand what I meant, then I could shut that shit down nice and fast. 'Do you want to pick a fight you can't win?'

'Wolfgang says we can.'

'Wolfgang thought this was Voodoo five minutes ago, he's getting ahead of himself.'

Su-Yin glanced over her shoulder at the man who was still locked in quiet discussion with the youth. 'He's usually right about this sort of stuff.'

'Been with him long?'

She crossed her arms. 'No, not really. Just a few weeks. But long enough to get the measure of him. He sees a lot of potential in you, you know.'

'Lots of people seem to be able to see my potential,' I sighed. 'Makes me feel a bit naked. But I get my share of insight, and it's telling me we can't fight our way out of this.'

'Why not? You killed one, Wolfgang said so.'

'*By accident*. Not keen on trying to reproduce that scenario, let me tell you.'

Her brow wrinkling in confusion, Su-Yin went quiet for a moment and turned her back on me. When she spoke again, her voice was flat and chillingly cold. 'Wolfgang is always right, you'll see.'

With that, she trotted back across the room to her little group of weird mates, leaving me alone with my thoughts.

*

My head was still very noisy when Wolfgang waved me over, and it took a moment to get my attention. Once I snapped back to reality, however, I could see he was almost giddy with excitement.

'Millie,' he said as I walked over. 'I think we need a plan of attack, don't you?'

I replied with a thoroughly non-committal, 'Hmm?'

'Well, locking this place down was just a temporary measure while you got back on your feet. Emergency triage.'

'Naturally.'

'But we can't just leave those things running amok out there.'

Clasping my hands behind my back, I pulled a deep stretch that pleasingly popped a couple of muscles at the base of my skull. 'And I thought you were here to support me on my day at big school, not take all the classes for me.'

'I'm not taking over,' he said, hurriedly. 'Just doing what a good lieutenant ought to do — putting out some suggestions, ideas, that sort of thing.'

Oh, I was sure he'd have no shortage of suggestions. There it was again, that little twist to his words. Son of a bitch was trying to top from the bottom, make me think all his ideas were mine and get me doing things his way. I'd missed that with the bullshit Voodoo lead, but I wasn't about to let him drag me into a fucking fistfight with horrors from the Nth dimension just because he had his puppy dog eyes on and that disarming grin.

'You going to tell me you know how to fight Outsiders?' I asked. 'You didn't even recognise them until about five minutes ago.'

His expression soured. 'And if we don't, how many kids are going to die out there?'

Let me be clear, my reluctance to kick open the door and start blasting wasn't me thinking the kids were expendable. Wolfgang had been very quick to throw that notion out there, though, and those labels are hard to shift once the glue dries.

Eat The Rich

The smart move was to wait it out, that was obvious. What good would we do the kids if we just got fucking stomped to buggery the moment we opened the door? The one thing Wolfgang was right about was the need for a plan, but I couldn't see even the *seed* of one that wouldn't get us all killed for nothing.

But, despite his charming little words to the contrary, Wolfgang and I were both very aware of where the decision ultimately lay. Sure, he was all about me making my own messes apparently, but of the four of us hiding in this weird little bunker, three were so firmly on Team Wolfgang they may as well have been humming *Deutschlandlied* every time he opened his mouth.

Look it up. Wikipedia is your friend.

Anyway, *the point* is that everyone present knew that, no matter what I might have wanted to do, we were all going to do whatever it was the suave German wanted. The only real question left was whether I was going to put up a fight about it — and look like a whiny bitch — or make the best of it.

I'd had my fill of whining.

'Fine,' I said, practically spitting venom. 'But I'm not exactly combat capable in the old magic department.'

He smiled smugly. 'Don't worry, we've got you

covered.'

It was very well rehearsed, what followed. The three of them fell effortlessly into formation, Wolfgang at the centre like some lauded general and the other two flanking his shoulders. I felt the familiar tingle across my skin as they drew on their magics, the arcane equivalent of limbering up, as they prepared to throw open the door.

It was very clear that Wolfgang was trying to look cool now, really digging into the need to portray himself as some inspirational figure. I can't even say he wasn't good at it either — he cut a pretty sexy silhouette, and the confidence and swagger in his step went a long way in explaining why Su-Yin and Walid might have hitched themselves to that wagon. Hell, he didn't so much walk now as blend between the sort of poses only achievable in a propaganda poster.

When he finally threw open the door, I'm a little ashamed to admit that I found myself a bit excited too. It was a very much unwelcome excitement, and while not at the level of the ear-splitting fangirlish or fanboyish scream that might bubble out of the soul when you get swept up in something powerful, it definitely grew from the same seed.

That all evaporated pretty bloody quickly, however, once I watched Wolfgang stride out all *heroically* and very much ready to do battle, only to be met with kids casually going about their business.

No screaming. No horror. No sexy peril. Just another normal day at school.

Wolfgang and his entourage faltered, all the piss and vinegar draining from them at the sight. Then he muttered something under his breath in German which, while I'm far from fluent, I'm pretty sure translates as:

'What the shit?'

Ten

No-one ever likes the shitty cop-out of *it was all a dream.* Whenever some otherwise talented writer bashes out that old cliche, you can feel the rotation of the Earth slow a little as all those eyes rolling up into all those heads take a bite out of the onwards momentum of life itself.

But, and this is crucial here, nothing quite fucks with your head so much as walking into a situation so unbelievable that you think you might as well be dreaming.

When I had passed out, the college was in chaos. I'd seen the Outsiders, and while I hadn't seen the extent of their numbers I had definitely noticed enough to judge that we were in the shit. There had *definitely* been more than the one I had burst, for instance. Stepping onto the field of what should have been a massacre but *wasn't*, that's a shift in gears that most brains aren't prepared for.

Mine wasn't, and neither was Wolfgang's. For a moment, that heroic image shattered like Waterford Crystal — a fragile cascade, leaving a razor sharp remnant that could very easily be dangerous if poorly handled. His face was a fascinating read.

Whatever spells he had been holding fizzled away in that moment, though it only took an instant for him to force his brain into a fresh gear and start to concoct some new spell. Not that I would let him. Didn't need a general if there wasn't going to be a fight, now did we?

Pushing past him, I snatched up a stick from the ground, snapped it in half, then lobbed both halves up into the air. He started to object, but I shushed him. 'Let me work here, big lad.'

The sticks landed in a wonky cross, the pivot being near the rough edges of the break. It's the sort of piss-baby magic that arcane casters never learn but can be very useful if you know how to read it.

Which is to say, if you know how to convince people you know how to read broken bits of wood as if they are powerful tools of augury.

'Right, we're awake,' I said to no-one in particular. Squatting down on my haunches, I studied the sticks. 'And we were awake before. That means this is regular weird, not dream weird.'

Beside Wolfgang, Walid's fingers were twitching and I recognised the practised movements of someone feeling their way through the background magic for clues. 'This doesn't make any sense.'

'Yeah, no shit,' I laughed. 'We've all come to that conclusion, genius.'

He cocked his head my way in frustration. 'Smart arse.'

'Go do a lap of the property,' I said, taking charge before Wolfgang could piece himself back together. 'I want to have a mooch around, see what I can find without you three looming over me and putting the kiddos on edge.'

A shit order with a shit reason, but it served to mask the real reason and it got them out of my hair. Wolfgang's overwhelming charm and confidence was going to need a few minutes to come back online, and I'd be off on my own by then.

I set off before they had a chance to object. I was reasonably sure that Su-Yin and Walid wouldn't follow me without Daddy Wolf's say so, and if I was gone fast enough he wouldn't have time to react. Seemed to work well.

The resulting mooch about was largely fruitless, sadly. Classes were back on, which meant the kids were out of reach and the few teachers that I felt might have given me the time of day — which is to say about three of them — were too busy to deal with me fluttering my over-mascara'd eyes at them for information. I couldn't

Eat The Rich

even find De'Ath, pompous little windbag that he was.

It didn't take me long to give up on any hope of finding someone that could fill in the gaps for me. Instead, I ended up back at the classroom where all the crazy shit had gone down. I'm not really sure how — I certainly hadn't intended to wander back up there, but it had felt a little like I had been ushered through the college by some invisible current, nudging me just enough that it tricked me into thinking it was my idea. My feet went wherever the hell they wanted and my body was just along for the ride.

Not a magical effect, at least no more so than animal instinct was in general.

Whatever had calmed the rest of the college didn't appear to extend this far. Everything was prim and proper and in its rightful place — a noticeable lack of scattered desks or young man's blood, for instance — but the air was thick with anxiety. Some of it was my own, but not all. Most of it was that grey haze that clogs up your pores when you walk into somewhere you know you shouldn't be, that suffocating heaviness that gets your nerves screaming at you to run.

I'd already run once, wasn't about to pussy out again so soon.

Studiously, I did several laps of the room. I ran my fingertips over the surfaces of the desks, feeling for anything that might catch my attention. Then I did the same over the floor, paying special attention to where Gracemere's blood had pooled, and again where I had fucked up the Outsider.

Nothing stood out, except for the fact that nothing stood out. If you were going to cover that shit up without magic, there'd be the smell of cleaning products, a dedication to mopping up grime that you don't get from people who clean up after children and know they'll have the same mess to deal with tomorrow. Surely there'd be a similar feeling if magic had been involved.

I slumped down into the teacher's chair and stared out the window for a while. I could see Walid in the distance, doing the rounds I'd barked at him to do. No sign of the others.

Something was very wrong with this school. I know, that seems pretty fucking obvious at this point, but there hadn't really been the *feeling* that things were overly *out there*. Like, I get that, from the outside the notion of some spooky bitch flaying those little buggers one by one and leaving their gory corpses behind is probably not the sort of sight you'd find at any school you attended, but also when was the last time you had to kick a ghost in the balls?

Point is, that was all concerning and *out there*, sure, but not so far that it was brain-breaking all things considered.

I mean, a Norse god talks to me. I've palled around with Medusa. Oh Christ, I'm one of those people now, aren't I? *But for me, it was Tuesday.*

Ergh.

Still, there *is* a line between that sort of stuff. Reality being rolled back to a point where none of what I'd literally seen had happened was about where that line turned into a fucking *dot.*

I could see Su-Yin outside now, padding along about a hundred metres behind Walid. Still no Wolfgang.

There had to be some trace, some speck of a clue that could help me understand what was going on here. I pulled out the notes Azizi had given me and arranged them on the desk. Without much in the way of rhyme or reason, I slid the papers over each other, listening to the soft sound of paper scraping over paper rather than trying to read anything. I'd read them all, they existed in that stupid brain vault of mine, but the hope was that something would leap out at me and tell me where to focus in.

It didn't, obviously. That would have been nice and easy, and you've seen how nothing about this wanted to be easy for me.

But the lack of anything useful did tell me something. I'd been focused on the recent events, which did make sense, but I hadn't thought bigger picture until now. It had made sense to think that something had changed recently, something that summoned or lured or otherwise enticed our murderous little scamp. But this new weirdness? That was the kind that soaks into the very foundations of a place — maybe this all wasn't as fresh and tasty as I'd been led to believe.

I needed to know the history of the place, which meant I'd need to go back to the library and have another chat with the Dee Society. Plus, I did need to have a word with them about what De Pfeffel's ghost had told me.

Shuffling the papers one more time for good measure, I left them on the desk and made for the library. It was safe to assume no-one would be going in that room for a while.

It turned out no-one was going to be heading into the library anytime soon either, though.

The unassuming door — cheap wood with one of those two-way hinges — sat so firm in the frame that I couldn't get the damned thing to budge. At first, I wondered if someone had barricaded themselves in there, but even the best barricade has a little give in it, even just the scantest millimetre of movement as the fortification strains against itself. This was as solid as a wall.

I closed my eyes and tapped into my arcane senses. They're limited and foggy, like squinting through smoked glass, but this close I didn't really need 20:20 vision to spot the wards woven into the door frame. Delicate, but hasty, work.

That meant wizard.

And that meant that someone in the Dee Society was a little bit more than they had been letting on.

Considering that my arcane warding needed work, I didn't think it was safe to tamper with the work of someone with actual skills. The last thing I needed was to have all my hair burnt off or the consistency of my bones and skin inverted. Instead, I opted for the polite approach and knocked loudly on the door, being sure to jump back a good step and a half afterwards just in case.

The wards flared and I felt the very unpleasant sensation of being stared at by a thousand sets of eyes, all of them seeing much more than I was comfortable with. Then something changed in the air, a low hum — that I hadn't even noticed until it ended — fell silent and my ears popped as the pressure in the room changed ever so slightly.

Comically slowly, the door to the library started to

creep inwards. As soon as the crack in the door was wide enough, an arm shot out holding a chunky metal talisman. '*Abi, intruder! Revoco invitationem tuam, ius hospitii tui, licentiam tuam ad existendum in hoc plano. Exsul es.*'

I slapped the talisman aside and pushed through the door. 'I do love some gratuitous Latin. Move over, you dork. I need a word.'

Azizi had been the one on the other side of the door, but he wasn't alone. I recognised some of the others from the first time I had met the Dee Society, sleepy students that had been splayed out around Azizi like spotty greyhounds. Now they were kneeling on the floor, eyes closed, muttering something that sounded just close enough to Latin to turn a priest's head.

But, most importantly, in the middle of their little prayer circle *floated* a man surrounded by a fucking silent tornado of books. His eyes had rolled back into his head, possibly in a futile attempt to track down his hairline, which had receded so far back along his head that I can only assume it had looped around again to reinforce his prodigious beard. A proper wizard's beard, that one — long enough to reach his knees and bushy enough to block out the sun.

'Oh, Ms Thatcher!' Azizi said, pulling my attention back from the spectacle. 'We thought that—'

Eat The Rich

I flicked his nose to shut him up. 'Yeah, one second, my guy. Want to explain to me what the fuck *this* is first?'

He turned and looked at the old man as if it was the first time he had noticed him and his whole Wizard of Oz shtick. 'Hmm? Oh! That's just the Professor.'

'He's a mage.'

'And a powerful one, yeah,' Azizi continued. 'We're lucky to have him. Right now he's keeping us safe from those things out there.'

'You mean the Outsiders. They're gone. It's almost as if—'

This time, he interrupted me. 'They were never there at all? That's the Professor's doing. Give him a second and I'm sure he can explain it all to you.'

I'd been polite and patient so far, so why rock the boat now? It wasn't like I had anywhere else to be.

The Professor didn't keep me waiting too long, thankfully. Azizi rejoined the group, muttering that same almost-Latin, and the storm of literature started to calm. The books riffled shut before returning to their shelves in a chill and orderly fashion. As the last book slid into place, the old man floated back down to the ground, silvery eyes sliding back into view.

He shivered, and suddenly the old man was gone,

replaced by a much younger and more vibrant figure. 'You must be the Thatcher lady. Sorry it's taken such circumstances for me to be able to find the time in my schedule to meet you. Excuse the glamour. When you get to my age, vanity's grip on the soul can get a little tighter.'

I folded my arms across my chest. 'And how old would that be?'

'Old enough that it's rude for you to ask,' he said, eyes shimmering. 'And ruder still for me to answer. Professor Roland Constable, the officially unofficial magus of the college.'

Magus. Distinct from *mage,* though the specifics of that distinction escaped me. Definitely something I should have known, but Wingard had never force-fed me a glossary of self-aggrandising magical nomenclature, so it's really his fault.

'Apparently you know who I am.'

'I know your name and that you're here to clean up our mess.'

'Looks like you've cleaned it up plenty well enough, Rolo,' I said, putting on my most pantomime of fake smiles. 'Would have saved me a lot of trouble if you'd just done whatever you were just doing from the beginning, you know.'

A cold smile touched the corner of his eyes, though it never graced the rest of his face. 'And who says I haven't?'

I must have looked confused — I mean, I *was* confused, after all — and Azizi once again tried riding to my rescue. 'We've not been quite as open with you as maybe we should have been.'

'That's quite evident.'

'In our defence,' Azizi said, blushing. 'It's kind of hard to put into words in a way that—'

'I'd appreciate it if you tried.'

Constable placed a hand on the kid's shoulder and gently pushed him aside. 'The Outsiders have taken more souls from the students than the faculty knows.'

'More than the handful they told me about?'

He nodded. 'Considerably more.'

The junior members of the Dee Society suddenly found the tops of their feet extremely interesting indeed, all of them shuffling away and staring at them. Even the otherwise unflappable Azizi wasn't immune, awkwardly retreating a couple more steps from the magus.

'Do I need to sit down for this?' I asked.

'I doubt it would help,' Constable said. 'But before I tell

you exactly how deep this goes, I need you to understand that there is some room for error here. It might not be *quite* this bad.'

'But I'm getting the impression that you are expecting it to be on the worse side.'

The cold smile was back in his eyes again. 'Yes.'

'Okay then,' I said and took a deep breath. 'Hit me.'

'Five hundred thousand.'

My brain lurched like a car slipping a gear. 'Do you want to try that again?'

'Five hundred. Thousand. Children.' Constable repeated, wearily. He'd done the legwork of pondering the numbers for me, of chewing them over, of forcing them into a shape that the brain could understand — his face told me as much. I couldn't muster any doubt in what he was saying now.

'Okay, different angle then,' I said, grasping for any straw that would have this make even an ounce of actual sense. 'How?'

Constable waved his right palm over his left — the tried and tested stage magician sleight of hand gesture. A small gem shimmered into view, cupped comfortably into the centre of his lifeline. 'Do you know what this is?'

'Going to go out on a limb here and say it's magic.'

He chuckled. 'Just a bit. It's a diamond, made from the sands of time themselves, compressed and crushed until solid. Extremely powerful spell focus, especially if you have a need to fold time in on itself. Say, to stop hundreds of thousands of children getting ripped apart by extra-dimensional travellers.'

Now, I'm not an idiot. Yes, as far as my skills with the arcane go, I'm not what you'd call *well-versed*. I was a C student at best, not blessed with much in the way of natural aptitude, and a bit of a coaster at the end of the day. But, and this is very important, I've never been gullible, and I've tried very hard to not fall into the same trap as some others wizards I could name — specifically, just because you can piss fireballs and jizz acid, doesn't mean that there are no limits to reality.

Time travel is bullshit. At least, swimming against the flow of time is. History exists as memory, not as some other state you can step into. Anyone telling you different is trying to get in your pants or get in your head.

And I was ready to laugh right in Constable's face, slap that piece of costume jewellery out of his hand, then get all up in his grill about this bullshit. *Oh look at me, I'm a big sexy wizard DILF and I can turn back time with a shiny rock, fancy a ride in my convertible?*

But, I didn't.

'That's not possible,' I managed to say.

Another stage magic gesture and the diamond was gone again. I was half expecting him to try and pull it out of my ear. 'I confess, it's possible that the provenance of the item is embellished. Its power, however, is quite real. For the last, well, God knows how long, I've been using this thing to fold time and undo as much of the damage as I can. But I can never get all of it, and I can never stop it outright. I've tried.'

Constable was making a play for the patron sainthood of stoicism. There was a lot of pain lurking behind his words, but you wouldn't have known it from the delivery — wouldn't have surprised me to find out that Azizi thought this guy had bollocks of stone, emotions buried so deep that you'd need a canary and a pickaxe to go looking for them.

I didn't need the canary. Constable had made sure I didn't. He wasn't baring his soul, but he had a way of looking at me that could guide me down those mine shafts and let me know just how serious he was without seeming to give anything away. People like him are dangerous — it's not even subtext, it's something else, something you feel. Authority maybe, or gravitas.

Either way, it was doing a lot of work.

'So you treat the symptoms, not the cause.'

'Palliative care.'

I frowned. 'I don't understand. You're trying to get me to believe in time travel, which is obviously utter bollocks—'

'Not time travel,' he said. 'Not really. It's *folding* time. Here, let me explain. You got any paper on you?'

I fished around in my bag and pulled out some sheet from one of the dossiers or something, along with a pen, and handed it over. 'Here.'

He took the paper and scribbled manically on one side of it. 'This is reality — Outsiders causing chaos. I can't put the ink back into the pen, no making this paper nice and clean again.'

'Mhm,' I mumbled. 'With you so far.'

'But you can *hide* it,' he said, folding the paper in half. 'All that chaos is on the inside, but on the outside you've just got a pristine surface. Nothing to worry about.'

Annoyingly, this was making sense to me. 'Folding time around the murders, making a bypass. A *pocket*.'

'Exactly,' he said, slipping into full teacher-mode. 'It all happened, but it didn't happen. But, like with paper, the more you fold it the harder it gets to fold.'

'And the smaller the area you can see.'

'Precisely.'

I had to sit down — turns out that isn't just a thing people do on TV or in books, the world really did feel far too heavy for me to remain upright at that moment. Azizi, astute as ever, knew this before I did and cleared off one of the nearby chairs for me, just in time for the plastic to catch me as I slumped down.

Jesus Christ, this guy was the real deal. This was like Oppenheimer putting in a call to Jane Shitbag, life-time supermarket cashier and ASBO-haver, and asking her to come check his maths and wedge a few more atoms into the bomb.

The more he talked, the more out of my depth I was feeling — and I was already so deep I needed armbands.

But, you know, *fake it till you make it*. Surely though, he had to know this was beyond me?

I cleared my throat. Another thought had popped up from the darkness. 'I might need a moment or two to digest this... *complication.* Tell me the truth, I'm not the first person you've roped in to help with this, are you?'

'No.'

'The others are trapped in those *time pockets*, or whatever?'

He nodded.

I nodded back. 'I was bottom of the list, wasn't I?'

'Well it's not—' Azizi started.

Constable interrupted. 'Last choice. Last chance.'

'Huh,' I said, falling quiet for a moment. 'Well, that makes more sense, I guess.'

Eleven

I'm under no illusions — I'm usually the last choice. Not to fall into that maudlin brooding bullshit, but you don't get picked if people don't know you. Or if what they do know of you makes you look like a moody fuck with a bad attitude and the aesthetic to match. But, usually, people have the tact to not say it out loud, you know? The social covenant requires that you don't go blabbing things like that, even if everyone knows it's true.

That's a magic all its own, and Constable had shattered it with a sentence.

Now, I have enough confidence in myself to not usually let that sort of thing bother me. There's no greater authority on my capabilities than me, after all — not about to start second-guessing myself because some bloke I've never heard of kept me off his fantasy footie team. Key word there, though, is *start*.

It felt like every step of this case just made it more and more daunting, painting me as less and less capable of seeing it through. Blind confidence and bollock-crushing bravado had masked those doubts so far, but nothing had really tested that paper-thin facade. Well, plenty had tested it, but nothing *substantial.* Nothing that felt like authority.

Constable was rocking the same sort of authority that Wingard had had, and it was fucking me up.

I'm not pretending I don't have a few hangups to work through here, catch up.

Things had been quiet in the library for a few minutes, everyone taking the time to soak in what Constable had said. Azizi and the others had known it already of course, but it was clear that it had never been *said* to them, just imparted in the way the British are so good at doing. Saying things without saying them, a national pastime. Constable had spent the entire time watching me though, waiting to see how I was going to take it.

'Try not to—' he started.

I cut him off. 'How many times, roughly, have you folded these events back on themselves?'

'Hundreds, possibly thousands,' he said, changing tack far too fast for my liking.

'Must be to rack up the numbers you're suggesting.'

'Some of the incidents are more bloody than others.'

I scrunched up my face. There was a thought brewing, and I was trying to work out if it was a helpful one. 'All rolled back to just one death, the *stitch in time* I guess. It happens but it doesn't happen. Very convenient.'

'I wouldn't call it that,' Constable said. 'The pain lingers, festers. It takes a lot of work to sew the wound shut, even more to sterilise it so it stays that way.'

I sucked my teeth at him. '*Sterilise* it? What does that mean?'

'Well, let me put it this way: we had a list of very competent wizards to work through. And we worked through them all before you. They all died. And yet—'

'I never heard about huge swathes of wizards dropping off the face of the Earth.'

'Exactly,' he said, eyes flashing. 'Because they didn't. Or, rather, they no longer did. They tried, they failed, they died, and then I folded everything in on itself so they never tried and, therefore, never died. Apart from a few bad dreams, they'll probably never know.'

'One and done, that's all they get?'

He shrugged. 'If we want to keep the wounds closed, it is. It's hard enough to tie things off nicely without the added complication of resonating magical auras. It's getting to the point where it's taking the lion's share of my concentration to make sure Monday comes before Tuesday at this school now, no need to over-complicate things.'

'But one kid still dies.'

'Scar tissue on the timeline. It's the best I can do.'

There was *something* important about the fact one kill could never be cleared up then, the infected wound. All those timelines slotted away outside of realities, each one a charnel house of boarding schools, but the first kills were following a pattern. They were the goal, everything else was a bonus — crimes of circumstance.

Yes. That was a good thought. Solid. *Professional*. It was the sort of thought that makes you feel like you know what you're doing, built on the kind of shaky foundations that wouldn't hold up to a chipmunk's fart, let alone any real application of logic. But you can do a lot with that, and I was determined to use it to avoid giving in to self doubt.

Space travel is just falling so fast that you never hit anything, managing to stay functioning when you've got *issues* is very similar.

'Take me back to the beginning,' I said in my best take-charge voice. 'Just the extant victims, the ones that didn't survive your temporal haberdashery.'

'It is my understanding that Azizi gave you a list.'

'He did,' I said, pulling it out. 'But seeing as my best

guess was our killer was doing people in alphabetically, I'm starting to think I need to go over it again. Start at the top.'

Constable reached for the list and time started to turn to porridge. Or jam. Thick and sticky, the magus ground to a halt with his hand reaching out for the paper. His fingers brushed the top of the page before coming to a complete stop, resting there for a second or two before another hand — slender and fair with long, thin fingers — reached over my shoulder and pushed Constable's aside.

'Come on, Millie, this is painful to watch.'

I turned. It was like moving underwater, I could feel the currents in the still air resisting me. 'I aim to displease, Laufeyjarson.'

The trickster god of lies had dressed up for the occasion, though I wasn't sure why. His hair was slicked back and tied behind his head in a tight ponytail, his beard was freshly trimmed and tidied, and he was wearing a suit with the cut of a precious gem, and the scintillating pearlescent colour to match. No tie to hide the button at his throat, instead there was a lozenge of pitted stone with a rune etched into the surface.

'No song and dance today, kiddo,' he said, regarding me. 'This is put up or shut up time. You're drowning out here.'

'I'm doing fine.'

'You're doing shit,' he said. 'And I'm running out of ways to keep your plates spinning while you get yourself together.'

'You're never normally this frank.'

'Never normally this disappointed,' he snapped. 'But I can't watch you turn back to page one and start over without saying something, now can I? This isn't an exam you can resit.'

'Oh, it's an exam now, is it?'

'Of course it's an exam!' In a second he was in close, eyes wide with a dash of rage. Then he was calm again. 'It's always been an exam, and that's not something I've been coy about. *You need to pay attention*.'

I frowned at him. 'You're concerned.'

'Concerned like a father, maybe,' he said. 'Concerned that you are going to waste your potential going around in circles. You're mucking about in a sandpit when there's a whole beach behind you. I'm concerned that you *actually* don't know what you're doing. Tell me, what's the point of your investigation here?'

'Oh, great, the patronising rhetorical questions bullshit. My *actual* dad never had much headway with this, but sure, fill your boots.'

'Humour me.'

'To stop all these murders.'

He balled up his hands in frustration for a moment. 'No. *No no no*. That's the *hook*, the point of impetus. It's not the purpose.'

'And here I was thinking that saving the lives of kids was a noble goal.'

He swatted my point away like it was an annoying fly. 'Eh, the story always ends the same way. The point, as I have told you many times, is in the journey. Making the journey your own, not this boring shit you've been doing.'

'I've been trying to save *fucking* lives, you dickhead,' I shouted. 'Terribly sorry my investigative techniques are too boring for you.'

'Think. Like. A. Runeskald.' He tapped me on the forehead with each word, the air was too thick for me to stop him. 'Not a wizard. Not a detective. If this was a story for one of them, one of them would be here.'

'One of them *is* here,' I said. 'Constable is a magus.'

'He's a twit,' Laufeyjarson snorted. 'Doesn't know what to do so just ensures that he does nothing, and does it slowly. Never solve the problem when there's an opportunity to look flash, that's wizards for you.'

I found myself scrabbling to defend Constable — not out of any sense of loyalty, mind. It was instead drawn from some innate need to tell Laufeyjarson to get fucked, whether he was right or not. In this case, the fact that he *was* right only made it worse.

Asking around, following clues, chasing down leads. That was the *proper* way to do things, and I bloody well bet it was exactly how all the others on Constable's list would have gone about this. Follow the rules, be smart, build things up a step at a time.

And look at where that had gotten them.

I locked eyes with Laufeyjarson. 'What's really going on here?'

'You tell me,' he said, flashing one heart-stopper of a smile. 'You're the *detective*.'

'Nah, I'm in the role of one,' I said. 'And you're in the role of the wise and vague mentor, usually. When we first met, you made an art form out of dancing around your point but now you're here giving me a tough love pep talk. Doesn't fit.'

The smile faltered, then grew to a sinister size. 'This is important.'

'Yes. But *why*?'

'Work it out,' he said, giving me one last flick on the

forehead. It was like a gunshot, slapping me back to reality and making my head spin all at once.

Time was moving again. Constable had grabbed the end of the paper in my hand and was trying to take it from me. My fingers were clamped tight.

Start again? Like I said, that was definitely the smart move, but it was rapidly starting to feel like it wasn't the right one. To be clear, this wasn't all Laufeyjarson's influence either — he's so far up his own arse he could suck on his own uvula, and he's not as smart or as manipulative as he likes to think. But I'd be lying if I said he hadn't given me the push.

Been doing an awful lot of reacting since I'd arrived at this Tory factory. Reacting to the faculty, reacting to the kids, reacting to the evidence other people had collected for me. Awful lot of leads, all handed to me by someone else. Very *procedural*.

And, honestly, not very *me*.

Love a good epiphany, me. People talk about them like they're rare, miracles or something, but you can have one everyday if you get drunk enough the night before. In that moment right there, I was for all intents and purposes sobering up.

I blinked and yanked the paper away from Constable. 'Fuck the list.'

Eat The Rich

'Excuse me?'

'Fuck the list,' I said again. 'I've read the damn thing front, back, and sideways. Nothing useful. Going back to that well is just going to be a waste of time.'

Azizi was looking confused. 'But... You asked for it in the first place.'

I shrugged. 'So? Now I'm saying we bin the fucking thing. I've got a better way to move this forward. I'll just need a few things.'

Constable nodded sagely and crooked a finger. He moved to the edge of the little library clearing and ran that beckoning finger across the spines of a couple of books before selecting one and pulling it from the shelf. 'I keep some magical accoutrements on hand, for emergencies. You're welcome to take your pick, if any will help.'

He went to offer me the book, but I shut him down. 'Yeah, no thanks. I don't need to flick through your copy of the Argos Catalogue for ancient tat. Just give me a ballpoint pen, a fresh packet of chalk, and a pencil sharpener.'

*

Constable had sent Azizi out to grab me the supplies I had wanted, then shown a great deal of restraint by steadfastly refusing to ask me to elaborate on my whimsical request. Dickhead, I was really looking forward to being able to keep the whimsy wagon rolling by being coquettishly evasive.

Once Azizi returned, I took the goods and fucked off back up to the classroom where I'd exploded the ever-loving piss out of an Outsider. Constable might have rolled up time like a snot-encrusted tissue so the rest of the day hadn't happened, but that gross spectacle would still be untouched. What better place to start?

The blood was starting to dry on the floor, halfway through turning that earthy brown that is somehow even more disconcerting than the fresh red it should have been. As a puddle it had spread further than I remembered, but as a drying clot you could track the moisture rolling back towards the centre as the skin on the surface shrivelled away in mock veins. Luckily for me, I only needed a bit.

You guessed it, I was going to do more runes. If you're going to complain about that, just give me the benefit of the doubt a little longer.

See, I know you've watched me work some rune magic before here. Whipping out an old spell or two, going through the motions, and there's very much a place for that sort of thing. Shortcuts don't exist for the sake of being lazy, they exist because we all value a bit of directness once in a while.

But what Laufeyjarson had said had gotten me thinking: he was so *keen* on me being a runeskald, perhaps it was time to really play up the *skald* part.

Mages don't really make their own spells often — their magic is, ultimately, shaped by the scope of their imagination, and the average person's imagination is much more limited than you'd think. Don't believe me? Fire up a dating app and see how quickly you get the same message. Variations on a theme, sure, but a theme everyone shares into.

Fireballs, tracking spells, all that shit. They use foci and incantations to put their mind in the right shape.

Runeskalds make all their own spells. You can share some around, sure, hand over the runic formula, but the good stuff has to come from you. You have to use the runes to shape the universe to your mind.

Which I had been very much not doing, I think we will both agree.

To remedy that, I was going to whip up a nice little spell to stitch the Outsider back together so I could ask him a few questions. Because, fuck it, why not just jump right to the end and ask the bloody bad guy what the hell was going on?

Fuck the smart play, it wasn't working. Let's give the dumb one a try.

Personally, I don't think it counts as necromancy if you're doing it to something from another dimension. That's probably a little bit racist, but considering this guy was flensing a kid, I won't lose any sleep over that. Besides, necromancy is hard. This was surprisingly easy.

I've summoned a lot of wandering ghosts, but this was the first time I had tried to drag something back from beyond the veil. There's resistance there, like trying to push a hard boiled egg through a tennis racket — push too soft and nothing's going to happen, push too hard and the egg's going to implode and get *bits* just *everywhere*. Got to find the right pressure, that's the art of it.

Theoretically.

Being my first shot at this in practice, it went pretty well. Some of that I can put down to the strength of my rune work, though not all of it. My runes were doing a lot of heavy lifting — I'd used a little bit of arcane persuasion to fill the ballpoint with some of what little wet blood was remaining, letting me daub my workings on the wall with it. Maybe it was a bit too heavy metal a choice, but the blood of a victim — and I'm speaking *narratively* here — makes for a great focus if you frame it right.

Eat The Rich

I did most of the runework with my eyes closed. The spell wasn't one I had kept in my back pocket for emergencies, and definitely not one I'd given *any* thought to over the years, so all seeing it would do is give me more reasons to doubt my plan. There's always plenty of opportunity to doubt, not so much when it comes to believing in yourself. If you're set on a plan, best to avoid thinking.

Besides, I didn't need to think, not once I got going. My pen strokes were slow and hesitant at first, but I quickly found myself falling into a rhythm. An actual rhythm, I mean, like I was conducting rather than writing. There was a flow to it, a flourish to each line I was sketching, that hadn't been there before. Magic by way of stream of consciousness.

Once I realised what was going on I found myself reining in the flow, choking it off. That wasn't the plan, but the more I noticed what I was doing, the less I could just *let* it happen. Slowed me down a little, and killed a lot of the excitement that had been building, but I don't think it affected the spell in the end.

When the last rune was complete, I finally opened my eyes to take in my work. It was a goddamned *treatise*, an essay of demands and requests and proposed payments that, when read together, meshed into the spell I had been going for. All it needed now was a spark.

Placing my thumb against the first rune in the sequence, I smudged the line that bound the mote of magic that would power this whole thing. I watched as it dashed through the gap and along the line of runes, dancing and spinning from symbol to symbol, the spell itself reshaping as it passed through each one. Then it hit the end and the door to the room slammed shut.

The temperature started dropping. My breath turned visible, thin crystals of ice started forming on the windows, and the hairs on my arms started to tingle.

Taking the fresh chalk from my pocket, I jammed it into the pencil sharpener and shaved myself a handful of dust. Holding my hand outstretched, I waited as a gentle breeze rose and started to carry the dust from my palm. It blew from my hand and painted a shape in the air in front of me.

The shape of a very tall man with porcelain eyes.

Realisation dawned on its face, knobbly hands reaching up to trace its own expression. 'Curious. You caused me to cease.'

'I blew your fucking head off, you mean,' I said. 'I killed you.'

The temperature started to rise again. 'You ceased my instance. In time, I will return anew.'

Eat The Rich

'Not if I hold you here,' I said, as if I knew what I was talking about.

If the Outsider had nerves, I definitely touched one. 'You cannot.'

'Sure I can. I summoned you back from the dead with a *story*, sunshine. Stories last as long as they need to, and if I need this one to last until the end of time...'

The Outsider's face went blank, which I assume meant it was thinking things through. 'I know this word. This is *extortion*, correct?'

'I suppose.'

'Impeding the work is unacceptable.'

'Then answer some questions for me and I'll let you get back to hitch-hiking your way to the next cycle or whatever it is you do.'

That same blank look fell over his face again, for longer this time. The Outsider's lips, or the thin leathery flaps that served as lips, twitched and quivered as if the thing was talking to itself. All the while, the eyes kept grinding in a soundless circle around the chalky eye sockets.

The lips stopped twitching. 'I will acquiesce.'

'Very big of you,' I said. 'You can even keep pretending

like you had a choice, if it will make you feel better.'

'I am choice,' it said with a thinly contained sneer. 'I am an agent of true freedom.'

'The freedom to have your skin ripped off agonisingly slowly, I suppose.'

'More than that,' it said. 'But ask your questions.'

The temperature was still rising, and I wasn't enjoying that. Ghosts make things cold, as a rule — heat is life, cold is death, at least as far as the rules of this whole *thing* is concerned — so a rising temperature couldn't mean anything good. Probably best I didn't waste any more time than I needed to.

I got right up in the thing's face, ready to read every micro-reaction. 'Who let you in?'

'Inconsequential,' it said, face blank and unflinching.

'I'll decide what is inconsequential, thanks, fuckface.'

The lips pulled back to reveal a flash of razor-sharp teeth. 'The Reaper of Old. He demanded my services, but no contract was ever signed. Once the way was clear, I could attend to my duties.'

'Those duties being murdering school children?'

The Outsider steepled its fingers in thought. 'I would consider it... What is the appropriate word? Ah, yes, *triage.'*

You expect vagueness and the like from bastards like this. It's easier when they are doing it to get on your tits though — much harder to deal with when their brains aren't the same shape as your own. 'Are you joking?'

'I am not from Mirth. Those skills are beyond me. I have but one duty, and that is to pick clean the wounds that fester on the veil. Without me, the infection will ripen.'

The temperature had risen another couple of degrees now. The Outsider was straining against the skin of the spell, pushing back at the energy holding the spirit together. The spell would crack if it kept that up. 'What infection?'

'The school,' it hissed. 'The children are bacteria, borne on waves of effluvia into the world at large. There they fester, spread pestilence, pollute. Their grasp is far-reaching, and those of us from Pragma felt the need to cut out the sickness. Pull it out by the root, purge the incubator.'

Pragma. Mirth. They were new to me, though from the context I was going to hazard a guess that they were planes, or dimensions maybe? I made a note to ask someone with more book learning than I had, maybe they'd have a clue. 'They're goddamned *children*. How can they be a threat to you?'

'Because,' the Outsider said, straining to lean forward and bring its hand up to clutch at me. The spell kept it still, just. 'They are a threat to *you*.'

I dread to think how fast it would have moved had the sheer weight of magic not slowed it down then. As it was, I nearly didn't need the other hand until it was less than an inch from the side of my head, the long fingers fixing to claw at my face. With a scream, I threw myself backwards, landing hard on my back and knocking the wind out of my sails. Adrenaline flared, ready to get me rolling and kicking if the damned thing followed me, but it didn't.

It only had the one lunge in it, and now that it had missed its chance it had nothing left to bear the brunt of the magic. The form of the Outsider was collapsing in on itself.

Without the threat to keep the adrenaline pumping, I had to resort to determination alone to get back up, which I managed, and then angrily limped over to my array of runework that was fuelling the spell. 'Look at that. I get to kill you twice.'

I smudged a rune and the spell ground awkwardly to a halt. The chalk dust that formed the visage of the Outsider fell to the floor and kicked up a small cloud. And that was that, Outsider gone.

Again.

But this time, I had a little more to go on. I had a vector now, sort of.

Now I had a place to *goddamn* start this *properly*.

One (Properly This Time)

If I was going to start acting like a proper runeskald, I figure that counts as a fresh start.

Even so, I *did* need a bit of help. Now that I knew what the Outsiders were up to — or, at least, what they said they were up to — I needed it translated into *Sane Human* rather than *Insane Monster From Another Dimension.* Context would help with that.

Wolfgang and his little brood of two had finished their perimeter sweep long before I found them again, but with no real idea of what to do next had wound up clustered under a tree on the far side of the college. They were watching the kids from afar, and doing so with the sort of silent authority that would convince most people that, in fact, they weren't even there that all. *That over there? That's just a big shadow.*

'I was going to look for you,' Wolfgang said as I approached. 'But I figured you'd find your way back to me when you were done. How did it go, whatever you were doing?'

'Fine. Listen, how good with magic are your little pals

here really?'

Walid and Su-Yin perked up, as if they hadn't been listening before, but Wolfgang didn't give them a chance to speak. 'Fair to middling. I assume you're talking arcane here?'

'Yeah,' I nodded. 'Got an idea that's going to need more juice than I can muster.'

He sat forward. 'Fill me in.'

'Rather not,' I said. 'You'll go getting ideas.'

'What does that mean?'

It means I don't trust you. It means There's something off about you that I don't have time to look into right now, but you better believe I will as soon as I have a chance. 'It means that the fewer strong minds involved in this, the less chance they'll trip over each other and something horrible will go wrong.'

'And if it does,' he said slowly, piecing things together. 'Then I'll still be here to try and pick up after you. That about right?'

'Exactly.'

There was absolutely zero chance he bought that horseshit, but I had been willing to bet he wouldn't call me on it. After all, there were two possibilities with him: one option held that he was on the level, in which case he probably *would* buy what I was saying because that's how people like that think — compliments that aren't, but sound like that might be. The other option was that he was a shady shit, in which case he'd let this play out just to see what I was up to.

He snapped his fingers. 'Su-Yin, go with Ms Thatcher. Help her with whatever she's up to. I've got an idea of my own, but I'll need Walid to help me. Will one do you?'

'More than enough,' I lied. Honestly, for this plan to work, even both of them was unlikely to be enough. No sense in pissing the bed before it's made, though.

Su-Yin shot me a look as she wandered over to my side and slapped me on the shoulder. 'I'm a lot stronger than I look. Where do you need me?'

Bidding the boys a polite, if brusque, farewell, I led Su-Yin away to the first bit of open space I could find that was out of eyesight and earshot of Wolfgang. 'Right, so, there's a magus on the faculty here. Did you know that?'

'No,' she said. 'But then Wolfgang deals with the people. I just do as I'm told.'

'Is that, you know... Healthy?'

She shrugged. 'I've got no complaints.'

Is it bad that, as much as I recognised this was a big old red flag, that sort of mindset was exactly what I needed right now? 'If you say so. Anyway, this magus? He's been folding time in on itself to undo as much of the damage from these attacks as he can, that's why all the Outsider seemed to just piss off out of nowhere. You following?'

'I'm going to assume I'm not supposed to ask questions about things like folding time and just accept that this is completely normal?'

'Exactly.'

'Then yes,' she said. 'Following along completely.'

'I need to see what they're doing.'

'The Outsiders?'

'That's right.'

'They're killing kids, I thought that had been established.'

There may have been something off about Su-Yin, but I did love the way she managed to state the bloody obvious as if it was something I hadn't considered. Like, she *knew* that I was pushing at a bigger point here, but she just had to take the slyest of digs when she had the chance. Her face may have remained deferential the whole time, but there was a tiny twinkle there in her eye, just desperate to shine.

'Yeah, but they don't see it that way,' I said, my gaze zeroing in on her twinkle. 'So I want to see the whole picture, and I don't want to wait for the next time they start slicing someone up to do it. I figure a nicely air-gapped bit of reality should do nicely for that.'

Her face twisted through a number of emotions — mostly flavours of confusion — while she tried to understand what it was I had said. It didn't take her long. 'You want me to shunt you into one of those closed off loops.'

'Exactly,' I said. 'I would have asked the magus, but something tells me he's not going to be open to helping with this. Besides, that would give him a chance to tighten the defences and fuck everything up.'

Su-Yin blinked a couple of times. 'Did you ask for my help because you knew I wouldn't say no, or because you actually need my magic? This sounds like something that could go very wrong, very easily, so—'

'Sure, it's a little reckless, but less so than going over old ground and learning sweet fuck all like Wolfgang wants,' I snapped. 'But, yes, I need your magic for this. And I need to leverage your weird fetish for being bossed around like a shapely marionette. Two things can be true.'

Her expression shimmered for a split second before locking into a chipper and cheerful smile. 'Ok! What do you need from me?'

I filled her in on the details while preparing the space.

Essentially, what I wanted to do was squeeze through the gaps in Constable's little time pockets and see how things had developed. That much I think I've been pretty clear on. The hard part is working out how to actually do that, which means I'm going to get a bit technical. It's fine, take a deep breath and I'll give you a hug on the other side.

Ready?

Right, so, you can mix and match all the different magics easily enough if you know what you're doing, but you usually want to do that at the moment of casting. Swan up after an hour or so and the spell is all confident and secure in itself, it's liable to shit the bed if you go messing about with it and trying to jam a rune in there or something. As a result, breaking into Constable's time pockets like an ASBO nightmare would need arcane magic, and there was no chance I had the skill to pull that off. Hence Su-Yin.

The plus side though? I didn't really need her to *do* anything, just sort of provide a bit of a sheath for my stuff, enough to open the door a crack. Once my fingers were in, metaphorically, I could pry that bastard open and slip inside. If I was lucky, she'd be able to hold it ajar long enough for me to get back, too.

I guess I did need her to do *one* very important thing, then.

Su-Yin kept insisting she had no problem with any of this, that she had more than enough juice to spare, and was downright enthusiastic to get started once I told her the nitty gritty. I wasn't even enthusiastic about this, and it was my idea, but her unbelievably bubbly glee was a little infectious. By the time everything was arranged, I almost believed that things were going to go nice and smoothly.

'You know what you're doing?' I asked, more for my own benefit.

The space we had picked was the bedroom of the first victim — the kids were all in class, so it didn't take much in the way of stealth to sneak in. Half the dumb idiot babies didn't seem to know they could lock their doors. Su-Yin was standing beside me while I sat on the dead boy's bed.

Without taking her eyes off of me, she started plucking at the arcane weave with her fingers, warming up. 'A crack in the door. Simple enough.'

'In theory.'

'In theory,' she repeated with that gleeful grin.

'Just don't pull too hard, we've not trying to rip the bastard open. And not—'

'Not too softly or it'll snap shut and you'll be stuck,' she interrupted. 'I listened. I always listen.'

'My bad,' I said, then took a long, deep breath. 'Little nervous.'

'Are you sure this is the best idea?'

Of course I wasn't sure. How could I have been sure? This was an incredibly dangerous and stupid idea. There were so many other less direct options I could take, clues to follow, but as we all know I had already decided that I was done with all that shit. 'It's the coolest idea, so it's the best idea.'

'I really hope you don't die.'

'Girl, me too.'

The pair of us couldn't help but laugh. Just a soft little giggle, burning off the surface tension, but sorely needed. Reaching up, I squeezed her hand softly, hoping against hope she'd squeeze back and give me a bit of wordless reassurance. She did.

One more deep breath. I pulled another stick of chalk

from my pocket and set to work shaving it into dust again, letting it coat my hands and fingers. Then I gave Su-Yin the nod and watched as she started to work her magic, glistening strands of flamingo-pink energy knitting around her fingers. One by one, her magic snapped out, drawn to the residue of the magus' own spell, and latched onto the seam.

I hadn't taken Su-Yin for an expert magician, especially considering her age, but she was really showing me up here. If I wanted, she probably could have worked out how to do the whole thing on her own. Might take longer, though.

Once her magic was firmly latched to the seam, I waited for her to drag it open just a little before I made my move. Clapping my hands together, I kicked up a cloud of dust and quickly started etching sigils into it — I wasn't even sure this would work, if I'm honest, but the moment I started I could feel the power thrum into being in each smoky swirl. Drawn into the opening, my spell lodged there, a wedge to force the crack wider with each blow of the metaphorical hammer. I sketched out a few more sigils, each one forcing the mouth of the opening a little wider, until I could feel it creaking against the desire to either snap shut or fracture entirely.

I wafted away what was left of the dust. 'Right, that'll probably do. You good?'

Su-Yin almost went for a thumbs up, then thought better and merely nodded. 'I can hold it. Just so I know: how long do I need to hold it for?'

'Fucked if I know,' I said. 'Willing to lay odds that time is going to flow weirdly inside a little pocket dimension thing. Just hold it until everything goes tits up, then slam it shut.'

'Understood.'

Flat obedience, I knew she'd follow through if it came down to a question of me or everyone else here. Worst came to the worst, I'd rather I was stuck in there than all those horrors got spat back out into the world — something you can cover up, while far from ideal, was at least better than a complete bloodbath. There's, like, a scale of terror you've got to think about here.

I rolled up my sleeves and threw myself into the seam.

*

There was a storm brewing. The air was thick and humid, it had the damp smell which brings down moods and aggravates mental health conditions. Off in the distance somewhere, a wind was picking up, whipping around the stones of the buildings in a tired scream.

Technically, the buildings were the college. They were all the right shapes, had the doors and the windows in the right places, all the little pathways that snaked across the communal areas. But you can always tell when everyone in a building is dead, even before you step foot inside — if you're not topping up the life force of a building regularly, it settles and becomes *too real*. The world washes round it like a rock in a stream, making it a thing life happened *around*.

Of course, the fact that my arrival had been loud as hell and no-one had come to see what was going on might have informed my decision a little as well.

I picked a building at random, hoping to find something I could work with. Given what I knew, I wasn't holding out hope for any survivors but someone I could question would have made me very happy. More likely, I'd run into an Outsider or two and have to try and come up with a way to get them to talk to me before they tried to peel my flesh off like a pasty banana.

There were *so many* of the ugly bastards, though. I passed room after room packed with them, folded up and freakishly still in a way that brought to mind those massive fuck-off spiders that show up in summer and just *lurk*. Not an image I wanted in my head, but there you are.

Some of them were still moving, albeit sluggishly. Every few rooms I would spot one staring down at its hands, watching its fingers move as a wet string of viscera stretched and squashed with the movement. Typical horrifying monster stuff, really. So much for their noble triage bullshit.

Before long, voices started to make their way down the hall towards me. They were little more than ragged whispers, but they carried and I managed to follow them all the way back to the source. I moved carefully, practicing this sneaky way of walking I'd heard about in a videogame — if you're interested, you walk toe-heel instead of heel-toe — and hoped against hope that it wasn't the sort of bullshit that sounds impressive but doesn't actually work.

It seemed to work; nothing came to kill me.

The voices were coming from a trio of Outsiders that were camped out outside the bland navy blue doors of the admin offices. Two of them were crouched inside a cage of their own long limbs, watching contentedly as the third was carving intricate designs into the remaining flesh of someone I really hoped was very much dead.

'Has any progress been made?' asked one of the sitting ones. 'The mortality rate approaches its zenith.'

The one that was working on the corpse tutted loudly, continuing its *carving*. 'It is confounding. There simply must be a cause we can identify, a seed that can be extracted. I have looked deep, time and again, and found nothing.'

'We have all looked,' the first one said. 'Perhaps it is time to consider that there is nothing to find?'

There was a loud crack and a crunch as the second thrust his hand into the chest cavity of the corpse without the fluid grace he had been using before. 'There *must* be something. The very fact that you would ask that question proves it. The infection spreads to you, colours your thinking, pollutes it.'

Glacially slow, the first unfolded up to its full height, its face locked with that of the second. 'You are displaying frustration. Is it not you that has been infected? To speak threats to your own is a greater sign of pollution than a mere question.'

The second wrenched its hand free from the corpse, dispelling whatever magic was holding it aloft. It squared up against the first, both of them bristling with barely contained rage now.

'Enough,' It was the third. It spoke quietly, calmly, and with a chill of the grave about it. 'This infection tests us all, but it cannot take us unless we allow it. Do you intend to give it leave to do so?'

The first let out a low grumble. 'I do not.'

'Nor I,' said the second.

The third's head slumped back into the slackened stasis it had been in before. 'Then *do not*.'

The other two shrank back, and the one that had been elbow-deep in the corpse went back to work. The bastard didn't do so without complaint, though — if it had been human, I would have said it was sulking, pouting and making a big deal out of everything. You know the type. I *am* the type, on occasion. Never done so with quite that level of brazen menace though.

I did my best to creep closer, sticking to whatever cover there was — which is to say not much. The Outsiders may have caused a lot of damage to anything with a spleen, but they hadn't seemed to be concerned about smashing up the architecture. Very conscientious that way, but it did mean a lot of me skulking behind bins and huddling up behind potted plants and fire extinguishers like a cartoon.

If they had been looking for me, I have to believe they would have seen me. But they weren't expecting any survivors, that much was clear, so they weren't at their best.

The third Outsider's eyes grated pensively inside its skull. 'How many samples are left?'

'Few,' the amateur surgeon said, accompanied by a wet crunch. 'Not enough to isolate the cause of the pandemic.'

Samples? Did that mean there were some survivors maybe, prisoners? That made a certain kind of sense — they didn't kill Gracemere straight away, and the other victims had been immobilised long before they died, so it wasn't entirely unexpected that they would have a methodical approach. Wasn't as if anyone could go anywhere anyway, right?

Carefully, I crept back down the corridors and slipped out of sight again. If I wanted to get an understanding of what was going on here, survivors were going to be a much better source than eavesdropping. If I could find them.

On reflection, they wouldn't have been too hard to find. All I had to do was think like a big gross murdering monster, put myself in their shoes, and work backwards. Thing is, I really didn't want to get into that habit. This meant it took me longer, but I got to see a lot more of the aftermath.

I worked really hard to try and make that sound like a positive thing in my head.

I found the survivors by looking for the guards. Most of the Outsiders had gone into a sort of strange hibernation like the ones in the rooms, but as I moved around the buildings I found a few pockets of activity like the trio I had dropped a few eaves on. They were equally as frustrated and lax as each other, easy enough to avoid.

But then I'd spotted *four* of the fuckers, and they were *alert*.

I mean, actually, what I had spotted was a whole host of kids all corralled against the border wall of the compound, the Outsiders lurking around them like big spooky lamp posts. That didn't really go with the flow of what I was saying, though.

Anyway, these spooky bitches were again not so concerned with what was going on outside the group, but they were deeply fixated on the kids they had left. It was hard to tell how many they had in their little pen — maybe a dozen, possibly two — but no matter how they had rounded them up it had clearly broken the poor buggers. I didn't need to get close to see all the fight was gone from them, they didn't even have it in them to cry. All they could do was sit there and wait for death, like cattle.

Pretty sure something irrevocably shrivelled away inside me at seeing that. Not sure what it was, but I definitely felt a lot less whole.

One of the kids stood up and started to walk across the pen with purpose. The guards didn't give a fuck at first, but they did start to take notice when the kid reached his destination and smashed another child in the face with the heel of his shoe. The second kid fell back limply, not even putting up a fight, and the first went down on top of him, shouting something I couldn't make out from that distance.

The guards closed in, but didn't intervene. I took that as an opportunity to get closer — a lot more cover here, what with there being actual trees to hide behind — and managed to get within twenty metres by the time the Outsiders decided to break up the scrap.

One of them had the first kid by the shoulder, lifting him up with ease and dragging him backwards. Two of the others watched the docile flock while the third knelt over the kid who had just had his teeth pushed in. It was the quietest playground ruck I'd ever seen — only the instigator was saying anything, the poor lad bleeding on the ground wasn't even groaning.

'Get off me,' he was yelling. 'I *command* you to let me go.'

The Outsider dutifully released him. The kid immediately tried to dash back into the fray, the bony fingers seizing him before he could get three steps. 'Cease.'

The kid screamed with rage, lashing out against the Outsider's grip. It seemed unconcerned and held him until he tired himself out. He sagged, defeated. 'Fine. I'll stop. I'll stop...'

The fingers uncurled. 'Your bloodline gives you authority, Little Reaper, but we cannot allow this to interfere with our duty. Kindly remove yourself.'

The kid muttered something, then turned and started to walk away from the pen. Just totally free to go, didn't even need to fucking jog. Just a chill and calm — for a given value of calm, all things considered — stroll out of the group and off along the wall.

Right in my direction.

I'd been a bit too cocky and moved too far forward. I had a tree to hide behind — a trusty little tree — but it wasn't much of one. It worked well for masking my silhouette for a passing glance, but the kid was looking right at me as he walked.

I saw his face change at the exact moment he spotted me — the eyes widening, the mouth falling open — and realised that behind the grime and the dried blood was a face I recognised.

The Little Reaper.

Bertie De'Ath.

Two (Or Thirteen, I guess? Whatever)

I didn't give De'Ath time to sound the alarm before I turned tail and fucking legged it for the seam. No looking back, no listening for the sounds of long strides and grinding eyeballs, just the sort of sprint you can only manage when your heart is beating like a bastard.

My exit wasn't far, but it certainly felt like it was miles away. Every step I was certain I could feel bony fingers tickling at the back of my neck, tempting me to turn around and take a look. I focused my gaze on the rip in reality and stayed the course until I was close enough to throw myself through it.

'Close it, close it, *closeitcloseitcloseitcloseitCLOSEIT!*' I squealed articulately as I face-planted the floorboards.

There was a loud snap behind me and the crisp smell of ozone. I rolled over and looked up into the concerned face of Su-Yin, wisps of magic dissolving in her hand. 'I closed it. You ok?'

'Just going... to need... a minute,' I choked out between

breaths. Being skinny does not automatically mean you are fit and healthy, so keep that in mind when you try to understand how knackered such a short sprint had left me.

Su-Yin lowered herself down onto the floor next to me, legs crossed. 'Guessing things were about as bad in there as you expected?'

'Mhm,' I managed, along with a backup nod just in case. 'Pretty bleak.'

'You get something useful, though?'

'I got something,' I said. 'Whether it's useful, that remains to be seen. Good work on holding shit open, by the way.'

She smiled. 'You made it sound like it was going to be hard. It's the delicate stuff I struggle with, but I've always been good at the brawny business. That's what Master Wolfgang sees in me, I guess.'

The utter reverence she put on his title was never going to stop making my skin crawl. Best to just ignore it. 'I need to have a word with someone. Want to stick around and play good cop to my trash cop?'

'Sure. Who we looking for?'

A cloud shifted outside, shining sunlight directly through the window and into my eyes. I winced. 'Little

Tory tosspot called Bertie De'Ath.'

'You think he's got something to do with all this?' she said. She shuffled an inch to the left and blocked the sun from my face. It gave her a charming little halo effect.

'The Outsider I *had a word with* mentioned a reaper. The ones trapped in that hell dimension there called him the *little* reaper. Figure that's worth looking into.'

'Bit on the nose, isn't it? Calling him *reaper* because his surname is *De'Ath*.'

I shrugged. 'Not as on the nose as the kid called De'Ath being responsible for a whole lot of corpses. Nominative determinism is a very real force in the upper classes, I think.'

She giggled and held out a hand to help me up. 'Going to go class-by-class until you find him?'

'That was what I was thinking, but...' I trailed off, taking her hand and letting her yank me up to my feet. It was like I'd strapped a rocket to my wrist and had it jerk me upright. Winded me a little, if I'm honest. 'No, I think we don't go straight at him. He's not in a rush yet, we've got time. When I go at him, I want to floor the little fucker, not let him get a chance to squirm.'

There was that feeling again, the sensation that there

was something really important just completely absent from the picture I was painting in my head. *The Old Reaper*, that's what the Outsider had said, right? They'd shown some deference to De'Ath, but he clearly wasn't the *Old* Reaper. Family connection then, more than likely, which would be complicated.

Besides, I needed to get off the campus. The hellish time pocket hadn't looked so very different, but I think that just made it worse. It's easy to tell yourself you're not looking at the same shit if there are chunks taken out of the wall or innards unfurled like net curtains everywhere — you know, spot-the-difference shit — but it's much harder to shift when everything looks broadly the same.

'Just tell me where to go,' Su-Yin said patiently.

'We'll start at the records office.'

*

Despite boarding on site, little Bertie's home wasn't all that far away from the college. I slipped out without the chauffeur this time — didn't want word of my excursion getting back to *the little reaper*, after all — and let Su-Yin drive. The back of her little VW camper was bulging with luggage and nick-knacks, but the front was spacious enough.

It did have a lingering smell of old socks, though.

The De'Ath estate made up the majority of the nearby village of Goule, which again seemed very much on the nose to me. Then again, if your name is *De'Ath* it would probably be rude not to live in a place that sounds like some undead horror. Likewise, if you didn't grow up and get some sort of doctorate you were a tit.

Anyway, Goule was made up of like three houses — servant's quarters, Su-Yin reckoned — and then about four hundred cubic fuck-miles of fence that served to keep the great unwashed masses so far from the manor that the house was a little nub on the horizon. The main gate was very imposing, hammered out of the thick, chunky iron designed by Victorian blacksmiths to repel anyone who'd never known the decadent taste of fermented ostrich egg. There was an intercom with a camera, an empty shack for a guard, and a small metal sign riveted to the tastefully — and very deliberately — overgrown brickwork of the gate arch:

You're not welcome, unless you're welcome.

'I was kind of hoping for a cheerful goth family,' Su-Yin said. 'You know, like the Addams family or the Munsters?'

I smirked. 'Hell, if I had this much money I wouldn't want to have to deal with people either.'

'Yeah, well, you're an introvert,' she said. 'Talking to ghosts feels like something an introvert would love doing. Should I buzz?'

'No, better not,' I said, frowning at the little camera over the intercom. 'They won't let us in anyway. No point waking them up. I want to go over the fence.'

I watched Su-Yin's face as her eyes mapped the wall. Bless her, she was really trying to find a way to say something supportive about my idea, and the cogs in her head were getting gummed up.

See, the wall was big, obviously. It was a *proper* wall. But the size wasn't the problem. Even the razor wire at the peak wasn't the problem — the usual coils had been carefully coiffured into a beautiful filigree that ironically made it much easier to snip out nice chunks. No, the issue was that the fence had such a massive electric current running through the ironwork that even being a few metres away was close enough to have our hair frizzing like Cousin It in a tumble dryer.

There's your second Addams Family reference. I'll rein it in now.

I learned a lot of things from Wingard — pretty much all of it was magical shit. The non-magical shit, though, that's largely self-taught. Not to perpetuate the stereotype that people who grow up in the inner city are utter reprobates who eat, breathe, and shit crime, but I may happen to know a little about breaking into a house. Enough to be dangerous in any case.

You need to be a little dangerous when it comes to dealing with an electric fence. If I'd been in the correct wizardy mood, I'd have given Su-Yin the whole lecture about how you really want to lean into the *breaking* part of *breaking and entering*. But I wanted to seem impressive, so you're getting it instead. Be thankful it's the short version.

The *very* short version, though, is this: electric fences are great, but they tend to be owned by people who just fucking love privacy. Also, those people have to pay for that electricity, as much as they would love to live in their Objectivist dreamworld. This means energy meters, and that means meters that need reading sometimes, and the whole point of a big fence is to stop weird strangers from mooching around your stupid garden.

Ipso facto, all the important electrical shit is going to be outside the walls where any smart-arse with a bitching hairdo and boots bigger than her ego can kick the shit out of them. If you're lucky, you only have to go as far as the first bush near the gate.

Sometimes you might have to go as far as the nearest substation — which I grant you is stretching my cocky definition a bit but not so much it breaks.

The De'Ath family kept theirs behind the empty guard hut, is the takeaway here.

'The real skill comes in knowing just *how* to kick things,' I said to Su-Yin as she pried off the protective cover from the electrical box. 'It's more stomping, really.'

She watched as I brought my heel down on the fragile dials and counters and circuit boards inside the box, her arms crossed. 'There is absolutely no way this is going to work.'

'Maybe you're right,' I said, the crunch of a very important bit of kit punctuating my words nicely. 'It wouldn't work if someone else was doing it, but I'm blessed. No-one knows how to kick shit quite like me.'

Plus, I'd etched some runes into my boots to disrupt things if I had cause to kick them — electrical circuits, testicles, anything really. Su-Yin didn't need to know that though.

After a couple more stomps, the sizzle from the fence died away. Su-Yin ran a hand over her hair, brushing down the strands that had really taken to the electricity in the air. 'Okay, fine, well done. But did you happen to bring some wire cutters for the razor wire up there?'

I started to take off my jacket. 'Not as such, but I figure I can just throw this—'

Su-Yin, apparently not one to be upstaged, was already halfway up the ironwork. The index and middle fingers on her right hand were wreathed in that same flamingo-pink magic as I'd seen her wielding before. Reaching up, she casually snipped at the metal with those fingers a couple of times and pulled away a great chunk of the wire.

She dropped the wire to the floor and hoisted herself up onto the top of the fence, straddling it. 'Sorry. Needed to feel useful. Want a hand?'

'If you're offering.'

Reaching down, she once again hoisted me up with such strength that my shoulder felt like it was going to pop out. She dragged me up, over, and deposited me softly down on the far side before leaping down herself. It was all very smooth, very impressive.

It got me thinking things. Things like *huh*, and *oh dear, it's happening again.* Then I had to blink a couple of times, clear my throat, and compose myself.

If Su-Yin noticed, she did a good job of not mentioning it. Instead, she gave me exactly long enough to catch myself before breaking the silence. 'Right then, boss. What now?'

'Now we head for the house, I guess,' I said, shielding my eyes from the sun and surveying the scene. 'Bastard's got a bloody big garden, though.'

'Think they make the servants walk it everyday?'

Eat The Rich

'I think they *try*,' I said. 'Follow me.'

The garden was flat and featureless, a perfect monument to order that boring bastards seem to think is an art form. No way that was all done by hand, not if it was going to stay this pristine. And the sort of people who work for boring bastards like that wouldn't want to be walking to do the bloody shed every morning, and would look for any excuse to piss all over that order.

The gardener had hidden the mower well, but not *too* well. From a distance, the carefully placed shrubbery that lined the bottom of the wall masked the little ride-on nicely enough, but once you got closer the shiny green plastic body of the thing stood in stark contrast to the deeper, verdant leaves.

'How could you possibly have known that was here?' Su-Yin asked as I rolled the mower out of the hedge. 'You been here before?'

'Places like it,' I said. 'But mostly it's knowing people. Everyone's as lazy as they can be at work, so once you know the sort of places the people in charge are going to be looking—'

'You know the places they *won't* be looking.'

'And that's where you find all the good shit,' I said, grinning.

I was bent over the mower now, stomach flat against the seat, fishing around for the keys in the gaps between the body and the chassis. Given the need, I could probably have forced the thing by wedging a bottle cap in the keyhole — the keys are more for safety than security on these things — but what had the gardener done to me to earn such a fate? No, the keys would be there, tucked away somewhere.

Just needed to reach the buggers.

'Can I help you, ladies?'

It took a moment for it to register that this was not Su-Yin speaking. A bit embarrassing, I know. Then I looked up and saw a man in a guard uniform a few metres behind us. Middle aged and with greying hair, he had a build that screamed *former military* and a haircut to match. There was a travel mug steaming away in one hand, and a taser in the other.

He was making a show of keeping the weapon lower than the mug.

I pushed myself upright again, then turned and sat on the seat of the mower. 'We're new. Work experience week, you know what I mean?'

'I like that one,' he said. 'As lies go, that's a good one.'

Su-Yin cocked her head to one side. 'How do you know

it's a lie?'

The guard took a long, slow sip of his coffee. 'Because you're both too old for starters. Plus, there is a minimum IQ requirement for this job, and I managed to just squeak on by. So, the way I see it, you've got two options. One: you scarper and no-one says anymore about it. Two: I have to remove you, and quite a bit more will end up being said about it than any of us would like.'

'I look too old to pass for school age?' I asked. 'Thank fuck. Might finally stop getting ID'd at the pub.'

I watched for his reaction to see if I could get a read on him, work out how I was going to play this. He turned his eyes on me to reply, but before he could he was hitting the grass like a sack of shit.

Somehow, and I still have no idea how, Su-Yin had taken that microscopic opening and turned it into a full breach. He'd been good enough to see her coming even without looking, but she had managed to be better, swivelling around his side and flipping him over her hips, twisting his arm and snatching the taser from it before he even finished falling. I heard the wind leave him as he landed, followed by the jagged attempt to suck something back into his lungs as she fired the taser into his chest.

Never actually seen someone tased before. Bit horrible.

Bit sexy.

Su-Yin shocked him until he was groaning, then tapped him on the forehead with a glowing finger. 'Nighty night.'

The guard was out like a light.

'Jesus cartwheeling Christ, Su!'

She shrugged. 'Was that wrong?'

'Little bit,' I said. The guard was smoking, but at least he was alive. 'Little bit. I guess it solved a problem though?'

Her finger stopped glowing. 'Should be out long enough for us to do what we're here to do. Pretty reliable, learned it back when I was a babysitter.'

'The magic, right? Not the tasering?'

'Depended on the kid,' she said and winked.

Not wanting to waste any more time, I spun around again and finally located the keys. I fished them out and started up the mower. There was only one seat, but Su-Yin managed to get comfortable on the back, adapting a technique I think I recognised from bombing around on the back of a friend's bike when I was a little younger.

Got my own bike now, don't need to share.

Eat The Rich

Driving the mower across the grass wasn't too much faster than walking, but it was a great deal less exhausting. It took ten minutes of straight driving — and only a little harmless vandalism of the patterns on the grass — to get close enough to the house. We didn't drive right up to the door, not wanting to announce our arrival or anything, but we got close enough that we could spot movement in a few of the windows.

'There's more than just De'Ath inside,' I said. 'Was kind of hoping the place would be empty and full of cobwebs.'

'Just the old man rotting away in a rocking chair, all prepped for interrogation?'

'Yeah. Think you've got the juice to *nighty night* anyone who might count as a complication?'

'Am I here to be the muscle?' she said.

I laughed. 'That wasn't my original plan, but you do seem to be good at it.'

'Well, don't get carried away. Only got so much of my fairy dust to sprinkle around. The more people I put under, the less potent the magic.'

Made sense, at least so far as I understood arcane magic. Only so much space in your head to hold a spell, and the more you were holding the harder it was. Besides, I didn't want to go relying on someone else's magic unless I absolutely had to, and there was always an alternative.

I frowned up at the windows, watching the movement inside. 'Big house like this, how many family members you reckon we're looking at compared to guards and staff?'

'I reckon the whole thing is guards and one old coot in the most difficult to reach room, just because.'

See, Su-Yin wasn't a natural pessimist. She had to work to come up with a fuck-you scenario like that — you could tell because in her situation De'Ath was still on site. Being that I am adept in pessimism, I was aware that you can't go working on assumptions. You'll be wrong.

'I'm going to take a look. You stay here, I want to do some sneaking.'

'Sneaking?' she said. 'We just drove a noisy lawnmower across a flat and empty garden. They will know we're here by now.'

I was still watching the windows. 'Some might have, but no-one important. If someone important had seen us, we'd know about it. As it stands, I think everyone who *has* spotted us has just assumed it's someone else's problem.'

'That *sounds* like bullshit,' she said.

I rolled my eyes. 'If people cared, we wouldn't have gotten this far in. We had a long trek over open ground to get here, plenty of time for people to come and kick us out. Absolutely no way they don't know we're here.'

'But you said—'

'I wanted to put your mind at ease, didn't I?' I snapped. 'Them not knowing we're here is a lot less menacing than them knowing and not doing anything.'

'I guess,' she said, frowning.

I nodded as sagely as I could. 'I *know*. It's either their arses hanging out or ours, I figure one of those is better to hope for than the other.'

'Because if they've got the drop on us, nothing we can do anyway?' she said. I could see the nascent migraine starting to form, all from trying to get her head around my logic. 'I guess that makes sense. Sort of.'

Just another sign that someone has seriously fucked with your head then, I thought. 'See if you can put the mower out of sight just in case.'

An impossible job, all things considered, but I wanted Su-Yin out the way for the next bit. It was going to get a little bit *uncool*, and it would be even more tragically uncool if she was close enough to see it.

Creeping low, hoping to stay out of sight, I made my way to the front door. It was as obnoxious as you'd expect; a huge oaken thing that would have looked more fitting barring the entrance to a castle. De'Ath manor had many similarities with castles, but if you wanted to have a stonking great door like that and not have it look stupid, have fewer windows.

There was a huge knocker in the centre of the door — no laughing at the back, please. It was gaudy and I loved it. The iron had been carefully molded into the shape of a screaming gargoyle, its tongue wrapped around the top of the knocker and working as the hinge. I slammed the thing on the door a couple of times and it made a pleasingly deep sound.

I could *feel* it vibrate through the house.

By the time the door opened, I was gone — I'd thrown myself into one of the privets that flanked the doorway. I didn't get a good look at the man who opened the door, but I heard him grumble and mutter to himself as he looked around, spotted Su-Yin in the distance, and shuffled off to intercept her, leaving the door wide open.

Ding-dong Ditch is often overlooked as a way to sneak into a house, probably because doing so requires a sacrifice. It's not like I was selling her out or anything — what was he going to do, give her a stern talking to? — and she had already shown she was more than capable of taking care of herself. But the best distraction is one that doesn't know they are the distraction, and I needed a distraction if I was going to go snooping around.

Ducking into the house, I closed the door behind me and set about looking as though I belonged. This was another tip from the Jameson Parker school of fucking about and finding out, namely that you can get away with a lot more than you'd think if you just carry yourself like you belong wherever you are. Granted, a tiny goth disasterpiece was never going to match the aesthetic of the place, but that was why I needed the distraction.

I spotted the servants quickly enough, beavering away dutifully, but their attention was wandering towards the windows. I'd timed my knock perfectly; Su-Yin had been perfectly framed in the windows, giving the staff a prestige view of her argument with the gentleman who had answered the door. She already had him by the throat.

This left me with a lot of time to casually search the De'Ath manor, disgustingly large as it was. It had four floors, and the lower three seemed to be largely devoted to being *pristine.* No-one lived on these floors, that became apparent very quickly. You can clean a place everyday, but if you *live* in it there are going to be signs. Even the most incentivised cleaner is going to struggle to get out every last biscuit crumb, each speck of dust floating in a sunbeam. De'Ath's crew had managed it.

The top floor, however, that was the living space. It was basically a whole separate apartment, though still a fuckton nicer than any I had ever set foot in. It also seemed to be the dumping ground for the rest of the building's dust and cobwebs — it looked like a layer of grey snow had settled over everything, bar a small but well-trodden pathway through the centre to one of the rooms in the back.

Obviously, I followed it.

The path led to another heavy door, this one a more modern design than the others downstairs. It was one of those faux-wooden fire doors you get in hotels and hospitals and care homes, the kind that always looks a little incongruous no matter where its put. It wasn't locked, and I pushed it open slowly — couldn't have done it fast even if I had wanted to, the self-closing mechanism was extremely resistant.

The spells came in like machinegun fire, rattling down the wall above me towards my head. If the caster's aim had been better, I'd have been hit before I could blink, but as it was I had time enough to bring up a shield on instinct to absorb the shots that would have hit me.

When I brought the shield down, I was greeted by the hacking giggle of a very old man, staring at me from a padded leather armchair. Only one finger was raised from the arm of his chair, though it lowered back down as he spoke. 'An instinctual response. Enough training to survive, not enough to thrive. Puts you better off than most.'

'You nearly took my fucking head off!'

'You're in my house.'

My blood was burning with arcane magic that was demanding to be cast somewhere, but the advantage of not having much talent is that shit like that can't whisper in your ear so easily. 'Well, I needed a word. About wee Bertie.'

'Ah, of course,' the old man said, shuffling in his seat a little. 'I must admit I expected this visit from the moment he told me about you, Millicent Thatcher. Your reputation has preceded you.'

'What reputation is that?'

'The reputation of someone that may well be worth knowing, one day,' he said. He pushed himself up to his feet, a movement that was unsettlingly sprightly for a man of his years. 'Harecourt De'Ath.'

He took a few steps closer and held out a hand. I eyed it suspiciously. 'Awfully welcoming of you, seeing as not ten seconds ago you were trying to blast my head off.'

'Obligation,' he said. 'I knew you'd have the moxie to survive, but I couldn't allow you to think you can break into my house without any consequences. Now, come along, young lady. Won't you shake a poor sinner's hand?'

'I'd rather not. Got some questions to ask you, though.'

Harecourt's fingers closed like vines, they might as well have bloody *creaked*. Then he withdrew his hand and sat down with much less gusto than he had when he stood up. 'Smart. Very well, ask what you're here to ask. I expect you've got a lot of questions about *my friends from the other side*.'

Fourteen (Fuck it, we'll go back to normal, it's less confusing)

'I have made many a deal with many a devil,' De'Ath said. 'Not literal devils, but close enough, one supposes.'

I had brushed the dust off of one of the other chairs in the room and taken a seat, making sure my back was to the wall and I was facing the door. 'So you don't even deny that you're the one who invited the Outsiders in?'

'Why would I deny it? I made them a very compelling offer.'

'Yeah, see, that's where I'm drawing a blank,' I said. 'I get why a wilted old raisin like you would want to make some grubby deals, but I can't work out which one you'd think to make here.'

He lent forward in his chair. Something creaked, though I couldn't say whether it was the furniture or the old man's bones. 'My, my, my, you are a little behind. I'll be direct, for your benefit: I was looking for partners in my long-term endeavour to keep you in your place.'

'You fucking what?'

'Not you personally, you understand,' he said. 'People like you. The ones of lesser breeding, of lower class, of *insignificance*.'

I felt my spirit leave my soul in disappointment. 'Oh, so it's typical classist bullshit? I was hoping for something cool!'

'And there we see it, the problem with your kind but writ small: lack of curiosity. The chips you have stacked upon your shoulders weigh you down so that you can only see your feet. Can you *imagine* how bad that would be for the country, or even the world, if you were left unchecked?'

'Bad for your bank balance, maybe.'

His demeanour changed, shifting towards an almost nostalgic glee. 'Did you know that there has been a De'Ath at that college from the moment it was founded? It's true, an unbroken line right through to Bertie. We are the *foundation* of this area. It's a privilege but a duty too, to make sure the future rulers of the country are prepared, we steward them to greatness. The changes in circumstance in recent years have altered the establishment to the detriment of this goal, but such is the way of money.'

'Poor people got in and started ruining things by simply existing in your private rich twat playhouse?'

He sniffed. 'Not poor in the way you mean it. I don't care about the financial in itself, I care about the *moral*. They are *morally* poor, and they need removing. I was content at first to force them out the old fashioned way, but then that damned Dee Society was founded. Subversive. Rebellious. They drove me to this.'

'Not really seeing the connection in all this moaning, mate,' I said.

'If there is one thing worse than the fundamentally lack of curiosity in the lesser classes, it is the poisoned curiosity of those very same troglodytes when directed somewhere they have no business of treading. They are opening doors that are not meant for them.'

'Magic? You're talking about *magic?*'

You can't swing a cat in my neck of the woods without hitting a racist or a bigot or some manner of twat that hates you because of how you look. What I'd never properly run into was a S*orcerer:* a blood purist that grew out of old money and older bloodlines, so far up their own arseholes that they decided it was a good idea to try and stratify wizard society.

I'd never run into them because they were the first ones Whitehall had dealt with during the war. So cocky and full of beans, they were invariably the first ones to try stand up and place themselves at the head of the snake. We've got our fair share of Wizard Hitlers, as I understand it, but the ones that lasted long enough to warrant more than a footnote always kept themselves confined to *us and them* politics.

The sort of people who ended up called Sorcerers liked to go a little further. They ended up in the realm of *us and them, and them, oh and them too, yep, that one over there,* **oh definitely them,** *I'd be embarrassed if my child was one of* **those***, just keep going and we'll tell you when to stop.*

De'Ath nodded sagely. 'The *correct application* of magic. We are responsible for so much more than we see, and it is up to those of us with the ability to bear the weight for those who are ill-suited to the task.'

'Oh good, you want to throw some paternalism in there too? I've got to say, your personal philosophy is *delicious*, mate. Really loving this.'

'So flippant. Fine. I shall be even more direct. We as a species are fundamentally obliterating life in other planes with our actions. Want to be flippant about that?'

'I want you to cite your fucking sources, that's what I want.'

'The Outsiders are my sources.'

He reached a hand up slowly and made a small gesture. A book dislodged itself from a shelf behind him and floated over into his palm. It was an old and very heavily battered journal, bound in faded leather and held shut by a leather strap. The strap had been tied into a tight knot, one too strong to unpick, so De'Ath simply unhooked it from its moorings, slipping it through a cut in the leather.

Flicking through a few pages, he turned the book around and offered it to me. Curious, I took it off him. 'What's this shit?'

'The expedition journal of my grandfather,' he said. 'And his before him. Explorers, one and all. Look, they tracked the changes in the realms they crossed.'

I scanned the page. It was, indeed, a series of observations about what appeared to be other planes. It was hard to read — different hands had scrawled all over the page, correcting the previous author and then being corrected in turn, until there as barely any white space left on the page. From what I could make out, it certainly seemed to tell of a society in decline, providing it wasn't all horseshit.

De'Ath didn't reach for the book back, so I took that as a sign to flick through a couple more pages. Sketches, hand-drawn maps, even whole treatises on the civilisation encountered. Honestly, I had to hand it to them, this was excellent work. De'Ath might have been a bigoted fuck, but he did come from a solid line of skilled and adventurous wizards. I'd give him that.

'Impressive, but I'm still not seeing it.'

'Last page,' he said. 'Perhaps diagrams are more your thing.'

Flipping through, I turned to the last page and was greeted by a ludicrously intricate alchemical diagram. There's a bit of overlap between alchemy and rune magic, but not enough that I could decipher the whole thing. I could make out something about balance, a thing that looked like an equation, a word that might have meant *pulse*. What was clear, though, was the entire diagram was built around the idea of a flow of energy, like a tide, knitting between the planes.

Across the bottom of the page, someone had hurriedly scribbled a message:

Not A to B, a to A. Not a mirror, a *lens*.

A wizard wrote that, had to be. Cryptic fuckers.

Worse still, it was starting to make sense to me. 'Fuck. That's the contagion.'

De'Ath smiled and cocked his head. 'Go on.'

I pointed to a series of circles in the diagram, all orbiting another, larger ball in the centre. 'These are other planes, right? All interconnected, feeding off each other, but mostly feeding off *this* one.'

'The nexus of all things,' he said, seeing that I was pointing at the central circle. 'The material plane. Us.'

'They're all defined in opposition to ours.'

The old man's eyes closed for a moment. 'Not always opposition, but close enough. Some oppose, some reflect, others emulate. But yes, in short, the realities of these planes are all dependent on ours. I understood this when I reached out to the denizens of Pragma and made a deal with them for our mutual benefit.'

'Oh, this is going to be rich, I can already tell.'

'Order,' he said, ignoring me. 'Those Outsiders were crying out for order, but the tides by which they set their clocks were elusive. While over here regimes rose and fell, the shockwaves would hit much larger across those outer planes. They scarcely had time to adjust to the new order before a ripple of discontent from someone in our plane would turn into a tidal wave in theirs.'

I threw the book back at him. 'It's always order with you types, isn't it? The world as a tidy little machine, everyone a fucking cog. Except for you, of course.

You're the hand on the switch, right? That was the deal you made, I expect.'

'You'd prefer chaos, I suppose? If you'd finished your training in the arcane, I think you'd have a better understanding of how dangerous unfettered chaos can be. You're looking at the world without having all the facts — I *do* have those facts, and that is how I knew the best way to move forward.'

'I swear to god, if this is just you leading up to saying that arrogant toffs are made to rule then—'

'Don't be so reductive!' he snapped. 'They are *expected* to rule, and expected to rule in a specific fashion. Every country has its traditions. Order doesn't come from stamping out discontent, it comes from codifying it. You grasp it and force it through channels that you control, keep it where it belongs. And if things go awry, then you bring in outside help to repair the machine. That was the intent behind the deal.'

Not going to lie, it took me a moment to put everything together as he was saying it. Old white dudes have a way of talking that runs on expecting you to just defer to them — full explanations are reserved for wives and priests, everyone else should just bask in the glory that is a dude speaking. But it did start to make a kind of sense, pieces sliding very slowly into place, my brain smacking them in millimetre by millimetre with a rubber hammer.

Still, the words were hard to force out. 'The college is explicitly designed precisely to produce stereotypical scumbag Tories?'

'My family has been moulding the output of that establishment for years, though I admit I was the first to do so with loftier goals. The recent changes have misaligned the mechanism.'

'Loftier goals than just being an arsehole?'

'Yes,' he said. 'The application of soft power to ensure stability and security for our world and those beyond. The perfect detente. My life's work.'

'Your life's work is piss,' I snorted. 'Bullshit pseudophilosophy to try and justify feeding children to monsters. You're just out here buttering your toast with dog shit and insisting it's Nutella. Pathetic.'

I touched a nerve there. De'Ath's face twitched as he folded it into an expression it should have been used to, at least if the lines mapped across the skin was any indication. It was a killer scowl — made his forehead look like a scrotum but the eyebrows were sharp enough to crack open oil fissures in the deepest ocean. It was a glare that could collapse stars.

Then something changed. A laugh bubbled up, and I

realised it was one of pity. He was laughing *at me*. 'Oh! Oh I see! You think this is all my doing.'

'You just said—'

'It was my *intention* to make a deal, that I will readily admit,' he said between sniggers. 'I would have gladly opened that door and ushered the beasts across the threshold. Alas, I was soundly rebuffed.'

'What?'

His face was twisting into a grim sneer. 'They don't think like we do, young lady. The very idea of negotiation and compromise wounds them. To even propose a deal, it turns out, is the equivalent of a slap across their hideous faces. They *are* order. Any attempt to bend them from their designs is, in their mind, no different from chaos.'

'Wow,' I said, stifling a giggle. 'That must have really stung, huh? To get on your hands and knees for the big daddies of order and tradition, only to get told you're just a big old pile of shit in human form. Did you cry?'

'It was a learning experience, that much I will say,' he replied. My cutting barbs failed to wound, apparently. 'I put too much of myself into attempting that deal, and I left my garden unattended, as it were.'

'Someone took advantage while you were distracted

Eat The Rich

and nudged you aside.'

'Let's call it what it was: a hostile takeover,' he said, rolling his eyes. 'For a time, myself and other like me had quite a run indeed. Had I managed to avoid such a prolonged distraction, I daresay that run would have continued. But we missed the opportunity to nip the threat in the bud, and there are prices even we could not afford to pay. Our pockets were deep, you understand, so consider what I am saying when I state that these had fathoms on ours. I would have been impressed, had they kept the school up to code.'

'Who's calling the shots now?'

He shrugged, one with so little energy in it that the sheer dismissiveness of it can't be overstated. 'No clue. Once I noticed what they were doing, the vast resources at their command had already been leveraged to provide a degree of anonymity I was disinclined to penetrate. I knew it was time to turn my attention elsewhere. I have been, and continue to be, at the top of the pyramid, young lady. I know the power wielded by vast sums of capital. And that also means I know when those sums are insurmountable. The smart play was to move on, to reassess my goals for a legacy.'

'A legacy?' I said. 'Like your grandson, perhaps? Your own saboteur inside the system. Got ya.'

'Bertie?' he laughed again, the tone even more mocking than the one levelled at me. 'He's a disappointment, not a successor. I offered him the chance to develop his powers as my grandfather did with me, proper tuition from a proper source. All he could talk about was that damned Dee Society. He carries my name, but it is his mother's blood that runs in his veins. No balls, that kid. I am fully divested of that decaying husk of an establishment, as I am with my grandson.'

'Someone has to be guiding the Outsiders though.'

'Must they?' he said. 'Even if that is the case, it has nothing to do with me. Our deal died in the cradle, they owe nothing to me nor my bloodline. Continue to grasp at straws if you like, but you'll find no connection here.'

I was so sure he was lying, and badly too. That grim sneer had turned smug, like he was trying to feed off my confusion. I had come in the room ready to wring the truth from his old ragged throat, and here he was trying to shut me down. He wanted to see me slip a gear, to fumble, to show him that his blood purity bullshit had bred a perfect brain that was far superior to the working-class mongrel meat in my head.

It was so goddamned obvious that it was laughable.

Bertie De'Ath had to be involved somehow. The critters had been too deferential to him in the time pocket, too friendly. They'd been respectful, given him

Eat The Rich

free rein. And why would they possibly do that if they *weren't* working in concert?

He had too much freedom to ignore.

Unless. Fuck, was it all an illusion of it.

Christ, he was still in the chain gang wasn't he? Rounded up and corralled with all the other kids. Maybe he was the big daddy of the cell block, but he was still *in the pissing cells*.

Bertie De'Ath clearly had a very important role when it came to keeping the others in line. He had their respect, a touch of authority, and just enough slack on his leash to keep that image alive. He was, after all, the head prefect — a source of order. Didn't it just make sense for that they would exploit that and use him?

He wasn't the mastermind, he was just another fucking Quisling — a weak pissboy hiding behind what privilege he could and ensuring his life was as least bad as possible.

Fuck! How had I missed that? Oh, brilliant work, Millie, well done jumping to a conclusion. All because a handsome posh-boy twatted someone in the face. Great job.

Still, two steps forward, one back.

'You've been very helpful, Mr De'Ath,' I said, being as

saccharine as I could manage. 'Thanks for your time. I'll leave you to your slow rot into oblivion.'

He drummed his fingers on the arm of his chair. 'If only he was more like you. You could be moulded into something really special, you know.'

I managed to let that comment go without reply, which I contend is a pretty big deal actually. Evidently, I have a face that screams *adopt me* to a certain kind of person, and I was either running into them an awful lot or it was a very broad pool indeed. Instead, I got up to leave.

And made it all the way to the door before I pulled a Columbo.

'One more thing,' I said, turning slowly. 'How long ago were you forced out, allegedly?'

His eyes twinkled. 'Oh, a decade. Perhaps two. I've long since given up caring about keeping track of time. Why?'

'And you've had a bee in your bunghole about the Dee society for how long?'

'Even longer than that.'

'Hm. Thanks.'

*

I had expected to need to do a full on sincere apology

when I caught up with Su-Yin, but she didn't seem bothered. The staff had, eventually, convinced her to allow them to escort her off the grounds, and I found her leaning against the little guard hut in pleasant conversation with the man she had tazed. Not one to interrupt, I watched for a few minutes as she ran him through the moves she had used to put him down.

Honestly, I needed a moment to get my shit together anyway. On the face of it, Old Man De'Ath had been a big bust, but that Columbo moment had shaken something loose in me that was rattling around insistently.

The timelines didn't add up, for one thing — but perhaps that was expected given all the fucking about with time that Constable had been doing. Judging from his age, he couldn't have been there long enough to make an enemy of the Elder De'Ath, but also the society lacked the gravitas and legitimacy of a proper legacy organisation. They still held their meetings in the back of the library, for gods sake. More Buffy the Vampire Slayer than the Skull and Bones Society.

The more I looked into things, the more loose threads I was uncovering. Not ones worth pulling, but like the frayed edges of a rope hacked apart by a sharp rock. Obvious, dirty, and really fucking suspect.

Working theory? Constable had fucked up time really

badly with all his little stitches and sutures, and this was just one symptom of it. I was willing to bet that I'd find more if I looked hard enough — students who had spent too long or too little at the school, boring shit like budgets not adding up or weirdness in staff numbers. Another curiosity. Another wrinkle.

Another twist.

Hmm.

Once Su-Yin was finished with her impromptu martial arts class, I made myself visible and we shuffled off back to her car. Like I said, I tried to apologise but she wasn't annoyed or anything, so instead I filled her in on what had gone down with De'Ath.

'I can't work out how useful that information is,' she said. 'But hey, it's information I suppose.'

'It feels like everyone I talk to is just throwing obstacles at me. Like, are they doing it on purpose?'

'What do you mean?'

I thrust my hands into my pockets and walked in silence for a moment. 'First, I was looking at all this like a detective, right? Following clues and leads and everything, and it wasn't going anywhere. Got the basic picture, got a red herring or two with Wolfgang's insistence that there was Voodoo or something involved—'

'But they *were* using Sangfroid, right?' she interrupted.

'Yeah, they were, but—'

'And the Voodoo guy did help a little, and we did save you from the Outsiders and put up a sanctuary to keep you safe.'

'Yes, but—'

'Wolfgang *helps,*' she said.

I held up a hand to calm things down. 'Okay, I'm not saying he didn't. What I'm saying is that *despite* that, new complications were coming into play. Then I tried doing things the runeskald way, and the same thing is happening.'

'I don't understand.'

We were at the car now, and I sat on the bonnet, lifting one knee up to my chest. 'A corner looks like a dead-end if you come at it straight on.'

'What?'

Got to admit, I wasn't really sure what I meant there either at first. Sounds profound though, right? A little hint towards the importance of perspective. This whole investigation had been about switching perspectives, but no matter how I rotated it I couldn't quite get the pieces to line up. Every corner led to another corner, all of them also a dead end. And that meant one of two things: I was either really shit at this (a possibility), or someone was actively steering me in circles even now.

Thinking like a runeskald had brought me to the second point, and that same thinking kept me there. It wasn't like someone was twisting history to keep me off balance, but they were out there sewing all sorts of unnecessary shit to clutter everything up.

Was this what Laufeyjarson had meant? Was approaching this like a runeskald supposed to mean stripping everything away and finding the *narrative spine* of everything, the core? Maybe. Or maybe I was overthinking things.

But here's the the real thing, and the thing that only really hit me when I was having my little Columbo moment: there's absolutely *no way* a private school in the heartlands of Upper Poshtwattington has a wizard openly on staff. Not a single chance.

Oh my fucking god, that was the *core.*

'Can I ask you a question?' I said as we got into her car.

'Another one?' Su-Yin said. 'Sure.'

'Do you know who was Prime Minister when the dark times kicked off?'

She frowned for a moment. 'Not really, no. I mean, I didn't really give much of a shit about politics at the time.'

'Me neither, was very much blissfully ignorant.'

'Hadn't even come into my magic then, you know,' she said. 'Why do you ask, anyway?'

'Just wondering how likely it is that whoever was sitting in the big chair went to a school like this one. Or this one exactly. I bet, at least, several of his cronies did.'

'I guess it's likely?'

'Almost certain, I'd say. And you know one of the many things I know about people who end up in Whitehall, one of their universal qualities? They are shit scared of magic.'

'So?'

I slapped my leg, hard enough that it hurt — punishment for my stupidity I guess. 'So why the fuck didn't I immediately realise that it's *really fucking suss* that there's a wizard training club at this college? Even moreso, that it's entirely staffed by *the poors*.'

'It is?' Su-Yin said. For a second, her eyes glazed over, as if something in her brain had hit a wall and was resetting. 'I try not to think about the weird shit that goes on at posh schools, if I'm honest.'

I'm starting to suspect that you try not to think about anything at all if you can help it.

I did my best to roll with the punches and kept talking. 'Point is, I didn't even question it until now, not really. That's not like me, I think. I hope it's not like me, anyway, because that's a pretty amateur thing to ignore.'

'I mean, we were here for a bit before you arrived and we didn't find anything weird about it. Wolfgang said—'

'I'm sure he did,' I said, cutting her off. 'But *I'm* saying something else. Come on, there's something I want to check.'

'Back to the school?'

I snorted. 'Fuck no. I've had enough of that place. I want to branch out a little.'

Fifteen

I didn't tell Su-Yin where I wanted to go until we were basically already there. You'd think that would be a problem — the driver not knowing where to go — but there were only like two roads out of Goule and they both intersected after a couple of miles of frankly gorgeous countryside anyway.

It wasn't that I didn't want her to know where we were going, not really. If she had pushed back even a little, I would have told her exactly where I wanted to go, but she didn't. You'd think she would have, right? Maybe it's just me, but the only time I could see myself driving blind like this was if there was a dude in the backseat with a gun to my head like in a bad movie. I wanted to see if she'd *react*.

She didn't, and that really wasn't much of a surprise at this point.

'Why did you want to come here again?' she asked as she wedged her car into a gap between two others that was definitely not big enough. 'I thought you said the Voodoo woman was a con artist or something?'

'Yeah, basically nothing she told me panned out at all.'

Su-Yin turned off the car. 'Right. So, why come back?'

I shrugged. There wasn't really an answer I wanted to give her. It didn't even really make sense in my head, but I just knew that there was *something* I needed to look at again. My investigation — such as it was — went all bonkers-batshit-askew once I let Wolfgang steer me over this way. That didn't really sound like a proper argument that would justify my going back to see Mistral, but luckily I didn't have to defend my actions because fuck you.

'Stay in the car,' I said. 'I won't be long, I shouldn't think.'

'You sure? I don't mind tagging along.'

'I'm sure,' I said, flashing a small smile. 'Chill out for a moment, I'll scream if she tries to smash my face in with a shrunken head or something.'

Exiting the car, I made my way back up to the weird little house so perfectly sandwiched under the bridge. There were no needles in my pockets this time, but still I felt myself scrabbling for something to run my hands over, a totem that would have this feeling make sense. If this was just all based on some dumb intuition, some childish internal whining that everything was *just being too hard*, then I was going to feel like a right tit.

I knocked on the door and it dutifully swung open in

that spooky way they do when there's a dead body lurking somewhere inside. Smart move would have been to just turn around and leave then and there, but it seemed to me that it was probably fine — what were the odds there would be a killer in there at the exact moment I had decided to come swanning back in? Exactly.

And, you know, I was right. There wasn't a killer in there. No body either. Mistral the Voodoo charlatan was still alive, sitting bolt upright at her table with her hands neatly folded in her lap. She didn't look up, far too busy enthralled by whatever she was looking at on the tabletop.

'Mama Mistral?' I said, hoping to get her attention. 'It's Millie Thatcher. I was here before with Wolfgang. We brought the Sangfroid?'

Nothing, not even a glimmer of acknowledgement. I cleared my throat and tried again, but still she didn't look up, her thousand-yard stare remaining aimed at the table. Had to be something super interesting there, right?

Now, I've seen films — imagine that! — and I know that this sort of scenario is *bad fucking news*, right? Always struggled to understand why the people in those films always get closer to the spooky thing, and that's coming from a girl whose bread and butter is in getting close to spooky things. But Mistral sitting there like a fucking doll, staring off into space like that? It's like there's a little voice in your head telling you to get closer, the same one that whispers things like *jump* when you peer over the edge of a tall building or to shout *eat my entire ass* at the top of your lungs in a quiet library.

So, I got closer. Step by agonising step, waiting for the inevitable jump scare of her leaping to her feet and going for my throat.

She definitely had the look of a crazed zombie. The closer I got, the more I could see signs that she just wasn't right — you know, beyond the obvious catatonia. Her skin, already pale, had taken on the off-yellow hue of a bruise, with dark rings under painfully pink eyes. It was a look of utter exhaustion, her lower lip pocked with marks of her having chewed them and her mouth itself hanging open.

Those very pink eyes were really the focal point of the whole ensemble, though. They were rocking a dry sheen that made me think of the porcelain orbs shoved into the Outsider's faces, but they were very much real human eyeballs. That said, they *were* sickeningly dry. I got close enough to snap my fingers right under her nose, close enough that I could have reached out and touched her if I wanted, and I didn't realise quite how reflective an eyeball is until it *isn't*.

Eat The Rich

Oh, and there was nothing on the table. I think we all expected that.

I pulled out a chair and sat down next to her, watching her. She looked so very fragile, as if the only thing holding her up was the immense good fortune to not have come into contact with the slightest breeze, like balancing a coin on its edge. Very little difference between her and the walking dead, at this point. Which works in my favour, when you think about it.

The room echoed as I slammed my hand down hard on the table. It was a short, sharp shock, and enough to finally tickle the edges of her attention. Slowly, her head lolled back and she looked at me, her face blank and slack as if she was half-asleep.

'Oh, it's you,' she mumbled. 'The wizard girl. Hello.'

Her eyes didn't move to meet mine, but I expect that's because they were too dry to swivel comfortably now. I hunched down into her line of sight. 'Call me a cynic, but I think something shady has happened to you.'

'Is he with you?'

'Who?'

'The other one. I need instruction. Please.' A hand unlatched from her lap and snaked up beneath her hair to scratch at the base of her skull. 'I need him to instruct me.'

I leant a little further forward. 'Instruct you how?'

'To blink,' she said, her voice breaking. 'I need him to tell me how to blink. I don't remember. I can't do it.'

'You just close your eyes.'

'But *how*?'

If you've got an answer to that, you're a better woman than I. 'Mistral, what happened here?'

'Why are you here? I did such a good job. The best job. Tell him I did a good job, then maybe he'll come back and remind me how to blink. I was worried he'd make me forget how to breathe, but he said it would all be fine if I stuck to the script.'

'Are you talking about Wolfgang? What did he tell you to do?'

The fingers beneath her hair scratched frantically. 'Sell the story.   Set the scene. Classic parlour trick, convince the mark to believe what you want them to believe. Sound insightful, talk bollocks. Spin the yarn, follow the script. I said that was easy, that's why he promised punishment if I failed. *False confidence is no confidence at all.*'

Hell, it took a good con artist to con you by telling you

they were a con artist.   But that's exactly what she had done, and I'd been happy to gobble it all up. 'He gave you a script?'

'Basically,' she said. '*Tell her what she wants to hear*, that's what he said. *What I want her to hear.*'

'So everything about Nightmares was bullshit, was it?'

'No. Yes. I don't know! I didn't ask! Would never ask! Just did as I was told. Will only do as I'm told. Please ask him to tell me to blink again.'

So, not a Nightmare then. That had just been a way to usher me onto his path of bullshit make believe — like a street corner drug pusher, he wanted to rope me in with a taste of something soft, then crank up the severity. The Nightmare was the gateway drug that let my mind buy into the Outsider shit; it didn't matter if the pieces didn't fit neatly together, what mattered was he got me properly hooked on the flow.

Every lie built upon the last. Must be exhausting to spend so much energy putting all that together.

A dark thought crept into my mind. 'Mistral, how long have you been sat here?'

'Since you left.'

'And how long has it been since you last blinked?'

'Since you left. I count the seconds now. You can stand anything for ten seconds. Reach ten seconds, start again. So many tens.'

Well then, I guess I had an answer now for what happens to the ventriloquist's dummy when they're locked away in their box. You know, provided the dummy is a literal human being. The poor woman had been wiped so clean that she simply couldn't function without his hand up her arse now. How had he even done that?

I mean, sure, I'd known there was something off about him from the beginning, but I'd been thinking some weird cult of personality thing, your standard masculine charismatic mindfuck bullshit. This though? This was way beyond that.

I reached for her hand and pulled it away from her neck. The fingers came away with blood coating the nails, but she didn't resist. Gently, I folded her hands in her lap again.

'Can I take a look?' I asked. I would have looked anyway, but she deserved the chance to consent. If he had left her with that.

'Yes.'

I stood up and moved over to her, softly taking her chin and angling her forward until her forehead lay against

Eat The Rich

the table. Then I took her hair, probably the only visible part of her not yet affected by whatever this was, and flicked it over her shoulder.

At the base of her skull, just underneath the hairline, was a round and bloody scab. This was clearly what Mistral had been scratching at, and she had succeeded at tearing off a bit of the surface scarring. There was a design beneath the blood, something etched into the skin, but I couldn't quite make it out.

Leaving her laying on the table, I went and searched the house for a first aid kit, something I could use to pry off the rest of the scab that wasn't just my disgusting human fingers. I found a small kit tucked away under the kitchen sink, dug out what I needed, and set to work. If it hurt, Mistral didn't appear inclined to show it. Probably couldn't have hurt worse than bone dry eyeballs, anyway.

Once I peeled away the last of the scab, I dabbed the wound clean with a damp towel and tried to get a look at what we were dealing with before the blood swelled again and drowned out my view.

If you were guessing some sick rune magic, then I give you permission to feel a bit smug. Go nuts.

The work was beyond my skill level, that was about as much as I could tell. It was tiny, no more than the size of my fingernail, but it was so intricate. The lines were each thinner than a hair, but overlaid in such a way that they complimented each other perfectly, layer after layer of illustration just to build one final piece. That they had managed to end up carved into flesh was impressive in and of itself — the design may have featured a load of layers, but they had been carved in one go. Looking closer, I could see the slightly jagged edges of flesh being torn rather than cut lining the circumference. The inner design was smooth and perfect, as though a steady hand and a knife thinner than a razor had been used.

Like I said, the design was utterly indecipherable, but I could hazard a guess as to what it was doing. If Mistral was going to be able to blink again — hell, if she was going to keep the use of her eyes — she'd need the damned thing removed. That gave me a couple of options.

As possible avenues go, the most wizardy one would be to counteract the magic. I was pretty confident I could do that if I needed to; it doesn't require you knowing what the spell is exactly, just roughly what it does. Whip up something with a reverse resonance, they'll butt against each other, cancel each other out.

And, you know, that's *fine,* at least in the short term. As long as you keep that balance perfectly managed, nothing to worry about. But you'd worry, wouldn't you? I know I would, knowing the only thing keeping me sane is the the waning magic stored in my skin. If the balance is off by even the smallest margin, shit's going to get bad.

Again, this is *mostly fine* and the chances of something going wrong are pretty small when a skilled hand is in charge. So, yeah, with me I was thinking a 50/50 shot at best if I took that route.

But I wasn't going to go down that road. I had a better idea.

I pulled my small penknife from my pocket and unfolded it, wiping the blade on my thigh to clean it.

'I'm going to help you, okay, Mistral?' 'I said. 'Ten seconds, right? Just count to ten.'

She didn't respond, but whatever.

I had to cut through more flesh than I thought to get the whole thing out, but at least I didn't have to cut deep. The scabbing helped to guide the knife, and Mistral didn't even speed up her breathing or anything. May as well have been slicing up a chicken breast.

The instant that flesh was torn free, a pained squeal bubbled out of Mistral's throat and she fell sideways off her chair. I caught her and lowered her down gently to the carpeted floor, doing my best not to stare. I mean, it's really hard not to just gawk at someone who is so very fucked up, especially when you want to help.

I sat on the floor next to her and let her cry silently for a while. It didn't seem right to leave her, though I didn't have a clue what else I could do to help. Call an ambulance I suppose? Yeah, sure, I would do that but I needed to talk to her first, get some more coherent answers. She already seemed a lot more alive, if weepy, so I wasn't too worried that there was any irreparable damage that would be made worse now by delaying a little.

Eventually she rolled onto her back, eyes closed, her face slick with fresh tears. 'Are you still there? I daren't open my eyes to check.'

'I'm here,' I said. 'How you feeling?'

'Shit. But I'm very glad you came back to shout at the fraud.'

'That's not why I came back. I was having a small crisis and wanted to strip away all the bullshit.'

'And everything I told you was bullshit,' she said. Her thumbs were pressed against the side of her nose, massaging the tear ducts in the corner of her eyes. 'But you bought it for a while, right?'

I stood up and moved over towards the kitchen. 'You did a good job, I'll give you that. Just enough truth in there to get a girl going.'

'That's what he wanted,' she said. 'I was supposed to put on a show for the new girl, that's what he said.'

'Yeah, I got that part,' I shouted from the other room, running a hand towel under the cold tap. 'Not really sure on the why of it. Not asking you for that, I know you don't know.'

'I don't,' she called back. 'But I can tell you what I do know. I know that I was part of a larger plan.'

I walked back over with the wet towel and placed it over her eyes. 'Yeah? How do you mean?'

She shivered as the cold water touched her skin, then sighed as it started to moisten her eyelids. 'Once he had... *branded* me, he held a brainstorming session with me and a couple of other people to help make sure everything was planned out perfectly. Surprisingly businesslike.'

'What others?'

'He didn't introduce them. A young couple.'

That would be Walid and Su-Yin then, had to be. 'And that made you think there was a bigger plan?'

'Not just that,' she shook her head. 'I came up with a lot of ideas on how to con you, but he shot them down because they wouldn't *fit*.'

'I get you. This act was meant to slot into a larger narrative, back it up somehow. Curious.'

Now, yes, it's possible this was still part of the con. Mistral had already shown she had the chops to spin me round with the old honesty ploy, so it was conceivable she was just doing it again. Not likely, but definitely possible. But, that said, she was filling in a lot of blanks in my head.

The way this investigation had been fucking me about had, I've previously said, got me thinking that there was something wrong with the whole thing. Every twist and turn was leading me the wrong way, and now I had a bit of evidence that this was actually true. One of the very first things Wolfgang had said to me had been a complicated lie — no, more than a lie, a full-on performance — and that cast everything in doubt, now didn't it?

'He's a sneaky little fuck, isn't he?' I asked, continuing. 'How did he get to you?'

She shrugged, still dabbing at her eyes with the towel. 'Bought me. I'm a professional con artist, he only had to pay me.'

'Paid you enough to let him carve into your flesh?'

Eat The Rich

'Oh, no,' she said. 'The money got him through the door. Branded me the moment my back was turned. Like you said, he's a sneaky little fuck.'

Right, so she hadn't chosen the word *brand* idly then. He'd cut that design into her quickly, before she'd had time to react — anything else, she'd have mentioned a struggle. Was that good? Maybe. If he'd done it that fast, it meant it was prepared well in advance, meaning I didn't need to worry about him just rattling off a mindfucking spell in my direction without notice. Provided I was careful, of course.

He'll have had the design carved into a ring, mystical dudes loved their rings.

She was still dabbing her face with the towel, and I noticed now that it was coming away stained. A crust was beginning to form in the corners of her eyes — the muddy reds of dried blood and pale yellows of pus mixing together.

I put a hand on her shoulder and gently pushed her down into a laying position. 'Okay, that's enough excitement for you. I'm going to go call you an ambulance. Just stay here and enjoy the dark for me. Can you do that?'

Mistral nodded, and whatever fire was burning in her chest started to dim. Tiredness was flooding in, taking what it was owed with interest. It was hard to argue that she didn't deserve a nice long sleep.

I stepped out into the hall and dialled 999. The operator on the other end of the phone handled things with much more aplomb than I had — evidently someone with *dried out eyeballs* isn't up there on the weird shit board for them — but they said they'd have an ambulance to me inside of ten minutes.

Good old NHS.

If I let myself stop to think, I was pretty sure my head would burst. It wasn't as if things were too complicated to follow, far from it, but if I slowed down long enough to map everything out it was going to need a lot more mental space than I had on offer. You know back in the ancient times when people would buy one of those fuck-off big folding maps for their car journeys, and they'd unfold it a row at a time until it was so massive your dad couldn't see over the steering wheel and your car would end up upside down in a cow pasture and your mum is shouting at him and calling him a stupid bellend? *That*.

The possibility space was growing all the time, and the temptation was to get lost in it instead of dealing with what was happening *right fucking now*. I just needed a moment to focus, wait for the ambulance to show up, then see if I could pump more info out of Mistral before they put her on too many of the good drugs.

Eat The Rich

I slid my phone back into my pocket and returned to Mistral.

Someone was crouched over her, their back to me. They must have heard me enter the room, because they shifted on the balls of their feet and turned to look at me, moving just enough to the side that I could see their hand clamped down hard over the woman's nose and mouth. I'd barely been gone a minute and Mistral had been suffocated to death.

The killer stood up slowly, muscles taut and jaw set, their expression so blank that I couldn't tell if they were looking at me or through me.

'What did you go an do that for, Su-Yin?' I asked.

Su-Yin blinked but her expression remained blank, her voice a dull monotone. 'Written out as she was written in: suddenly. Motivation.'

A cold chill formed at the base of my spine. My fight or flight was screaming at me, begging me to acknowledge that a decision needed to be made here. I barely knew the woman, but seeing her now I could tell I didn't know her at all. I'd seen the woman she was now — funny, witty, ever so *tired* — but the Su-Yin that had just killed Mistral was kicking out shades of who she must have been before.

An urban barbarian.

Whatever this barbarian side had going for it, there had to be a way to skirt around it and find her other half.

But that split second of indecision would cost me. Before I had time to settle into either flight or fight, she'd already crossed the room in one large step and had me up against the wall by the throat. The impact knocked the air out of me, leaving me flailing weakly against her as she just held me there, eyes unfocused and staring through me as the world started to turn grey.

I wasn't going to die here. If that had been the plan, there had been plenty of opportunity to snuff me before now. But it's not like I was going to just leave it to trust that I'd wake up, right? Looks like a duck, walks like a duck, strangles like a duck: it's a fucking duck.

'Are you motivated now?' Su-Yin whispered, but there was an accent undercutting her words — Wolfgang's gentle German twang. 'Are you *listening?*'

Su-Yin's face moved in close to mine as she spoke, her breath warm on my face. I could feel my eyes ready to roll back into my head, feel the blood thundering around my brain as it tried to push past her vice grip at my throat. I wasn't listening, but I was *waiting.*

She moved even closer, her nose almost touching mine, blank face coming back into focus as it cross through the grey fog of suffocation. Close enough for me to aim for.

I brought my hand up, pulling my penknife from my pocket and driving it into the side of her nose. As it was closed, the wooden handle worked nicely as an impromptu knuckleduster, cracking bone and cartilage, sending her nose horribly askew. Blood exploded down her face — the only colour left in my vision — and her grip faltered.

Gasping, I fell to the floor and scrabbled away. I looked back in time to see her snap her nose more or less back into place and glare at me.

I was so very, *very* fucked.

Sixteen

There's only so far being slippery and fast can get you in a fight. Being small and quick gives you certain avenues to exploit for sure, and you've already seen I know how to do that, but there's a lot of moving part to account for there. It's all glass cannon without the cannon, just glass and big stonking rocks trying to smash the fuck out of your beautiful panes.

This is all predicated on the ability to breathe, of course.

Cracking Su-Yin's nose had gotten her to drop me, but I was still gulping for air by the time she'd recovered. I stumbled on my first attempt to dodge past her and she grabbed a handful of my hair, yanking me backward. If you're looking for the full blow-by-blow of me getting my little arse kicked, I'm going to disappoint you — not out of any sense of propriety, but purely because it all became a blur very quickly.

Pulling me back, she curved my back over her knee, propping up my head perfect for a flurry of blows from her free fist. That's when everything stopped being an experienced reality and morphed into this cubist nightmare of blasts of thudding pressure and whirling vortexes of awareness. If it helps, imagine that thing cartoons do when they get smacked and their eyes spin around like tumblers on a slot machine.

I could feel my brain slapping against the inside of my skull.

My saving grace was that even in this state I had enough about me to squirm. There's not a chance I could have mounted an actual defence, all things considered — and even less chance I could have escaped — but what I *could* do was just enough to wriggle out of any more choke holds. Those snapshot moments of coherency always seemed to accompany Su-Yin trying to lock a hand around my throat again, or attempting to smother me with a pillow. Just enough of a twist from me to convince her I needed some more pounding first, thus keeping me alive.

This was all delaying the inevitable, of course. I had no smart plan to get out of this, nothing up my sleeve to pull a sneaky escape. Su-Yin had to *want* to stop breaking my face in if I wanted to survive, and even if she did want that, it was clear now that she wasn't pulling her own strings.

I could taste blood now, smell copper. She wouldn't need to choke me out at this rate, she could just beat me to death. Maybe that was the way out, to just accept that was the way this ended and just drift away before she finished getting me there. Check out early.

Each dull thud pushed me further away from myself, punting my consciousness deeper into the dark. Swimming back to my eyes was harder and more desperate each time. Best to just relax now, go limp.

After another thud, I switched off. No more wriggling, so squirming, just a blood-stained rag doll bent backwards over a meaty thigh, blood running up my face and over my eyes, dripping onto the floor.

Su-Yin stopped hitting me, and there was just enough life left in me to feel the movement as she rolled me up, vertebrae by vertebrae, into a sitting position. I felt her rough hands grab my chin, feel for a pulse, then coldly pull away when they failed to find one.

And that gave me an opening I didn't even know I was waiting for.

Looking back on it now, it was a stroke of genius — the perfect possum play. Take that beating like a champ, let them think they's won so they let their guard down, then *pow*. Rope-a-dope, or whatever boxers call it. For me, it meant lashing out as fast as my dying body could manage, reaching around to the back of Su-Yin's skull, and clawing at the base of the hairline there. I don't have the best nails of the job, but you can do a lot with very little if you have to.

Eat The Rich

If Wolfgang had chosen any other location to hide his brand, I would be dead. Hell, if I had been completely wrong about things and he hadn't carved his little domination sigil into her flesh, I'd be dead. If Su-Yin had chosen to rattle my skull one more time with that fist of hers, or drive her boot heel into my face, *I'd be dead*.

But no-one's got luck like me, I guess. The bad luck of getting your face smashed in, balanced with the good luck of getting your nails right into the design in one go, ripping the damn thing clean in one sloppy movement. I felt the skin tear away, and then I felt myself falling away. Deeper and darker, darker and deeper, until everything was black clouds and white noise.

*

When I woke up, Su-Yin was holding my hand and I felt like I was bobbing around in a swimming pool full of piss. That creeping warmth that you get when some shitbag kid with a gap in his teeth and a horrific cowlick lets rip at the lido? Felt like my body was bathing in that sensation.

'Thank fuck,' Su-Yin whispered breathlessly. 'Don't try to move. I really don't know if I'm doing this right. Let it settle in for a few seconds.'

My skin tingled as the warmth spread, almost like fire ants were crawling across my face. I felt *things* shifting, settling, laying down anchors to hold them steady. A long, slow crunch bounced around in the depths of my skull, and I felt some moist coagulation slither free and down into my throat. It made me cough, but Su-Yin's firm hand was pressed on my chest, holding me still.

This time, I didn't fight.

After a moment, the warmth began to recede. In its place, a wave of throbbing pain and agony crept out of the dark space and flooded me. Too much pain for me to even want to scream — it completely locked me out, overloading every possible pathway in my brain. I had to wait for it to adapt, reroute, before I could react.

'I did the best I could,' Su-Yin said. 'I mean, I... I don't really know medical magic, but I didn't think it was a good idea to move you either... You looked... You looked...'

She trailed off, and it didn't take a genius — or even two unblacked eyes — to tell she was on the verge of tears. Personally, I was so far over the verge that I'd be at danger of dehydrating if my eyes hadn't swollen too much to let them all out.

'It's all right,' I said. My voice didn't even echo in my skull, must have been a leak somewhere. 'I'm pretty sure you didn't know what you were doing.'

She shook her head. 'I knew. At least, I knew enough that I had something lurking in there I had to dance around. Triggers.'

I tried to get up, but thought better of it. 'That explains a lot, actually. I thought you seemed a bit… changeable.'

'I run hot and cold, that's just me. Not usually this badly, though. I've never…' she drifted off, eyes slowly turning towards Mistral, then back to me.

Yeah, I wasn't about to let her sink herself into that shame spiral. 'What were you doing to me when I woke up?'

'Uh, medical magic,' she said. 'First aid, really. I set a few bones, turned the clock back on some breaks so they reverted to fractures. Stopped the bleeding and dulled the pain. Enough, fingers crossed, to get you mobile.'

'You're a bit of a beast, huh?'

'Apparently.'

Cracking a smile hurt, but she needed to see it. She had to know I didn't blame her, and words wouldn't do it. A good liar can say anything with words, but it takes an exceptional one to do it with looks. If she suspected for a second that I put any blame on her for this, something would give in her head — her looks said as much, and she was most assuredly not an exceptional liar.

And don't ask me to explain why it mattered. If you haven't worked it out, I can't help you.

Again, I tried to get up. This time, I felt something shift in my chest, the warm rush of something coming loose, and sank back to the floor. In a panic, Su-Yin had her hand on my chest again, that soothing warmth spreading out from her palm one more time. Her lips were moving, but I was already detaching from reality again, sinking down into the dark one more time.

The next time I woke up, I was in the back of an ambulance and feeling, well, not *better* exactly but considerably less deathly. Su-Yin was there still, gripping my hand tightly and with that same pleasant warmth, but a hectic paramedic was there too now. He was a young man with tired eyes and a scruff of stubble that shaded his already dark face. He had his limbs spread out, securing himself against the walls of the vehicle as we went over a bump.

'Can you hear me, Millie?' he asked. 'Don't try to speak, you've got a fractured jaw. A fractured, well, pretty much everything.'

Is it ironic to get picked up by an ambulance you called for someone else? I'm not sure I really understand what irony is, to be honest. But then, I had more than enough time to think it over, all things considered. Even with Su-Yin's attempts at magical first aid, I was going to be in for the night.

She stayed with me the entire time, to her credit, sort of lurking behind all the doctors and nurses and social workers — wasn't expecting one of those to show up. A few times, I tried to tell her, or mime at least, that I was okay, she could get some air, she didn't owe me anything, but she was having none of that.

I might have felt less forgiving of her if she had, though.

Eventually, they set me up in a bed and pumped me full of enough drugs to knock me spark out. It was lovely, a thick, milky sleep that swallowed up the rest of the day. I got to watch the sunset through the window in a sort of timelapsed haze — there are worse ways to end a day. Found the one silver lining, I guess.

There was a streetlight outside my window that kept flickering on and off. Now and then, I would hear a car drive up the road outside and the vibrations of its wheels across the tarmac would toggle the lamp, filling the room with soft white light that slashed through the blinds on the windows. Striped of light and shadow, really appealing when you're high on painkillers and everything is suddenly very *profound*.

Another vehicle, a truck by the sound of it, rumbled past the window and sent the light flickering again. This time, it wasn't the dazzling zebra stripes that caught my eye, it was the man standing at the end of my bed. He was leaning on his elbows which were planted on the foot board, a thumb idly tick-tick-ticking on the metal hook of my chart.

'A+ for effort,' he said. 'But I'm going to have to give you a D when it comes to results. I'd grade on a curve, but I don't know what that means.'

Even as I lay there, doped off my tits and in more pain than there are words to describe, I had enough life left in me to flip Laufeyjarson one hell of a bird.

His teeth caught the light as he smiled. 'I never learned sign language either. My bad. As, I suppose, is Wolfgang, if you think about it.'

I had been thinking about it. A lot. This was one of the few times I actually welcomed the god of fuckboys showing his face — I had questions, but owing to all the bandages and plaster casts and *fucking metal rods* now wasn't the time to ask them.

'I did warn you,' he said. 'I mentioned the *wolf at the door*, right? A little on the nose, I know, but I needed to try and find a nice balance between subtlety and just giving you the answers. The hardest part of being a god is giving people a chance to work things out for themselves. If I go giving you all the answers, that doesn't make for a very good story. You need the struggle to grow, and if there's one thing that should be very clear now it's that *I really want you to grow.*'

Eat The Rich

He folded himself up from the end of my bed and tiptoed comically across the room to Su-Yin. She was asleep, pretzelled over a chair in the corner of the room, facing the door. Sinking down to his haunches, he studied her sleeping face.

'She's had a bad time, this one,' he continued. 'Old Wolfgang's words rattling around in her head like that. Horrible stuff, but ingenious. He took the gift I gave the world and found a way to use it I never even conceived of. Then again, I'm all about consent, so why would I? But *that's the point*.'

He placed one of his hands on her head, the fingers steepled and pressing against the skin like spindles ready to be driven deep into her skull. Despite appearances, his touch must have been gentle because Su-Yin didn't seem to notice — or she was just so fucking zonked from smacking the shit out of me that it would take more than that to jolt her awake.

There was a sizzling sound and the smell of burning hair, then he pulled his hand away. 'There. My gift to her by way of a small apology — shaved a few years off the therapy and rejiggered things to keep anyone else from getting in her head like that. The whole mental fortress package. Can't have you thinking I'm a callous old bastard, right?'

I grumbled and shoved myself upright in bed. They'd

wired my jaw shut, but I'd be able to growl out some words if I tried hard enough. 'What do you want now, Laufeyjarson?'

'Just to give you perspective,' he said, slithering back to the end of my bed. 'Look, I sat back and watched for a long time as my gift drained out of the world, and there were so few of you that looked at it with any real artistry. You see the runes, you use the runes, but you don't experiment. If, as a species, you don't have it in you to be curious, well, then who am I to intervene?'

'You're literally intervening now,' I dribbled. 'All you've done since I met you is intervene.'

He shrugged. 'Nah. All I do is shout at the screen from my comfy couch. No effect, just a lot of histrionics. At best you could say I send a lot of story ideas to the producers, clog their inboxes with fanfiction. But intervene directly? Girl, that's boring.'

'Sure,' I said, slumping down. The pain in my jaw was swirling up into the pain in my head, mixing like a storm front. As always, Loki was giving me a migraine.

A glimmer of concern flashed across his face. 'I could extend some mercy your way, if you want. Finish what the lass over there started and knit your bones back together. No catch.'

'Eat piss. I don't want your mercy.'

Eat The Rich

The glimmer gave way to a cold smile. It was hard to read, but I felt myself leaning towards it being one of pride. 'Of course, you've got to do it all alone. Why take the highway when there's a perfectly good country lane saturated with nettles and thorns and, fuck it, rabid hedgehogs made of razor wire? Quite right.'

I sighed. The migraine was real, drilling its way out from the dark centre of my brain and tugging on my optic nerves. Ultraviolet starbursts were blotting out my vision. Closing my eyes, I lay down. 'Leave me alone.'

'As you wish, princess,' he said gently. 'You only had to ask. Keep heading down this path and you'll see that writ large. After all, he did.'

*

I was in and out of consciousness for another day or so, but Laufeyjarson didn't bother to pop back. At some point, Su-Yin left and came back again — a change of clothes, some food, probably a shower — but she was looking tired again when they finally let me leave the hospital.

Her attempts to use magic to undo the damage she'd inflicted had definitely hastened my recovery, but there was a lot left to heal naturally. Still, she'd done a lot to heal the breaks and whatever she had done to my jaw had confounded the doctors enough that they felt it necessary to blast me with so many X-rays I started to worry I'd end up as some massive green-skinned rage monster.

'I think he knows you unplugged me,' Su-Yin said, loading me into the back seat of her car.

My joints were creaking like the beams of an old galleon. 'How can you tell?'

'Walid won't take my calls,' she said, as if that was explanation enough. I gave her a look of confusion and she continued. 'He's always been very *diligent* when it comes to responding to my calls and texts, you understand? Very *keen*.'

'Ah,' I said. 'I've known a guy or two like that.'

'He wouldn't ignore me,' she said, climbing into the front seat. 'Not unless Wolfgang made him.'

'Think he'll come after you?'

She shook her head. 'I doubt it. I've been thinking about how we ended up with him, and there's nothing in that which makes me think he'll be desperate to try and slap a brand on my brain again.'

'What do you mean?' I said. My jaw had a new click to it now and I could feel it trying to lock on the harder consonants.

Turning in her seat, Su-Yin faced me. 'Walid and I, we're

nothing really. We did some self-defence classes for minor talents falling between the cracks now that everything has gone batshit over at Whitehall. And, well, we made a little money on the side selling information. That was the only useful thing we had going for us, and Wolfgang had us burn our network down to the embers trying to find you.'

Obviously the guy had one hell of a hard-on for me, that was never in doubt. 'So, now he's got what he wanted, you think he'll be content to just leave you alone?'

'More that I'm not worth the effort,' she said. 'You, though. I'm surprised he hasn't come looking for you yet.'

I had to admit, while I hadn't exactly been properly conscious for long, I'd been wondering the same thing. If his plan had been to take me out, having me laid up in a hospital bed was pretty much an open invitation. But then, if that had been his plan he could have crushed me the moment we met — it was clear he had a better command of rune magic than I did, not to mention the arcane muscle to back it up.

But, obviously, he'd had something different in mind. Recruiting me, maybe? Was he going to try and carve a brand into me too? Again, it felt like that was something he could have done without all the pageantry. Hell, I'd been knocked out in his presence —

ample opportunity.

'He wants something else,' I said. 'But I'm fucked if I can work out what it is. Or how any of this ties together. The Outsiders killing the kids? Do you have any update on that?'

'Another kid died last night, so I heard,' she said. 'Local papers finally got hold of the story. Only a matter of time now before the big boys from London come knocking. They'll end up closing the school soon, I should think.'

I wasn't going to find the connection between Wolfgang and these Outsiders by overthinking things, especially with my growing concussion blossoming in my aching head. 'You know what, fuck this noise. I'm doing wrestling with two mysteries at once — I'm going to go and shut one of them down right now. Mind running me up to the school?'

Seventeen

It won't have escaped your notice that the school had more than a few unanswered questions hanging over it. Kids dying, Outsiders showing up, there just happens to be an ancient and powerful magus on site. *No-one is doing anything.*

Hella suss, right? I mean, obviously, because why else would they have needed to call in someone like me? Wolfgang was already there, apparently, and he knows more than I do — or at least paints himself that way. Every time I had an answer, something would show up to change the question.

It's a lot easier to notice from the outside, all right? Don't roll your eyes at me.

If I was going to make any progress here — real progress that actually mattered — I needed to follow through on a threat I had made days ago and actually strip this all back to basics. I hadn't known what that meant at the time, and I still wasn't exactly sure, but I really needed to get at the marrow of all this.

Christ, Laufeyjarson was right. Don't tell him.

Su-Yin was almost a little too happy to drive me back to

the school. She'd slipped into love-bomb territory almost, trying too hard to apologise for something I'd already forgiven her for. At another time that might have been something to complain about, but those scales needed balancing.

I asked her to drop me off at the gate, which she did, and then sent her to drive towards the centre of the campus. For most of the drive, I had been carving a set of honking great runes into the scratchy fabric of the door panel and the cheap plastic of the dashboard. I needed her to park those runes in the right place, to be my pivot point.

One of the reasons I love rune magic a great deal more than the shitty arcane magic most wizards use is the flexibility. If you're persuasive enough, you can make it do anything — and that meant I didn't even need to know if there was a similar spell to what I wanted to do, provided the logic of the language held up.

Watching Su-Yin head off down the road towards the campus, I flexed my hand in her direction, attuning to the energy of my big of automotive vandalism. It was easy enough to find, just a load of blank, welcoming runes that would shake hands with anyone that asked. Open sockets for any connector. Just needed to whittle out the right connectors.

Out came the pen knife again. In theory I could have

used a permanent marker, but I wanted as strong a connection as I could manage — I'd carved one half of the equation, it made sense to do the same with the other half. Halfway through scoring the first rune into the pad of my left index finger, I decided this was not an experience I'd repeat in the future.

But I'd started, so I finished.

Four runes, one on each finger, creating an abstract link between me and the car. Invisible but tangible, and it didn't take more than a small effort of will to draw it taut, causing me to lift my hand palm-up towards the campus. I tested the connection a couple of times, yanking on it, and then started walking.

I circled the property a couple of times, my fingers plucking at the energy like it was a collection of harp-strings. In reality, it was more of a dragnet than anything else. I'd pulled the connection tall and thin, dredging across every building, every student, every *inch* of the school as I walked in circles around it.

The net snagged a number of times, peeling the surface level motes of magic off of *something*. It wasn't designed to identify what was causing the snags, just to collect them, detach them. It needed constant reminding of that, hence the plinky-plonky harp plucking, but I was surprised to find how easy it was to do.

After the fourth rotation, the net felt heavy and sluggish. It was full, the contents straining against the fabric of the spell. A few more finger-plucks tied the energy up on itself, closing the net securely around its dredgings. I tied it off tightly, pulled it to breaking point, then gave it one firm twang.

I felt the note reverberate up the strands of energy, reach the pivot point, and shatter, sending a sickly echo back up the dissipating net. It lashed at my fingertips, stinging as the connection severed.

All I had to do now was wait, and it didn't take long.

The changes were small at first, barely noticeable until the larger ones started to fade in. The buildings changed first, the facades melting away like old wax. Then the students, the little black pinpricks that I could see flitting about even from this distance, snapping out of existence. Not to get all dramatic on you, but it was the curtain finally dropping.

See, the school had made for such an intriguing set for this whole thing, I'd not taken the time to remember that sets are a thing you *dress*. My little spell had gathered up everything that didn't belong, all the props and shit that had been added by a certain German dickhead, and let me bin the lot of them. It was indiscriminate and dirty, not at all subtle, but it worked very well.

Eat The Rich

Like, think of it this way — I'd snaked my fingers deep into the school's toupee and yanked that fucker clean off, along with a few patches of scalp. Now neither of us were under any allusions that this place was anything but bald as shit.

What that meant was the rustic veneer of Edwardian toffery had been stripped from the campus, leaving behind a far more realistic rundown aesthetic. The buildings were largely as they had been before, at least on the surface, but where they had been old-but-charming, they were now just *old*. Even from the front gate I could tell the student body had cratered — the air turned cold and heavy, like it wasn't used to being breathed, and I felt it pull back a little in what felt like shyness. Plus, you know, one of the dorm buildings had a mouldering hole in the roof, the damp tiles long having settled into their precarious new positions.

I stepped through the gate and started down the road I had sent Su-Yin down. How much of this place had been a fiction? There had to be, at some level, a working school here, right? Could the lie have spider-webbed out so far that it stretched beyond the campus? That was the problem with thinking big, all the thoughts were *big*.

Su-Yin was struggling with the car when I reached her, trying to wedge the passenger-side door back into place. 'That was really trippy. You could have warned me.'

'I can't warn you if I don't know it's going to happen,' I said. 'What *did* happen, by the way?'

'The car door fell off.'

'Probably whiplash from the spell. What else happened?'

She let the door go. It fell loudly onto the floor. 'I mean, look? Everything is different.'

'Not everything,' I said. 'Just the bits he changed.'

'You mean Wolfgang?'

I nodded. 'He took the skeleton of this place and draped a big fucking blanket over it. Then he scribbled all over that blanket so I'd see what he wanted me to see. *And he kept changing it* so I'd keep seeing things.'

'Fine,' she said, her brow scrunched up in confusion. 'I mean, I can't argue that he did that, looking at all this. But why?'

'That... I don't know,' I conceded. 'Keep the car warm, though. Now I can actually do some snooping.'

'Aye aye.'

It didn't take long to get a good look at the actual state of the school. From afar, I could tell the place was knackered, but it was only when I was up close that I could see the repairs that had been made to keep it usable despite all that. They just made it all look a little sadder, really putting a nail in the coffin sort of thing.

Ok, so, it wasn't like the real version of the school was some entirely rotten shit hole. It was *fine*. The main problem was it was *real*. Before, it had been Hogwarts — a theme park version of a posh twat school, where everything looked the way boomers remember and everything worked, marred by only a couple of pesky murders. Now, it looked lived in, like a normal building that has to deal with routine repairs, budgets, and little shits who write "Dave-o Giant Cock loves Big Dinners" on the brickwork.

Crucially, though, it was still a working school. I could see classes going on through the windows, lit by sturdy yellow strip lights. Had that made it easier to build up the illusion? So many new questions!

No-one popped up to bother me as I made my way to what had previously been the library. It still was, but the previous version had been better. For one thing, it had been manned — by a magus, as I'm sure you remember. No students nor staff in this one, just a pair of self-scan machines to check a book out with. The room they had given me wasn't there either, but then neither were most of the dorms as we've previously established. In fact, a lot of what I had dealt with when it came to the school simply didn't exist.

Wolfgang really did have me all strung up like a fucking marionette, huh?

I had decided that my best option would be to find James Dayne — he knew me, essentially hired me, and while Bertie De'Ath had been the one to meet me off the train, Dayne had a proper grown-up position. If he knew who I was, then I'd know the limits of Wolfgang's fuckery. If he didn't then that opened up new questions anyway.

I let myself into Dayne's office in the admin building, only to find it empty. Empty of him, not empty-empty. My heart did a little tap-dance of terror until I saw the decor. It was the usual trash of academia that follows university people around like a fine mist — a framed diploma, *hilarious* comic strips clipped from an actual newspaper, more pens than a man has reason to own, you know what I mean. Proof he existed, but not proof I interacted with him.

A cursory rifle through the drawers of his desk uncovered nothing useful either, and I don't have the skills to crack a computer password if it isn't *12345*, *password*, or the inexplicably popular *swordfish*. I'd entered the first two when the door handle started to turn slowly.

Split-second decision: project confidence. I hunched

forward onto my elbows and glared daggers at the door — this was my office now.

Walid sidled in sheepishly and closed the door behind him, leaning his back against it as if to brace it shut. 'Hey.'

'Hey.'

'I was supposed to get here before you,' he said, and I noticed he was a little out of breath. 'There was supposed to be a dramatic chair spin.'

I rattled Dayne's chair. 'It's not a swivel chair.'

'It would be.'

'Was that supposed to be a threat? It sounded like you were going for a threatening tone, but you're talking about a swivel chair, so—'

His eyes were scanning the room awkwardly, but his tone was ice cold. 'He's teaching me to weave the context into the working. It's fascinating. I always thought that magic was a middle finger to reality, but it's really astounding what you can do if you work with it.'

'Ah, I see,' I said, slowly daring to push myself to my feet. 'Hey, you want to come over here and let me take a look at the back of your neck? Totally normal request, no need to overthink it.'

He shook his head. 'I'm good. The drama is kind of the point, but it does get a touch overwhelming when it's dialled so high. But the creativity!'

I took a step around the desk. 'Yeah, runes are great, you're preaching to the choir. Just let me take a wee look at your hairline…'

His expression dropped, out the bottom of his twitchy paranoia and into stern disappointment. 'You still think this is just about runes? Oh, no, I understand! You still think this is just a school, even despite tearing down the veil. I get it. He did write everything specifically to steer you that way, it's only fair.'

All I needed was a moment, a split second where he wasn't looking at me. 'Fair would be for someone to finally stop talking in circles, my dude.'

'I agree! I agree! But he likes the dramatic realisations, says it unlocks your mind faster. I don't understand, but I'm getting there.'

Ever so gently, I slipped a piece of chalk from my pocket and flicked it to the side. His eyes followed it, giving me time to dash forward and grab him by the hair. A knee driven into the gut bent him over, and I yanked his hair up to reveal the base of his skull. In the same motion, I snapped open my penknife, ready to quickly — and painfully — carve out the control rune.

But there wasn't one.

He twisted out of my grip and snarled at me in a voice far too deep to be his own. '**Back.**'

I felt a pair of unseen hands forcefully shove me backwards, almost sending me toppling over the desk. My balance was fucked, and I couldn't slow myself in time to avoid ending up sat on the desk, but at least I *was upright*. Walid was much smaller than Su-Yin — if I needed to fight, at least I had a bit of a chance.

He didn't follow up like I had expected. Instead of rushing in, he pressed himself back against the wall again, seemingly as much in shock as I was, perhaps even more. He clapped his hands to his mouth, eyes wide with fear, and froze.

'You all right there, dickhead?' I asked, climbing down from the desk. 'Looking a little peaky.'

'I did it,' he whispered as his hands came away from his face. 'I actually did it.'

'You put on your big boy voice, great job.'

Something, some emotion that I didn't recognise or like, crept over him. 'It's real. It's really real!'

I clicked my fingers to grab his attention. 'Oi, over here, mate. We're not done here.'

Cold eyes turned on me. 'This changes everything. I need to talk to him. He needs to know.'

'Talk to me first,' I snapped. 'I'm due answers and I'm not letting this shit get all fucking spaghetti'd again. You're not walking out this door until I get what I want.'

'If I'm right, you can't stop me.'

'And if *I'm* right, I'm going to kick you so hard in the bollocks you'll spit jizz.'

The moment self confidence kicks in is a delicate one. It's not instant, there's a short window where it has to set once it's all in place. If you can interrupt the signal during that time, you might just have a chance of putting someone on the back foot.

Like, yeah, it goes both ways. I was about ready to start fucking reeling mentally over whatever that shit was he had done to me — might look and sound like magic, but that wasn't the sort of magic I knew about — but while I still had the balls I had to use them. He was clearly discovering something about himself, and yeah it was giving him a right kick up the arse, but he wasn't sure about it yet.

When he glanced down at my boots for a second, I knew I had him. At least for the moment.

'What do you want?'

Eat The Rich

I took one long, slow, deep breath. 'I want to know what the *fuck* is happening. Please.'

'Fair enough,' he said. 'Fair enough. Obviously you've worked out that everything to do with the school is a fiction, right?'

'Obviously,' I replied. 'I ripped up that veil.'

'It wasn't an illusion in the traditional sense. If it had just been an illusion, you'd have felt it eventually.'

'I did feel it.'

'No, you didn't,' he said quickly. 'You felt something was off with the investigation, but not the school. Not until things got weirder. The actual mechanics of the situation worked perfectly.'

I nodded reluctantly. 'Or, I'm so burnt out when it comes to magic that I can't sense shit, and you're trying to big up your boss man.'

'He said you'd do that,' Walid said, pointing at me. 'He said you'd play yourself down. That's why this would work.'

'I underestimate myself so I'm easy to fool? Bro, I think you're reaching now.'

'None of this was to fool you. It was to position you.'

That did send a few blocks shifting in my head, I won't

lie. Kind of reframed things. 'Position me how?'

'Do you really not see it?'

I had seen it, but it was a difficult thing to force myself to accept. Loki had been saying it from the beginning, harping on about the need for me to start thinking like a runeskald. The believe in the stories. To think less like a wizard. 'You can't be serious.'

'It's a multi-step process. The first step alone does make it sound a little weird, but I'm totally serious.'

All of this shit was designed to piss me off. Like, actually properly designed to mess me up and get me all up in my head, to manufacture an epiphany. 'You wanted me pissed off and stressed out. You wanted me to start believing my own bullshit, giving in to self-delusion.'

'He wanted you confident, that's all,' Walid said. 'Confident that you were right. About everything.'

'By making everything I thought wrong? Don't buy it.'

He shrugged a little. 'I didn't quite get it either. But it's something to do with giving you a reason to think. If it's easy, you don't think. You just do. He said it was like shaking the rust loose so the cogs can get whirring again. Then once they're turning, you just crank up the speed bit by bit.'

'Make or break.'

'Something like that.'

'This is a really fucking convoluted way to smack me with some tough love and a pep talk.'

'He said you were a special case,' Walid's confidence was starting to set in now, his gaze was turning to steel. 'A lot of damage to work through. I've barely met you, and I already know you're not going to get on with a therapist. You think simple and straightforward would work for you? It needed to be elaborate.'

'So it was all bollocks?'

'I don't think so. The school is real, the deaths of the kids are real. I think. It's not Outsiders, none of that stuff, but kids are dying here.'

'What?'

'One a year, usually. No-one cares. There are schools in central London with higher death rates, and no-one cares about *those*. But there was enough truth to embellish with magic. And I think Wolfgang had other reasons for picking this place, but I know better than to pry.'

Fuck. Fuck fuck fuck. Kids were still dying here? I had really hoped that the whole dead children thing was part of whatever bullshit veil Wolfgang had concocted, but of course it was real. I'd said it before, he'd laid a blanket over things, built his fucking escape-room-grade mad plot on top of the bones of what was actually happening. He'd made the deaths a big thing, but they had to have been a thing in the first place for him to do that.

Suddenly, whether I had been brought to the school by someone real or not didn't matter — the reason I was there definitely *was* real. Just slot that at the top of my list of priorities, I guess.

I crossed my arms. 'Where is he? I think I need a word with him.'

'Here somewhere. Waiting for you, probably. He's very keen to finish building you up. It's all he's talking about now. Maybe he'll change his mind when he's seen what I can do now!'

'Yeah, about that—'

He cleared his throat, interrupting me. '***I'm out.***'

Bastard didn't even have the decency to vanish in a puff of smoke, he just bloody vanished. The air tasted metallic and coppery, like blood, but earthy and moist too. A very memorable residue to leave from a spell, but not one that properly fit with arcane or runic magic. It was like trying to think of a greenish yellow-purple, or smelling a sound.

Basically, it was fucking weird and it made my head hurt.

But, on the positive side, I'd got the scent now — quite literally. Given a bit of time, I was sure I could sniff him out; it was lodged firmly in my mind-nose and it wasn't going to shift anytime soon.

If I was going to actually work out what was going on here and save those kids, I'd need reality to just fucking stay still for a minute. And for that to happen, a certain handsome German shitbag was going to need a smack in the face.

Time to start my run-up.

Eighteen

'How many ghosts have you sent packing?' Su-Yin asked.

It was a little out of the blue, as questions go, but it was clear that it had been burning a hole behind her eyes for a while now, and it had reached a temperature now that meant she couldn't ignore it. Not that I could blame her; Wolfgang was the target for sure, but I needed an avenue of approach. My mind was whirring, cogs clicking and grinding against each other. There were ideas there, gestating in the dark, but they needed time. That meant a lot of waiting around while the little goblins in my head slid a few blocks around.

That sort of thinking leads to *pacing* up and down corridors in silence, which is not a very sociable endeavour. All that silent stomping up and down, it stood to reason she'd get thinking too. When her brain reached critical mass, we were near one of the many empty classrooms, and she'd pulled me inside for the privacy. Now, she was leaning against the door, her face all screwed up in thought.

I perched myself on one of the desks, one foot up so I

could rest my chin on my knee. 'Where's this coming from?'

'I've been thinking about all this,' she said, blinking slowly. 'I don't really know that much about you, obviously, but I know a little about Wolfgang.'

'And you want to try and match his pseudo-insightful mumbo jumbo against facts.'

'Something like that. Unless you're too busy pacing aimlessly.'

I let my eyes narrow. 'It's not aimless. I'm just not exactly sure where I'm aiming yet. There's a super important distinction there.'

'So, that means you've got enough time to humour me a little, yeah?'

'Okay, fine. I'll bite.' I said. 'How many ghosts have I kicked to the curb? More than I can count. And I can count into three whole digits.'

'Right, so, loads of them; that's what you're saying, yeah?'

I sighed. She wanted a serious conversation, then. 'More than most people, sure. Most wizards, even. It's not glamorous or anything, so it kind of gets overshadowed once you get a firm grip on twisting the fabric of reality.'

'It's not even a little exciting?'

'Eh, once you've done that a couple of times it gets pretty rote,' I said. 'It's actually easier with the bad bitches because you don't have to talk to them. The ones that can still think are trickier, but even then it's pretty simple over all. Are you trying to make a point here?'

Su-Yin folded her arms and smiled. 'Look at you, talking about *ghosts* like you're dealing with a Jehova's Witness at the door. It's really that easy for you that it's become *boring*?'

'Don't go pointing that out at me,' I half-snapped. 'You'll have me thinking Wolfgang was onto something.'

'Well, maybe he was,' she said, undeterred by my withering glare. 'He's definitely made some highly questionable choices—'

'Questionable? That's the word you're going with?'

'I'll use language you're more familiar with if you like.'

'Please.'

She smirked. 'Fine. His brain might have been churning out premium-grade batshit scumfuckery—'

'Way better.'

'But he's not completely wrong, is he?' she asked.

'Would it have worked so effectively if he had been? It's possible to be both shitty and insightful, I think.'

There was a glimmer in her eye, one that made it very clear she had so much more to say. Yes, she had declined to talk about my run-in with Walid, but the embers of her pointed questioning had kicked into life the moment I filled her in on what he had said about Wolfgang. It was extremely annoying that someone I had only just met had been able to get such a good read of me that she could start *sassing me* with a look.

Naturally, I lashed out. 'You're definitely managing it.'

'I'll change the subject then,' she said with a smile. 'What's next? I know you think you can sniff out Walid or whatever, but have you thought about what to do when you get to him?'

'I figured I'd leave him to you while I have words with Wolfgang.'

'Fair, but—'

'No, look, I know,' I interrupted. 'But if I think for too long about what Wolfgang can do, it gets too big for my head. *Yeah, go and take down someone who can apparently just rewrite reality so he wins,* easy fucking peasy.'

'I'm still not clear on that.'

'You and me both. Like, if he's that powerful, how did I break the spell so easily?'

'You apparently kick ghosts to death pretty easily.'

I shook my head. 'It's not even close to the same thing.'

'Isn't it?' she said. 'I don't know much about all that rune magic stuff, but I do know a little about the arcane. And I know that all the technical talent in the world is secondary to will. You've got to fuel a spell or it doesn't work.'

'Doesn't really apply here. Rune magic fuels itself, that's what the runes *are*. They're the magic, the talent comes from how you put them together.'

'But does it, though?'

I climbed down from the desk, crossed the room and slumped down to the floor near the whiteboard. 'Pretty much. It's complicated. You've got to take the context into account, how each rune fits together...'

'Aren't you the context, though?'

'That's the skald part, yeah.'

'That's what I'm saying,' she lowered herself down next to me. 'Give Tom Waits and Freddy Mercury the same song, you really think they're going to sing it the same way?'

'I'll ask. I've met Freddy's ghost.'

'Stop it.'

'Really nice, actually. Very chill.'

'We're going to put a pin in that so I can ask you whether it's bullshit later,' she said, bumping me with her shoulder. 'But come on, be serious. You know I'm making sense here.'

I felt my eyes dart away. 'Please don't start on the whole confidence is power line. It feels so gross. It's one step from that to singing Kumbaya to spin up a wind turbine or something.'

'What?'

'I'm very uncomfortable talking about my feelings and its damaging my analogies. Go easy on me.'

That glint again. 'I will when you will.'

'Very zen. Thanks so much.'

Fucking fucking *fuck*. Like, I know she was right and I know you know that. It's so much easier to admit that here than with actual human words in a human conversation. There's not some objective arbiter of magic that you have to convince of the logic of your spells, runic or otherwise, it's just you, in your own head, believing so hard that you're right. Yes, ghosts will fuck off to the afterlife if you kick them hard enough, because that's just how I've decided it is. You can protect someone from harm by shoving a pebble under their tongue because I've *decided really hard* that that's what it does.

Sure, you can undo a massive fucking illusion by walking round and round the garden like an edgy goth teddy bear *because you spun the story in your head and believed it would work*.

And that's super easy when you don't have time to think too much about it, when you're caught up in the moment. But if you're not in the moment any more, then you're thinking. If you're thinking, you're doubting. If you're doubting, you can't stop.

Then you have a stupid gorgeous weight-lifting barbarian who you've just met telling you that you need to believe in yourself more, like this your first day inside your own head and it's *so* easy to do. But if you start doing that, then that opens so many more doors you might not be ready to open, so many questions you've carefully locked away in your brain and...

And...

And fuck me, I need a therapist.

As if she'd somehow read all that on my face, Su-Yin wisely opted to let silence reign for a little longer while I jammed all the crazy back into its boxes. A whole lot of introspecting was going on there, let me tell you.

Eventually, she placed a hand gently on the back of my neck. 'So, what's the plan?'

'Fuck if I know,' I muttered. 'Maybe I'll just duel him. He's so in love with fiddling about with stories, maybe he'd love that.'

'What, like walk twelve paces, turn, fire? That sort of duel?'

'But with magic, yeah.'

'See, there's that confidence I was talking about.'

'I'm going to cheat, obviously.'

'Oh.'

'Do I look like a fighter?'

She took a moment to size me up. 'A bad one. All the bruises and stuff.'

'That you gave me, exactly.'

'Technically, you won that fight, you know.'

I laughed a little. She did have a point — being able to walk out of that fight, even after a hospital stay, did feel like a victory.

But I'd need more than that if I was going to go up against Wolfgang. Hell, I'd need more than that if I was going up again Walid now. I hadn't forgotten his weird little fancy magic that gave him such a mad stiffy.

'Real talk now,' I said. 'Why here?'

'Hmm?'

'It's out of the way, forgettable, a blank canvas. But there are loads of places like that. Why did Wolfgang pick this one?'

Su-Yin bumped her head back against the wall a couple of times. 'I hope you're not asking me because you think I know. I was a good little brainwashed soldier. He'd made sure I didn't need the explanations. Or even want them.'

'But Walid did. He wasn't branded, which means he was talked around. Can't talk someone around without explaining things, even a little.'

'Or he was branded somewhere you couldn't see.'

'Gross,' I said, screwing up my face. 'Come on. Wolfgang might not have had to spit his poison in your ear, but there's no way you weren't close enough to sometimes hear him doing it to your bestest buddy.'

Her face fell. 'He told me not to listen, so I didn't listen. He kept using the school as an example though, went on and on about how it's important to match the narrative significance, whatever that means. Honestly, Walid was eating it up, that much I remember.'

'I wonder if he even listens to himself when he speaks,' I said, rolling my eyes. 'Narrative significance? What the fuck?'

'Man loves the smell of his own farts, what can I say?'

'I'd never heard of this school before I got the job, so it's not significant to my bloody narrative.' I frowned. 'Fuck me, is he classing me as a part of another narrative? That's rude. What's this school called again?'

'Fury College these days, I think,' Su-Yin said, pulling out her phone. 'Used to be called The Wyvern School. Any of that ring a bell?'

'Nothing,' I said, taking the phone.

She had pulled up the school's Wikipedia page. It was considerably more detailed than it had been when I'd done my *extremely thorough* thirty-second research a few days ago. Signs of another tendril of Wolfgang's power, no doubt.

The school was as old as the illusion had purported, that much was true. The Wyvern School was a *much* cooler name though, so why wouldn't he pick that if he was rewriting shit to set his stage? Fury College lacked the old money gravitas that was meant to be baked into the stone of these posh places.

'I didn't see anything special about it either,' Su-Yin said.

'Changed its name to Fury College about ten years ago,' I said, scrolling through the article. 'After some dude donated a stonking huge pile of cash. That little nugget wasn't in here before.'

'Wolfgang edited that out in setting up his illusion but kept the name? What's the point of that?'

I didn't reply, I was getting dragged into a rabbit hole.

See, the article didn't name Richtwat McMoneybags, but it doesn't take a genius to work out his name had to be Fury. I ruled out the beefy boxer boys because duh, and then I had to scrape real deep to find anything that might fit.

'Hey, ever heard of this guy?'

I showed her a news article from a small local paper. The paper didn't have the look of one that was particularly well-read, and this article bore the brunt of that — it was all squished and blocked, like it was designed to be read on one of those boxy bastards that every school computer lab always seems to have.

She scanned the page. 'Raoul Fury? Never heard of him,

and I'd remember someone with a name that boss.'

'You think his name's cool?'

'You don't?' she said. 'Sounds like the hero in a super shitty 80s cop film.'

'Sounds like a man who picked his own name to sound cool,' I said. 'But also the guy that funnelled a load of money into this place?'

Su-Yin shrugged. 'Does that tell us anything useful?'

'Probably not,' I said, sighing. 'Or possibly something? There's got to be some connection there. Don't suppose you've got any of your old information gathering network left, have you?'

'Doubt it. Walid was the brains there anyway. Even if we hadn't burned it to the ground trying to locate you, I doubt they'd talk to me without him there.'

'They don't trust you?'

She smiled sheepishly. 'They're shit scared of me. Walid hyped me up as his muscle.'

'Fair enough,' I muttered. 'Then we'll have to go to my sources instead.'

'You have sources?'

'Of course I have sources. Surely you've noticed I'm not

a fucking amateur at *all* of this, right?'

I didn't let her reply — she'd only start asking questions and that would interrupt my flow. If I was going to talk to my sources, I was going to need to tap into that bombastic confidence I was just discovering I actually had, and having someone telling me what a terrible idea it was — which she would do, because I would do that if I wasn't already utterly stoked — would cock things up.

Scrambling into the passenger seat of the car, I snapped open the glove box and had a good rummage. Su-Yin hovered beside me, one arm leaning on the roof, bent double to watch what I was doing.

'Ah yes,' she said. 'The all knowing oracle of miscellaneous car junk.'

'I love the sass, just so you know.'

'Are you looking for something in particular?'

I ignored her and carved a path through the assorted wires and empty tissue packets that were stuffed into the thing, yanking out my prize. 'You've got GPS on your phone, right?'

'Yeah, but—'

'So you don't *really* need this A-Z map thing, yeah? Modern woman of the world, you, right?'

Eat The Rich

'I don't like—'

Harnessing my unearned confidence, I pushed past her and started to rip page after page out of the little atlas. The first few pages fluttered sadly to the ground next to my feet, and I stomped on them for good measure. 'Haha, eat shit, knowledge!'

'Are you ill?'

'Just shush,' I snapped, tearing out more pages. 'I'm making a scene.'

'Yeah, you are.'

The next few pages I removed fell as limply as the first, and I stomped them just as dutifully into the mud. The third lot did the same, and that warm feeling of embarrassment started brewing in my cheeks, just readying itself to make me feel like a real stupid tit. It wasn't ready to make its play yet, though, it needed an opening and I was hoping I wouldn't give it one.

I was about a third through the book when things started to happen.

The pages were catching on the breeze as they fell now, swooping around me a few times before hitting the dirt. The stomped pages were smouldering at the edges, glowing embers kicking out a heady, smoky smell. It snaked its way up my nostrils and wrapped around the back of my eyes, dragging my conscious back and away the more I breathed it in.

Another handful of pages and I was drunk on the fumes, swimming in an inky blackness.

And something else was swimming in it, something unfathomably massive but impossible to see. The pressure of it moving nearby was the only way I could perceive it at all.

'***Welcome back, little Runeskald of Midgard.***'

The voice boomed through the darkness, threatening to crush my skull. It made my ears ring with the foreboding resonance of a beaten up old grandfather clock, and I'm pretty sure my eyes would have watered if I was still attached to them.

'Hello again, you spooky bitch.'

'***You wander once more where you don't belong, wearing your false bravado like armour. Paper armour. Paper tiger. Paper heart.***'

'I see you haven't changed much.'

A cold chill crept up my spine, vertebrae by vertebrae, from coccyx all the way up to the base of my skull. A sharpness pricked at me with each small step up my back. '***I change. Knowledge changes. I undulate with change.***'

I fought off the urge to slap at whatever was tiptoeing up my spine. 'I need information.'

The presence went quiet, and I could feel it thinking. I'd only dealt with it once before, and I hadn't even meant to at the time, but I understood it in ways I didn't even understand myself. It had made sure of that.

See, the first time I had talked to it I'd been tagging along with a demigod and playing the dutiful sidekick. The intention had been to talk to Sigrun — alleged queen of the valkyries and professional nosy bitch — but I'd shown up a few centuries late. This *thing* had eaten her.

'**Precocious little Runeskald,**' it said. '**You come and make demands, as you did before, so confident that you have foreseen everything. You know the rules. You know the price. Still you think it worth paying. Amusing.**'

I did my best to do the astral plane equivalent of a derisory snort. 'Okay, look. I'll admit I got a little shit up last time we talked, but I'm giving this whole confidence thing a try and, I have to say, it's making you a lot less scary.'

'**If it was my wish to scare you, I have more than enough means.**'

The sharp chill traced a path around my throat and up

under my chin. It pressed into the tender flesh, tilting my head up, threatening to pierce into the bottom of my mouth. Another was scoring up my chest and began to gently fasten around my throat.

'But I know the rules,' I choked. 'And you can't hurt me if I don't break them. We've been through this dance before.'

There was another long pause. '*That is true. Should I choose to follow the rules. I did not write them. I did not agree to them. I inherited them through gluttony and consumption. They do not constrain me.*'

Huh, well, shit. 'They did last time.'

'*Last time was one choice. This time is a new choice. Every choice is unique, every decision sacred. Every moment your last. Or not.*'

The icy fingers, or whatever they were, cinched tighter at my throat and I could feel my skin start to split as the icicle under my chin slowly started to press harder. 'Why is Raoul Fury so important to Wolfgang? That's a direct question, *you are obliged* to answer.'

'*Like as like, a pact is made. A secret for a secret. If you invoke the rules, you are as bound as I.*'

'I'll give you a secret,' I whispered. Despite it not being my actual throat, the pressure was making it hard to breathe. 'But not before you tell me what I want to know. Buyer's privilege.'

'*That is not the rule.*'

Every fibre of my being was begging me to claw at my throat and prise those icy fingers open. I mean, sure, there was no chance I'd be strong enough to move them even a millimetre, but when has that ever stopped someone?

Well, then, actually. It stopped me then. The only leverage I had was in my complete indifference to his bullshit. I'd realised this sometime after my first encounter with this presence — it loves rules, but only as a trap. Give the fucker an inch, he'll take a mile. He thinks you don't know all the rules, he'll squeeze the piss out of you.

So you bullshit the bullshitter, and you do it without fear.

I gritted my teeth. 'It fucking is. Anyone paying for something sight unseen is a fool, and despite appearances I'm not a fucking mark.'

A ripple made its way through the darkness. The cold fingers remained still, but the pressure around me lessened just a tad, as if something had distracted the presence for a split second. It was enough for me to gulp down a strained breath before it pressed down on me again, giving me the sensation of an invisible face mere inches from my own, teeth bared.

'*Like as like. Ironclad and riveted. Deadbolt sealed. Perhaps you deserve to know,*' it said, the voice booming once more. Then it dropped down to a sinister rumbling whisper, as though it was right at my ear. '*He wants you to know.*'

The fingers at my throat shifted, grabbing me by the hair and holding my head still as the claw under my chin slid slowly over my jaw and up my face. It traced the bag under my left eye and came to a rest at the corner by my nose. Again, everything in me was screaming for me to pull back, to recoil, to just fucking run. And, again, I managed to make myself seem a lot less outwardly terrified than I was.

See, I know you've worked out something horrid is about to happen to my eye. It's obvious, yeah? You'd probably be a little squeamish too, right? But think about it this way — you probably don't know exactly what's coming. I did. I knew exactly what that icy digit was about to do, how much it would hurt, and quite how much I couldn't show it.

I don't often go begging for bad bitch coins, but frankly, I fucking deserve them here.

One more deep breath, then I felt the fingers in my hair grow tighter still, locking me steady. Then slowly, agonisingly slowly, one finger forced itself behind my eye.

Nineteen

The pain was excruciating. It felt like something inside me was tearing, a cobweb made of nerve-endings. With each horrific tear, new memories were coming into focus. They were bright and vibrant, carved in deep like trauma, so there would be no hope of being able to forget them.

The presence was showing me Raoul Fury. Despite the name, he was quite an unremarkable man to look at — he had the tired and wiry form of a geography professor, complete with the slightly-too-long hair that was just dying to be cool, and the sort of beard that would have looked roguish if it was on a more handsome face. He looked sad and pathetic, like someone who would wear a fedora and show up in a compilation of cringe posts online.

Then something changed. Nothing changed in his appearance really, but he filled himself out more somehow. His eyes came alive, and I saw him walking with a woman — the memory told me her name was Ertras — through a forest that felt oddly familiar. They reached a clearing and stood in front of a building I didn't recognise.

Until I did.

It was the Wyvern School, but it wasn't. It was an office block, but it wasn't. It was both.

Ertras placed her hand on Fury's shoulder and he started to cast a spell. A spell that wasn't a spell. It made the memory rattle around my head, something in there trying to reject it, pushing it right down until the only thing that remained was one word bellowing at me from the darkness.

And, naturally, the smugness of the presence asking me if it had earned its price. There was no way I could conjure up the resolve to turn it away after this, and I felt myself go limp as it extracted its payment.

The darkness faded and my eyes snapped open, burning against the daylight. Mate, it's worse than a ketamine hangover. Probably. Never actually done ket, but stands to reason, right?

Once my pupils remembered how to work, my eyes focused in on Su-Yin's face and I realised she was cradling me in those very strong arms of hers, her face etched with terror. On reflection, I probably should have told her a little bit more about my plan before I let my consciousness get dragged off to another dimension, huh?

'You back with me?'

I practically vomited the word out. 'Diplomancy.'

'Huh?'

'*Diplomancy,*' I repeated, throwing myself out of her grip and onto the floor. I was one step away from proper convulsions. 'Diplomancer. Raoul Fury was a Diplomancer.'

Su-Yin crouched down and hoisted me upright again. The manic energy was already starting to drain out of me, and I could feel the emotion welling up to take its place. 'Millie, I don't know what that means.'

'Me neither,' I said, choking back tears. 'But it's what he was, and its important, and it's why Wolfgang cares.'

Then my legs gave out, my tears burst out, and I just sort of shut down for a while. A lot of emotions, a lot of trauma, and a *lot* of pain to deal with all at once. Best way to deal with all that is to cry it out like a bitch, and I'm not ashamed of that.

Mercifully, Su-Yin didn't seem to mind either. It's a hell of a lot easier to deal with when you're bawling up your snot in someone's arms rather than a bathroom cubicle, let's put it that way.

*

Back when I had been an actual student of magic, Wingard had taught me a lot of the alternatives to arcane magic. Was pretty shitty when it came to my confidence for casting arcane stuff, but I can't deny it had given me a more stable grounding than most wizards. The broader your horizons, the more open your thinking. In theory.

He'd never taught me anything about Diplomancy, though, and by the time I regained my composure I was starting to understand why.

Names are important for basically all kinds of magic, including the magic of the internet. I knew someone once who was really into search engine optimisation, which is exactly as boring as it sounds, but he could just go off for hours about how the job is done for you if you just fucking know the name. It's a shortcut.

This account hasn't done a great job of upselling my competence at my job, I'm aware. We've all got to start somewhere, and I started up to my neck in Trash Alley, as I have recounted here. But, despite appearances, I do know what I'm doing. With the name, I could find everything I needed about Diplomancer with just a few searches.

But Su-Yin could do it faster.

'I don't like how deep I had to go on the net to find this stuff,' she said, thumbs hurriedly tapping out a symphony on her phone screen. 'We're talking Mariana Trench depth. So many weird-looking terror fish.'

'I thought you'd burned all your intel bridges.'

'I did. But you don't always need to ask questions, just read things. Take a look.'

She handed me her phone. On the screen was a website so simple that it had more than a bit of low-fi charm — chunky white text on a deep black background, like someone had just uploaded a notepad file and called it a day.

'Okay, so, this looks like something you'd show a doctor to get your tinfoil hat signed off as a medical expense,' I said. 'You sure?'

She nodded. 'It's vouched for. Intel brokers leave signs for each other as professional courtesy when they verify something that's useful. I'm non grata these days, sure, but I can still read.'

Trying to read the damned thing, I realised why people went to professionals for their intel. Finding stuff like this took some talent, sure, but that was very much a skill you could start learning in an afternoon — after all, I said Su-Yin did it faster than me, but I know for a fact I would have still gotten there. But understanding it? That was where you needed the professional.

Stream of consciousness writing is one thing, but this was all the way to a river, one raging and overflowing its banks. Sentences began an ended at random, inside other sentences, twisted around each other and bounced between upper and lower case aS iF wRiTtEn By SoMeOnE wHo ThInKs ThIs LoOkS EdGy aNd SpOoKy.

I thrust the phone back at Su-Yin. 'I can't read this. It's in code.'

'Code?' she said, taking the phone back. 'This isn't a code, it's "dangerously online millennial", that's all.'

'It hurts my brain. I want to burn it.'

'That's a natural reaction. Give me a sec...'

She tapped at the screen a couple more times and handed the phone back. Everything was lower case now, much easier to follow.

'You're a witch.'

She rolled her eyes. 'There's a browser setting for this. How do you not know that?'

'Leave me alone. I'm researching.'

It still read like a conspiracy theory, but it did at least sound like one formulated by your standard lunatic and not a criminal one. Everything you'd expect was there: secret societies, hidden bases, shadowy individuals pulling the strings. My absolute favourite bit was the insistence that you could use Diplomacy to philosophise someone to death which, as anyone who has talked to the sort of tight-arsed dickbag that *really wants you to know he's been to university* will tell you, is hardly a secret.

Do you know how many guys have sidled up to me at the pub and tried to impress me by wittering on about Bertie Camus? It's enough to make me wish for death, and that got me thinking that maybe, just maybe, there was something in all this.

I scrolled through the page a couple of times, making sure I'd absorbed everything of worth. 'There has to be something I'm missing here.'

'Hmm?' Su-Yin, in a fit of boredom, was idly kicking the heads off nearby daisies.

'There's nothing here that says *why* Wolfgang would be *here*,' I said. 'Like, sure, there's a lot of shit here about Diplomancy being really scary shit, reshaping reality with words at a fundamental level—'

'And who wouldn't like that sort of power?'

I nodded. 'Exactly. But why come here, to a school? Just because Raoul Fury's name is on it? This batshit website doesn't have the decency to completely spell out the conspiracy — where's the bonkers legend or ultimate power or unhinged scavenger hunt to find an ancient relic?'

'If you give me back the phone I could probably find—'

She reached for her phone and I felt myself yank my arm away from her. 'You know what, fuck it. I'm going to ask.'

'What?'

'I'm going to ask him. His number's in your phone, right?' I was already scrolling through her contact list.

'Is that wise? I mean—'

'He's not under W for Wolfgang. Where is he?'

Su-Yin's face went ashen. 'M.'

I scrolled back up. M — for Master. Yuck. 'He's a real prick, huh?'

'Yup.'

I hit the call button and waited for him to pick up. There's a weird magic involved in using someone else's phone, a disconnecting discomfort in how weird it feels in your hand, and that was something I was hoping to use to my advantage. You can do weird shit with magic, so just be patient.

Wolfgang answered after four and a half rings. 'Hello, Millie.'

'Hello dickhead,' I replied. There wasn't a shred of

interest in me concerning the fact he knew it was me on the phone and not Su-Yin, but I knew he'd want to tell me, and I wanted him in a talking mood. 'How did you know it was me?'

'Su-Yin texts. Plus, I've had an enlightening conversation with Walid.'

'Yeah, I had one of them too. Very chatty guy. Told me all about this Diplomancy shit.'

I could hear the smile forming on his face. Ergh. The wet slither of lips over teeth. 'Yes! You're finally there! At last! I was beginning to worry you'd never make the logical leap.'

'I mean, your underling told me, so...'

'Come on, don't give him all the credit,' Wolfgang was bordering on overjoyed now, a very strange tone to connect with such a harsh accent. 'He gave you a final push, but you'd been suspecting for a while, I am sure.'

Nope. 'Maybe a little.'

'I'm just scratching the surface myself, but it is *fascinating*. The forgotten history of runeskalds, unfolding bit by bit.'

'You're very chummy all of a sudden.'

'I've been chummy this whole time, Millie,' he said.

'You're a peer, chosen by Loki himself. Just like me. All I've done has been to pave the way for you so we can share in this. I just needed to give you a little boost up to my level, and if you're asking about Diplomancy then it's safe to say you are where I need you to be.'

From the beginning, Wolfgang had been a bright neon red flag, flapping in the wind. Everything he had told me had been shady as fuck, obviously untrue, and very obviously manipulative. It was like he had been following a handbook.

But I wasn't getting that sense from him now, and that made it all the more disconcerting. Again, he was telling me this had all been some weird tough love, teachable bullshit stuff, and again it rang true — or, at least, rang true in the sense that he *thought* that was what he was doing.

'I think I've reached my limit,' I said, slipping a little helplessness into my voice. 'So, if you're ready to teach...'

'You're ready to listen?'

'Mhmm.'

'Then let's make you who you were born to be. Meet me in the basement, under the admin building. You'll know where to go. I'll leave the door unlocked. Oh, and don't bring Su-Yin. She's not welcome.'

He hung up. I handed the phone back to Su-Yin and she looked at it suspiciously. 'I'm going to assume you were bullshitting him there and not actually about to go all teacher's pet.'

'Obviously.'

'You think he knows?'

I shrugged. 'Doesn't matter, I have to play it as if he does either way. If he's not suspicious of me, then the fact he's been a few steps ahead this whole time makes me look really fucking dumb, right?'

'Doesn't make me look much better.'

'Well, he fucked with your mind. You get a pass.'

'So kind of you.'

'I'm worried too,' I said. 'Only time anyone is as aggressively friendly as he's trying to be is when he's already got a trap all laid out. He's really bad at hiding this shit.'

Su-Yin crossed her strong arms across her chest and frowned. 'But just because you know it's a trap doesn't mean you're safe from it.'

'I'm not that big of an idiot, you know. I do know that. But I've still got to go, don't I? I mean, I'm tapped out here. Either I stroll into his evil lair and hope for the best, or I slap on a pair of nerd glasses and click through dark web Wikipedia forever and leave him to his nefarious business.'

'Nefarious?'

'A smart-sounding word used for effect. Would you prefer I said *villainous wankery*?'

She giggled. 'That sounds much more you, yes. So, what's the plan?'

'He doesn't want you there, for one thing.'

'Okay, fine,' she said. 'But do you?'

I didn't even need to think about that. 'Yes.'

'Then I'll find a way to be sneaky. Just tell me what you've got in mind.'

Taking her by the hand, I led her down onto the grass and sat next to her. 'Okay, but bear in mind that I'm expecting things to get really fucking weird. He's weird, so it just stands to reason.'

'Understood. Hit me.'

*

The basement didn't even have the decency to look all spooky and shit — it had proper lighting and some ambitious architect had avoided the bunker-chic claustrophobic walls. It was actually quite disappointing.

Wolfgang, however, had been true to his word. The basement wasn't big, but it would have been confusing enough to get lost in if there hadn't been something pulling me in. It was like a tingle across the hairs on my arm, almost a breeze but not quite. It was quite a gentle bit of guidance, all things considered.

I followed the sensation through the twisting bowels of lower-upper-middle-upper class education until the corridor gave way and opened out into a strangely cavernous space. Like, yeah, any cavern underneath a building is going to be strange, no matter what's in there.

But it's even stranger if that cavern houses an office block.

Which, to be clear, this one somehow did.

It wasn't a small one either. The thing was several storeys tall, gleaming glass windows and all very hyper-modern design. Even if it hadn't somehow been squashed into the basement of a school, it would have looked odd anywhere but the middle of a city — somewhere that had airs and graces and *finance districts*.

Stepping out of the basement corridor, I felt the ground

shift beneath my feet. From lacquered concrete (or whatever) to moist earth and the damp mulch of autumnal leaves. No sky, though, just a featureless black void hanging menacingly above.

You know, I had to allow myself to be a little impressed. 'Huh, fuck me.'

There was a tug at one of my belt loops. 'What? What is it?'

'The weird shit is happening faster than I thought,' I said, over my shoulder. My hand crept down to my waist, playing over the invisible finger looped through where my belt would have sat.

'How weird?' Su-Yin said. 'I can't see shit!'

'Did you need to make the veil quite that thick?'

'The less I can see out, the less likely someone can see in,' she shot back. 'We've been over this.'

And we had. Several times. It was apparent almost immediately that sneaking Su-Yin along with me to see Wolfgang was going to be extremely difficult. He'd be prepared for that sort of betrayal, and seeing as he controlled the location we didn't have the luxury of doing proper stealthy shit. So, that left magic, and not the kind I was good at.

Sure, you can definitely come up with a set of runes to

mask your presence, but they're not exactly portable. Lot of rules to define, so only really feasible if you've got a fetish for full-body tattoos. Even if Su-Yin had that, we didn't have the time.

So, I bowed to her greater knowledge of the arcane which, on reflection, was starting to sound a little more bullshitty than I would have liked.

Veils are classic magic, everyone knows that, but we had hit a bit of a sticking point regarding the very-adult-and-not-at-all-childish logic of *if I can't see him, he can't see me.* But, hey, what do I know? Maybe that is how it works. Or maybe she just wanted an excuse to tug at my waistband constantly. Who can say?

'It's an office building,' I said, avoiding dredging up the same argument one more time. 'Just sat there.'

'Just sitting underground?' she said. 'Oh. Ohh! Borrowed space! Very clever.'

'Hm?'

She took a breath, the same kind Wingard used to do when he was about to give a little lecture. Seems it comes naturally to wizards. 'Borrowed space. It's, like, mid-to-high level arcane fuckery. Basically, you bend space-time in hundreds, even thousands of tiny little out of the way places so they all interconnect in one place. You steal room from somewhere else and use it to stitch together some Frankenstein location elsewhere. Gather enough tiny specks from all over the place, you can make your own little kingdom.'

'Big enough to store an entire building?' I replied. 'And the immediate area around it? That's a lot of work, surely.'

'Well, I can't *see* it, can I? But sure, it would be theoretically possible. I don't know how much work it would be to hold it long term, though.'

An idea sidled into my brain. 'Hold on.'

I took a few steps back towards the entrance to the clearing, where the basement corridor ended and the moist earth began, and kicked aside some of the liquidised leaves. Underneath were sigils, stamped into the earth like moulds and filled with poured metal. It was pretty likely they would span the entire circumference of the clearing, though I wasn't going to take the time to check.

'What you got?'

The metal was cold to the touch. 'Binding circle of some kind. Runic, not arcane. I don't recognise the runes at all, though.'

'Is that unusual?'

'Kind of. Like, even if I don't understand what the runes

are *doing* there's usually *something* familiar there. I guess it's kind of like trying to read Cyrillic?'

Su-Yin was quiet for a moment. 'Ok. I think. But what does it mean?'

'I'm not sure yet,' I said, tracing my finger around the edges of one of the runes. 'Definitely a binding circle, though. Taking the weight of that borrowed space shit you were talking about, maybe?'

'Someone's stolen your thunder and gone and mixed arcane and rune magic. Wolfgang?'

'*Considerably* better than I've ever been able to, so maybe,' I said. 'But I doubt it was him. Can't think of a reason he'd do this, even if he could. Besides, feels like this has been here for a while. I think I *know* this building.'

'Oh, come off it.'

But looking at it now, I did. It didn't look quite the same as I remembered — the lighting was all wrong, and the edges of the clearing were lacking the thick treeline that had originally served to shield the place. The windows, while still somehow gleaming against the non-existent light, were fogged in places too, just enough to throw off the image at a first glance.

I'd seen this place in my head as part of the memories

Eat The Rich

I'd taken from that extra-planar spooky boy, the ones crammed in to ground me on Diplomancy. Raoul Fury had been here, the Ertras woman at his side. I was standing in the same place, at the same angle, getting the same view. There was no memory of him being the one to seal the building away down here, but I couldn't help but think that fit a whole lot more than Wolfgang doing it.

Now, the German dickhead digging the place up on the other hand? Much more plausible.

'We're going in. Stay quiet.'

There was the gentle thrum of stale magic in the air that only got more noticeable the deeper into the clearing we moved. It crackled over the hair on my arm in a way that was dangerously close to being enjoyable. Didn't want to spend any time thinking about the implication of that if I could avoid it.

By the time I reached the actual building, that aura was so thick I could taste it — like licking a burned out battery, if you're interested. True to his word, Wolfgang had left the front door wide open, and stepping into the building I could feel the pressure drop instantly. I could still taste the metallic tang in the air, but breathing was mercifully easier.

Naturally, the place had that tomb-like quiet you'd expect — the lobby had polished stone floors and high ceilings, so every footstep echoed for about half-a-fucking-hour, tickling at the anxieties that kept insisting I was being watched. You know how nothing is scarier than walking into a place that *should* be absolutely busy as fuck but is completely dead? Like everyone just sort of vanished in the middle of their boring routines? That.

A reception desk sat comfortably at the far end of the lobby, wide enough to staff three or four people. Behind it, carefully moulded into rear wall, a door that looks like chiselled plasterboard and a thin slit of glass next to it. A barely concealed security room? Worth a look.

I did check the desk first, though. A computer that wouldn't turn on, scattered files seemingly bleached white from exposure to the non-existent sun, a cold and half-drunk mug of tea. No mould on the tea, though, so it was either somewhat recent or weird magic shit was to blame. I was still putting my money on the latter.

The door to the security room was locked, but Su-Yin's invisible hand didn't have any trouble forcing it. All she had to do was grab the handle and twist — a sound of something brittle snapping and, voila, an insecure security room. I squeezed her hand in silent thanks, not knowing who else might be listening.

The CCTV was still working. A bank of flatscreen monitors was focused on showing a lot of empty

Eat The Rich

corridors, though a couple had their monotony interrupted by the strobing of an alarm. If the light show had any accompanying sirens, they didn't reach this far.

No sign of Wolfgang on the cameras either.

Across from the monitors, a cross-sectional map of the entire building had been mounted on the wall, each room marked with a little red LED. Beautifully low-fi next to the wall of flatscreens. Only one of the LEDs was lit — the vault.

Because, of course, office buildings have vaults. Just like they're worth jamming in a little pocket dimension. Totally expected.

Pretty obvious where I was expected to go then, don't you think? I just had to find my way down there. X marked the spot, and the spot was in the basement. Down, down, deeper and down it was, then. Wolfgang was getting a lot of mileage out of the atmosphere and the setting, that was for sure.

Su-Yin was starting to lag a little as I moved, and I could feel her trepidation. Not much I could do about it, but I could sense it all the same. Another reassuring hand squeeze to keep her calm as I stepped back out into the lobby was the limit of what I could manage without risking blowing her cover.

A pair of elevators were tucked away in a corner, perfectly placed so that the reception desk would draw the eye away from them. I hit the call button and the doors slid open immediately, so I ducked inside and hit the button for the third basement. Fourth basement, really, if you take into account the fact the whole building was *in a basement*.

I know I keep banging on about that, but honestly, wouldn't you?

The third basement lobby was one of the places that had been strobing on the monitors. The screens had been monochrome, so I hadn't had the full experience of rotating bulbs beaming bright yellow hell into my eyes before the lift doors slid open again. Mercifully, I had been right about the lack of a siren.

I had to move around a corner to see the vault entrance, out of the range of what the camera had seen, and I wasn't prepared to see signs of actual life. Or death. I guess it's both?

In any case, the corridor that ran up to the vault door was the only place that didn't look like everyone had just got up and left in the middle of all their shit. There had been a battle here — the walls were pockmarked with bullet holes and spiderweb cracks from bodies hitting with great force. A few of those bodies were still there, cold and lifeless but seemingly fresh enough. Just like the tea upstairs: no mould. Thankfully. They were your typical tactical lads, all body armour and chunky helmets, scary-looking assault rifle things vaguely near their beaten and bloody remains.

The vault had a comically large door, one of those massive steel numbers with locking bars as thick as your head. It had been folded in half on itself and torn open, those same thick bars sheared in half. The ones that sank into the floor poked up out of their resting places, whereas the upper ones had long since slid out of their sockets and dented the ground.

I had to risk a whisper. 'There's been a fight here.'

'How bad?' Su-Yin whispered back, her voice right by my ear.

'Fucking awful. Like, monstrously awful.'

'That doesn't sound like Wolfgang.'

'Doesn't it? In any case, be ready and be careful how you walk.'

Her voice turned cold. 'Blood?'

'And corpses.'

Her grip on my belt loop tightened, and I felt a second hand trace across the small of my back to grab at a loop on the other side. 'Lead on, MacDuff.'

Slowly, I picked my way across the battlefield, making sure to give Su-Yin time to follow just as carefully. Fortunately, there's no way anyone watching would have found that suspicious; after all, I was slipping in thick pools of sticky blood every other fucking step.

By the time I reached the remains of the vault door, my thighs were blazing from the awkwardness of keeping my balance while dragging one of nature's barbarians blindly behind me.

Exactly how you want to be feeling before a showdown with the big bad, I'm sure you'll agree.

Twenty

The last time I was in a vault, it didn't even have the decency to look like a vault. I guess I'd gotten my hopes up a little with this one, expected something a little more traditionally grand. You know, like piles of gold coins, precious jewels, something like that. Yet, almost all the loot that had been stored here had been spirited away long ago, and apparently in as much a hurry as everything else. Empty storage racks and lock-boxes lined the walls, with the centre of the room being the only bit not completely cleared out.

Wolfgang and Walid were there, milling around a statue that had carved its own little niche amongst the remaining cash, coins, and loot bags. At first, I thought I'd managed to sneak in unnoticed, but without looking at me Wolfgang threw up a hand and waved me over.

'Miss Thatcher, here at last! Come take a look at this.'

Su-Yin gave a cautious tug at my waist, but I didn't need reminding to play this cool. 'I didn't think you were going to be quite so literal when you said you'd leave the door open.'

'Hmm?' he still wasn't looking at me. 'Oh, that wasn't my doing. If you're looking for those responsible for the state of things outside, you'll find them here.'

He beckoned me closer again, his hand almost brushing the statue. Being the cool-ass boss bitch I am, I approached.

They were *really* interested in the statue. Wolfgang's eyes never left the thing as I drew closer, and Walid only managed to glance at me for split seconds at a time. Once I was close enough to get a proper view of it, I kind of understood the appeal, though.

Like all sexy statues, it was chiselled from milky-white marble, though there were veins of something glittery set deep into the grain. It was an action scene, a beautiful woman in the middle of a violent rage and a tired-looking middle-aged man scrambling away from her, stabbing an ornate dagger fearfully up into her chest. The glittering veins seemed to converge around the wound.

The dagger wasn't marble. 'All this for a fancy letter opener?'

Wolfgang blinked and finally raised his eyes to my face, if only for a moment. 'Pardon? No, I don't give a shit about the dagger. Look again. Properly.'

'I really don't—'

'Just humour me this once.'

Before I could object again, a memory clunked into place inside my head once more. I didn't know the woman in the statue, but I did recognise the man. 'Is that Raoul Fury?'

'Yes,' Wolfgang said, beaming. 'In the flesh, or near enough. Which means this is the last remaining trace of Diplomancy in this world.'

'What?'

Walid hastily shuffled around the statue, and I noticed he was rapidly scribbling out a rough sketch of the thing. 'Diplomancy is gone. Written out of existence.'

'*Almost*,' Wolfgang interrupted. 'If it had been written out entirely, we'd have a paradox. You can't use Diplomancy to erase Diplomancy if there's no Diplomancy, can you? The best you can do is trim and prune it, *edit it*, right down to the marrow.'

'So, you hide it away under the earth, bury it deep, and hope nobody finds it?' I said. 'Even so, I'm not seeing the big deal.'

'You don't see the similarities?' Wolfgang replied. 'What is Diplomancy but the power of a Runeskald taken to its logical conclusion? It's all stories, at the end of the day, all persuasion. Got to walk before you can run.'

'Yes, a statue is really going to help you run.'

Wolfgang rolled his eyes. 'Again, I don't care about the statue. I care about this building. It's a *library*. There's not enough information about Diplomancy out there to reverse engineer anything but the barest of parlour tricks, but in here we've got the holy grail — *information*. This is our inheritance.'

'What the hell does that mean?'

'How many Runeskalds are there in the world today? Proper ones, other than us two.'

I shrugged. 'How am I supposed to know that?'

'Master Laufeyjarson,' Wolfgang snapped. 'He will have told you. Perhaps you weren't listening, though? In any case, it's a very low number. A handful. I've met them all, his trusted few, and we all have one thing in common.'

'Sure we do.'

'Untapped potential,' he continued. Evidently my input wasn't required for this portion of his lecture. 'We never think big enough, act confidently enough, ever truly *shine*. And of course not, because we're not playing with a full deck. Diplomancy can give us that, it was always meant to.'

'Right, I get you. So, world domination, then?'

Wolfgang frowned. 'How on earth did you get that from what I was saying?'

'The bombastic self-aggrandising did a lot of the heavy lifting there.'

'I don't want to dominate anything—'

I cut him off. 'You literally carved a mind control rune into at least two women, so...'

'That's a wilfully reductive way of looking at things.'

'Is it, though?'

'Yes!' his eyes were wide and close to frenzy. He really, *really* wanted me to understand his point here, and he could see he was failing. 'I told you before, this was all to make sure we got you where you needed to be. There's too much here to do alone, I'll need help.'

'And Walid can't help? You had to go through a very convoluted rigmarole to recruit me?'

'Walid wasn't chosen by an actual god,' Wolfgang said, sparing his acolyte a sympathetic glance. 'We were.'

'No, we weren't.'

'Are you going to stand there and tell me you haven't had numerous conversation with Loki Laufeyjarson, an actual Norse god? Because he insists you have. He sees something in you, and he wants you on board with this.'

This is the part where I'm supposed to tell you how it was a very tempting offer. On the face of it, it does kind of sound like something enticing, I guess. Doubly so for people of a magical disposition, which I technically am. I'd spent a lot of time and energy learning what Wingard had to teach, all in the hope of being able to feel in control of myself. The transition to rune magic hadn't done much to hit that goal, and what better way to put a capstone on those dreams than by levelling up?

The problem, of course, is that this was hardly the first time someone had come offering me salvation that they thought I wanted. It was starting to be a theme in my life: people telling me that they knew what was best for me, how I should move forward, telling me I was special or chosen. Funny how *special* quite often seems to mean the worst possible definition of *worth something to me* for these people, huh?

So, yeah, I wasn't really tempted at all by this German dickface's grand scheme of mothering in a new world order.

That said, I am capable of learning. The scales were very much not leaning my way right now — if I kicked off, I'd be on the back foot. The fact that his desperation was showing gave me a bit of an in, if I wanted it. All the better to learn a little more, right?

'Convince me,' I said, folding my arms.

A disarming smile started to form on his face. 'Come here, let me show you something.'

'I can see well enough from here, thanks.'

'Suit yourself,' he said, then ran a hand over the statue. 'What do you know about Raoul Fury?'

'Only what's on the internet.'

He laughed. 'So, nothing useful then. That's fair, there's not much about him left out there thanks to his deleting everything. The few facts that remain paint a very disappointing picture indeed, however. Weak, idiotic, but blessed with power of a kind he couldn't truly comprehend. And, like all such men, instead of trying to use it he set out to destroy it. But he couldn't, not completely, because deep down he knew that it was too important to remove completely. It had to be preserved for a successor.'

'This isn't convincing me, just FYI.'

Wolfgang passed his hand over the statue, up the arm of the male figure and across the blade, coming to a rest just above the stab wound. 'Germany never had a problem with wizards, did you know that? Until I came over here looking for you, I didn't understand how bad things were in this country. If the things that had happened here had happened in my country, I'd be desperate to find a way to rewrite that history.'

'So you don't want to rewrite the whole Hitler thing? You're going to just leave that out there?'

His fingers traced the edge of the blade again, down towards the hand holding it. 'That's ancient history now. That's got tendrils that encompass the entire world — far too many things that could go wrong, fiddling with that. If it had been more recent, though... Walid, are we ready?'

'I believe so,' came the reply.

'Ready for what?' I asked.

'To convince you,' Wolfgang said. 'Just watch and pay attention.'

With a swift and fluid motion, he grabbed at the blade's handle and pushed it deeper into the statue, up and into the woman's chest. As it slid out of the fingers gripping the hilt, Wolfgang's grip shifted to take their place, yanking it up in an arc until he could withdraw it easily. It slid free of the woman's chest and then, instantly, she was moving — a blur of gnashing teeth and snarls — leaping at the other half of the statue. The man.

The man who was now very desperately skittering backwards.

So, not a statue, then. Some sort of stasis?

Petrification? Weird magic shit, either way.

The sudden reanimation had seemingly left the pair a little off balance, however. The man fell flat against the floor as she pounced, but the woman flipped over him and landed a few feet away, pivoting in the air. Setting her feet to leap again, she slammed up against an invisible wall.

Next to where she had landed, Walid was crouched. He had a finger pressed against the floor and he was muttering something under his breath, eyes rolled back into his head. I didn't recognise the craft, but I could identify the result: a binding spell.

'No!' the man-who-had-been-a-statue shouted. 'Whoever you are, you don't understand—'

And then he fell silent as Wolfgang plunged the blade between the man's ribs, snapping him back to that same gorgeous marble state he had previously enjoyed. It seemed as though the woman enjoyed this sight too; she stopped crashing against the walls of the binding and downgraded to quiet seething instead.

Wolfgang positioned himself between me and the woman, blocking my view of her. 'Don't look her in the eyes.'

'I've met Medusa,' I said. 'This isn't her.'

'Quite right. But you don't want to challenge her all the same.'

'And why is that?'

'Because I'll rip your bitch-eyes out and crush them under my bare feet,' the woman snarled.

'Miss Thatcher, meet the last repository of Diplomancy,' Wolfgang said. 'Miranda Ertras.'

I opened my mouth to call bullshit — this wasn't Miranda Ertras. I had memories of her, at least I think they were of her, gifted alongside what little knowledge of Diplomancy I'd been granted, and she didn't look like *this*. She was mousy, normal, extremely tired. That was a look I could respect.

What she didn't look like was a rabid version of Jessica Rabbit, ferocious and bestial and very much still somehow a starlet from the golden age of Hollywood.

Then again, seeing her in motion, there was something else off about her. It was like she was wearing a second skin — not in a Hannibal Lecter way, but like someone would wear armour. Every now and then a movement wouldn't quite line up and you'd catch the gaps — the fractured emerald irises would shimmer the same shade of grey as a Scottish summer, the voluminous red hair would fall lank and slack for a split second, the bronzed skin and ruby lips would dull. And she'd lose something in her stature too, the caged violence in her bones would shiver away like static and then snap right back into place.

'Jesus *fuck*,' I managed to say. 'What's wrong with her?'

Wolfgang took a few steps closer to Ertras. 'I can't say for sure. But I suspect that for Raoul Fury to do what he set out to do, he needed to make sure the story worked. Think like a Runeskald.'

'He needed a monster to slay.'

Ertras raked a sharp nail over the bounds of the binding circle. 'Monster to slay. Monster to lay. Men can only write two characters. Raoul was no different.'

'He wrote the last remaining ions of Diplomancy into her bones, Miss Thatcher. She is our Rosetta Stone, the bouncer guarding the door to the new world Laufeyjarson wants. So, shall we get started?'

'Oh, please do,' Ertras snarled. 'Don't leave me here quivering. The anticipation, it's *too much*.'

Something brushed across the small of my back. I did my best to not react and kept my attention focused on Wolfgang. 'The thing about the Rosetta Stone, though, is that it was studied for years by smart dudes who already knew, like, a thousand languages already. How would we even start here?'

'We call on an expert,' he said. 'Or, rather, you call on him for us. I'd do it myself, but he's never been open to the idea of a two-way relationship in my case. Not like with you.'

'Pardon?'

The snide little fuck almost rolled his eyes at me. 'Laufeyjarson. You need to summon him.'

'Yeah, right, like I can just snap my fingers and a god's going to show up.'

'We both know you've done it before.'

Sure, I guess you could have referred to that as *summoning a god*. In my case, I very much thought of it as provoking him enough that he had to come and have a good sneer at me. Summoning made it seem much more grown up.

It also raised a few too many questions about why he bothered to listen to me at all.

'So you don't actually want me here as a partner,' I snapped. 'You want me as a divine switchboard or something, that about right?'

'You're misunderstanding—'

He was interrupted by a voice over my shoulder. 'It's a half misunderstanding at best, Wolfy.'

I didn't even need to turn to recognise Loki's voice. Likewise, I didn't need to see him to know how he would be standing — astride the petrified man like something out of an old painting, the brave explorer at the prow of his ship. When I did turn, I saw that I was right of course.

Fucker had even dressed up for the occasion in some mockery of what I could only assume was meant to be a military dress uniform. Extremely extra.

'Master Laufeyjarson,' Wolfgang said, snapping off a quick bow of the head. 'It's been a while. I didn't realise you were still watching me.'

Loki dismounted with a flourish. 'Oh, I wasn't. I was watching *her*, as you well know. Getting a little envious were we, my boy? Daddy issues run rampant amongst you mages, so don't get embarrassed. Still, this is very good work!'

'Your wish is my command,' Wolfgang said.

Loki slapped him on the shoulder. 'And my commands are your wish. I remember the wording too, dear lad.'

'You've been stalking me?' I interrupted. 'Following me this whole time?'

'Wasn't that obvious? I thought I said as much. Didn't I? It was definitely implied.'

'It wasn't bloody implied,' I snapped. 'And it definitely wasn't ex-plied. *Explicit,* that's the word. What the fuck, man?'

'Yes, *fuck the man,*' Ertras crooned. 'Ripe and juicy, ready for a good *peeling.*'

Loki's head snapped to her, seemingly noticing her for the first time. 'Oh! Nice. Very nice indeed! That is some masterful craftsmanship.'

Ertras grinned hungrily. '*I am art.*'

'Hush,' he snapped, wagging a finger at her. 'Talking about you, not to you. A cage around a cage, inspired design. No need for a guard if the vault can guard itself. How long were you infected before Fury locked all that power away inside you, hmm?'

For a moment, Ertras faltered. 'I don't—'

'Hold on,' he said, walking over to the binding circle. He pulled a small coin from his pocket and flicked it up into the air. 'Watch the birdie.'

With the speed of a predator, Ertras' gaze snapped to the coin as it tumbled. It only held her attention for a split second, but that was all Loki needed. His other hand sliced through the air in an arc, carving through the barrier and slapping her hard across the cheek. He hit her so hard that he slapped the armour right off her

— almost like a ghost, the arresting and violent starlet detached from the woman beneath, drawn into the coin. It hung in the air for a second, smoking, before landing in the Norseman's open hand.

Inside the circle, the tired and mousy form of Miranda Ertras remained, much more human and lacking in that larger than life quality she had been so expertly rocking. She looked to be in shock, shaky hands tracing over the chest. 'Did he stab me? Did I hurt him?'

Loki ignored her. He was rolling the coin over his knuckles. 'Did he infect you or just take advantage of an opportunity, I wonder. The latter, I expect. Memetic pathogens are tricky beasts to wrangle, probably beyond him. Anyway, Wolfy, let's see what you've got.'

Wolfgang, to his credit, didn't seem overly fazed. 'Just tell me what to do.'

'You already know. After all, you're the one that said it's in her deep, right to the marrow. Extract it.'

'Her *bone marrow?*' Wolfgang asked, but it seemed more out of surprise than revulsion.

Loki nodded. 'Shouldn't be a problem to get at it now I've removed that pesky little passenger of hers. Rip out all that power for me, there's a good dog.'

Without a word, Wolfgang's fingers started tracing sigils

in the air. At first I could sort of read what he was doing, but he ramped up the speed of it all so fast I lost track pretty bloody quickly. It called on a lot of raw magic though, of that much I was certain.

It took only a few seconds to reach the focal point, the climax of the working, and at that very peak Loki interrupted him.

'Changed my mind,' he said. 'Let's just leave everything as it is.'

'What?' I said.

'*What?*' Wolfgang said.

'I've gone off the idea of this Diplomancy stuff,' Loki said, picking at his teeth with his fingernails. 'It bores me. And seeing as you were only searching for it to impress me, and impress me you very much have, objective achieved! Right?'

'I've been searching for this for years,' Wolfgang said, his voice shaking. 'I've devoted my life to this search.'

The corners of Loki's mouth twitched. 'Because I told you to. Now I'm telling you to do something else.'

I've seen a lot of people lose their cools, and I've even lost my own more than once. Surprising to hear, I know, but it's true. Thing is, I've never really liked the phrase — *losing* your cool implies a level of passivity that simply isn't there. It's a choice, one you make in a split second, that leads to you cranking those dials to eleven and letting the rage in.

Everyone, from bellicose hooligan to saintly pacifist, goes through the same range of expressions when they snap that olive branch inside their head — everyone except Wolfgang, apparently. He went cold, robotic even, and his voice went flat to match.

'All this time, and you'd still play with me like a toy?'

Loki sighed. 'There it is. Watch this, Millie. You'll like this.'

'I've done nothing but devote my life to you, you know that?' Wolfgang said coldly. 'I honed my craft *for you*. I put this whole convoluted nightmare together, *for you*, because you said Thatcher needed a push.'

Loki laughed. 'A push, yes. That's all I said. The rest, you did that on your own. And, now let's be honest here, you were never in this for me, now were you? You were in this for you.'

'I am loyal.'

'You're a liar,' Loki sighed. 'And I normally love that, but when you're lying to yourself it's just a little sad. Little Thatcher here doesn't lie to herself. She needed a push, yeah, but this was never about a lesson for her. It was a lesson for you, Wolfy. You think she'd do any of this mad bullshit because she thought I wanted it? Come on.'

Normally I'd get a kick out of seeing a pompous prick get his dick stomped flat by someone — and there was a definite bouquet of pomposity to Wolfgang, don't get me wrong — but this was like Laufeyjarson had punched the core of his being right out his arsehole. The poor bugger had built his whole understanding of the world on a foundation that simply wasn't there anymore, and that sort of shit messes you up.

I should know, I've been there.

Thing is, until that moment, I'd never thought of Wolfgang as fragile. There was the sort of fragility present in anyone with a penchant for self-aggrandising showmanship, sure, but now I could see how deep those cracks actually ran. Laufeyjarson was playing with fire.

'All of this...' Wolfgang began, his words catching in his throat. 'It all meant nothing to you?'

Laufeyjarson shrugged. 'Eh. Not nothing. A curiosity, I guess, watching how it unfolded. I was hoping you'd be a little less fucking wet, if I'm honest. A shame, really. If you *had* the balls to resurrect Diplomacy for your own sake, maybe you would have stayed interesting. As it is, not so much.'

Eat The Rich

The Norseman was laying on the mocking tone so thick you could mortar bricks with it. Frankly, it was almost comical — no way it would be working if Wolfgang wasn't already wound tight, but the words were deep under his skin now. I had to hand it to him, Laufeyjarson was schooling me in how to *really* provoke someone.

Wolfgang's cold rage turned to a boil, and he lashed out. A flash of crimson energy burst from his palm and slammed into Laufeyjarson like a hammer, but he didn't even stagger. Undeterred, Wolfgang tried a second, then a third, each time letting out more of his anger, screaming, pumping more of himself into whatever the spell was.

The most he managed was to force Laufeyjarson to shift one foot back a fraction of an inch.

'Let it out, Wolfgang. Let it out,' Laufeyjarson said. The cockiness was stripped away now, leaving something disarmingly sinister. 'I can take it.'

Panting, Wolfgang managed one last outburst before sinking to his knees. 'What's the point?'

Laufeyjarson walked over to him and crouched down, lifting the man's chin until they were eye level. 'For a real moment there, I thought you might have a breakthrough. Oh well. Hold this for me, would you?'

Wolfgang's eyes turned to the coin dancing over the

Norseman's fingers. Seemingly before he could register what was going on, Laufeyjarson's other hand slid from Wolfgang's chin and wrenched his jaw open. He unceremoniously popped the coin into the open mouth and forced the jaws shut.

'Time for another lesson, Thatcher!' Laufeyjarson shouted over his shoulder. 'Remember, you've been the teacher all along.'

With that he stepped aside, giving me full view of Wolfgang going full on Hulk mode.

It was a spectacle I did not care for.

Twenty One

Whatever Laufeyjarson had pulled out of Ertras, it didn't hit Wolfgang the same way. She had looked beautiful in a predatory way, all sharp angles you could cut yourself on. On Wolfgang, it just looked painful.

He did have that same shimmer she had, though — like a double-exposed photograph, a faded veil hanging off his skin. It was hungry, dangerous, and just as enthralling as Ertras had been, albeit for much different reasons. The only true point of similarity was the eyes — the irises torn and blown out as if buckling under some great pressure.

Honestly, the room suddenly felt really fucking small. Like, the light may as well have dimmed until it was just me and Wolfgang in a bloody spotlight. By the time he started moving — long legs unfolding far too geometrically for my liking — there was no space in my head for anyone else. He hadn't even done anything, and he'd already punted me so far beyond fight or flight that I'd hit *fight or die*. Wolfgang was *the problem* now and nothing else mattered.

Fucking Laufeyjarson. Seriously.

What could I do here? I didn't even know what *this*

even was. Bringing up a shield could work, fight on the defensive, but there was nothing I could slap together that could rival a binding circle. It would buy me seconds, and I didn't need *those*. The longer the fight went on, the more likely I was to lose — that was as true in a standard fistfight as a magical throwdown.

Some sort of haymaker, then? Yeah, sure, fucking magical Mike Tyson my way through this. Very me. Oh fuck. Fuck fuck fuck.

I let my hands make the decision for me as he approached, simply shut off my brain and let instinct take over. He moved fast, but I was faster, using my little arcane prowess to try and shove his first blow away. His nails grazed my cheek, but whatever I had done had managed to save my eye. Didn't give me much space to think, though, and he was following up with a second strike before I had even recovered my balance from deflecting the first.

This time it wasn't anything I did that saved me. Instead, Wolfgang suddenly lurched to the side as if hit in the ribs by a truck. He landed awkwardly but rolled through it so fast it was almost balletic.

There was a glimmer of dust in the air as my knight in shining armour faded into view.

Su-Yin, obviously. Just in case that wasn't clear. She'd detached herself from my belt-loops when I felt that hand on my back a few minutes ago, apparently to put herself into just the right place to save my arse.

And dammit if that wasn't a good look on her.

The splintered magic from the shattered veil washed down over her like starlight, perfectly framing her muscles and scowling face in such a way that even a hardened gang-land bastard would have thought twice before squaring up against her. But not Wolfgang. He didn't hesitate — he was on her again instantly with the kind of ferocity that made me think of someone being savaged by a bear.

With the strength and speed advantage, he had Su-Yin on the defensive. But better her, than me — this way I had the time to *think*.

Not enough time for a spell, rune or otherwise, so I needed to be practical. Empty vault, not much to work with. Just the one thing, and I could be certain that it would have some effect.

I sprinted around the writhing morass of combat, darting awkwardly when the pair of them rolled in my direction. Losing my balance, I dropped to one knee and pushed myself across the floor, sliding on the polished floor until I was just out of reach. Then, back up, my hand reached for the hilt of the blade lodged in the chest of Raoul Fury.

It came free easily, slid from the man's marble chest as if it was silk. Pivoting, I hurled the fucking thing right at Wolfgang's face — the thing felt like it weighed almost nothing, so I didn't give myself time to second guess what I was doing. Find the centre of mass, grip, yeet it. That would work, right?

And, in a beautiful display of good luck and untapped skill, it very nearly did.

Picking out Wolfgang's head for the throw was stupid. The fight was so chaotic that nothing stayed in one place long enough to really aim. From his position on top, he was gnashing his teeth at Su-Yin's throat, trying to get at an artery or rip the damn thing out entirely, and her panicked wriggling meant his bonce was yo-yoing all over the place.

With all that going against me, though, still the blade soared beautifully, spinning end over end, catching him right on the bridge of his handsome Germanic nose with a sickening crack. That's the almost part — it hit hilt first, clattering down to the floor just out of Su-Yin's reach.

A hand grabbed my arm and pulled me round. 'The blade won't be enough.'

Raoul Fury looked up at me, his face pale and haggard. His eyes were staring past me, in fact, as if locked onto the blade even when he couldn't quite see it. The man's grip was so tight I could feel pins and needles in my fingertips. I shook off his grip.

'Why the fuck not!' I snapped.

'The annoyingly capricious nature of Diplomancy. Would take too long to explain now.'

'Can you at least explain what the fuck *he is*?'

The real Wolfgang — the image behind the spectral veneer — was a mess of blood thanks to his broken nose, but whatever was riding him didn't seem to care. If anything, that veneer was less ghostly now, more opaque, almost like it was subsuming him in a way it hadn't with Ertras. The more pronounced it became, the harder it hit.

Su-Yin was having real trouble getting her arms up.

'In a word, complicated,' Raoul said. He was on his feet now, next to me. 'He's infected with an idea. A parasitic strain of emotion.'

'Which fucking one?'

'Vanity. He's got a vainglorious delusion at the wheel right now.'

'Vanity is this violent?'

He shrugged. 'Anything's violent if it's potent enough. Diplomancy can make anything potent.'

There was a roar from across the room, rage with such purity that it turned the air crimson. With a second wind, Su-Yin had forced herself to a standing base and had Wolfgang by the throat. His fists were a blur, pummelling her chest and arms, but she still managed to deliver   one hell of a ferocious chokeslam.

She stood up straight and cracked her knuckles, staring down at Wolfgang while he was so briefly stunned. Groggily, she sat astride him, using her knees to pin his shoulders, and started raining down punches on his face. Her fists were glowing white-gold, leaving streaky afterimages in my vision as they moved.

Maybe we wouldn't need to do anything after all.

Then, as if to smack down my hope before it could take root, one of Wolfgang's hands burst free of Su-Yin's knees and pushed her blow aside, following it up with a headbutt. She went limp, swayed for a moment, then slumped to the side. I half expected to see cartoon birds circling her.

'Fuck,' I whispered. 'He's going to kill her.'

Raoul was floundering. 'Give me a minute. I need a minute to think.'

'She doesn't have a minute!'

'It took months to work out how to lock this shit away

last time!' he shouted. 'I don't... I need...'

And then it hit me — possession. Ghosts possessed people all the time, and I was good at that. A few runes in the right place, a cocky demeanour, and those spooky sods would get evicted right back to the afterlife. Was this really *that* different a situation? It looked like a possession, walked like a possession, quacked like a possession. If it was similar enough...

'Buy me time,' I shouted. 'As much as you can!'

I didn't wait for him to agree, I was already running back out of the vault. Had there been a desk or something outside the door? Somewhere for the guards to sit? There had to be guards, right? And they would need somewhere to sit. And they'd have sign-in sheets for the visitors — proper office people love those — and if they had *those* then they would have pens.

And if they had pens then maybe, just maybe, there would be *pencils*.

There was a desk outside the vault, and it did have a sign in sheet and, mercifully, a whole pot full of pencils. I snatched up a couple of the pencils and a sign in sheet, flipped it over, and started scribbling.

The usual runes would make for a good starting point, but they'd need adjusting. Tweak the formula, bend the composition, fudge a few rules to make the net a little broader. But not too broad! A delicate balancing act. I had to rely on my artistic eye, there wasn't time to *plan*.

A couple of pencil leads snapped under my not-so-tender ministrations — it was frantic scribbling, there was no time for subtlety. The finished piece was exactly as horrible to look at as you'd expect too, mad grooves almost carved into the paper, the sheen of graphite pushed to the very limit. Runes and sigils were stacked on top of each other so haphazardly that there was very little differentiating them from a messy blob to the naked eye.

But that's the beauty of pencils — the lines cross over but, look close enough, and you can see them. It's like brush strokes; you're never eradicating something by painting over it, you're building atop it.

Or, at least, that was the narrative I'd been spinning myself. Looking at it now, maybe it was all hot bullshit, but it sounded pretty boss when you don't have time to think about it. I'm not saying you can do dumb shit and get away with it through ignorance and self-confidence alone, but I was willing to accept that there may have been a bit of a crossover here.

I took one last look at my runic disasterpiece, judged it good enough, then grabbed one last thing from the table and booked it back to the vault.

I'd been gone all of a minute, possibly two, and Raoul

was already fucked up. Su-Yin was still kicking, so he'd done his job, but it had come at the cost of seemingly an ankle, three fingers, and probably a rib. Wolfgang had him by the nose, fingers lodged into the nostrils and hoisting up the man's limp and battered body. On the floor under one of the German's feet, Su-Yin squirmed and beat impotently against the very long leg.

At best, I'd get a single shot at this. Of course, if all went to plan, I'd only need the one.

Setting my feet, I tightened my grip on the paper, feeling it crinkle in my fingers. In my other hand, my fingers flexed on the metal lever of the last thing I had grabbed from the desk outside: a staple gun.

Grinning madly, Wolfgang raised his hand a little higher, lifting Raoul's knees off the floor. He was enjoying himself too much to notice me. Perfect.

I broke into a sprint and, once I was a few steps away, belted out a sharp whistle. 'Oi, dickface!'

He turned as I leapt, his arm whipping around ready to catch me by the throat. Not a problem, I had enough momentum to knock him off balance for a second, and that was all I needed. As his fingers closed around my throat, I brought up the paper and held it over his face before stapling the fucking thing right to his forehead. I got off five staples, rapid fire, before his fingers slackened and released me. As I fell, I tried for a sixth but missed. Five would do.

The room filled with the smell of burned hair and the cloying taste of chewed fingernails. Wolfgang was jerking about awkwardly, frenzied hands trying to scratch at the paper dangling from his forehead, every attempt to grab it slapped away by an unseen magic.

The mad grasping hands went searching for something else to grab hold of, twitching and shuddering their way through the air as the smell grew ever stronger. I was in no danger at this point, but I still put a staple or two into the back of his hands.

Click-clunk. Click-clunk. Click-clunk. 'Just. Fuck. Off!'

The designs on the paper started to sizzle and smoke as they finished their warm up. The graphite markings sparked up like strips of Magnesium, little sparklers tracing the sigils in the air now as well as onto paper. Then it all burned away in less than a second, taking the air out of the room with it. A perfect vacuum for all of five seconds — no sound, no breathing, no life.

Then reality snapped back, hard.

Wolfgang's face was blank, his eyes glassy and unfocused. The shimmering veil was gone, and in its place was an emptiness it would take his mind some time to refill. He sank slowly to his knees and let out a single wet cough. The coin slithered from between his lips and tumbled to the floor, clinking against the marble and rolling over towards me.

It came to a stop about thirty centimetres from me, right as he flopped unceremoniously onto the floor.

I tore out the lining of one of my pockets and wrapped it around the coin, securing it in the other pocket for safe keeping. Even through the fabric, I could feel the coldness of the metal.

On reflection, Laufeyjarson might have pulled off a more skilled exorcism or whatever, but there was no denying that mine had looked so much cooler.

Su-Yin was laying on her face, panting so heavily that the movement made it look like she was belting out a few post-battle press-ups. I lent her a hand getting up, and she squeezed my shoulder before dropping her full weight on me. 'Gave you enough time to think up a solution, huh?'

'I liked your solution better,' I said. 'Watching you punch the bad thing means I don't have to do stuff like running. You okay?'

She winced and I'm pretty sure I heard the creak and pop of damaged bone. 'Not really. You?'

'I'd feel guilty complaining,' I said. 'So, I've been worse, I guess.'

'What about him?' she asked, nodding over in Raoul's direction. 'He saved my life, I'm pretty sure.'

'Let me have a look.'

Making sure Su-Yin was able to stand on her own, I knelt down over the limp body of Raoul Fury. He was alive, barely, but it was like looking at a bag of giblets — too many weird lumps and not enough places for them to fit together.

Su-Yin leant over my shoulder. 'Well?'

'Do I look like a doctor?' I snapped. 'Wolfgang fucked him up, that's my professional opinion. He looks like someone who might die, I guess.'

I went searching about in my little bag of tricks. Somewhere, near the crumbs at the bottom, there had to be one last little rune tablet that had some semblance of healing in it, right? Even something for hangovers would have enough juice to do something.

My fingers found a tablet that I hoped would work, and I ground it under my thumb until it was a patina of loose dust in my palm. I held my palm against his nose until he snorted it all up.

'What's that going to do?' Su-Yin asked.

'Save his life, hopefully,' I said. 'Hit of magic right to the brain, might get lucky. Like I said, I'm not a doctor.'

Eat The Rich

Raoul shivered as the magic kicked in, and some of the smashed up giblets started to slowly melt back together. Turns out I'm better at first aid than I thought, huh?

One puffy eye opened a crack and swivelled lazily in my direction. 'Miranda…'

The eye slithered closed again and, with a single ragged sigh, Raoul Fury passed out. Yeah, for a second I thought he was dead too, but the gentle rise and fall of his chest convinced me otherwise.

I'd forgotten about Ertras — she hadn't been a priority while shit was getting crazy with Wolfgang, after all. Now I thought to look, though, I realised she was gone. I mean, obviously, of course she was. Why wouldn't she have just fucked off during all that? The only thing holding her had been Walid's magic circle, and it was very clear that had not been sufficient.

Walid was in a heap on the floor, whimpering and clutching at his eyes. No idea when that had happened during all the kerfuffle, but you can't expect a guy to keep up concentration on a spell when his eyes are melting out of his face.

Don't think I know a rune to fix that, either.

Su-Yin didn't notice Walid at first — she glanced over in his direction, but I reckon some defence mechanism in her brain just redacted him entirely from her view while her adrenaline levels reset. It took a moment of prolonged staring before she seemed to notice him, and then she was over at his side like a shot.

She crouched down over him, uncertain of whether to touch him or not. 'You're okay, Walid. You're okay. Try to calm down.'

Reacting to her voice, one grasping hand came away from his face and pawed at her shirt. His fingers knitted into the fabric, flexing with obvious pain. There were words between the sobs and the quiet howls, but I didn't understand them — they were probably in a language I didn't know, but the speed he was speaking made it hard to tell for sure. Su-Yin didn't seem to have that problem, nodding away as she stroked his head.

Eventually, all he had left in him was quiet sobbing. Gently, she lowered his head back onto the floor, wiped the tears from her eyes, and limped back in my direction.

'How is he?' I asked stupidly.

She bristled. 'Bad. I need to get him to a hospital. Fury too. You need to go after Ertras alone.'

I didn't need to ask why she wouldn't come with me, the answer was written in her eyes: she was too angry. 'Okay, fine, but I don't even know where to begin.'

'Yeah, you do,' she said, glancing over her shoulder at Walid once again. 'Who else isn't here?'

The penny dropped embarrassingly slowly. 'Oh my *god*.'

Twenty Two

Loki *fucking* Laufeyjarson.

Despite everything, I still didn't understand shit about how his brain worked or even what he wanted. Not really. Beyond the fact he was clearly a little sweet on me, everything else sort of ebbed and flowed.

It didn't *feel* like he was the big bad here, though. He had really slapped the shit out of Wolfgang's confidence, exposed him, but still run off with Miranda Ertras and the power etched into her bones. It was all one big stupid distraction to keep me occupied.

But why did distracting me even matter to a god?

I took my time leaving the building and heading back to the surface. My head was swimming and the pressure was starting to solidify into cluster migraines. It's not the years, it's the mileage, and I'd done more than my fair share of miles in the last half hour.

Despite the pain, I tried to call out to Laufeyjarson, provoke him into showing up again. It didn't work, and I hadn't expected it to, but I had to try something.

Not that I had any clue what I would have done if it *had*.

Shout at him again, maybe? Try and give the all powerful god of fuckbois a proper bollocking? Wolfgang had tried that, and look how he ended up.

Not to get all introspective and mopey, but I have to admit I did spend a lot of that walk wondering how things had gotten quite this weird. Granted, I'm technically a mage so things were always going to get weird, but even the magical heavyweights I've run into don't get to tangle with literal gods and shit.

Then again, look at it like a Runeskald and it all makes sense in a weird way. Socially maladjusted orphan with a chip on her shoulder the size of the soles on her platform boots, dead father figure, tightrope walking the line between self-destructive apathy and cheeky-charming punk-bitch irreverence. That had classical chosen-one written all over it, so I guess I shouldn't have been surprised so many people kept harping on about my *potential*. Not *surprised,* sure, but that didn't mean I had to accept it.

Would have been easier to stomach if all this talk of potential had just been a smokescreen for attempts to get in my pants. But that was too neat, too simple — now I was starting to really think like a Runeskald, I couldn't stop.

My ears popped as I climbed my way back up to ground level. There hadn't been such a pressure imbalance on the way down, but there hadn't been migraines and nausea either — the nausea followed on from my ears popping, by the way, but it didn't last long — so I didn't much question it.

It was raining outside and I let the water soak me through until my hair was drenched into a very different type of mess than it had been and my makeup started to run. No idea why I did that, but it felt like something I had to do and, at this point, I was too knackered to fight those little impulses. Besides, a cold shower does wonders for waking you up, and what I saw when I reached the surface had me wondering if I had somehow fallen asleep on my ascent.

The school was gone. In its place stood something so incongruous that it didn't register as real — a gleaming citadel of gold and platinum, beautiful carved arches like a Fritz Lang movie, unfolding across the horizon like a pop-up book. A set of burnished metal steps led up from where I emerged, ushering me towards a disgustingly ostentatious gate that was three times as tall as I was. It was wide open.

That sign was about as neon as you could get, right? If the invitation had been any more obvious he would have needed to tattoo it on my eyeballs.

With a sigh, I climbed the stairs one by one, my legs protesting with each step. At the top, there was a dull ringing in the air, like a distant tuning fork buzzing away. It sent my balance a bit loopy and the back of my throat filled with a familiar metallic taste. Didn't slow me down, though.

Inside, the citadel was just as unbearably extra as it had been outside. And just as lifeless.

The unbearable tackiness of the precious metals had been tempered inside thanks to a liberal scattering of exquisite rugs and carpets. They carved a path through the other furnishings — varnished wooden constructions full of fanciful curved carvings and fleur-de-lis designs — encouraging a look-but-don't-touch approach to their appreciation. Half the room looked like an antiquarian's storage room, the other like someone had exploded a king and distilled his pomposity into a kind of paint.

Laufeyjarson was easy to spot. The room at the end of the fancy carpet path was designed to draw your eye towards him. He was lounging across a wooden throne like he was in an old painting, arms and head flopping loose over one of the arm rests, back arched, his chest presenting to the sky. His dark hair was tickling the floor — a black marble with misty veins of white-grey running through it — casting longer shadows than the light should have allowed.

'How did it go?' he said. I was barely into the room, but

his voice sounded as if it was right next to my ear. 'Did you teach the old dog another new trick?'

'I don't really feel like having a friendly chat, Loki.'

He lifted his head a little. 'Ah, I've upset you.'

'All you do is upset me,' I snapped. 'This is worse. You've confused me.'

'Everyone wants to be the centre of attention until they finally are. I never expected you to be an exception.'

'Where's Ertras?'

'You disappoint me now,' he said, sitting up. 'I didn't think the old boy's taste for power would rub off on you.'

I shook my head. I was still only halfway across the room, but I was getting closer. 'I don't want the power, but I think you do.'

'I told Wolfgang I didn't want it.'

'But you took it with you anyway, and you used me as a distraction to do it. Or distracted me while you did it. Either way, I think you did want this Diplomancy bullshit.'

Laufeyjarson got up from his throne. It was even less fancy than I had thought — cracked, rough wood with no varnish, no cushion, and only a well-used animal skin for padding. So well-used, in fact, that the fur had gone black and shiny in places. 'For safe keeping.'

'Going to go out on a limb here and say that making a fucking Wizard of Oz palace doesn't count as safe keeping.'

'Ha, you got me,' he said, flashing that charming smile. 'Just a small indulgence. I'll set everything right before I seal this away much more properly.'

I was within arm's reach of him now. 'Please, *please*, just dispense with all the bullshit. For once.'

Something changed in his expression. The haughty god melted away, replaced with tiredness and, good grief, *sincerity*. 'Okay. Just this once. Look up.'

I did. Floating in the air above his throne was Miranda Ertras. No, not floating, there were chains binding her, but they were so fine that I couldn't see them until she struggled and shifted a little, letting the light glance off them. 'What the fuck?'

'I'm reversing a terrible mistake, Milicent,' Laufeyjarson said. 'One of my worst. And I've made a few really bad ones, so trust me when I tell you this one isn't good.'

'Diplomancy?'

He was staring up at Miranda Ertras now, hands in his pockets. 'I did the worst thing a writer can do. I published my first draft.'

'What?'

'Diplomancy,' he said. 'My first attempt at bringing a little flair and excitement to this dull plane of existence. I put a lot of myself into it, too much actually, and didn't properly think things through. Made quite a mess, let me tell you.'

'So much of a mess that no-one's heard of it,' I said.

'Exactly. Had to be written out of existence to stop people using it to fuck things up. Runes are much neater, far less arbitrary. But you can't go back and patch up something you've already let loose into the world — better to just replace it. And I couldn't replace it if I couldn't find it. Got to run it all through the old typewriter again, stamp over the letters a few dozen times.'

'What are you doing to her?'

His gaze never faltered. 'A delicate and painful procedure, but a necessary one. Every word of Diplomancy has to be peeled out of her marrow.'

Yes, that's what those chains were. Words and letters all hooked together, admittedly not in any language I recognised, being unwound from her flesh. Why wasn't she screaming?

'Wolfgang was right.'

'No.'

'Yes, he was,' I shouted. 'You've been steering us around on some big bullshit quest for you, not even telling us, just manipulating us and playing with us like your own little toys.'

He turned on me, his eyes icy blue and cold. 'You *are* my toys. Every Runeskald is. Every power you have is born of me, that's *the point*. But... Make no mistake, I treat my toys with care. Why do you think I've had an interest in your development, Millie?'

Oh Christ, here we go. 'Because of my *potential* or some shit like that, right?'

'The potential to call me a dickhead, maybe,' he said. 'You're being stalked by a literal god and your reaction is annoyance. Not terror, not anxiety, *irritation*. Do you know how rare that is?'

I shrugged. 'I can't be the only one who would react that way.'

'Why?'

'Huh?'

'Why can't you?'

'Because, um...' I stammered.

'Look,' he said, the otherworldly charisma starting to seep back into his pores. 'There's a lot of people with the bravado to put on a really good front in your situation. Wolfgang used to be one of them, for example. Talk big, walk big, but think small. They think small because they think that I want them thinking big, you get what I mean?'

'Not really.'

He snapped his fingers and Miranda Ertras jolted as the shimmering lines being drawn from her body sped up. 'They can't help but shape themselves around what they think I want, even if they don't realise it. And not just me, they'd do it for any god. It's damn near written into human DNA to worship power, that's why so many of you do it. Talk big, walk big, think small. Getting it yet?'

I wasn't about to get into a philosophical debate with the collective fantasy of every teenage Tumblr girl, especially because there was an element of truth in what he was saying. But then, these guys always started from a tiny kernel of truth, didn't they? Fucking Barnum Statements and circular logic, always shoving you where they wanted you to be. Laufeyjarson was just clever enough to do it while making it seem like he was shitting on the whole idea. Next level fuckboi magic.

'What I'm getting,' I said, slowly. 'Is that you like the

sound of your own voice.'

'Of course I do. I'm a god. Whereas you, you're so painfully human. Possibly the most human person I've ever met.'

'Christ. What does that even mean?'

He drew a line in the air, sizzling golden power like the afterimage of a sparkler. 'The spectrum of humanity. Up top, the confident ones, the ones with the balls to stand up to people like me. The heroes. Down below, the rank-and-file who know their place, and their place is to rock the boat as little as possible. Then, here, right on the line, sits you.'

I rolled my eyes. 'Oh yes, special me, the chosen one. Sure.'

He snuffed out the line. 'You're really hung up on that phrase, huh? *Chosen one*. Hollywood has really fucked you over with that. Writers love that nonsense, easy shorthand. Who is choosing you, Millie?'

'There's been a lot of people trying to get me to sign on with their shit.'

'You choose yourself, dumbass,' he said, waving my words away. 'Chosen. Choice. You're not someone with an iron will or bullish stubbornness, you're just someone so fucked up in the head that you sit perfectly on the line between apathetic acceptance and self-destructive arrogance. You care just enough to act, but not enough to think about it. Walk big, talk big, don't think. And all of that is because of your choices; you chose to be you.'

'Everyone chooses to be themselves, you pompous idiot,' I snapped. 'And I think we're getting away from the point of this conversation, namely you flaying a woman for the primordial power etched into her bones.'

He sighed. 'Maybe. I'll leave you to chew on it for a while. As for this one though, I think I'm done with her.'

Another snap of the fingers, and the final shimmering strands snaked their way free of Miranda Ertras' flesh. A sharp gasp bubbled its way up her throat, then she unceremoniously fell to the floor, hitting the marble with a dull crack. The shock of the impact snapped her eyes open — they were unfocused and dilated.

The *stuff* extracted from her body was still hanging in the air, metallic threads weaving around each other like shiny ropes. It had spread out into a circle, almost like an elaborately constructed chandelier. Rotating slowly, at the nexus of its orbit was a knot of the same stuff, an anchor point. All in all, the design fit the rest of the surroundings quite well.

It radiated power — like, every cell in my body was

screaming that this was unnatural, a thing to be bowed to. 'You're not leaving with that.'

'Sure I am,' Laufeyjarson said. 'It's mine. Why, do you you want it or something? I might even let you have it if you ask nicely.'

Look, even if I hadn't been standing in a big gold palace created by that power, I'm not going to lie and say I wasn't tempted. Of course I was tempted — you don't get into magic because you're content with your lot in life, you know what I mean? But there were too many strings here. The manifestation of the power was *literally strings*, which really should be enough to set off alarm bells.

'Eat an entire shit.'

He clapped his hands and the Diplomantic diorama vanished in a needless puff of smoke. 'There she is! See, you always keep me guessing. My perfect little failsafe. You'll want to take Ertras and head outside now; I told you I'd put everything back nice and tidy, and I'm sure you don't want to be caught up in the celestial Roomba.'

Turning his back on me, he started to walk away towards the far end of the room. I should have grabbed him by the shoulder, forced him back, shouted at him to explain himself. But then, what was the point? Protracting a shouting match with him wasn't going to do any good, and I didn't know enough about this whole Diplomancy business to really want to push him on the issue.

I hadn't even been that against Wolfgang having it beyond the fact he'd been messing with my head and gas lighting me. Fine, for now Loki could keep his bullshit to himself.

Somehow, Ertras must have weighed even less than me because I didn't struggle to hoist her up. With one of her arms wrapped over my shoulders, I awkwardly marched her out of the golden castle and down the steps with only a couple of embarrassing stumbles. By the time I had laid her on the grass at the bottom of the stairs and turned around, the castle was gone and the school was back.

Su-Yin emerged, immediately showing me up by carrying a man over each shoulder while somehow dragging a third along behind her. She dumped them down when she saw me and ran over.

'Figured I'd bring everyone up to the surface,' she said. 'Couldn't work out a way to give directions to the ambulance crew that wouldn't sound like a prank call.'

'How's Fury doing?'

She glanced back at one of the unconscious men. 'He's alive, I think. Not so alive that I didn't call an ambulance, but alive enough that he should survive until it gets here. I see you got Ertras back?'

'Just about,' I said. 'She probably needs an ambulance too.'

'And me,' Su-Yin said with a smile. 'They'll think we're taking the piss.'

'I bet we get a loyalty card or something.'

'So what do we—' Su-Yin began before I cut her off.

'We'll work that out later,' I said. 'Let me just catch a breather, all right?'

*

The breather lasted about as long as it took for the ambulances, plural, to come and take Walid, Wolfgang, Raoul Fury, and Miranda Ertras off to the local hospital. The sheer number of dirty looks I got from the paramedics, mate, I'm not sure how they managed the mental gymnastics to blame it all on me — they looked like a group of car crash victims, and our car wasn't that fucked.

Su-Yin didn't go to the hospital in the end. She took one look at the fleet of emergency vehicles that all showed up at once and figured that was far too much of a scene for her, and I can't blame her. The sirens drew the attentions of the kids and the teachers, and having her as my personal bouncer ended up being a godsend — children are to flashing lights as flies are to fresh shit, apparently.

She couldn't stop everyone, though. The vice provost prick slithered through, Bertie De'Ath at his heels.

'What in the blazes have you done to my school, Thatcher?' Dayne all but screeched over the departing sirens.

'The magical equivalent of bringing it up to code, I think.'

There was a vein bulging in his forehead, one I had seen countless times on my own teachers over the years. Old faithful. 'This is... This is... De'Ath, you assured me that this woman could be discreet!'

Poor Bertie went to respond, but I cut in before he could. 'This is about as discreet as was possible, mate. Do you even know what was going on under your nose? God shit.'

Dayne folded down towards me, straining to bring his nose down level with mine. 'You charlatan piece of filth. First it was ghosts, then Outsiders, now it's gods? I've had enough of your... Your *shit*.'

'Investigating dead kids is a process, pal. It takes you places. The places it took me was all the way to the power of a god buried right under your pissing school.'

His face turned chartreuse. 'Get out. Your assistance, such as it is, is no longer required.'

Honestly, he didn't need to tell me twice. I was done with the whole place — let it burn, see if I cared — but I wasn't going to give him the pleasure of watching me leave. I'd leave on my own time, when I deemed everything was squared away and not a moment before.

'Sure,' I said. 'How many dead kids is it now? I'm just asking because I want to make sure the papers get it right when the news gets out, that's all.'

'You haven't even dealt with that problem?' Dayne spat. 'After all this?'

'Sure I did,' I said, putting on my best air of indifference. I was about to play a hunch, but I didn't want him knowing that this wasn't an iron-clad fact I was about to smack him with. 'But then a *god* was here, messing shit up with his celestial mumbo jumbo. There's going to be a loose end or two.'

De'Ath took a brave step forward. 'Sir… She really is the only expert available and, while I acknowledge she's not been as efficient as we would have liked—'

The vice provost let out a long, defeated breath. It

smelled distinctly of Earl Grey tea. 'Yes, yes, your point is made, De'Ath. Finish what we brought you here to do, Thatcher, and then leave. My tolerance for you is at an end.'

He had an excellent flounce, I'll give him that. The man moved like a goth flamingo, his long legs moving with just a smidge too much prominence. De'Ath didn't go with him, lingering about until the older man was out of earshot.

'I don't appreciate having to go to bat for you like that,' he said. 'But the unfortunate fact of the matter is that there really is no-one else.'

'And that will be reflected in my fee,' I replied. 'Also, do me a favour and answer my question.'

'Which question?'

'What's the death toll up to now?'

He blinked. 'You don't know? Have you been paying so little attention that you seriously don't know?'

I placed a hand on the side of his face, giving it a couple of playful and gentle slaps. Completely brain-locked him — he had no idea how to react to it. 'Just humour me, mate.'

'Three,' he said, finally pushing my hand away. 'Eric Vernaise, Harry de Pfeffel, and Milton Gracemere.'

Hunch confirmed. 'Of course, just three.'

'*Just* three?' De'Ath said. 'How many were you expecting me to say?'

'Doesn't matter,' I said. 'Run along now. I've got a job to finish.'

Mouth flapping like an overly confused fish, he set off in Dayne's footsteps, leaving me blissfully by my lonesome once again. The nosy children were already starting to thin out too, caught up in the sweeping wake of a very unhappy teacher — a wordless promise of detentions to come if they didn't get back to their classes this very instant. The stragglers were the ones too dense to notice such a subtle message, and the ones who thought they had it in them to rebel. In both cases, they were easily handled by Su-Yin.

She sent the last member of the group packing — a careful but forceful shove sending him staggering in front of his pals, just enough embarrassment to make him think twice — and I waited until her stance loosened before I called her over.

'These kids are really nosy,' she said as she approached. 'And weirdly horny. A few were really keen to get my phone number.'

They're not alone, I caught myself thinking. Let's just put that away for now. 'I was wondering if you'd like to tag along and see the sort of shit I actually do.'

'What do you mean?'

'It'll be easier to just show you.'

Twenty Three

The old *let me just show you* thing never really works outside of TV. If you're lucky, you'll get maybe halfway to where you're going before the person you're showing gets fed up and asks anyway.

Su-Yin let me get like three quarters of the way there, which is pretty much unheard of.

'Millie, I'm real tired,' she said, almost whining. 'Can you just tell me what we're doing now? I need some tea.'

I'd gone back to the mercifully empty dorms and was stalking the halls looking for the right room. 'I'll take you for tea when I'm done here. But everything got so big, I nearly forgot why I was here in the first place.'

'The kids?'

'Exactly.'

'So that's not sorted then?'

All the fucking corridors looked the same. 'There were a lot of deaths at this school, all hidden away in folded pockets of reality. Now though, we're down to just three.'

'Isn't that good?' she said, stopping to lean against a door. 'I mean, not *good*, but better.'

I stopped too, taking a seat on a small table piled high with unopened mail. 'Yeah, but it raises questions that I need answering. Namely: how much of what went on here was your boy Wolfgang fucking about with Diplomancy?'

'I'm a little fuzzy on that myself, what with the mind control and everything.'

I nodded. 'It's not just that. Laufeyjarson made this whole basic bitch castle to flex about how powerful Diplomancy is. Then he promised to undo it all, hit the big reset button. If he actually kept his word, I'm wondering…'

'If all the shit left over is unrelated.'

'Bingo,' I said. Fucking bingo? 'That's the stuff that was here first, before our genial German started trying to court me.'

It was a bit of a reach, but hardly a leap. By his own admission, Wolfgang had been tinkering with events to push me into a particular mould, but there was no way of seeing the seams from the inside. It wasn't that he had some prodigious skill at what he was doing, but the tools at his disposal did a lot of the heavy lifting.

Eat The Rich

Give someone enough paint and they could smooth out the Grand Canyon. A fuck-ton of paint, but still.

So, that had to mean that the dead kids weren't all part of Wolfgang's bullshit, right? Ipso facto, Latiny Latin, I still had work to do. Best place to start, or end, would have to be the room of the latest victim. Except it wasn't where I had left it.

Then again, Milton Gracemere hadn't been dead before, either.

'Right, so, if your theory is right and this is all unrelated to Diplomancy,' Su-Yin said. 'What *is* it?'

I frowned. I'd been asking myself that same question even before all the reality bending bullshit kicked off. 'Not a ghost. Definitely not fucking Outsiders.'

'Vampire?'

'Would explain the lack of blood, but not the lack of flesh,' I said, as if I knew shit about vampires beyond what I'd read. 'Picky eaters. More drinkers, really.'

'So what, then?'

'I'm sure that will become apparent once we check out the latest killing.'

Jumping down from the table, I took Su-Yin's hand and pulled her away from the door, leading her onward.

Milton's room definitely wasn't where I had left it — not a great feeling — but there were only so many rooms per floor, and only so many floors in the building. With everyone being in class, it wasn't too much of a pain in the arse to scout out the entire building.

Milton's new room was more central than it had been, though still far enough away from one of the main thoroughfares of the building to give the lad a modicum of privacy. It was also the only door that was locked, which at first seemed weird until I remembered this was a school — just think of the shit kids will get up to if they know you can't just walk in at any moment and catch them in the act.

I managed to summon enough arcane power to jiggle the tumblers and open the door, bringing us face to face with Milton's skeleton.

'Fuck me sideways,' Su-Yin snarled. 'That's really fucking grim.'

I'd forgotten she hadn't been witness to one of these bodies before. 'Yeah. It's not an image that will leave you for a while, let me tell you.'

'I'm a little upset it's not Outsiders now. At least then the level of grotesque inhumanity would kind of make sense.'

Which had been Wolfgang's play all along, hadn't it?

Shape the story plausibly, rewrite what he could to drag things out and string me along. But he hadn't created everything, so there had to be something concrete here.

It was clear that Milton had been gnawed to death, like the others — no resistance, perfect compliance. If that was true then the whole tranquilliser theory held up too; if the sangfroid stuff hadn't been a red herring, but just one of the anchor points Wolfgang had grafted his tale to...

'Fuck sake,' I muttered. 'I was right the first time.'

'Fill me in?'

I plucked a bony quill out of the mattress. It was stained brown with dried blood. 'I could never make this one bloody thing fit. It was a fucking Nightmare all along.'

'But I thought—'

'The fucking sangfroid laid it all out easy peasy right at the start,' I continued, building up to a rant. 'Should have been nice and simple, but I let Wolfgang send me off on a bloody tangent. Look, you see these needles?'

'Sure.'

'Classic Nightmare shit,' I said. 'Keep the target compliant and obedient so they can take their time.

They don't want to kill you, not really. They want to scare you. Fear flavours the meat. Over and over again, it's seasoning. Outsiders don't need any of that, they're just horrible shits that chase you down and carve you up.'

'But you said it was Outsiders,' Su-Yin said, frowning. 'We *saw* them.'

I sighed. 'We saw them after Mistral told me that it was a Nightmare. When I went back to confront her, I thought Wolfgang had told her to lie about the Nightmare to mentally prep me for his bigger bullshit.'

'To soften you up, sort of thing?'

'Exactly, but something about that didn't sit right with me,' I said. 'Just felt like a lot of work to spin up a small lie as a jumping off point, right?'

Su-Yin's fingers were twitching as she tried to keep up with my rapid-fire burst of very sensible logic. 'Right. And you're saying…'

'That he didn't even need her to lie. In fact, it worked better if she was telling the truth, or at least a carefully curated amount of the truth so he had a solid foundation to smash up. He needed to play off her perceived authority to build up his. Of course he had the right answers, he was changing the fucking questions. All that banging on about memetic viruses and shit. Then I got back here, and there's an Outsider right there, having a lovely feast. Really made him look like he knew what he was talking about, to the point that I was willing to discount even the obvious.'

'Oh!' she yelped. 'I get it! Whatever Mistral said, it didn't matter to him whether it was true or not. He just needed to be able to scribble over it.'

'The Nightmare just made it easier for him, meant he didn't need to worry over that part of the story. It would serve well enough to get me thinking, and thinking in the way he wanted. I could never get the sangfroid to fit with the Outsiders.'

'Because it was never meant to!'

I nodded. 'He needed to know I was capable of overlooking something obvious like that. Exactly.'

'Because as long as you were overlooking it, you were following his story instead.'

'Makes me feel really goddamned stupid, I can tell you that much,' I said. 'I thought I just didn't know enough to make the connection. Never occurred to me that I knew enough to lean on the inconsistency.'

Su-Yin crossed her arms. 'He hijacked your insecurities. Up until that point—'

'I'd actually been doing things properly,' I snapped. 'I

was on the right track. Oh for *fuck's sake*. That utter, utter prick.'

Su-Yin gingerly took the quill out of my hand and started to roll it between her thumb and middle finger. 'It's really light.'

'Bones get surprisingly light when you hollow them out. Most of the weight's in the marrow.'

'Is that right?' she said, slipping the needle into a pocket. 'Gross. But you said they don't kill. This one's done a lot of killing.'

'Fucked if I know,' I said. 'Maybe it got bored, wanted to change up its dishes. You never get fed up of eating the same thing everyday and fancy a change? Lots of fear in a boarding school, I bet, basically makes it a big buffet. Maybe the killing part is the equivalent of licking the plate clean.'

'Maybe,' she said with a little reluctance. 'But if you were right the first time and this *is* a Nightmare, what's the next step?'

A very good question. In fairness, most of what I knew about actual Nightmares was what Mistral had told me, and she was a big fat fraud. It was possible everything she had said was true, but equally as possible it was all horseshit — there was no way to know.

Which meant I had to go with my gut. I might not have known much about Nightmares in the specific, but I did know a fair amount regarding the things that flanked them in the big book of spooky bastards.

I have approximate knowledge of many things, me.

'Find it, trap it, kill it,' I ended up saying. 'The basic steps to any dance.'

'Yeah, fine. But how?'

'Give it some juicy bait and lure it out, then sort of beat on it until it stops moving.'

She folded her arms. 'It's that simple, is it?'

'It doesn't need to be more complicated than that. Sure, with ghosts and stuff there are procedures and all that, but Nightmares are technically alive,' *I think.* 'And most living things can be stopped by smacking them about a bit.'

She didn't uncross her arms. 'If you're about to say that I need to be the bait here—'

'We'll both be the bait,' I interrupted. 'Plus, I know exactly where to set the trap.'

*

The little hollowed out clearing behind the dorm building was the same as it had been, which was nice. I don't know why, but finding out that Wolfgang had taken the time to whip up a teenage make-out spot as part of his charade would have set my teeth on edge.

Outside of the fact something had shot me up with a dart last time I was here, there was no reason to think this was any more likely a place to snare the beast than any other. Milton had died in his room, and neither of the other two kids had perished here, but even the loosest connection was, in fact, a connection.

I had taken Su-Yin via the teacher's lounge and stolen for her a lukewarm cup of brown grit. Whether it was tea or coffee was impossible to tell, at least for me, but she didn't care. She had pulled a half-inflated balloon chair out of the hedges — the transparent pink plastic mottled with algae that was forming inside — and sank into it with a pleased sigh. Now she had her legs out in front of her, crossed at the ankles, and she was sipping happily on her gritty water.

'This is better than I thought it would be, you know,' she said between swigs. 'The location, not the coffee.'

'What was the secret make-out point like at your school then?'

'Who says we had one?'

I flicked the last of the catkins off an upturned plastic lawn chair, set it upright, and sat down. 'Every school has one. At least one. Mine was behind the maths block. There was a couple of temporary classrooms there, called them the terrapins, but they didn't schedule many classes in there—'

'Because the temporary classrooms weren't so temporary?'

'Exactly,' I said. 'Been there for years before I even started, were still there when I left. Smelled like mildew and stale jizz.'

'Charming description.'

'Well it's the truth! What about yours?'

'One of the viewing balconies overlooking the badminton courts.'

'Excuse me? *Badminton courts?*'

'Hey, you asked,' she said, throwing up her arms in defence. 'No-one ever used the courts, but the building had a glass ceiling so the balcony got a lot of natural light, and no-one could see you up there.'

'I guess kids can do a lot with very little,' I said, smiling. 'Or a lot with a lot, in your case.'

'A badminton court isn't a class indicator, you know.'

'Isn't it? It really feels like it is. The fact that you went to a school where people could say *shuttlecock* with a straight face—'

She winked at me and, dammit, that shut me right up. 'Now, I never said *that*, did I?'

We had plenty of time to kill before we could enact my master plan, and the conversation never graduated beyond this. And I was fine with that. It was nice to take an actual breather for what felt like the first time in a week. The first actual, pointless, relaxed conversation in I don't know how long, too.

Not to gush or anything. Shut up.

Once the sun started to set, that's when we had to put a stop to the festivities and actually do some work.

I held out my hand. 'Give me the stabby quill thing.'

'Sure,' she said, handing it over. 'You going to tell me this plan or what?'

I started to scrape off the dried blood with my thumbnail. 'Oldest trick in the book, I think. We go to sleep out in the open like this and hope the Nightmare finds us juicy enough to trot over for a snack. It's already shot me full of sangfroid here before, so it should be happy to tuck in for a second go.'

'I'm noticing a flaw in this plan.'

'The whole being asleep thing?'

'Yeah. Not a tactically advantageous position.'

The needle was free of visible blood now. 'Only one of us will be properly asleep. The other one will pretend. Hopefully the scent of sangfroid on the air will make the Nightmare complacent enough not to notice.'

Her eyes widened. 'You're going to stab yourself with the quill?'

'Yeah, obviously.'

'What the *fuck*, Millie?'

I held the needle up in front of my face to get a good look at it. 'I reckon it's used most of its payload so I shouldn't be completely out of it. Should just be enough to make me realistically groggy.'

'It's got someone's blood on it you tit.'

'It's fine, I've scraped it off.'

'You've... That's not... Give it back. Now.'

Like a shot, she snatched the needle out of my grip and slipped it back into her pocket.

'Hey!'

She placed a hand on my chest, gently shoving me backwards. 'No. Do your stupid shit when you're on your own. I'm not going to sit by and watch you do something objectively fucking stupid because it's the first thing you thought of. I don't think it's a stretch to say there has to be a better way than risking *a potential blood disease*.'

'It's a kid's blood, it's fine.'

'You seriously cannot be this fucking dense, right?'

Look, obviously I knew where she was coming from. It's a fucking used needle, right, of course I knew the risks. But I'd also run the calculations in my head and was reasonably sure everything was fine. In fact, it wasn't even the most dangerous thing I'd done recently — that honour went to calling up an extra-dimensional entity for some forbidden knowledge. That turned out fine, and this was basically a step down from that...

It's weird how readily you can trick yourself into liking the smell of your own farts. I'm looking back at this now and totally agreeing with Su-Yin, but at the time none of it was landing. I didn't think I was invincible or blessed or anything, I just felt that it was all going to be fine in the end so why worry?

'Well, how else are we going to bait this trap?' I snapped. 'We can't just have a nice kip under the stars and hope that's enough. It needs tempting.'

'Then tempt it another way, you utter tool.'

I slapped her hand away and turned my back on her, interlocking my hands behind my head in frustration. 'Oh my *god*, fine. Let me think... I guess, maybe, it would be possible to replicate the effect of the sangfroid. It wouldn't smell quite the same, but it might be enough?'

'And you can do that without stabbing yourself with the needle?'

'Probably? I'll need it back though, for reference.'

It's pretty obvious what I was actually thinking, yeah? Even then, I felt like a total shit for breaking out that lie, and it's not gotten any easier to think about with time. Watching Su-Yin's face as she tried to work out how much to trust me, those are expressions permanently etched into my brain now.

None moreso than her expression when she made up her mind. 'Fine, but behave. Or I'll be cross with you for a very long time.'

She handed the quill back once again, and I started making a big show of not doing what I was about to do. Kneeling down, I started drawing some designs in the dirt, sketching out a little magical workspace.

'Don't worry, I'll be good,' I lied. 'Just need to find the right combination of runes to mimic the effect. Groggy but not comatose, compliant but not paralysed. And if I can make it weak enough that it doesn't completely take me... Oops.'

Curse my clumsy hands. In my haste to get everything set up, it seems I *accidentally* poked myself in the palm with the business end of the quill. What terrible luck.

'I can't believe you,' Su-Yin snarled. 'I seriously can't.'

The sangfroid was working fast. My palm was already numb and I could feel that sensation spreading down my veins. 'No use being angry with me now, it's happening.'

'I'll be extremely angry with you later, don't you worry,' she said. 'What do you need me to do now?'

'Be ready,' I said, slowly sinking to my knees. This time, I'd make sure I landed on my back. 'Don't think it's as big a hit this time, so I should be able to do more than be the bait. But just in case...'

I slumped backwards onto the floor, face staring up at the sky. The sun was almost gone, but the stars hadn't come out yet. The last little bit of feeling I had in me drifted away, just as an arm slid under my head and around my shoulders.

'I've got you,' Su-Yin said, her mouth next to my ear.

Closing my eyes, I drifted off to sleep.

I didn't enjoy it. The dreams were weird, like watching old TV shows through melted glass or some other Salvador Dali shit. A very passive approach to the inside of my own head, straddling that awkward cusp of sleeping and wakefulness. It was, essentially, like being on a bad drug trip, which I suppose it was.

A bit of a different hit than the last time, and I'm still not sure why. Diluted sangfroid perhaps? Or maybe I'd built up a little tolerance? Or, and I'm going to get needlessly *teenager* about this, knowing there was someone there with me was giving me a bit of a boost...

In any case, I drifted around woozily for god knows how long, until I caught a glimpse of the stars through my groggy eyelids.

But not just the stars. It was there too, the Nightmare. My eyes were still too heavy to open, so I couldn't see it, but I could feel it was there, hovering somewhere behind me. That sixth sense we all have, the painful tingle of vulnerability that follows unseen danger, was doing a pissing tap dance on top of my scalp.

Next to me, I could feel Su-Yin breathing. Every breath was slow and deep, relaxed in a way that told me she was properly, deeply asleep. Which was a bit of a problem, seeing as she was the one that I had hoped would stop the Nightmare from skinning me alive and eating me. That was the plan. She had agreed to that plan.

I tried to force my eyes open and will some semblance of energy back into my limbs, but it was slow going. One eye could open a crack, but it steadfastly refused to focus on anything. A single finger would move, but it felt like dragging my bare flesh across a mound of pins and needles. All the while, that tingle in my scalp was growing more and more insistent.

The earth on either side of my head shifted and I knew the creature had knelt down above me now. A shadow crept into view, blocking out the stars, but my eye still refused to focus on it. Probably for the best, all things considered.

A shape that somewhat resembled a hand stroked at my forehead while the rest of the shadow scuttled around me in a circle, climbing over me and straddling my chest. I'm not sure if it barely weighed anything or if the sangfroid had fucked my perception of things, but I couldn't feel it there.

'Ah, you're not asleep,' it said. The voice was silver gravel, privately educated stone-on-stone. 'Have we met?'

Tangled in the cotton wool filling my brain, I had a lot of responses. None of them could make it out.

It didn't wait for my reply, anyway. 'I've not tasted you

before. Did you baste yourself for me, little morsel? So polite, knowing I would be famished after my little jaunt.'

What jaunt? Had Wolfgang stuck the beast in timeout or something while he span his convoluted little story?

Had it been aware of that?

'Hush now, so noisy in there,' it said, running that shadowy hand over my head again. 'You don't need so many thoughts now. I will make this nice and simple for you.'

Now I felt the pressure on my torso pressing me down, constricting me, as the creature slowly loomed closer to my face. Naturally, that was when my eye finally managed to remember how to focus, just at the thing's face was inches from mine.

Its skin was ashen grey and heavily wrinkled, like a monstrous basset hound. The flesh was sloughing in puffy jowls, drawing out otherwise stubby features. The nostrils were dragged open by the weight of the hanging skin, as were the lips, revealing teeth mottled with yellow plaque.

The eyes were spirals the colour of dried blood.

The face slid out of view and I felt its breath on my ear. 'There is nothing so simple, so sweet, as terror. Sing me a song while I dine. You will make a fine *amuse bouche* before I decide upon my latest dish. And worry not, I always clean up after myself.'

The Nightmare's weight shifted a little and it sat upright again, shuffling forward so that its knees were pinning my shoulders. It's hands danced up my scalp, rifling through my hair until the fingers found flesh, and I could feel the grip tighten. The fucking thing was going to crack me open like an Easter egg, just peel me apart.

I felt the nails bite into my scalp and start to cut away. There wasn't any pain exactly, more an unsettling friction ringing around my skull. But also, the Nightmare was taking its time — it wasn't just unzipping me, it was starting to cut designs into me.

Fucking plating me like a Michelin starred chef.

I could feel the blood starting to drip down the back of my head.

That was curious, actually. Turns out, I could feel quite a lot now, all things considered. Two fingers on one hand, three on the other. An ankle. My heartbeat. The trickling blood pooling on the ground at the base of my skull.

Both eyes could open now, and focus as well.

I was waking up.

Fucking monster narcotics haven't got shit on my liver, or whatever organ's involved here. All I needed was to buy a little more time.

The carving stopped and the Nightmare cocked its head to one side. Its voice was a sing-song of amusement. 'You're singing the wrong song. You're going to ruin the ambience. Tsk tsk. Why is that? Why, why, why?'

Again, the hands came into view as, one by one, the Nightmare pulled fresh needle-like quills from underneath its fingernails. It really made a show of it, too, breaking out the flamboyant showmanship of a stage magician. If it had gone to pull one out of my ear I wouldn't have been too surprised.

'Ah, you're getting ideas,' it said. 'That won't do at all. Allow me to turn back the clock a little. Tell me, have you ever experienced acupuncture?'

Licking its dry lips, it traced down my chest and readied the first needle.

Twenty Four

The Nightmare was slow, deliberate. It wanted my heart rate up, I'm sure — get me shivering with anticipation and trepidation, get the blood pumping to spread the tranquilliser faster — and that was where it fucked up. It's a great idea when you're in complete control of the situation, but every moment it hesitated gave me precious time to get my body to wake the hell up.

Even as feeling started to trickle back in, there wasn't much I could do with the thing sat on my chest. My legs were free enough, but even on my best days I wasn't limber enough to get my legs high enough to get real power into a kick, and I figured I only had the one shot.

My fingers went searching for a weapon. I was scraping blindly in the dirt with both hands, hoping against hope that some grotty kid had left something useful nearby. If the Nightmare noticed, it didn't cause them to hurry — they seemed content tracing the tip of the first quill over my chest some more, scoring at the skin but not quite breaking it.

'Do you know about pressure points?' it whispered. 'I once ate a man who studied them intensely. The right little prod in the right nerve bundle, that's all it is. Directing the flow of the humours. If I can just locate the right ones, we'll have you back on track nicely.'

The thing loved the sounds of its own voice — then again, they always do — but the more it talked the closer it came to jabbing me with those needles, and I had no doubt a fresh infusion of sangfroid would be the end of me.

One of my hands found something. My sense of touch was still numbed, but I let my fingers feel around regardless. An opening, soft, deep. A pocket. It was Su-Yin's pocket — she'd laid down next to me and that had put her close enough for me to search. I just had to hope...

It was there, tucked away all safely. I just needed to grab it.

'I'm looking for the Vagus nerve. Do you know about it?' it asked. 'Fascinating thing. If punctured, it sends the most delightful electrical shocks to the brain. Excruciating, apparently. It brings a real succulence to the meat, it must be said. Though the temptation to over-season is hard to resist. I confess, in my exuberance I have spoiled a fair few dishes at this buffet, but I believe I'm learning to temper those impulses now. Shall I show you?'

Trying to force my hand free, the object snapped in my

grip. It wasn't much of a noise, but it was enough to draw the Nightmare's attention. It turned its head in time to see me yank a quill from deep in Su-Yin's pocket and ram it right into the creature's thigh.

Thank fuck Su-Yin picked up after me. Again.

I couldn't muster much in the way of force, but the quill was so sharp it slid through the skin easily. The Nightmare hissed and slapped at my hand, but that only pushed the quill deeper into the flesh until it was flush with the surface. Still hissing, the creature turned and shifted its weight from my shoulders, its hands clawing at the fresh wound.

That was my opening. I couldn't fight, I couldn't run, but I could awkwardly shimmy out from underneath it while it was distracted, put as much distance between me and it as I could. That wasn't going to be much, but it was still progress.

In its panic, the Nightmare had dropped its fresh quills and I took the opportunity to snatch them up as I crawled. A plan was forming. If I could just get closer to the bushes, where the earth was less compacted and a bit more pliable…

The Nightmare stopped hissing and began to chuckle softly to itself. It sank onto the floor and placed its lips down onto the wound, smiling and sucking. Like drawing poison from a snakebite, it extracted the broken quill, holding it in its clenched teeth. It plucked the thing free and flicked it away into the distance.

Dropping onto all fours, it started to slink towards me. 'You are right, morsel, I do play with my food too much. My mothers would be ashamed of my manners. But don't worry, you've taught me the error of my ways. Just lie still, I'm coming for you.'

I was so close now, another couple of inches until I could sink my fingers into the soil. The Nightmare's hand passed over one of my feet and up my leg worryingly slowly. It crept past the knee as I dragged myself one merciful inch closer. It tiptoed up to my waist as I moved that final inch.

And it was at my throat when I finished carving the sigil.

It was one of the simplest runes, which is why I could carve it so quickly despite everything. I had learned three simple runes when I started out — basic utilities that you couldn't do much with but you could do enough to practice your forms and even, if you were feeling daring, experiment a little with. Two runes were air, mostly used to conjure smells and pleasant breezes on a warm day; and water, for cleaning and refreshment.

But the one I had carved was light, used for fucking with the things that go bump in the night.

I'd thrust my fingers as deep as I could when carving it, but it wasn't just the size that made the thing go off like a god damned flashbang, it was the intention. I put a piece of myself into every runic working, and in this one I was going all out. I don't have much arcane skill, but I have enough to overcharge that one rune, make it glow brighter than the sun for all of half a second.

Even with my eyes screwed shut, I saw the flash and felt the heat on my skin. The Nightmare, though, hadn't been expecting it — it hadn't had the time to close those red eyes. It took the brunt of the light full in the face, flash-frying its optic nerve and sending it reeling.

Again it rolled off me, this time screaming like a dying cat. It scrambled onto its back, legs kicking at the dirt, slamming its head on the floor in agony. I managed to climb on top of it then, to hold the quills I had gathered in one hand, and slowly push them under the creature's chin and up into the base of its brain.

The screaming stopped. And the kicking. It went limp.

My arms went out from under me and I flopped onto the Nightmare's torso, my face in the dirt next to the creature.

'How's that for acupuncture, you son of a bitch?' I muttered, then passed out again.

*

Eat The Rich

When I woke up, it was dawn and I was fucking freezing. I was damp with morning dew, or what I had thought was morning dew until I pried my face off the ground and found myself staring into the decomposing corpse of the Nightmare. Sunlight had crept over the hedgerows and wherever it fell on the creature its flesh was melting away into a grim jelly.

I was going to need a change of clothes.

Rolling away, I took the long route around to check on Su-Yin. She was still asleep, a pair of sangfroid quills poking out of her neck — so that explained her sleeping through the whole thing, I guessed. I plucked the quills out and did my best to shake her awake. At this point the tranquilliser should have largely worn off, especially on someone with her muscle mass, but apparently she was a deep sleeper regardless.

With no other alternative, I stuck a finger up her nose. 'Wake. Up. Please.'

An eye opened the tiniest crack. 'No. I'm angry with you.'

'Okay, but—'

Before I could finish, she burst bolt upright, eyes blazing. 'Where is it? Is it time? Are you okay?'

'Easy, easy,' I said gently. 'Turns out I'm still a bad ass.

Who knew?'

'Why are you covered in goo?'

'The price of heroism,' I said. 'How did you sleep?'

She sighed. 'Badly.'

Getting up, she dusted herself off and started to look at the scene. The melting corpse got special attention, Su-Yin hunkering down over it and watching the flesh bubble away in real time. I kind of hovered behind her awkwardly for a moment.

Then I tried something I didn't think I was capable of. 'So, um, I wanted to say sorry.'

'Did you?' she said, still staring at the Nightmare.

'I think I might have fucked up a little? Exploiting your trust like that.'

'Mhmm.'

'It wasn't a very good plan,' I said. 'It worked, but...'

Su-Yin shook her head. 'It did work. But if it hadn't...'

'I know.'

'Do you?' she said, turning on me. 'Because if you had died last night, because I gave you back that quill... Because I *trusted* you... that would have been on me. I would have had to live with that, not you. Because you would have been dead.'

'And you already nearly killed me once, I get it.'

The level of confusion that washed over her face was almost comical. But it very much wasn't. 'This is not a transactional thing you utter bell end. This is me being human and caring about what happens to you. If you had died because of a choice I made—'

'A choice I made, not you.'

'I chose to believe you, despite everything. That's on me.'

I nodded silently. Like I told you, that was not one of my best decisions and it has lived with me for a long time. The thing is, I can still justify it to myself quite easily — the plan worked, the thing is fucking dead, I survived without any real lasting injuries — but the hurt in her eyes overrides everything else. That moment, her looking at me with such bare emotion, that took root in me.

It cut me off at the knees.

'Never again,' I said, voice trembling. 'Calculated and approved stupidity only. I swear.'

'Millie,' she stood up and crossed her arms. She wasn't looking at me. 'I'm not saying this with malice, but don't make promises you don't intend to keep. Back out there on your own, you'll go back to what you know. I can't blame you for that, but I can lament it, I guess?'

A lump formed in my throat. Guess it was now or never, then. 'I... Well, I kind of thought that maybe you'd want to hang out for a while. Kind of tag along?'

'As a bodyguard?'

'No,' I said, blood rising in my cheeks. 'As, like... Are you making this difficult on purpose?'

The barest hint of a smile. 'Yes. Continue.'

'Christ. Not as a bodyguard. A sort of friend. A partner. A *pal*. I was hoping you'd be my pal.'

I knew she wanted to say yes, that was never in doubt. It had been a long time since I had hit it off so readily with someone, and my radar is finely honed. She *wanted* to say yes, all she needed was to give herself permission. And that was where my anxiety kicked into overdrive — after all, I'd given her plenty of actionable reasons to turn me down and storm off into the sunrise, hadn't I?

Hell, I had wanted to avoid having to actually ask her. Ideally, she would have just glommed onto me and things would just develop without any of the difficult bits like having to use words or make decisions — surf the wave of possibility and never take any accountability. But she had me thinking that maybe, sometimes, you really do need to use your words.

Still scowling, she closed the distance between us and hugged me so tightly that I felt the soothing pop of tensions being squeezed from between my vertebrae. 'Pals?'

'Pals.'

'I can live with pals, for now,' she said. 'But I'm still angry. We can talk punishments and amends later, though.'

'I do still have some business left to attend to here.'

'More Nightmares to kill?'

'Nah,' I said, not making any effort to escape the powerful hug. 'Got to inform the poshos that I've slain their monster. Get my money.'

'You don't need me for that, do you?'

'I, um, suppose not?'

A real smile, warm and comforting, spread across her face and she waved her hand at me. 'I'm not ghosting you, you idiot. Put that worry aside. I just… I need to see Walid, talk to him. He's my friend and—'

'I get it,' I cut her off. 'I'll meet you at the hospital later? I should probably check in with Fury and Ertras, right?'

'Feels like something you should do, yeah?'

She released the longest hug in human history, looked into my eyes for a moment, and then made to leave.

'Su-Yin?'

She stopped. 'Yeah?'

'Are we okay?'

'We will be,' she said. 'By the time you get to the hospital later.'

Which, I think, is about as good an answer as I could have hoped for, all things considered.

Twenty Five

Dayne coughed up the cash much faster than I expected him to — apparently he wanted me gone a lot more than I had thought. He took one look at me, still soaked through with the viscous death-snot of the Nightmare, and judged that the job was complete, no further questions asked. De'Ath did the questioning for him, but it was nothing overly taxing or interesting. Didn't bother to give them the old spiel about keeping safe and deterring future infestations — they'd have ignored me anyway.

De'Ath offered to have someone drive me back to the train station, even followed that up with the promise to comp my ticket even. I filed that away as a useful skill for any future freelance jobs — be annoying enough and people will bend over backwards to get you to leave.

I declined both offers. They'd paid me enough, but also I wasn't done in town just yet and I didn't want their greasy private school fingers all over what I was doing now that things at the college were dealt with. After packing my things, I walked off the campus and waited at the nearest bus stop for a trip into the town. It was the first truly tranquil moment I'd had for days —

chatting with Su-Yin had come close, but this was honest-to-god *silence*.

Can't beat it.

My mind wandered, but not to where I had expected it would go. Usually, my brain couldn't get enough of bitching about me, a meat-grinder of self doubt and hyper-criticism. It should have been picking apart the whole Su-Yin thing, dissecting all her words for the signs that shit was going to go bad. It felt too positive, so surely my brain would find a way to ruin that.

But it was preoccupied with something else. It was really keen to go over Fury and Ertras.

I had come in well past the end of their story, that was obvious. There were so many unanswered questions about Diplomancy, Fury trying to write it out of existence, who the pair of them even *were*. None of it pertained to my job — that was done and dusted — but curiosity was getting the better of me.

Sometimes, it felt like the world was full of secret societies and shadow governments. Whitehall was doing its best to be one these days, nestled inside the real government. The Magisterium, or the Conclave, or whatever pompous name the mages had been using way back when certainly had delusions of being one. In a way, I'd been inside the bubble for so long that the word "secret" had lost all meaning.

But Diplomancy had been truly secret. It had been fucking *redacted*, and who knows what else had gone with it?

My hand had found the coin in my pocket, still wrapped in the torn lining. What had they said it was, a memetic virus? This had never shown up in the literature — and I would have found it too, it was exactly the sort of interesting shit I would have skipped ahead to read about, like looking up rude words in the dictionary.

How much damage could Laufeyjarson have done, or undone, with that power? The world was already big and scary enough, what new horrors would be set loose now? Maybe none at all.

Nah, it would be something. He'd hit the reset button like he promised, fine, but he'd pick the restore point, and he'd pick something interesting. Something dangerous but exciting.

Ah, there it was, the pessimism. Couldn't just rest on my laurels and enjoy a job well done, had to go looking for the next catastrophe.

Fuck it, it would come when it came. No need to dwell.

A bus pulled up in front of me and I boarded it. The driver was delightfully uninterested in any small talk, so I tapped my phone against the card reader and picked myself a seat on the top deck. This wasn't an area where people took busses, but I've got a reputation to maintain — that of the top deck scruff-bag that you don't want to talk to.

The bus didn't go as far as the hospital, so I had to walk the last twenty minutes. I did treat myself to a small detour into a charity shop to spend some of my newly acquired phat stacks on clothes that didn't look like they were covered in an ogre's cock snot. Couldn't do much about the hair, so I just let the gel work for me and slicked it all back.

It wasn't like the hospital was going to turn me away if I showed up a total fucking mess, but they might mistake me for someone who needed admitting. Again. And I was ready to feel a little more grown up and a lot less of a disaster.

I got some looks from the old grannies sat in the reception. Those coffin dodgers were lurking around the entrance to the little shop because they didn't want to buy a get well soon card for their friend in the palliative care ward, but they didn't want to show up empty handed either. What says *I'll miss you* more: the pathetic visual of a post-Brexit Toblerone or a packet of orange-flavoured Maltesers?

In any case, I grabbed myself a Wispa, paid cash, and ate it before I was back into the hallway.

The nurse on reception didn't bat an eye when I asked

to see Raoul Fury and Miranda Ertras, though she did roll those same eyes when I claimed to be family. She knew I was bullshitting, I knew I was bullshitting, but neither of us cared enough to press the point. Why bother — who was going to complain?

Not Ertras, that was for sure. I found her first, on a trolley being wheeled into ICU. She was more tube than woman, as far as I could see, and a gaggle of doctors and nurses were clucking around her and tapping at machines that each took responsibility for at least one of the pipes. I figured I'd come back to her later, no need to rush.

Fury wasn't too far away, swaddled in freshly applied casts and propped up on a bed so he could watch the world go by. When he spotted me, he threw me a nod and pointed to a chair next to his bed.

'Hello, saviour,' he said. 'Fancy seeing you here.'

I sat down, then noticed he was struggling to turn to look at me, so I stood up again. 'Saviour is a bit of a strong word.'

'You literally saved my life, so it's an apt title.'

'Yeah, so, about that—'

'Let me stop you right there,' he interrupted. 'I know where this goes. You've got a load of questions about

Diplomacy, right?'

'Obviously.'

'Well, get used to disappointment because I've got nothing to tell you.' He sighed. 'Nothing you don't already know, anyway.'

'I don't know much, though.'

He shifted his weight a little, grunting at the pain of the exertion. 'Let me redirect this for a second. What do you think it felt like, being a statue for so long, for years? Humour me.'

'Not great, I imagine.'

'Yeah, pretty shitty,' he said. 'At least, at first. Turns out, keep a mind disconnected from a body for long enough and it starts wandering. I managed to get a look at a few things, check in on some old foes, that sort of thing. Foes that, say, sell information to reckless idiots in exchange for memories.'

'You know—'

'We've met. Did you think you were the first person to tap that barrel? Well you're not, and that's how I know you already know enough to be dangerous. At least, if you wanted to be.'

'I really don't.'

He smiled. 'Then may as well keep it that way. But, listen, I'm not trying to be a dick here. You've got questions, and I'll answer what I can. At least, what it's safe to answer.'

'Very big of you.'

'Yeah, well, being too free with information hurts more than it helps.'

'Classic boomer logic, mate.'

'Okay, let me stop you right there,' he snapped. 'You've had a snoop around the office you found me in and got the impression that I'm some office jockey, right? What I am, *was*, is a highly-trained and extremely successful assassin, so watch your tone.'

I looked him up and down slowly. 'You look like a half-empty tube of toothpaste.'

'And imagine how much worse I would look if I wasn't what I'm saying I am,' he said, sinking back into his pillow. 'I didn't seal a memetic virus away in stone for fun, you know. It was the only option I had left.'

'I exorcised it pretty easily, just saying.'

'Think that through for me a minute, yeah? There wasn't something, some event, that might have weakened things sufficiently for you to make your play?'

'You're talking about Laufeyjarson.'

He nodded. 'Him smacking that thing out of Miranda weakened it enough for you to have a chance. At full strength... Look, we were basically the X-Files. We had all the knowledge, all the resources, and the best option we had was to seal it away in a vault. I like your moxie, but you're not on the level of these things.'

'Things, plural?'

'Like I said: we were the X-Files. We saw the weird stuff.'

'Bro, I'm a professional exorcist. I killed a Nightmare last night. I'm at home to mister and missus weird.'

'Ha, all right,' he started to fidget, trying to move one very stiff arm down to a pocket. 'A little help?'

Suspiciously, I reached into his pocket — extremely carefully, I might add — and pulled out a key. 'Want me to feed your fish?'

He let out a little chuckle. 'Kind of. Maybe I'm wrong and you're stronger than you look. Who am I to judge? I've been trapped in granite for a decade or something. You want your answers, this key will unlock them. Feed that curiosity in a slightly less self-destructive way than crossing dimensions and selling bits of your soul.'

I turned the key over in my hands. It had two sets of

teeth, one on either edge, and divots along the side. It was heavy too, cast from sturdy iron or something. 'Oh good, a quest.'

'Nothing so grand,' he said. 'Do it or don't, I'm past caring. But if you do do it, you'll be looking for a vault inside the vault. Nested security, all the rage. Or it used to be.'

'No-one ever gives me straight answers. It's extremely annoying.'

'Let your elder give you some wisdom, kid. You give gifts, you earn answers. Only way they're worth a damn.'

'That why you've yet to ask me for my name?'

'Does your name matter?'

'Matters to me.'

Another sigh and this time his eyes slid shut. 'Good for you. We're done here.'

For a moment, he tried to roll over. He ultimately thought better of it. Either way, he was committed to ignoring me now, which was pleasant. What a prick.

*

'He just gave you the key and went to sleep? Is your life always this weirdly mysterious?'

Su-Yin finally had herself a proper cup of coffee, squirted out of a branded dispenser that charged a little too much for the privilege.

'It's been getting that way lately, yeah,' I said. I'd bought another chocolate bar, I deserved it. 'But still, I'm thinking I might check it out anyway.'

'You sure?'

I shrugged. 'Maybe. A lost cause taking on a literal lost cause? There's some poetry there, right?'

'You're not a lost cause, Millie,' she said, peering over her shoulder and the door behind.

Someone had secured Walid a private room — I guessed his parents, but it didn't seem polite to ask — and Su-Yin had planted herself at the door as a kind of bouncer. Not a great one, mind; she didn't stop anyone going in or out, she just sort of glared at them intently until they were out of sight.

She hadn't been in herself, but she had looked through the window.

'Fine, a *misplaced* cause taking on a lost cause. That better?'

'A little,' she said. 'He's in a medically induced coma, did you know that?'

Eat The Rich

'I didn't.'

'I heard the nurses talking. They were saying none of the painkillers were working and he wouldn't stop screaming. They don't understand at all.'

'I barely understand either, but at least they're helping him.'

'They think they are, I guess,' she replied quietly. 'But they don't even have the first clue as to what happened. They're saying he must have been struck by lightning.'

'Oof. Wow.'

As explanations go, it was like the next page over from a gas leak in the big book of governmental bullshit. Then again, there probably isn't a certified mundane medical term for a catastrophic magical backblast — there wasn't even a proper term for it in the magical community.

Even waiting for the ambulance, Su-Yin and I had categorically refused to talk about it. We had known, of course, that Laufeyjarson had been the cause — he'd torn right through Walid's magic circle without issue — but focusing on that just reminded you that a god had fucked him up, and you didn't need that thought rattling around in your head.

That's the sort of thought that can take up a lot of space if you let it.

I had the space for it, sure, but not Su-Yin. She needed to concentrate on Walid's well-being, not the seeds of an existential crisis.

With a sudden shake of the head, she dragged her attention away from the door and back to me. 'What do you think you'll find?'

'No idea,' I said. 'But, if I'm honest, I kind of got a vibe from the place.'

'I know what you mean. It had that sort of history you can feel in the bones, right?'

That was definitely one way of putting it. All I knew was that something about the place had sunk its hooks into me, grabbed my curiosity hard. 'Do you think there's anyone who could see such a weird sight and not at least want to give it one more look? Like, I know curiosity killed the cat and everything but, come on.'

Seriously, think about it. A boring office block existing in the dark spaces underneath a private school in the middle of nowhere? Fine, Diplomacy put it there, sure, but I can't be alone in wanting to explore that delicious weirdness, right?

'Well, so far it's a 100% curiosity rating. Did you check

in on Wolfgang?'

'Fuck no.'

'Me neither. His welfare doesn't really matter to me now, but you can bet he'll be right back down in those hallways if he survives.'

'I doubt there's anything useful to his Diplomancy obsession,' I said. 'Not now, anyway. Laufeyjarson will have it all squirrelled away someone else.'

'Yeah but what did Fury tell you? That they were like the X-Files? Definitely some other cool stuff down there, right?'

Well, yeah, obviously. That was why I wanted to take that key and check it all out — I hadn't thought about the potential Wolfgang problem, I just didn't like the idea of who knows what just sort of laying out in the open like that. If it was going to come back and bite my arse, I wanted to at least know the shape of the teeth, you know?

'You don't need to sell me on this, Su-Yin. I was thinking I'd be pitching it to *you*.'

She glanced over her shoulder again. 'Well, maybe. But I need something to do. Sitting here, all I can do is hear his screams.'

'He's not screaming.'

'He is in my head,' she whispered. Her attention snapped back to me and there was a little more joy behind her eyes. 'Besides, it's either that or we have a *conversation* about you stabbing yourself unconscious.'

'Yeah, I choose the office of mystery, thanks.'

'Right now, so do I.'

That said, she still needed a full hour before she was ready to leave. Nothing changed in that time — no doctors came with an update, she never went into the room — but I guess she had a lot of thoughts to square away. I didn't know the history the pair of them had, but they definitely *had* it. I wasn't about to get in the way of that.

So I waited for that hour, and then a little bit more while she worked through detaching herself from outside his room, and then I called us a taxi to get us back to the school one last time. We spent the entire journey in silence, but at times I felt her hand reach for mine, give it a firm squeeze, and then retreat back into a pocket.

The scenery had changed little under the school. The office was still there in its little forest clearing, though the trees looked a touch more autumnal than they had. Without the time constraints of tracking down Wolfgang, the place felt a lot less foreboding too. It was so ordinary as to radiate a complete lack of interestingness.

Would I even have noticed the place if there was anything else to see down there?

We went back down to the vault, once again taking in the signs of chaos and bloodshed. Even knowing this was the work of Miranda Ertras — or, more accurately, the thing that had possessed her — did little to dull the low level musk of terror in the air. If anything, knowing the realities of the cause just made it all worse. It was making me want to   grab at the coin   — a subtle nudge to make sure that *thing* was safe and secure. I stopped myself; the last thing I needed was to start feeding the   paranoia   and become all twitchy and distracted.

Again, without any looming danger I was able to take in a lot more of the vault than before. The studded doors on the far side, complete with heavy-duty keyhole, were the first things I noticed this time.

Su-Yin gave me a nod of approval and I slid the key into the lock, giving it a quick turn. The mechanism was heavier than the key had suggested, but that didn't lead to any noise from the innards. The door sank down onto its hinges and pushed open easily.

Now this was more like a proper vault. The outer room had been cavernous, clearly designed to just pile shit up all higgledy-piggledy, but this one was orderly and carefully arranged. It had the feeling of a museum or a gallery — walls lined with plexiglass display cases, those little white cards with information on each piece, the works — and while I'm not that brand of nerd, I couldn't help but feel a smile worm its way onto my face.

'So this is where they kept the cool shit, huh?'

Su-Yin took one side of the room, me the other. She was already running her fingers over the surface of the cases. 'Maybe. It's all empty now, though. Just like the other room.'

I grumbled. Of course the room was empty, I hadn't expected otherwise. But it wasn't just like the other one. 'I don't think so. They'd been rushing in the other room, but someone took their time here, look.'

It was an easy detail to miss, and one that ordinarily I wouldn't have bothered noticing — none of the cases were open. They were all empty, barring their detail cards, but the doors had been securely fastened by their electromagnetic locks.

'I'm not seeing it.'

I was pacing my way up one bank of display cases now, something at the end had caught my eye. 'If you're ransacking, you don't close the doors and drawers behind you. Smash, grab, fuck off, that's the order.

Sure, they were in a rush with the stuff they kept in the other room—'

'Because they had to be?'

'Probably. Possibly. Either way, the stuff in here? They moved it out long before it became a necessity. Which makes this thing a real curiosity, don't you think?'

The display cases spanned the length of the room, coming together at one wall in an elongated U-shape. It had the effect of focusing the entire room on one very specific display, and it had drawn my eye before I even noticed that it was the only case still containing something.

Sat on a transparent plexiglass shelf, a rotund piggybank stared down at us, surveying its kingdom. It was about the size of my head and made of stone rather than porcelain, though it was finely polished and carved so the overall appearance was quite similar. Its little piggy eyes were bulging and its sides looked warped, like it had been overstuffed.

'That's oddly sinister,' Su-Yin said. 'I don't like it. What's it doing here?'

'Let's take a look,' I said.

The description card said it was a *containment vessel*, allegedly forged from the lining of Pandora's Box — not likely — but that wasn't overly interesting. Underneath the text, however, were photos of the underside of the pig, which was much more exciting.

A message had been chiselled into the stone, circling what appeared to be an opening filled with hardened wax or something. Considering the effort that had gone into making the thing, it made sense they wouldn't want it smashed to shit if they ever wanted to empty it. Then again, judging from the message it seemed strange that they had ever intended the thing to be opened.

This artefact holds nothing of worth. No treasures reside within its form, no everlasting mysteries to uncover, no truths to be revealed.

As to wealth, it contains only a wealth of harm, both mental and physical. The contents are a contaminant, as dangerous is your time as they were in ours.

Contained herein is a dishonourable monument to our own vanities and should be treated as such. Shun this object in its entirety, save for this warning.

There is nothing of value here.

'Pretty good English for something carved from ancient stone, right?'

Su-Yin was peering over my shoulder at the pictures.

'This sounds familiar.'

'It does?'

'Kind of, yeah,' she said. 'Reads kind of like the messages people wanted to put on dump sites for nuclear waste. You know, to keep future generations from disturbing them'

I frowned and read the message again. 'Huh, I guess you could read it that way. A bit damning though, seeing as it clearly didn't work. Although I'm guessing it didn't contain radioactive waste.'

'Christ, I hope not!'

Something in the corner of the case caught my eye. A sheet of cardboard had been folded into the crack between the door and the rest of the display, creating a barrier between the electromagnet and the locking plate on the door itself. It wasn't much of a barrier, but it broke the circuit well enough. I forced my nails into the gap and popped the door open.

I could see Su-Yin open her mouth to say something, so I jumped in before she could. 'Chill. I'm not disturbing the terrifying pig-beast. Look.'

The card fluttered out onto the floor, and I bent down to pick it up. I unfolded it.

'What is it?'

'It's a message. For me. Naturally.'

Again, Su-Yin was hovering over my shoulder. 'Saying what, though?'

'Where do you think I got that coin from?'

I crushed the cardboard in my hand and immediately climbed into the display case, sliding my way underneath the pig. The waxy stopper had been removed, as had whatever had been the contents of the thing. Son of a bitch.

'What coin?' Su-Yin asked.

'It's Laufeyjarson,' I replied. 'I thought he was showing off, being all flamboyant like usual. Fucking hell. He used a coin to pull that *thing* out of the Ertras woman, but I thought it was just, you know, a coin.'

'A coin and not *a coin*, you mean?'

'Exactly,' I said. 'I didn't think it was something important. Fuck sake.'

Clambering out of the case, I almost slammed the door behind me. Probably best to leave it open for now, though.

My hand was already in my pocket, grabbing at the cloth that held that same coin. It felt wrong — something was missing. Frantically, I pulled the scrap of cloth out and unfolded it. No coin. What the fuck?

'Millie,' Su-Yin said, her voice shaking a little. 'I've got a question.'

'Yeah?'

'How many of those coins do you think could fit in here?'

Plans within plans, that was Laufeyjarson. The god of lies and stories, misdirection and half-truths. Wolfgang really had been right about one thing — we were all playing pieces to him, and we didn't get to see the board.

But I did know one thing for sure, no matter what his overall plan was.

'Enough to be interesting.'

Epilogue

That really had been a lot easier than she had expected it to be — she had barely needed to do anything other than being in the right place at the right time.

Well, that wasn't strictly true. Being there wasn't enough, she also needed to twist a few neurons, tie a knot or two in the part of the brain that managed attentiveness. But that was hardly a challenge, at least not on someone like Millie Thatcher.

The girl was doing a lot better, she couldn't deny that. But she wasn't ready yet, and leaving the coin in her incapable hands would all but guarantee she'd never get there. The ease of getting it off of her had been proof of that.

She had hidden in the staff toilets when she saw Millie leaving the hospital — disguised as the cashier for the hospital shop gave her the ability to duck in there no questions asked, but few people bothered to question your authority when it came to shitting. Simple suggestion and magical manipulation had gotten Thatcher to pay with the coin, but there was no certainty that she wouldn't notice the misdirection and that was something Loki didn't have the time or energy to deal with right now.

That was why he had made his play into her play. Loki Laufeyjarson was a known quantity, but Millie Thatcher had never seen Loki Laufeyjardottir. Few had.

Loki had always preferred her female form. It came with different expectations, different freedoms. Subtle, clandestine, cloak and dagger stuff came much easier in this guise — that burning need to be seen was turned on its head, replaced with an ice cold obsession with going unnoticed. Even if she had wanted to, she couldn't have carried herself with the same bravado and bombast as he did.

They each had their strengths. She felt hers were stronger than his, naturally, but she was aware she felt the reverse when she was him. It was complicated.

She didn't even realise she was rolling the coin across her fingers. The creature locked inside was very angry, but it was already slipping into dormancy. It didn't have anywhere close to the power needed to break her protections, but neither did she feel comfortable giving it the chance to drip-feed from her. Better to keep it moving, disoriented.

The other coins slumbered in her backpack. The chavtastic pink yoga pants and puffy jacket had been quite a choice, but she had to admit the backpack had been an inspired choice. It was almost entirely concealed by her obscenely long ponytail, the jet-black hair acting as a natural barrier against wandering hands.

And there would be wandering hands. Hers would already have wandered if they could reach into the bag without taking it off, the sheer concentration of temptation was too high.

One coin wouldn't have been an issue. A handful? Better not to find out.

Once she was sure Thatcher had left, Loki shook her hair loose and made her exit. She had a car waiting in the parking lot — parked gratis thanks to a flutter of her long eyelashes — and she dumped the pack into the boot before pulling away. The SatNav whimpered a command at her demurely, fully aware of who was in charge here, and she settled in for the drive.

This was a big risk, but she still had faith in Thatcher. The Diplomancy incident had been a great test of her convictions and capabilities, as it had been of Wolfgang. Thatcher hadn't exactly passed necessarily, but the important thing was that she didn't fail. Wolfgang failed, but Loki was finding it hard to hold it against him — from the outset, she had guided him precisely to fail. A weak link conditioned to snap at exactly the right moment.

The perfect tutorial.

Eat The Rich

Things would get harder for Thatcher now, by design of course. There would be more eyes on her shortly, though the trick was going to be in making sure it was the right ones. Medusa was already aware, thankfully, but she hadn't done much to draw the interests of the rest of the Pariah Club yet. And if things were going to go the way Loki wanted, well, she was going to need to make sure Thatcher had one hell of a cotillion.

A real banger of a coming out party.

She swerved to avoid an oncoming car — an ancient Rolls Royce driving with nearly as much reckless abandon as her — and took a corner a little too sharply. A little lingering masculine energy, making her drive far too much like a dickhead. She lifted her foot from the accelerator and let the car breathe.

Another meek outburst from the SatNav told her she was at the first of her many destinations. She slid the car perfectly between another two parked at the side of the road — a modern mini and a classic mini, making her sleek Japanese four-door look massive — and killed the engine.

This outfit wouldn't do. A wave of the hand replaced the chavtastic ensemble with something a little more presentable — a smoke-grey pantsuit with heels to match, shoulder-length hair, eyeliner applied with a calculated amount of inexperience. Professional, but out of her depth, that was the look.

Believable, but exploitable.

Kicking open the glove box, she fished around for a small plastic case, slightly larger than the coin. She had hundreds of them, so it didn't take long to pick one out and snap the cursed coin inside it.

The coin rattled about inside, making a pleasingly inviting clack-clack. Which had been exactly why she had chosen these cases to begin with.

Slipping the case into her pocket, she climbed out of the car and made sure to lock it behind her. Double locked it. Triple.

Wandering hands.

Better to get started, she supposed. She had a lot more stops like this to make before the day was over. A lot more.

One last little adjustment to the height of her heels, and then she stepped inside the offices of Albert Tepping, collector and purveyor of antiques, premium collectables, and, crucially, vintage coins.

Thanks For Reading

I hope you enjoyed the book (if you made it this far then I'm going to assume you at least didn't hate it), and I'm very thankful for you taking the time to read through Millie Thatcher's first big adventure.

If you enjoyed it, or even if you didn't, please consider writing a little review. Writers can't grow without constructive feedback, and pretty much every comment received will give me something to work on in the future. This is especially useful for series like this one; I want to make sure I'm giving you what you want to read, after all!

So, please consider leaving a review on Amazon or Goodreads if you want, and if you're interested in keeping up to date with what I'm doing and future releases you can find me at @stevetheblack on twitter or even sign up to my newsletter from my website at stevekpeacock.com (you'll get first pick when it comes to giveaways, exclusive content, all sorts of things like that!)

Other Books By Steve K Peacock

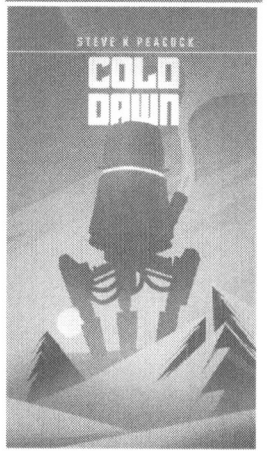

Printed in Great Britain
by Amazon